Jack,

Thanks for your support and encouragement but most of all for your friendship

Tom

Something Else Entirely

Something Else Entirely

A Novel

by Thomas M. Hall

iUniverse, Inc.
New York Lincoln Shanghai

Something Else Entirely

Copyright © 2007 by Thomas M. Hall

All rights reserved. No part of this book may be used or reproduced by any means, graphic, electronic, or mechanical, including photocopying, recording, taping or by any information storage retrieval system without the written permission of the publisher except in the case of brief quotations embodied in critical articles and reviews.

iUniverse books may be ordered through booksellers or by contacting:

iUniverse
2021 Pine Lake Road, Suite 100
Lincoln, NE 68512
www.iuniverse.com
1-800-Authors (1-800-288-4677)

This is a work of fiction. All of the characters, names, incidents, organizations, and dialogue in this novel are either the products of the author's imagination or are used fictitiously.

ISBN: 978-0-595-44859-3 (pbk)
ISBN: 978-0-595-69035-0 (cloth)
ISBN: 978-0-595-89183-2 (ebk)

Printed in the United States of America

For my best friend, my wife Marcia. She has been with me every step of the way, not only in writing this novel, but more importantly as the love of my life for the past forty years. She has truly been the inspiration for this book; my favorite sound in the whole world is the sound of her laughter.

Acknowledgements

Nobody truly writes a novel by himself. You are always influenced, encouraged, and supported by others. Many of my family and friends were essential to this process. However, I especially want to thank the people who went above and beyond—my wife Marcia, my daughters Kim MacMillan and Beth Slattery, my sister Bonnie Pendleton, my niece Lori Pendleton, and my friends Jack Umstatter and Jim Pryal.

The author has pledged that 50% of his proceeds from the sale of this book will go to charity.

Chapter 1

Hi, my name is Benny Curtis and I'm twelve years old. I'm pretty sure that in most cases when people read a book, they don't really care how old the author is. But in this instance, it's quite germane. (I know, I know—what twelve-year-old uses the word germane?) But actually that's a big part of what this story is all about. You see, since I was little—around three or so, I've had adult ideas and words in my head.

Since my very first recollection, I always thought like an adult. If I heard a word that I didn't know, I figured out its meaning by the way it was used, and I made it part of my vocabulary. I saw connections in everything around me. I was able to understand life like adults do. (Of course, many adults don't have a clue about life, so maybe that's a bad analogy.) Let's just say that however much of life adults **can** understand—I get it too.

When I was three, however, I didn't think all of this was any different from what other three-year-olds could do. (No frame of reference) It was only later that I realized I was making connections that little kids don't usually make.

I've done some research on this topic, and there doesn't appear to be a medical term for what I have. I suspect a lot of it has to do with my memory, however. I have what's called an eidetic memory. (Yeah, I had to look it up too.) It's not the same as a photographic memory, but it's close. One of the school psychologists I got to know, said to look at it this way—the more you remember, the more connections and relationships you can naturally make. And as much as anything else, life is about connections and relationships, about understanding how things fit together.

The thing is, this ability that I have doesn't make me smarter than anyone else, it just might appear that way because my mind works like an adult's, and I'm only a kid.

My mom and dad (that would be Lillian and Joe) didn't know what to make of me. I was talking at seven months, reading at two and a half, and employing sarcasm at three. (Actually, it was irony rather than sarcasm most of the time, but why split hairs?)

I'm sure there were other incidents in my early childhood that could be classified as defining moments, but the two I'm about to relate to you, have to be at the top of the list. These two incidents elicited the same exact response from Lillian and Joe—"Something has to be done." (Doesn't that seem to be a favorite phrase of parents, no matter what the issue happens to be? But, notice the use of the passive voice—nobody's willing to take ownership of the "something", or volunteer to do the "something".)

Many times when parents use the phrase "something has to be done", it has a negative connotation. That wasn't the case here. Lillian and Joe wanted the best for me, but they weren't sure how to provide it.

Anyway, back to the "incidents". The first one occurred on my third birthday. My parents had a small party for me. They invited a few family friends and some older neighborhood kids along with their parents.

Bob and Kathy Smythe lived two doors down. They were about the same age as my parents and didn't have any children. However, I did overhear my mother say that they were "trying very hard to have a baby". (I'm not sure, even to this day, what that phrase means—Do people make grunting noises while they're making love to show they're trying harder—kind of like a tennis player hitting a backhand? I mean, I've heard of ovulation and fertility cycles, but I'm still not sure how anybody can "try harder".)

Anyway, back to the party—the kids were sitting in the living room playing board games, and the adults were sitting around the dining room table. The rooms were connected and open, so we could hear the adult conversation, and the adults could hear and watch us. Of course, the decibel level coming from the living room would have caused hearing loss in most adults, except for the parents of the kids making the noise; it didn't seem to faze them. (Who knew that Chutes and Ladders could produce such rancor?)

Anyway, my dad started to make some drinks for the guests. When he finished pouring Kathy Smythe's drink, her husband Bob spoke up and said, "Kathy, do you really think you should have any 'l-i-c-k-e-r'? After all, you may be 'p-r-e-g-n-e-n-t'."

I overheard this whole thing, and my mind started racing in about twenty different directions. Why did Bob think he needed to **spell** those words? Did he think the mere mention of them in the presence of children would trigger something, and make us more susceptible to becoming alcoholics … or parents? However, without even looking up from the rancorous Chutes and Ladders, the only thing I said was, "Mom, don't you spell liquor 'l-i-q-u-o-r', and pregnant ends in 'n-**a**-n-t', doesn't it?"

When I finally did look up, I saw that Mom's jaw needed a forklift to bring it up to its appropriate position on her face, and Dad was just staring at me. A full ten seconds went by and then he said, "What did …?" I started to repeat it, but Dad said, "I … uh … never mind, Benny, I heard you."

At that point, Mom and Dad were faced with a real dilemma—I had just embarrassed one of our neighbors, and yet they probably should somehow acknowledge that my spelling effort was the preferred version. But most of all, they had to try to figure out how the heck a three-year-old knew anything about any of this.

In that situation though, Mom was amazing. She kept her cool and knew exactly what to say—"How about some birthday cake, everyone?"

Looking back, I realize that I shouldn't have corrected Bob, but at the time, I was just getting used to the whole "seeing the world as an adult thing", and tact wasn't yet part of the equation. But I don't like it when people get embarrassed, and I try my best not to do that to anyone. I mean, Bob was obviously.… (Select one from the list below)

A. not the sharpest tool in the shed

B. not the "go-to-guy" for the editors of *The Oxford English Dictionary*

C. not going to be in "The Tournament of Champions" on *Jeopardy*

D. not going to bring the baked beans to the MENSA pot-luck supper

E. (*Feel free to insert your own*)

But he didn't need a three-year-old to remind him of that.

Immediately after the guests left, Mom and Dad had a "pre-discussion conference" in the kitchen before summoning me. (Note to parents and kids: Generally, pre-discussion conferences are useful; they actually can aid both parties in preparing for the upcoming negotiations—parents can plan out what they are going to say, and it gives them a chance to cool down, if necessary. And since most kids know the discussion is inevitable, it gives them a chance to formulate counter-arguments.)

Dad started the proceedings: "So, how did you like your party?"

"It was great, thanks."

Mom chimed in: "Did you like your presents?"

"Yeah Mom, I got some really neat stuff."

Back to Dad: "Son, there's something your mother and I want to talk to you about."

Note to kids: Nothing good has ever come from a discussion that begins with the phrase "There's something your mother and I want to talk to you about." You see, if it were something good, one of them would just blurt it out. There wouldn't be this preliminary, softening-up stuff. So, my advice in these situations is to go for the preemptive strike, which is what I thought I was doing.

"Dad, if it's about the grape juice I spilled on the rug. I ..."

Mom looked aghast. She now had the jaw-dropping thing down to an art form. "Oh no, Benny, where?"

"It's just over ..."

Dad interrupted. "No, Benny, it's not about grape juice."

Mom was still staring into the living room, anxiously. She sort of looked like an ostrich bobbing its head, trying to see around furniture and lamps in a frantic search for some huge, amoeba-like purple stain. (Actually, the initial outline of the spilled grape juice **did** look like Barney the dinosaur had had a meltdown.)

Dad was watching Mom too, and said, "Lillian, why don't we deal with the grape juice issue after we finish this?" Reluctantly, Mom, at least physically, returned to the discussion.

Dad finally got to the point: "Son, what was with the spelling business?"

I paused for a moment, only having processed the words "spelling" and "business". I shrugged my shoulders, "Okay—'b-u-s-i-n-e-s-s'." (I wasn't being a wise guy; I thought he wanted me to spell it.)

Dad must have realized I wasn't trying to yank his chain, because he smiled and said, "No, no, Benny, I meant when you spelled 'liquor' and 'pregnant', when Bob and Kathy were here. How do you know how to spell those words? Do you even know what they mean?"

"Can I answer the last question first?"

Dad started to chuckle and Mom began to smile. (I think she would have been laughing too, except the Exxon Valdez grape juice spill was still on her mind.)

Dad said, "Sure ... go ahead."

"Well, liquor is alcohol. If you drink too much of it, you can get drunk. 'Pregnant' means you're going to have a baby." I actually had some additional questions about that last topic, but those inquiries would have to wait for another day. (Can you imagine the pre-discussion conference that Mom and Dad are going to have before broaching **that** subject?)

Dad's jaw dropped slightly, but he was nowhere close to being in Mom's league. "Where did you hear those words? You're only three—**today**!"

"Actually, I probably read them in the newspaper, or some magazine. Usually when I see something in print, I can spell it correctly after that."

Dad stared at me. "You really are something else, you know that, Benny?"

I shrugged my shoulders. "I guess." (What else can you say to that description?)

I turned to Mom. "I'm sorry I didn't say anything about the grape juice earlier, but I didn't want to interrupt you at the table. If you want, I'll show you where it spilled. I think it's all right though. I cleaned it up. I read the ingredients on the side of the cleaning bottle that was under the sink to make sure there was no bleach in it. I didn't notice any discoloration in the rug when I finished."

I looked back at Mom, and she was stunned into silence. Dad wasn't much better off, but he found his voice first, "It's been a long day, son. Why don't you go and get ready for bed? I'll be there in a few minutes to read you a story." He paused. "Or do you want to read me one?"

"No, you can read …" Then I realized he was kidding. (Hey, I was only three, gimme a break.) Note to parents: Even when your kids can read by themselves, keep reading to them. No matter what they might say, they love it. Of course if you're still reading to them when they're in high school, you should probably back off.

So, can you imagine the pillow talk between Lillian and Joe that night? For certain they must have been confused—"Who is this little person living under our roof, and what do we do with him … or for him?"

A couple of months later incident number two took place.

Despite the fact that I had read most every children's book appropriate for a three-year-old, Mom decided that we should attend story hour at the local library. (Remember the advice I just gave you about kids being read to? Well, for the most part, that only applies to family members and baby-sitters.) Nevertheless, I liked the library; there would be other kids there, and it wasn't as if having a story read to me by the librarian was tantamount to a root canal.

We arrived just before ten o'clock. All the good seats on the rug in front of the storyteller were already taken. (If I had only thought of it, I could have had Mom call Ticketmaster for reserved seats, although I wasn't sure whether they handled story hours or not.)

Anyway, even though she was billed as a storyteller, it was in fact the regular librarian who was going to **read** the story, not make it up. (Doesn't "storyteller" connote making something up?) I thought it was false advertising. I expressed this notion to Mom, who just stared back at me. That was my cue to be quiet and enjoy.

Miss Frist (first name Pollyanna) asked for our attention. (So, if you don't know who Pollyanna Frist is, and I ask you to guess her occupation, tell me librarian doesn't spring to mind?) There were a couple of four-year-olds in the good seats who were fooling around, but they quickly stopped, as Miss Frist showed us the cover of the book she was going to read—*Where the Wild Things Are* by Maurice Sendak.

I really liked that book. I probably had read it twenty times or more. As Miss Frist started to read, I pictured the illustrations on each page. Of course, I had to **picture** the illustrations, because I was too far back to actually see them. (As soon as I got home, I did put Ticketmaster on speed dial.)

Miss Frist's voice was somewhat high-pitched, so the scary parts weren't as scary as they should have been. It's a little tough to be menacing when you sound like you inhaled a balloonful of helium. (I wondered if any of her relatives were still receiving royalties from being part of the Lollipop League in *The Wizard of Oz*.)

Regardless, the other kids really seemed to be enjoying the story ... until the very end that is. Miss Frist got a pained expression on her face. My initial thought was that maybe she was going through helium withdrawal, but that wasn't it. Instead, she announced in a saddened tone, "I'm so sorry, boys and girls, but the last two pages of the book have been torn out. I can't finish the story."

You already know that I don't like to see people get embarrassed. Well, the same thing goes for people being in distress, especially if I can do something about it. Yeah, I was only three, but I had that whole memory thing I told you about. So, without another thought, I marched right up to where Miss Frist was sitting. Of course, it took me a while (you remember how far back I was).

I said, "Excuse me, Miss Frist, but I can finish the story", and I proceeded to recite the last two pages with all the intonation and inflection I could muster. (It also helped that I didn't have helium-breath issues.)

The kids seemed to take all this in stride, but the parents were a different story. You know the painting *The Scream* by Edvard Munch? Well, there were twenty adults with that same expression on their faces. And as far as Miss Frist was concerned—I was tempted to go on the library P.A. system and announce, "We need a forklift in aisle five—Children's Literature."

The parents remained in stunned silence for another 20 seconds. Nobody did or said anything. Finally, Miss Frist spoke up, "Young man, that was remarkable. How did you do that? What's your name? How old are you?"

"Can I answer the last question first, Miss Frist?" (Try saying that three times fast.)

Miss Frist just laughed, and said, "Yes, okay."

"I'm three. I'm Benny, and I'm not sure." Then everybody laughed.

"Benny, you certainly saved the day. Boys and girls, how about a round of applause for Benny?"

Everybody applauded, and I went back to where my mom was sitting. I thought I noticed some tears in her eyes when she spoke. "You're something else, you know that?" (There was that phrase again. I knew it was a rhetorical question, but I really wanted to say, "Mom, I'm not sure I understand what's the big deal, and no, I don't know that I'm something else.")

Now, some of you may be thinking, "When I read stories to my kids or grandkids, they memorize all the words too." But you have to remember, when I recited those pages I didn't have the book right in front of me like most kids usually do. (I'm not sure what I'm getting all defensive about; besides, that's not quite the end of incident number two.)

After things sort of calmed down in the library, and everyone was talking in small groups, Miss Frist noticed that one of the little girls was wearing a *Goosebumps* sweatshirt. If you don't know, *Goosebumps* is a series of scary children's books. Miss Frist said to the little girl, "Do you like *Goosebumps*?" The little girl, who was about four and very shy, just nodded.

I had overheard this whole exchange. (Can you call a nod part of an exchange?) And since Miss Frist and I were very tight, (I resisted calling her Pollyanna, however, not knowing the specific rules surrounding "tightness") I volunteered some information I had read somewhere. "Miss Frist, did you know that *Goosebumps* is being sued for copyright infringement?"

There went the jaws again, although Mom's recovery time was much improved. Of course, she'd had a lot of practice recently. She looked down at me and in a soft voice said, "Benny, I think it's time to go."

For the next several weeks my parents held a lot of pre-discussion conferences about what ought to be done for this precocious little person in their midst. On one occasion I overheard Mom say, "Joe, we have to find a 'school for the gifted' for Benny." As I was preparing my counter-arguments, I was relieved when it became obvious from Dad's tone that he had reservations about that idea.

Now, I hadn't even been to pre-school yet, so I had no idea what any kind of school was like, never mind a "school for the gifted". But there were some things that I did know—Have you ever seen those kids with the real thick glasses who graduate from Princeton at age sixteen? (Do they not have contact lenses in New Jersey?) Anyway, what kind of social life, or **real life** for that matter, do those kids have? I didn't want any part of going down that road.

It's interesting to me that really bright kids are called "gifted". If being that smart, with all the extra challenges it creates for them, is actually considered a **gift**, I wonder what God's return policy is? I would hope it's not just store credit.

The good news for me, however, was that I didn't have to worry about Princeton any time soon. (Actually, I'm not sure I'm going to get in anyway; I don't even wear glasses.) And then Dad postponed the idea of **any** school for the gifted. "Lillian, let's see what the local schools have to offer. If they don't seem right for Benny, then we can reconsider."

Way to go Dad!

My parents' reaction to the two incidents, followed by weeks of pre-discussion conferences, really put me on guard, however. Prior to that, I would just blurt out almost anything that came into my head (See third birthday party), but now I was beginning to censor a lot of things.

Just to clarify, I've got nothing against Princeton—I just didn't want to go there until the time was right. So, I figured if I reined in the adult comments and vocabulary, Lillian and Joe would say *ixnay* about rushing me to *ollegecay*. (Note to parents: Even if your children don't think like adults, it doesn't take them long to figure out the whole pig Latin routine.)

By the way, even though I frequently write "Lillian" and "Joe", instead of "Mom and "Dad", I never call them by their first names. Talk about pretentious. (Note to readers: If the "Lillian" and "Joe" references are making you uncomfortable, feel free to cross them out and write in "Mom" and "Dad". Please don't do that if this is a library book, however. Let's leave that to the professionals. After all, since we still don't know who tore out the last two pages of *Where the Wild Things Are*, getting caught defacing this book would certainly make you "a person of interest".)

As you've no doubt noticed, I tend to go off on tangents. I suspect I do this more than most people, although some of my seventh grade teachers have incorporated "going off on tangents" into the curriculum. (It should come as no surprise to you that they're my favorite teachers.)

I think the whole "going off on a tangent thing" stems from my eidetic memory and the connections I see. If I'm thinking about one thing, and in the back of my mind I see it has a relationship to another thing, I feel compelled to point that out. And then we're headed to Tangent City. I hope you like it in Tangent City. I think we're going to be spending a lot of time there.

A couple of more things about tangents and then I'll move on. Note to math teachers: You know how kids in math class are always saying, "But when are we ever going to use this?" Here's your chance—bring up the word "tangent"; it comes from math. And where would the world be without tangents? Come to think of it, where would **I** be without tangents?

Well, for one thing, this would be a short story, or at best a novella; and I don't think my first literary endeavor should be a novella. I mean, you should actually be an established writer before you tackle that particular genre, don't you think? Although Steve Martin did it. The only other author I can think of that writes novellas is Stephen King. (Do you think novellas are a "Steve" thing? Probably not.)

Still with me? This is your conductor speaking—"We are now leaving Tangent City. Thank you for visiting, and I hope you'll join us on our next excursion."

As I mentioned before, I don't think there's a medical term for the condition I have. I'm not just talking about the eidetic memory. I'm talking about the whole "thinking like an adult, and making connections thing". So, I thought it might be helpful if I gave it an abbreviation rather than writing it out all the time. What do you think about *Interesting Connections from Benny's Mind*—ICBM? (I know that particular abbreviation creates a lot of additional tangent possibilities. But since we just left Tangent City, I'm not going to head right back. However, you should feel free to talk among yourselves; and if you want to re-board the train—knock yourself out.)

So, if I'm in your shoes, I'm thinking—here I am almost finished with the first chapter and I'm still not sure where this Benny kid is taking me. (Aside from Tangent City, that is.)

Well, since I've never written a book before, I'm not exactly sure how this is supposed to go. But, I don't think this story can possibly make any sense unless I give you the entire background. And even with that, the events of last year, when

I was in the seventh grade, are still pretty hard to believe. So, despite my frequent visits to Tangent City, I really will make sure that there's some sort of chronology that will connect everything and eventually make it all come together. Otherwise, I don't think there's any chance you're going to believe it. (Of course if you don't, I guess I could always sell it to *Ripley's*.)

Chapter 2

Now that you know something about me and my ICBM, I want to tell you about my family. Mainly, because I believe everything has context. You can't really know why people are who they are, or why they act like they do, without context. And more than anything else, family is each person's context.

You've already met Lillian and Joe. (You can cross out their names and write in Mom and Dad if it still bugs you, but I'm not bringing it up again.) They've been married for fifteen years, and I'm their only child. I'm not sure why that is, except I know from age three on, I was a real handful. (Wouldn't the spelling incident alone give any couple pause ... or maybe even a permanent moratorium?)

Actually, I think my parents might have wanted more children, but it didn't work out that way. Mom's a big proponent of "God only gives you the challenges you're capable of handling". (Maybe God figured I was enough.)

Mom is forty-two, and I have no idea if she looks it or not. I think she's pretty, but it doesn't matter; she's my mom. Her maiden name was Evans, and she grew up on Long Island, New York.

That brings me to something else I'm puzzled about—why do people say "grew up *on* Long Island", not "grew up *in* Long Island"? People say "grew up *in* Rhode Island", so it can't be an "island thing", except Rhode Island isn't really an island. Could it be that you only use *on* with actual islands, like Staten Island? Although I think a lot of organized crime figures live on Staten Island. So in that case, maybe the crime bosses tell the people in their families (note the double meaning) which preposition to use. Of course given their line of work, "*under*" Staten Island may be more appropriate.

Anyway, back to Lillian Evans—My mom was an only child, just like me. She always did well in school, played the clarinet in the band, was the editor of the school newspaper, and wanted to be a journalist. (I think the blurb under her yearbook picture was written by Joe Friday from *Dragnet*—"Just the facts, ma'am".)

Mom's excellent grades in high school plus 1420 on her SAT's got her a partial scholarship to Boston College. (Some of you may not be aware that a number of years ago the College Board decided to "re-center' the SAT scores. I'm not sure what "re-center" is a euphemism for, but it probably means "made them way easier". There are a lot more 800's than ever. The other thing that "re-centering" did was to make it impossible to compare current scores with past scores. My mom's 1420 was an excellent score when she graduated; now it's not as outstanding.)

You know what all this reminds me of?—the movies. You know those lists of the top ten moneymaking films of all time? Well, shouldn't it be a list of the films that **sold the most tickets**? In 1939, when *The Wizard of Oz* came out, a ticket to the movies cost a dime; now it's approaching ten dollars. So, is anybody shocked to find out that the films that have grossed the most money came out in the last few years? But, do you really believe that *Dude, Where's My Car?* was a more popular film than *Gone with the Wind*? (I know—"Frankly, Miss Scarlett, you probably don't give a damn", but it just doesn't seem fair.)

Anyway, back to Mom—She majored in English, but she once told me that most of her elective courses were in philosophy, and she loved them. However, being the practical sort that she was, she decided not to major in philosophy. (Good choice, Mom!)

Picture this scenario: It's right after graduation and Mom's looking for a job. She's sitting on the couch reading the Sunday help wanted section. She reads down the list—Parking Lot Attendant, Patent Attorney, Pest Control Engineer, and then she sees it:

Philosopher wanted

Successful applicant:

- must have head in the clouds

- minimum two-year residency in Ivory Tower

- must have own sackcloth and ashes

You could be the next Socrates, Immanuel Kant, or John Paul Sartre.

Existentialism got you down? Make up your own meaning of life; share it … or impose it on others.

Compensation is competitive with the industry standard (not much).

There are no medical benefits (suffering makes you a better philosopher).

There is however, a prescription "co-payment" for hemlock.

So, instead of "I think, therefore I am", my mom decided, "I must eat, therefore I can't."

During junior year, Lillian met Joseph Curtis, whom she married six years hence. (I think the last word in the previous sentence should actually be "thence", instead of "hence". Note to publisher: If we go to a second printing, we should definitely change that last sentence. I mean, regardless of whether it's "hence" or "thence", doesn't it sound as if Jane Austen wrote it? As in "My sister Elizabeth can't see you presently, Mr. Darcy, but she will most assuredly receive you three weeks thence.")

I don't know if there is such a thing as love at first sight, but evidently Mom and Dad were in love at "first date". It must have been the real thing because for three years after graduation, they were involved in a long distance romance. Dad got a job in Boston and Mom got a newspaper job on Long Island. (Notice the "*on*" again. Note to organized crime figures *from* Staten Island: I hope you know I was only kidding before. Any preposition you choose is absolutely fine with my family and me—just wanted to clarify. I was also thinking that you might want to consider "*from*", as it was used above. It seems to do the job, and I've found that "*from*" is a very underutilized preposition.)

We're not quite done with my mom's side of the family, but before I tell you about Grandma and Grandpa Evans, let's talk about my dad.

My dad is forty-two, just like my mom. He grew up on the South Shore of Boston, and attended local parochial schools in grades 1–8. In grade nine he went to Archbishop Williams High School in Braintree, Massachusetts. (One of the odd things that people from Massachusetts do (and there are many) is that they shorten the names of things—particularly roads, places and schools. For example: there's a major thoroughfare in Boston called Massachusetts Avenue, except nobody calls it that—it's shortened to "Mass Ave". The Massachusetts Turnpike is just "The Pike". So, it became natural for Archbishop Williams to become "Archie Bills"—I hope that's not sacrilegious.)

Anyway, when Dad was at "Archie Bills", he excelled academically and was a good enough baseball player to get some scholarship money to play at BC. (That doesn't count as the Massachusetts shortened version—everybody shortens college names.) You already know about my dad meeting my mom junior year. What you don't know is that junior year was a real tough one for my dad. He lost both his parents that year—his mother to cancer, and his father to a heart attack. My dad has always thought his father actually died of a broken heart, but it doesn't say that on the death certificate.

Obviously, I never knew my grandparents on my dad's side, but in addition to whatever DNA I inherited from them, I got one more thing—my middle name. Someplace back in both my paternal grandmother and grandfather's families there was someone named Ignatius. Dad thought it would be a fitting tribute to the ancestors on both sides, that I be given that middle name. So, Benjamin Ignatius Curtis it is. And my initials became BIC.

Probably no one but me notices that I'm named after a pen company. But that's okay; I'm just glad it wasn't Papermate. (What would that look like?— Peter, Anthony, Paul, Elliot, Richard, Matthew, Allen, Thomas, Edward. Add two more names at confirmation and I'm my own football team.)

Anyway, back to Dad—Right after college he got a job at an advertising agency in Boston, where he's been ever since. I asked my dad once if he had applied to any New York ad agencies. (Remember, Long Island was where my mom had gotten a job.) He said if he thought at any time he was going to lose Mom because of the long distance relationship, he would have moved to New York, job or no job. He also said that working at a Boston ad agency kept him under the radar for the most part, and that's where he was most comfortable. (I'm sure I must have inherited the "below the radar gene" from my dad in that particular strand of the double helix. Although, being most comfortable below the radar, and being able to **stay there** are not necessarily the same thing, as we'll discover later on.)

Dad is the youngest of three siblings. Besides my dad, there's my Aunt Mona who lives in Los Angeles and my Uncle John who lives in Seattle. We don't see them very often because they live so far away (although I suspect we wouldn't see them very often even if they lived around the corner).

My Aunt Mona has been an **aspiring** actress for nearly forty years. (I don't think the adjective "aspiring" should be used if you're actually closer to "expiring".) But nonetheless, Mona continues to "aspire."

Early on in her aspirations (?) she was undoubtedly hampered by her real name, which was Jane Lee Curtis. Obviously, it was much too close to "Jamie Lee Curtis". So after years of soul searching, my aunt finally decided she should change it. Mona also kept insisting that things were even more complicated because she and Jamie Lee Curtis were often being considered for the same roles.

(Dad suggested—out of earshot from Mona—that that scenario could only be possible if Jamie Lee were playing a corpse that had been dead for 48 hours, and Mona showed up without make-up.)

Anyway, my aunt legally changed her name to (are you ready?)—Mona Lisa; she dropped the "Curtis" entirely. That was fifteen years ago, and the only part she's gotten recently was a small one in *The DaVinci Code*. The director was evidently a big fan of irony. (He should have known me when I was three.)

My dad's other sibling, my Uncle John, has also had his share of tough times as well. Quite a few years back, John decided to join a commune in Seattle and kind of "drop out" for a while. It wasn't that he detested the material world; it seemed, rather, that **it** didn't like him very much. He tried a number of small business ventures, none of which seemed to work out. Dad said his brother didn't have a good head for business. (But to tell you the truth, I don't think any other part of his anatomy was business-oriented either.) To be fair, however, sometimes a good head for business simply means good timing. My Uncle John didn't have good timing either. The week before he joined the commune, he sold his little corner coffee shop in Seattle. The next week it opened as the first "Starbucks". (The Tangent City options here are endless, but I'm going to resist. You're always welcome to indulge, however.)

Okay, back to my mom's family—that would be my grandma and grandpa, Ellen and Marc Evans. Outside of my parents, Grandma and Grandpa are my two favorite people in the world. I suspect part of the reason I feel that way is because, from the time I was three, I spent four or five weeks with them every summer.

Even with my eidetic memory, I'm hard pressed to think of any negative moments I've ever spent with my grandparents. As a matter of fact, the only flaw they have is that they're **Yankee fans**. You see, since we live in the Boston area, my parents and I are HUGE Red Sox fans. I mean, we actually bleed red … (Okay, bad metaphor, but you get the idea.)

I think what bothers Grandpa most about the fact that we're Red Sox fans is that Mom converted. (Yeah, it is almost a religious thing.) Mom was a Yankee fan until she went to Boston College. But I think it's hard to spend four years in Boston, two of them dating my dad, and not "see the light".

There's always a lot of good-natured kidding (at least I think it's good-natured) that goes back and forth, especially between my grandpa and my dad. Grandpa was riding high before 2004 when the Red Sox won their first World Series in 86 years. Here are two of Grandpa's better zingers aimed at my dad. (Grandpa told me he hadn't actually made them up; he heard them on TV):

In 1999—"Listen Joe, you shouldn't feel too bad about the Red Sox; after all, any team can have a bad century."

In 2000—"Joe, I really thought the Red Sox were going to win the World Series in 1992. I mean they won it in 1918. I thought maybe they were destined to win it the year after **every** Russian Revolution."

Dad didn't have a lot of comebacks until 2004—"So, Marc, how many World Series have the Yankees won this millennium?"

Back to Grandma and Grandpa—Grandma was a school secretary and retired a few years ago. Grandpa was a humanities professor at a local college. He still teaches part-time in the evening division.

Grandpa loves history—almost any kind—the history of art, the history of baseball, the history of rock and roll, the history of television—well, you get the idea. What a gift it was for me to spend a month or more every summer listening to my grandfather tell me about the history of everything. When I combine all this historical knowledge with my ICBM, I'm almost able to see the world through my grandpa's eyes, and the view is pretty terrific.

On most occasions when Grandpa was telling me his stories, Grandma would be there too. Often, she would appear to be reading, but she was obviously paying attention to our conversation, because she would correct Grandpa whenever he made a mistake, or exaggerated something. Usually the exaggeration involved the Yankees. So, whenever Grandpa talked about the Yankees, I learned to take it with a grain of salt (actually, more like a cellar of salt). The exception to this was Mickey Mantle; Grandpa loved Mickey Mantle. He knew every statistic about "The Mick", and never exaggerated. Of course for the most part, he didn't need to exaggerate with Mickey Mantle; the reality was pretty special.

There was one additional thing Grandma would do when the three of us were together, and I was listening to Grandpa's stories. She would say, "AM, Marc" or "FM, Marc". One time Grandpa was telling me the story of how my parents met. In the middle of it Grandma said, "Definitely, FM", and I started thinking—why does she want to listen to the radio? Grandma saw the puzzled look on my face and explained. "Whenever your grandfather is telling one of his stories, I let him know if he's remembering things correctly, by saying 'AM'—for accurate memory, or 'FM'—for faulty memory. (Gee, I wonder where my love of abbreviations comes from?)

So, Grandma and Grandpa got into a mini-debate about the "how my parents met" story. And despite Grandpa's attempt at revisionist history, Grandma's version prevailed. "I'm sorry, Marc, but it was 'FM'." (The good news is that Grandma says "FM", when most people would probably say "BS".) Following all this, I found out that my parents met on Boston Common. (Should that be *at* Boston Common?—darn those prepositions!)

In my grandparents' finished basement were bookcases, shelves, file cabinets, and closets filled with the history of all those subjects I mentioned before. Grandpa and I spent hours listening to old records (yes, the vinyl kind) from the 50's and 60's, and CD's from the 70's and 80's. Grandpa would tell me what was happening in the world, and what was going on in his life when various songs were popular.

He introduced me to Johnny Ray, Theresa Brewer, Patti Page, Nat King Cole, Perry Como, Sam Cooke, Tommy Sands, Pat Boone, The Everly Brothers, Ricky Nelson, and of course, Elvis. And even though I already knew many of the singers and groups from the 70's and 80's from my parents' collection, Grandpa and I listened to those too. Sometimes we would talk about what the lyrics meant, particularly after listening to protest songs and songs by Bob Dylan or Peter, Paul, and Mary.

One day Grandpa said that he wanted me to hear one of his favorite songs. And, while he really liked the music, he said the lyrics were what made it special. The song was *Hotel California* by the Eagles. And his favorite lyrics were "You can checkout any time you like, but you can never leave." You know what? I think I agree with my grandpa.

Of course we also listened to some songs that were at the other end of the "sensibilities spectrum". The lyrics in those songs were, shall we say, "inspirationally challenged". A couple of examples would be *Disco Duck* by Rick Dees, and *Yummy, Yummy, Yummy, I've Got Love in My Tummy* by Ohio Express. Actually, Ohio Express recorded a few dozen songs in the "bubblegum rock" genre. But I think it's safe to say, none of the other releases could possibly approach the group's masterful interpretation of the symbolic nuances and subtleties that are inherent in the "Yummy" lyrics. (Do you think sarcasm is a dying art?)

Besides listening to all that music, we also watched old movies and TV shows together. Sometimes Grandma would join us, and more than once she said, "Marc, let's take Benny to the beach/the movies/an amusement park". And sometimes we would do those things, but after a while, Grandma stopped suggesting it. I think she could see by the expression on my face that those "fun" things were never as good as being in that basement with my grandpa watching old TV shows.

Was this about "bonding" with my grandpa? Was it because of my ICBM? I'm not sure. I just know that I liked it, and I felt if I started to analyze why, it wouldn't be fun anymore. It would be like asking someone to explain why he likes chocolate ice cream. Sometimes, "because it tastes good" should be sufficient.

Two of my favorite old time TV shows are *Lassie* and *The Tonight Show* with Johnny Carson. (What were you expecting—*My Mother the Car?*) I'm not going to try to analyze why I like those shows. (I already told you I don't care for all this analysis stuff.) But, I am going to offer some observations. (Surprise, surprise)

In *Lassie*, the dog was obviously meant to be the star. Although Grandpa told me that he thought they used 13 **different** dogs in the show. (I might appear to be really smart also if I had 12 of my friends helping me.) Anyway, I really have nothing against Lassie, but I actually think that Timmy, Lassie's owner, should have gotten way more credit than he did.

Let's look at a typical story line, and I think you'll see what I mean about Timmy not getting the credit he deserved:

Timmy is looking at Lassie. She obviously can't speak, but he sees her wagging her tail and hears her barking. She then grabs his hand with her teeth. And from just the wagging, barking, and grabbing, Timmy is able to conclude that: Old Mrs. Wilson has fallen down the well out in the north forty.

See what I mean? Who's the real genius here? I think the show should have been called *Timmy*—and they wouldn't have needed 12 other kids to stand in for him.

As I said, my other real favorite old time TV show is *The Tonight Show* starring Johnny Carson. I especially like the "Carnac" segment in which Ed McMahon would give the answer, and then Johnny Carson as "Carnac" would "divine" the question. (Is that how *Jeopardy* got started?)

Anyway, here's an example:

The answer is—"Siss boom baa."

The question is—"What sound does a sheep make when it explodes?"

I laughed for five minutes straight after I heard that one. I suspect wordplay really appeals to my sense of humor, probably because of the ICBM. But I don't know what Grandpa's excuse was; he laughed longer than I did.

Sometimes Grandpa and I would make up our own "Carnac" routines. My favorite of those occurred after we watched a segment of *The Tonight Show* that aired on Friday the 13th. During that segment all of the answers were phobias of some sort, like "triscadecaphobia"—the fear of the number thirteen.

My grandpa made up this one:

The answer is: "BLT/ESP—phobia."

The question is: "What is the unnatural fear that your lunch knows what you're thinking?"

I laughed for way longer than five minutes.

So, now you know how come I have all this knowledge about things that happened decades ago. And although I can talk about these things with my mom and dad, Grandpa's the only one that has all the background and can answer all my questions.

Those weeks every summer are something I really look forward to each year. And every one of those visits with my grandparents has been special in its own way; but that first one really helped shape the next several years of my young life.

It was the summer after I turned three. My grandparents knew that Mom and Dad were considering a "school for the gifted" for yours truly. So besides wanting to spend time with their only grandchild, I suspect Grandma and Grandpa also wanted to see what all the fuss was about.

I also overheard my mom talking to Grandma, and the words "assess his intellectual ability" were spoken a number of times in the side of the conversation I was privy to. Of course, all of this made sense. Don't forget, Grandma was a former school secretary and Grandpa was a college professor, so they both knew something about education. And besides, they were my grandparents and I'm sure they wanted to have some say in what was going to happen.

Since I had overheard part of the phone conversation, I was not unprepared when Mom said, "Benny, how would you like to spend some time with Grandma and Grandpa?" (It's always interesting to me that parents phrase decisions that have already been made in the form of a question. I suspect it's an attempt to maintain the façade that the family unit is a democracy, and kids have a vote. Here's another one—"What do you think about going to bed?" Note to parents: Just say, "It's time for bed". No question needs to be posed. Additional note: Of course, none of this question business is actually employed at mealtimes—Parents never **ask** if you would like more spinach. It's always in the form of a command—"Eat your vegetables")

So anyway, when Mom asked the question about a visit to Grandma and Grandpa's, I decided to make it easy on her. I just said, "That would be great".

When I went to stay with my grandparents that first summer, I prepared myself to be subjected to Rorschach pictures, brain scans, and psychological batteries. (Why do you think they call them batteries, by the way? I have to say, that description really made me nervous. I mean, I was afraid of static electricity, never mind the idea of being hooked up to some gigantic Energizer Bunny machine.)

Anyway, none of the intense scrutiny I expected ever took place. Instead, we just got to know each other—and much better than we ever did during our brief holiday visits in the past. I was feeling pretty comfortable; but remember, I was still somewhat guarded about the ICBM and my adult vocabulary. So Grandma and Grandpa initially didn't get the full treatment.

After I had been there about a week, Grandma and Grandpa asked me to come into the living room and have a seat. Even though I hadn't noticed any pre-discussion conference (maybe it skips a generation), I still figured something was up. Grandpa started—"Benny, I think you know that your mother and father are considering sending you to a 'school for the gifted'. How do you feel about that?"

Before I responded, I thought to myself—wow, I like this approach. It's right up front, and he's actually asking me for my input. It didn't feel like those questions I mentioned before where the decision had already been made. Nevertheless, I still couched my response. "I'm not sure, Grandpa, it strikes me as somewhat ... elitist."

You know the "jaw-dropping thing" that Mom has? Well, she didn't get it from her father. Instead of Grandpa's jaw dropping, his eyebrows shot up. But then I looked over at Grandma, and there it was—the same jaw-dropping motion as Mom. (There's got to be a jaw-dropping gene that gets passed on. I wonder if Miss Frist is a distant relative?)

I looked back at Grandpa, who was fumbling for words. They finally came out in a sputter, "But ... when ... how ...?" And then he stopped trying to talk and just stared at me for about ten seconds. I could almost see the wheels spinning in his head, and then he calmly said, "You know what, Benny? I think maybe that says it all. I've actually been giving this 'school for the gifted' notion a lot of thought, and I'm going to suggest to your parents that they scrap the whole idea ... As far as I'm concerned, we don't need to discuss it again." (Of course, what just transpired could never really be defined as a discussion, but let's not nit-pick.)

Grandpa then continued. "I'm not sure it's the right thing for you, Benny." He paused. "I do have another idea, however, but I want to think it through some more, and talk it over with your grandmother. Then we'll discuss it with you."

I remember thinking, "Oh, I like this guy." Even if he weren't my grandfather, I would want to be around him. He seems to know just what to do. He treats me like a mini-adult, which is kind of what I am. It takes a special kind of person to see beyond my size ... and the fact that I've only been potty-trained for three months. (About the potty-training thing—it's difficult to be objective, but looking back, I probably should have been out of diapers by two, two and a half tops; I think it was pure laziness on my part. Of course Freud might suggest it was more psychologically based. But who made him such an expert? He didn't even have indoor plumbing, did he?)

So, only two days went by, we were all sitting in the living room, and Grandpa said, "Benny, here's my idea." (There was no need for any preliminaries; we both knew what this was about.) "I think you should start kindergarten a year early, when you're four. You'd still be in the public schools, where you seem to want to be, and it wouldn't be an … elitist situation." He paused as his eyebrows went halfway up, and he tilted his head to one side. "It still might not be all that challenging for you, but I've always been of the opinion—'What's the rush?'"

I waited about three seconds as my eyeballs darted back and forth. (I always do that when I'm processing information.) And then I said, "Okay", followed quickly by, "Can I have some juice?" And I headed for the kitchen. I didn't look back for any jaw-dropping or full eyebrow-raising.

I heard Grandma get up and start to follow me. And with more than a hint of concern in her voice, she said, "Sure." She paused. "We have apple juice and orange juice."

"Do you have any grape juice?"

Grandma said, "No", but I'm not sure that was exactly true. I think she might have hidden it away; I'm guessing Mom might have squealed. But I figured I wouldn't press the point. "Well, apple it is then."

Later that day Grandpa called Mom and Dad and offered his suggestion. They both liked the idea, but they still had to convince the officials at the local public school to enroll me a year early.

That would prove to be quite interesting, enlightening, and entertaining. (You'd be amazed at how many different body parts, besides jaws and eyebrows, can express shock and surprise.)

Chapter 3

▼

Before I tell you about the follow-up to Grandpa's suggestion about starting kindergarten early, there's some unfinished business.

Remember I mentioned about context and family? Well actually, there are a couple of other things that provide context for our lives as well—like our friends and where we live. And certainly as we get older, school, and eventually our jobs, provide context also. But since I wasn't in school yet and was still unemployed (what a slacker), the only other context for me, besides family, was friends and neighborhood.

And frankly, as far as friends are concerned, I think they have a much greater influence on us later in life, certainly from the teenage years on. I mean, if you think about it, how does a three-year-old even make friends?—Have your mom drop you off at the local juice bar, and then what's your opening line? "Hey, nice pull-up." (Plus, our local juice bar doesn't even stock grape juice; Mom must have told everyone.)

When you're three-years-old, your "friends" are usually neighborhood kids, if there are any, or children of your mom's friends. And usually, the only way three-year-olds get together is the "play date". This is the toddler version of the "blind date", and it's fraught with many of the same potential problems as the adult version. Maybe even more.

At least with the blind date you can prearrange to have a friend call you on your cell phone with some "emergency". And if things aren't going well, you can excuse yourself. What does a three-year-old do? (Note to toddlers: Since most of you don't have cell phones, here are a few suggestions you can use to short circuit a play date. I actually only used the first one, but I think both the second and third ones will work.)

- "Mom, I think I left the water running in the upstairs sink."

- "Mom, did I tell you about the phone call from 'Publisher's Clearinghouse' that said to make sure we're home by ___?" (Fill in an appropriate time.)

- "Mom, has this rash on my groin always been there?"

However, the problem with making excuses is that you can only go to the well just so often (although I suspect that Timmy, Lassie, and especially Mrs. Wilson, hope that's not true). I just figured that if I kept making excuses to get out of play dates, Mom might be concerned that I was socially maladjusted.

Mom and I were eventually able to come to a compromise, but only after a particularly painful play date. It took some doing, but I was finally able to convince her that it was okay not to arrange so many of them. It wasn't as if I was going to be traumatized for life if we cut down; and the "mother of the year" competition wasn't based on the number of play dates I had.

"Mom, could you ask me ahead of time, before you set up a play date? Sometimes I'd rather do something else. And as you know, I'm pretty self-sufficient".

Mom chuckled. "You know, you're probably right, as usual. I guess I should just ask you ahead of time. I probably have to start treating you more like a grown-up."

Me again. "I know it's not so easy being a mom, especially **mine**, but I think you're doing a great job. We probably just need to tweak a few things."

Now Mom laughed out loud. "Benny, where did you come from?" (For a minute I thought this was going to be "the birds and the bees talk", but I was wrong. And thank goodness, because I still hadn't formulated all my questions in non-technical language.)

Mom started shaking her head, and continued to laugh. She then opened up her arms and said, "How about a hug?"

I walked over to Mom and we hugged each other. After a short time, with my arms still wrapped around her waist, I lifted my head and looked up at her. "You know, just because I want you to ask me about play dates, doesn't mean you have to ask me for hugs. Those you can have whenever you want—no questions asked."

I thought I saw the start of some moisture in the corner of her eyes, but I'm not sure.

So, what precipitated this eventual meeting of the minds about play dates? It would be unfair to call it the "play date from Hell", but it probably qualifies as the "play date from Purgatory" or maybe from "Limbo" (the place where babies go, not the dance). Is Limbo still in operation, by the way? I haven't heard anything about it in a long time.

Anyway, back to the play date from somewhere—you be the judge. It was a Thursday morning in August, and I had just gotten back from my first extended summer stay with Grandma and Grandpa. (I sound like Joe Friday again.) Anyway, Mom came into my room and said with a twinkle in her eye, "Good morning, Benjamin." Usually the use of "Benjamin" is not a good sign, but in this instance the twinkle told me it was okay. (Mom would **not** be a good poker player—way too many "tells".)

"How would you like to go on a play date this afternoon? (Notice the use of a question again. Even so, I knew it was pointless to respond with something like, "No, thanks, I'd rather rearrange my sock drawer.") Instead, I managed an "Okay". Mom looked at me quizzically and said, "You don't seem very enthusiastic."

"Mom, can I be honest?" Mom knew it was a rhetorical question, but she smiled and responded anyway, "Of course."

"Well, the month I just spent with Grandma and Grandpa was really terrific, and I'm not sure anything is going to top that. Plus, sometimes I'm not all that comfortable with kids my own age". (This whole situation was a real dilemma. I did enjoy things that most three-year-olds enjoy, but sometimes the ICBM was at odds with me being a kid. Ah, the internal struggle. Is that philosopher's position still open?)

Mom said, "I'm really glad you had such a good time with your grandma and grandpa. They said they really enjoyed you being there, too. But don't you think you could also enjoy being with other kids?"

"Yeah, I guess so."

"Well that's not exactly a ringing endorsement, but I'll take what I can get. Let's get you dressed." (Now, I'm perfectly capable of dressing myself, but Mom picks out "what goes with what"—ICBM doesn't help in the fashion department.)

Around eleven o'clock we got into the car, and Mom headed toward Route 3A. She then started to fill me in about where we were going, and whom I was about to meet. (Yeah, it's *whom*—I checked. I have enough problems with prepositions; I'm not about to bring pronouns into the mix. Although in the future, I might just use "who" even if it's not correct. I mean, isn't "whom" way too pompous sounding?)

My play date was with Johnny Buckley, actually Johnson Buckley III. (No three-year-old should be stuck with that moniker.) Anyway, he lived in the next town over, which meant that his family was very rich. I don't usually care about things like that, but in this instance I didn't have a good feeling.

My mom had met Johnny's mom at the hospital where they both volunteered. Evidently, one conversation led to another, and when they found out they both had three-year-olds (although Johnny is almost four), the play date became a done deal.

Mom was checking house numbers and finally found the right one—4788 Whispering Pines Drive. (Is it really necessary to describe Whispering Pines Drive? Suffice to say, you won't find that street name in a trailer park; and if the pines were whispering, they were saying—"ostentatious", "pretentious", and "overindulgent". Each house on the block had to be over 6000 square feet.) But I put any pre-judgment on hold. Just because the Buckleys had a house that could double as an airplane hangar, didn't mean that they couldn't be down-to-earth. (Especially since their house was sitting on three acres of it.)

So, enlightened three-year-old that I was, I prepared myself to give everyone the benefit of the doubt. As it turned out, that was a good call for Mrs. Buckley, not so much for Johnny.

Mom rang the doorbell and Mrs. Buckley answered it. (What, no butler? All right, I'll stop; I said I was enlightened.) "Hi, Lillian—and you must be Benny. Please come in."

Mom and I both looked around, but we weren't really prepared for what we saw—a curved staircase, crystal chandeliers, **original** artwork, etc.

Mom finally managed to speak, "You have a lovely home. It's breathtaking."

"Thank you, Lillian. But honestly, it's way over the top, if you ask me. Johnson, that's my husband, says it's a good investment, and I'm sure it is. It's just that it's too big; it doesn't feel like a home. Johnson promised that we can move in a year or two when Johnny starts school. Actually, my husband expects to be transferred anyway, probably out-of-state, so that may force the move sooner."

Mom says, "Well, regardless, it's beautiful."

"Thank you, you're very kind. Johnny's in the family room; it's this way."

Mom and I followed. As we were heading down the hallway, Mrs. Buckley continued, "Thanks for doing this—the play date I mean. Johnny doesn't have many opportunities to be with kids his own age. I'm not sure he knows how to interact with them appropriately. We had him in a pre-school, but I don't think we're going to send him back in September; it didn't seem like a good fit." (I know that seems like a lot of conversation for just walking down a hallway, but you have no idea how long it was. I could have finished the New York Times crossword puzzle—the Sunday one, not the easier ones in the beginning of the week—before we even got to the family room.)

As we arrived, Mrs. Buckley said, "Here we are. Benny, this is Johnny; Johnny, this is Benny." I was able to get "Hi" out of my mouth, but just barely. To say that I was taken aback would be a huge understatement—Johnny was wearing a three-piece suit, vest and all, with a monogrammed handkerchief in the pocket. I'm not sure if Johnny said anything to me, because Mrs. Buckley interrupted the proceedings.

"Johnny, I thought we talked about dressing appropriately for today. Honey, that suit is really for special occasions, not a play date. You're kind of overdressed". (Ya think?—Johnny would have been overdressed for a coronation—**even his own!**)

Johnny then spoke up. "I know, Mother, but I really like this outfit." I was a little surprised that there was no additional discussion after that, but Johnny's statement just seemed to end it. A moment later, he pulled me aside, literally, and pointed to two piles of toys. "Yours", and then the other one, "Mine".

I wasn't exactly sure what to do, so I just headed for "my" pile of toys. Johnny sat with his back to me, so the chance of any meaningful interaction was non-existent. I think child development experts call this "parallel play"—but this could more appropriately be called "parallel **universe** play".)

We sat separately for about twenty minutes while our moms talked. The family room was enormous, and Mom and Mrs. Buckley were sitting quite a distance away, so I couldn't really hear any of their conversation. But finally, I did hear Mrs. Buckley say, "I'm going to fix lunch."

Mom offered, "Can I do anything to help?"

"No, not really, but if you'd like to keep me company, that would be great; I'm sure the boys will be fine."

Mom looked over at me and said, "Okay, Benny?"

Unfortunately, Mrs. Buckley was looking in my direction also, so there was no way to signal to Mom that I had any concerns. I mean, I didn't really think that "Little Lord Fauntleroy" was dangerous, but I still didn't necessarily want to be alone with him. I tried to think of something to say which might get them back more quickly. The only thing I came up with was—"I hope we eat soon; I'm kind of hungry."

The whole time they were gone I really did try to engage Johnny in conversation, but he only said two words to me.

I asked him which one of the Power Rangers he liked the best—no response.

I asked him if he thought the Rugrats cartoon portrayed toddlers in a favorable light—no response.

I asked him if he thought the Fed would raise interest rates next month. That time I got a look, but still no response. So, I tried a different tack.

"Can we go for a swim in your pool?"

"Can't—being cleaned" (Okay, I lied; he said three words)

Finally, after about fifteen minutes Mom and Mrs. Buckley returned. They each had a salad and there was a grilled cheese sandwich for Johnny, and a peanut butter and jelly sandwich for me. (I really like peanut butter and jelly, so don't knock it. Plus it was **grape** jelly; and since there was no way for me to get the taste of grapes in juice form anymore, this was the next best thing).

Mrs. Buckley left some extra bread and the peanut butter and jelly on the table. "If you want some more, Benny, help yourself. Your mom and I are going to sit out on the deck." Mom and Mrs. Buckley went to the sliding glass doors, and I was again left alone with Marcel Marceau.

So, needless to say, Johnny and I were eating in silence. But, to be fair, Johnny couldn't have spoken anyway because he had half of his grilled cheese sandwich stuffed in his mouth. His cheeks looked like a squirrel's, with winter fast approaching. Somehow he managed to swallow most of what he had in his mouth, and then proceeded to stuff the second half of his sandwich in there as well. It took him less than a minute to eat his entire lunch.

I, on the other hand, took a lot of extra time to savor the "grapeness" of my sandwich. (Is "grapeness" a word?) While I was still eating, Johnny decided to make himself another sandwich—a peanut butter and jelly one this time.

Unfortunately as he went to transfer the jelly to the bread, the knife fell out of his hand on to the rug, and a whole glob of jelly with it. Being somewhat of a grape spill expert (juice and a semi-solid glob are not that different), I figured I could help. But before I was able to make a move, Johnny picked up the knife, scooped out another glob of jelly and threw it down on the rug. He then added some peanut butter and some milk for good measure. That part of the rug looked like one of the Jackson Pollock paintings his parents had on their wall. (Maybe they're not originals after all.)

I'm not sure what sound I made, but whatever it was, it brought Mom and Mrs. Buckley rushing back into the family room. Mrs. Buckley looked at the Jackson Pollock wannabe and said, "Oh my gosh, what happened here?"

Johnny, being a man of few words, just pointed. Mom followed Johnny's finger with her eyes and they eventually landed on me. "Benny, are you responsible for this?" (I was sure that she knew that I wasn't, but she had to ask.) I did some quick thinking, and remembered something my grandma had said—"FM, Mom, FM!" I could see in Mom's eyes that she knew Grandma's code.

Mrs. Buckley was looking quizzically at both Mom and me. I thought she was about to say something, but Mom jumped in—"Benny says he didn't do it."

I'm sure Mrs. Buckley had no idea how Mom could possibly have figured that out from me yelling "FM", so she asked me directly—"Benny, who did this?" I pointed at Johnny. (Two can play at this silent pointing game.)

Johnny then erupted. "You don't believe me; you don't believe me!" And then he proceeded to hold his breath. Nobody did anything for about ten seconds, and then Mrs. Buckley said, "Johnny stop that; I want you to look at me; let's talk about what happened." Johnny continued to hold his breath, and then he folded his arms across his chest.

Mrs. Buckley said to Mom, "I'm so sorry about this."

"It's okay; but maybe we should go."

Mrs. Buckley just nodded, and Mom started to usher me out of the room just as the effects of diminished oxygen on Johnny's complexion were becoming evident. (Note to Crayola: Have you ever considered some really unique crayon color titles? I mean we all know what "fire engine red" looks like, and the same for "taxicab yellow". If you're interested, however, I could help you develop "temper-tantrum blue".)

I think Mom called Mrs. Buckley later that night to see how everything turned out, but she didn't give me the details. As I mentioned before, however, something good came out of the debacle at the Buckley's; it led to the renegotiation of the whole play date situation. And ironically, there would be one more play date that summer, and **I** was the one who pushed for it.

A week or so AB, (After Buckley—it actually is a demarcation line in my childhood; not as significant as PPT—Post Potty Training, but important, nonetheless), Mom took me to my pediatrician to check out a rash I had developed. (No, it wasn't in my groin area, plus it was AB anyway, so I couldn't have used it as an excuse.) It turned out to be poison ivy. The doctor gave me some lotion and sent us on our way.

My pediatrician's office is in another part of town about four miles from where we live. On the way home, Mom mentioned that she had to stop at the supermarket to pick up a few things. Even though she didn't usually shop at this particular store, it was on the way home, so in we went.

As I said before, even with the ICBM, I was still a kid; and I liked to do a lot of the things other kids liked to do. One of those things was riding in the shopping carts at the supermarket. But, only if they were made over to be racecars or chariots, or something like that.

At this particular store there was a shopping cart that looked just like the "Batmobile". Mom had to separate seven carriages to get to it, but she didn't seem to mind, especially when she saw the smile on my face.

As I was "tooling" around the store, (I know Mom was pushing the carriage, but work with me here—it's tough enough trying to act like a superhero with your mom pushing your "wheels"), I started singing the "Batman" song—you know—"da, da, da, da, da, da, da, da, da, da, da da da da Batman." (Talk about meaningful lyrics—Did Bob Dylan write that?)

Anyway, Mom picked up a few items and put them in the "Batmobile." (I'm not sure Bruce Wayne would have ever allowed asparagus anywhere near his upholstery.) As Mom was looking at some additional items on the shelves, I saw a woman and a small boy at the end of the aisle. As they got closer, the woman started staring at Mom. Finally, as she got within a few feet, she said, "Lillian Evans, is that you?"

Mom looked up at the mention of her maiden name, and from the expression on her face, I could see that she recognized the other woman. Mom's voice went up about two octaves. (She still wasn't in Pollyanna Frist territory, though.) "Janet Rice, I don't believe it." They moved toward each other and started to hug.

After a few moments they separated, and the other woman said, "Oh, Lillian, what's it been since graduation—eleven years?" (Must have been a math major.)

"Yes, Janet, I think that's right. Look at you; you look terrific. What are you doing here? Last thing I heard, you were headed back to Chicago after graduation."

"I did, but a year and a half ago, Bob—my husband, got transferred to Boston. It's Janet Davis, now."

"And I'm Lillian Curtis now. Do you live here in town?"

"Yes, about a mile from here. This is so funny."

"It is. I can't believe this."

Almost simultaneously Mom and Mrs. Davis realized that there were also two toddlers with them.

"Oh, Janet, this is my son Benny. Say hello, Benny." I could tell Mom was pretty excited about meeting her college friend because she actually **instructed** me to say hello. (Hey, I don't have all the social graces down pat, but I know enough to say hello when I first meet someone. Plus what were my other options—"Do you think the idea of the **Euro** will eventually catch on?")

"Hi, nice to meet you", I said. (Mom didn't seem to mind that I modified the greeting slightly from her instructions.)

"Nice to meet you also, Benny. Let me guess—you must be about three." (I told you—either a math major, or she works at a carnival. If she had gotten my age wrong, would she have owed me a stuffed animal?)

"Yes, I am."

"And this is my nephew, Derek; he's four." Derek said "Hi" to both Mom and me with a little wave. "And this is my...." Mrs. Davis was looking up and down the aisle, just as a little girl came around the corner.

"Oh, Vanessa, I thought you were right behind me. Anyway, this is my daughter, Vanessa. Vanessa, this is Mrs. Curtis—right? And her son, Benny."

Vanessa said, "Hi" and then she handed something to her mom to put into their shopping cart.

Remember when I said that I didn't know if there was such a thing as "love at first sight"? Well, the way I felt at that moment would have bolstered the "pro" side of that argument. However, I also realized that the way I was feeling toward Vanessa was probably exaggerated because of what she was carrying—grape juice.

I know that I seemed obsessed with grape juice (talk about "forbidden fruit"). But I definitely preferred it to the other fruit juices; and I really thought Mom overreacted to the spill at my birthday party. (The woman can hold a grudge.) I did try some logical arguments in an attempt to persuade her to lift the grape juice ban.

"Mom did you realize that grape juice is a strong anti-oxidant? It slows down the aging process." (Probably not a big selling point when you're three.) Mom just said, "Uh—huh".

Actually, I'm not sure how we ever got **any** kind of juice into the house, because whenever we went to the supermarket, Mom skipped the juice aisle completely. Did you notice that Vanessa came from around the corner with the juice? The "Batmobile" never even went down that aisle.

Okay, here's the deal. Just like I said I wouldn't bring up the "Lillian and Joe" and "Mom and Dad" thing again—I'm going to do the same thing with grape juice. I won't bring it up again, unless it's integral to the story. (Sort of like in the movies when actresses say they won't do a nude scene unless the nudity is integral to the plot.)

So, back to Vanessa, Derek, and Mrs. Davis—The conversation between the adults continued for about ten more minutes. Mom filled in Mrs. Davis about Dad, his job, her volunteer work, where we lived etc.

Mrs. Davis told Mom that her husband and Derek's dad were brothers, and that Derek's parents lived in town as well. She said that Vanessa was four years old (about two months older than Derek), and that they went to the same pre-school. Mrs. Davis then asked if I attended school yet. Mom said that she and Dad were looking into some options.

While this conversation was going on, I extricated myself from the "Batmobile." (It's not as easy as it looks on TV; and don't forget, they get to do multiple takes.) Vanessa and Derek talked to each other, and then they spoke to me briefly. I really liked the idea that they made the effort; but honestly, the whole situation was very awkward.

Think about it—what can three toddlers possibly talk about in the middle of a supermarket aisle—"Come here often?" "Only when my mom brings me." "Do you like my wheels?"

I was tempted to bring up the container of grape juice, but decided against it. I didn't want to appear to be needy. (Hey, that was integral.)

Finally, Mom and Mrs. Davis exchanged phone numbers and said goodbye, but I knew a play date was definitely in the offing. And how bad could it be—Derek wasn't wearing any monogrammed clothing, and Vanessa had grape juice. (Okay, I agree, that may have been pushing it.)

Chapter 4

▼

That night as I was lying in bed, I thought about meeting Derek and Vanessa in the supermarket. I really felt a connection to both of them. Of course, given my most recent play date experience with Johnny Buckley, there wasn't a whole lot of competition in the "Connection Olympics".

Some people might find it unusual that I could feel so connected to Derek and Vanessa after knowing them for only ten minutes. But actually, a lot of experts in the field of human behavior believe that this experience is quite common. In fact, that's the whole theory behind "speed dating".

I saw a segment on some TV show that was entitled "The Speed Dating Phenomenon". (Shouldn't the word 'phenomenon' be reserved for more spectacular things?—The **aurora borealis** is a phenomenon; I don't think speed dating even comes close to qualifying. It must have been sweeps month on TV.)

Anyway, here's how speed dating works: Twenty men and women come together in a large room. All of the members of one gender—let's say females—sit at individual tables scattered around the room. Each of the males then sits opposite one of the females. (Doesn't this sound like it belongs on "The Discovery Channel" or "Animal Planet"?) Anyway, the men and women talk to each other for five minutes, and then a bell sounds (or possibly a gong, if things aren't going well). Each male then moves on to the next female. (Now, I'm sure of it; I know I've heard those exact words spoken by a narrator on "Animal Planet".) Anyway, the process continues until everyone has spent five minutes with each person of the other gender.

The "inventors" of speed dating (It's not Thomas Alva Edison territory, is it?) subscribe to the notion that most people know within five minutes of meeting someone whether there's a connection or not.

It seems to me, if their hypothesis is correct, then with just a few modifications, this could be a huge cultural "phenomenon" for **toddlers** everywhere (Oh, so it's okay for adults to use the word phenomenon, but not kids?) Anyway, here's my idea:

"The Speed Play Date"

In case you're interested in organizing one of these, I took the liberty of listing some of the modifications I would recommend:

1. No three-piece suits or monogrammed clothing for any of the participants. (As you could probably figure out, this is more of my own personal preference than some of the other modifications). You know, on second thought, you can scrap that modification. If these toddlers have a chance to find each other, who am I to stand in the way?)

2. The speed play date must be held in the morning before naptime. (If the toddler you're meeting with falls asleep during your session together, the damage to your self-esteem could be devastating.)

3. No stuffed animals or action figures—If you're trying to find out if there's a connection with someone, you don't want to hear—" Say hi to my kitty cat, Miss Fluffytail". Or worse—" My Transformer can blow up Miss Fluffytail with his hand-held bazooka." (Note to adults: If you're involved in speed dating, I would recommend that you **also** adhere to the "no stuffed animals or action figures" modification—might seriously limit your prospects.)

4. There should be frequent diaper-changing breaks. If your mom comes up to you while you're talking with a potential play date and says, "Did you do 'poopies'?—Could be a mood-breaker.

I think this speed play date idea may have some real potential.

Anyway, back to my thoughts about a play date with Derek and Vanessa. The next morning, when Mom came into my room to see if I was awake yet, she sat on the edge of the bed, as she always did, and said, "How're you doing, Sleepyhead?"

I paused for just a moment and then said, "HAGS."

"Oh, that's an easy one, Benny; you've used it before—**Had a good sleep.**"

"Also, Mom, I-L-A-P-D."

Mom thought for a moment—" I'd like another play date".

"Right." (She was getting really good at this).

Mom again—"W-D-A-V?"

"Yeah—with Derek and Vanessa."

"I thought you might. They seem …" She was searching for the right words … or letters.

I jumped in—"M-N-T-J"

She looked puzzled for a moment and then said, "I wasn't thinking—'more normal than Johnny' … if that's what you meant." Then she smiled a huge smile, knowing that she had gotten caught. We both laughed, and she gave me a kiss on the forehead.

"Anyway, enough of this anagram stuff; it's time for you to get up. While you're getting dressed, I'll call Mrs. Davis and try to set something up for next week. I also have to call the school department to set up a meeting about your early kindergarten enrollment." She said this last sentence more to herself than to me.

She addressed me again. "Do you want to eat breakfast first or get dressed first?"

I thought for a moment and then said, "CATSPAWF".

Mom scrunched up her mouth and tilted her head, obviously trying to figure out my anagram. "Nope, I've got no clue."

"Cereal, and then surely proper attire will follow."

Mom raised her eyebrows and started to chuckle. "How long have you been waiting to use that one?"

I just smiled back at her as she continued. "So, I'm guessing that after all of this anagram stuff, you'll be having your usual for breakfast—Alphabits."

"Of course."

I got out of bed and followed Mom into the kitchen. She got me some cereal and some juice (nope, not integral). And then she took some papers out of her pocketbook, which must have been the phone numbers for Mrs. Davis and the school department.

By the way, I probably should mention that there are some house rules concerning the eating of Alphabits:

- The Alphabits must always stay in the bowl; I can't put them on the table to spell words.

- I can only make words with the letters floating in the milk; but I can add cereal if I need additional letters to complete a sentence.

- I can only use the spoon to move the letters around in the bowl, no fingers.

I adhere to these rules very strictly. I know they're for my own good.

The first time I had Alphabits, before the rules were enacted, it took me nearly three hours to finish my breakfast. In my defense I was trying to write out the entire text of *Good Night, Moon*, but the Post Cereal Company didn't put enough of the letter "o" in the Alphabits; and it became even more frustrating because when I borrowed some "o's" from the Cheerios box, they were in a **totally different font**.

Before we go any further, I probably also ought to explain about the anagram situation. I'm really not sure how it started, but nearly every morning when I woke up and every night when I went to bed, my parents and I played the anagram game.

Mom usually got me up in the morning, and Dad put me to bed at night, so I got to play the game with each of them almost everyday. There were some house rules around the anagram game, but they weren't nearly as stringent as with the Alphabits:

- If the anagram makes a word, or most of a word, then you just say it, like "HAGS" or "CATSPAWF". If the anagram isn't a word, than you say each letter individually—like "W-D-A-V".

- You can eliminate articles, pronouns, or prepositions (Don't get me started), if it makes it easier to form a recognizable word.

My mom is pretty spontaneous when it comes to the anagram game, but I have the feeling that my dad spends way too much time thinking about it. For example, a few days after my third birthday (you already know about the party), I asked my dad to make an inventory of all my cartoon videos. I had gotten a few new ones as presents, and I had decided to donate some of the old ones to the children's wing of the hospital where Mom volunteered. Dad was pretty busy, so he didn't get to the inventory right away.

About two weeks later, Dad was sitting on the edge of my bed. (I think my sheets had "Parents sit here" printed on them.) We were talking, and I reminded him about the inventory. He paused, and then said, "BATMOBILE".

This was prior to the "wheels" I had in the supermarket, so I had a hard time making a connection to anything. It didn't even dawn on me that it was part of the anagram game.

"Give up?" he asked.

"Yeah."

"**B**enny, (since it's) **a**fter **t**he **M**ay **o**bservation (of your) **b**irthday, **I**'ll list everything." Then he got this huge grin on his face that would have put the "Cheshire Cat" to shame.

"Wow—pretty impressive, Dad."

I didn't challenge him. I mean spontaneity was not a rule of the anagram game. And if the truth be told, I often spent time thinking about anagram possibilities. I mean, "CATSPAWF" wasn't really off the cuff. (I think full disclosure is good for the soul, don't you?)

Anyway, back to me at breakfast. Mom was on the phone, and I was eating ... and spelling. (I was adhering to the rules, just using my spoon.) I thought I heard her speaking to the school department, which I kind of tuned out. But when I heard her talking to Mrs. Davis, I was all ears. The pleasantries took quite awhile, but I was sort of glad. I figured if Mom got along with Mrs. Davis, then the chances of the play date actually happening were more likely. Finally, I heard the magic words—"Next Wednesday sounds great".

Mom got off the phone and confirmed that the play date was scheduled for next week at the Davis'. It seemed that Mrs. Davis was watching Derek next Wednesday, so he was going to be there as well.

"Also, Benny, the meeting with the school department is two days after the play date—next Friday."

"Am I going to that?"

"Yes, honey. They certainly want to meet you before they start to consider what to do."

"Okay."

"Benny, it's such a beautiful day outside, why don't we take a walk?"

As I was moving my spoon around in the Alphabits, I said—" That sounds good, Mom, but can I finish this paragraph first?"

If you remember, I mentioned earlier about family and friends providing context for our lives, and that where we live does also. The fact that there's no playground within walking distance of our house, and no elementary school for miles, had an impact on the composition of our neighborhood. And by extension, it determined the people we came in contact with each day.

For example, if there had been a lot of young couples with children my age in our neighborhood, then the "cross-town" or "other-town" play dates wouldn't have been necessary. (Right after the play date with Johnny, I called Century 21 to find out how old you had to be to be an agent. I figured if I cut my commission in half, I might be able to attract some young families to the neighborhood. Talk about win-win.)

You might not have thought about it, but where your ancestors came from probably helped shape who you are. Take religion for example—unless you've converted, your faith is probably a product of where your ancestors lived. If you're Irish, you're probably not a Buddhist, because Saint Patrick brought Catholicism to Ireland. But, if Saint Patrick had been a Buddhist, and your ancestors lived in Ireland, then you'd be a Buddhist too. (Although, since he's known as **Saint** Patrick, Buddhism wouldn't really be in his background, would it? So … Maybe that analogy needs some work.)

This observation isn't meant to be a knock on anything; it's just that I think geography has more of an impact on us than we sometimes realize. (Do you suppose that if someone promised to rid **our** neighborhood of snakes, like St. Patrick did for Ireland, that most of our neighbors would convert? Just wondering. Do you think that was sacrilegious? I suppose if Dad didn't get in any trouble for "Archie Bills", then I guess I'm okay.)

Anyway, back to our neighborhood—Despite what I may have implied in the last paragraph, we actually live in a snake-free zone. I mean there's no sign posted with a picture of a snake and a red line through it, but trust me there are no snakes around our house. Mom's not a real big fan, so I'm sure she would know. I don't think Saint Patrick actually visited our community, so I can't give him credit, but nonetheless, snakes are not something we concern ourselves with … at least not until I started writing about them. Maybe I'll just double-check with Mom, to see if she's seen any snakes around. As you can probably tell, I'm not a big fan either.

Anyway, we live on the South Shore of Boston in the house my father's parents left him when they passed away. We live on a street with fifteen houses in an "established neighborhood". (That's "real estate speak" for "the houses are old".) Most of them were built in the 20's and 30's, but in almost all instances they've been modernized. I mean, we all have indoor plumbing and everything. (Eat your heart out, Sigmund.)

Some sociologists believe that our lives have become so busy that neighbors rarely interact with each other the way they used to. Things like block parties and frequent visits back and forth among neighbors are a thing of the past.

And while I'm sure there's some truth to the notion that our busy lives have caused this, I think there's another major reason for the "disintegration" of the neighborhood—the backyard deck.

Decades ago when most homes had a front porch, people would sit out there, and as their neighbors walked by, they would be invited onto the porch for a visit. But now, the front porch has been replaced by the backyard deck. And it's not very inviting. In fact, the backyard deck has become like the old Studio 54 nightclub in New York City, where only certain people were admitted. Can you envision the scene?

The neighbors are all lined up behind a velvet rope:

"Sorry, Mr. Underwood, you can't come in; you haven't mowed your lawn in two weeks."

"Okay, Mr. And Mrs. Buckley, you can come in, but the kid in the suit and the monogrammed handkerchief is out." (Maybe I'll re-evaluate my position on this backyard deck thing).

And if the deck is big enough (aren't they all?) then some people might even be restricted to certain **parts** of the deck. I can picture some linebacker-type "bouncer" saying, "Here, put on this "invisible fence" dog collar. You're not allowed to go past the green chaise lounge; if you do, you're gonna feel it."

Anyway, let me take you back to our neighborhood for a couple of updates:

You remember Kathy and Bob Smythe. (He of the Dan Quayle School of Spelling; she of the potential pregnancy.) Well, they moved out about five years ago, just after their **quadruplets** turned three. (Maybe there's more to that "trying hard to get pregnant" thing than I thought.)

The neighbors that I've always felt closest to are Mr. and Mrs. Witkowski who live in the house next to ours. I'm sure a large part of why I like them so much is that they remind me of my grandma and grandpa. Whenever I need a grandparent "fix", I can just go next door. The Witkowskis are in their seventies, and even most of their grandchildren are adults. On occasion some of their great-grandchildren, who were closer to my age, would visit, but that was rare. So, I think the Witkowskis really enjoyed it when I would go over to see them.

Mrs. Witkowski made chocolate chip cookies that would make Mrs. Field drool. So with that in mind, I would always carefully choose when I visited. Noontime was the best—it gave Mrs. Witkowski time to bake in the morning, then I could visit for about an hour and leave by one o'clock so she could watch her "stories".

Mom called them "soap operas", but they were "stories" to Mrs. Witkowski. (I guess I understand where the name "opera" comes from, but there were no fat ladies, never mind singing ones, on any of those "stories" that I ever saw.)

Mr. Witkowski has every tool ever invented. If you need a "left-handed Palumbo wrench", he's your man. (For those of you who are "Craftsman-challenged", there is no such thing as a "left-handed Palumbo wrench"—they only come in a right-handed model). Whenever Dad needed to borrow anything, Mr. Witkowski had it. (Don't most "established neighborhoods" have a "Mr. Witkowski"?)

Sometimes, Mr. Witkowski and I would build things together. (I'm using the word "together" very generously. Mainly, I would just watch.) What I still remember, however, is that he never seemed to tire of answering my questions. I think that's another reason he reminded me so much of my grandpa.

If Mr. Witkowski was out of patience, he never showed it. And you know how many times a three-year-old can ask "why":

"Why are you using the hammer?"

"Why are you wearing those glasses?"

"Why is the saw so sharp?"

And to make matters worse for him, because of the ICBM, my questions weren't limited to carpentry:

"Why do we continue to use the Electoral College?"

"Why do people eat sushi?"

"Why did Prince change his name to an unpronounceable glyph, and before he changed it back, how did people ask to speak to him on the phone?" (I was usually allowed one follow-up question, not unlike presidential press conferences: If Prince had known about the anagram game, do you think he would have just used TAFKAP—The Artist Formerly Known As Prince, instead of the glyph?)

Mr. Witkowski gave me very good answers for questions one and three, but he offered no explanation for why people eat sushi.

So, back to our neighborhood walk—I'm not sure of my exact thoughts as Mom and I started down the street, but I probably was reflecting on who lived in each house as we passed it, and what might be going on inside. So, I'm sure there were some thoughts of "the Witkowskis" and "the Smythes", but most likely my mind was pre-occupied with the upcoming play date—W-D-A-V.

Chapter 5

▼

It's probably pretty unusual for a three-year-old to be able to focus on anything for five **minutes**, never mind five days. But that's what I did. All I could think about was the upcoming play date. It might have had something to do with the fact that I've always felt that half the fun of things is the anticipation. I'd much prefer for Mom and Dad to tell me ahead of time that we're going to do something exciting or special, rather than to spring it on me at the last minute. I love the anticipation.

Of course the opposite is true for less exciting events. In those situations I'd much prefer Mom to tell me about six seconds before we have to leave. "Benny, dentist, now!" (I know it sounds sort of "cavemanish", but it cuts down on any long-term anxiety.)

While I was really looking forward to the play date, I guess if I'm being honest, I was a little nervous as well. I definitely felt a connection with both Derek and Vanessa, and I thought they felt one too. But I couldn't be sure. Certainly, some part of my anxiety was that I really wanted them to like me. (Gee, there's a novel human emotion.) I mean, if things turned out the way I was hoping, it wasn't as if I was going to pull a "Sally Field" at the Academy Awards: "You like me; you really like me!" (Well, maybe if things went **really** well, and just as I was leaving.)

There was one other thing that I had some concerns about—should I bring up the ICBM? I mean, it's tough enough getting **adults** to accept my "condition", let alone kids. I finally decided not to raise the topic, and to just try to be myself. The problem with that strategy is that ICBM **is** myself. Nevertheless, I went into

GM. (Not General Motors, Guarded Mode). I was going to try to adhere to the words of Archie Bunker speaking to Edith, "Stifle yourself".

Even though I ultimately decided **not** to bring up my ICBM, I did think of some very strong counter-arguments during my internal debate. And they did raise a lot of doubt in my mind as to whether I was doing the right thing. I was torn because there are a lot of unusual conditions that people readily accept once they begin to understand them, even if there's no clear explanation for how they came about.

Take Tourette syndrome for example: When that condition was first identified, I'm sure people were skeptical. I mean, it is pretty hard to believe, don't you think?—There's this guy who has facial tics and swears all the time, no matter whom he's talking to—a policeman, a priest, his grandmother. And it's not his fault. He can't control it. Yeah, right.

See what I mean? I'm sure people had to be convinced that Tourette syndrome was real. They didn't just accept it the first time they heard about it. (Do you think there's something about shopping malls that exacerbates Tourette syndrome? I've seen groups of teenagers in the mall moving in really peculiar ways with what appears to be full body tics, while yelling the "f—word" over and over again, and they don't seem to care who hears them.)

Here's another example of what I'm talking about—hypnotism. If we didn't know hypnotism was for real, and someone explained it to us, wouldn't it still be hard to swallow, especially post-hypnotic suggestion?—"I'm going to have you focus on this locket I'm swinging back and forth. You're getting very sleepy. When you wake up, you won't remember any of this. But whenever I say the word 'preposition', you will jump around like a monkey and pretend to eat a banana. Are you ready to wake up now, Queen Elizabeth?"

Okay, one more. What about dreaming? Since most of us have dreams, we accept that dreaming exists. But what about those people who aren't able to dream? When somebody describes the experience to them, it must be pretty difficult to imagine that there really is such a thing. Picture this scenario:

"Yeah, I was asleep and this story was going on in my head. I think it was in "Hi-Def" because it was really clear. There was this murder witness who had to be transported in this jumbo jet, and the guy who he was going to testify against didn't want him to reach his destination. So, he arranged for hundreds of poisonous snakes to be released when the plane was in flight. And then all these **snakes on a plane** …"

(I hope the idea for that film came to the screenwriter in a dream. The possibility that he thought of it while he was fully awake just really scares me.)

Another interesting thing about dreams is that scientists have discovered that many of us actually experience the **exact same dreams**. Here are a couple of examples:

- You're in a very public place and you have absolutely no clothes on. (Of course for certain groups of people, being completely naked in a public place is actually a real-life experience, and not just a dream—like babies having their diapers changed, and Paris Hilton.)

- You're in a very large lecture hall where your mid-term exam is scheduled, and you haven't studied at all; you haven't even been to **one** class. (Again, being totally unprepared for an exam is probably a real-life situation for some people, and not just a dream—like college freshmen, and Paris Hilton.)

Anyway, can you see the dilemma I was faced with? I mean, if people could come to accept Tourette's, and hypnotism, and dreaming, shouldn't they be able to accept my ICBM. But since I felt as if so much was riding on this play date, I wasn't ready to take any chances.

Finally, Wednesday arrived, and Mom and I headed over to the Davis'. They only lived about two miles from us in a neighborhood that was a little less "established" than ours. When we pulled up in front of the house, I could see Vanessa and Derek looking out the picture window. I smiled even though they couldn't see me. It appeared, however, that they were eagerly anticipating today also. But it was still much too early to even consider doing my Sally Field impersonation.

As we were walking up to the house, Mrs. Davis opened the front door and said, "Hi, Lillian. Hi Benny". Then simultaneously, Derek and Vanessa, who were now standing next to her, waved to me. I waved back.

I've noticed that most small children wave like they're cleaning a window—the elbow remains stationary and the whole forearm moves from side to side; sort of like "wax on, wax off" from *The Karate Kid.*

Some other people also have distinctive waves—like The Queen of England. In her case, the elbow again remains stationary but the forearm and hand twist back and forth with all of the fingers touching each other. (Of course, if someone yells "preposition", then all bets are off.)

Mom said, "Hi, Janet. I hope we're not too early."

"No, right on time. Please come in."

Both Derek and Vanessa said, "Hi, Benny." And Vanessa followed up with, "Let's go into the family room to play." (It was only a short walk to the family room; not like Johnny Buckley's house, where you needed an amusement park conveyance—"Remember tram riders, you're parked in Minnie Mouse 17.")

As we entered the family room, I noticed that there appeared to be "stations" set up for various activities—one for drawing and coloring, one for watching videos, one for the computer, and one for board games. I wasn't sure whether Mrs. Davis or Vanessa had organized it that way.

Then Vanessa said, "How about we color?" (I know what the punctuation indicates, but it wasn't really a question.) She pointed to some chairs around a molded plastic table. "Derek, you sit here; Benny, you sit there."

I was now pretty sure that Vanessa was the one who organized everything. But that was okay with me. I like a woman who takes charge. It doesn't intimidate me. (I've been left alone with Johnny Buckley; now that intimidated me.)

In front of each of us was a new coloring book, and in the middle of the table was a bowl of crayons. My coloring book was about the circus. I kept turning the pages until I found just the right the picture. It depicted a small boy with his father. The boy was holding a bunch of balloons. The artist's rendition was okay, but since the title of the picture was "Balloons are Fun", I thought the balloons should have been more central to the composition. I mean, as you looked at it, your eyes weren't drawn to them. But I thought maybe with the right color choices, I could make it work.

However, the balloons would have to wait; I had something else more pressing. I took the two crayons I wanted from the bowl and began to color the face of the little boy in the picture. And in just a few minutes I was able to achieve the desired effect. I combined the "flesh" colored crayon with "royal blue" and there it was—"temper-tantrum blue". It looked just like the color of Johnny Buckley's face about a minute into the breath-holding incident.

(Note to Crayola: If you're still interested in this new color, have your people from "Research and Development" contact me. I'll be more than happy to give them the proper mixture percentages. It gets tricky when you try to replicate the color after someone holds his breath for more than a minute; the blue is much more pronounced than you'd expect.)

Even if Crayola never calls, it was still pretty exciting to have discovered a new color. Have you noticed that when people discover new things, they like to name them after themselves? I really didn't consider that for "temper-tantrum blue"; I thought the name kind of said it all.

Although, I do think if I ever discover a new **element**, I will name it after myself. I mean, don't you think *Benjaminium* at least **sounds** like an element? Not like some of those other ones, for example, "molybdenum"—who thought that was a good idea? "Yeah, let's spell this element with a 'y', 'b', and 'd' all following each other; that'll make it easy for high school chemistry students."

Anyway, back to the coloring—As I put the finishing touches on the face of "Balloon Boy" (That's what I re-titled the picture; I thought it was a good choice, especially since Gainsborough had already taken *The Blue Boy*), Vanessa looked over at my coloring book and said, "That's kinda silly."

I wasn't exactly sure how to respond. After all, I didn't actually have a signed contract with Crayola; I wasn't even working on consignment; I was just free-lancing. And since Vanessa didn't have any of this background, I'm sure the blue face did look silly. I decided to go with the truth. "I'm pretending he's holding his breath." This got a laugh from Vanessa. (Grape juice and a sense of humor—what a woman!)

Derek looked over at what I was doing just as Vanessa made the "silly" comment. He pointed to the words on the bottom of the page—"That says, 'Balloons are Fun'." I quickly figured out that my response in this situation had to be thought out carefully. Remember I was in "Guarded Mode", so I didn't want to say "Yeah, I know"; it would make me seem like a know-it-all. And, "I can read, too" wasn't much better. To take myself off the hook, I decided to turn the discussion around and make it about Derek. "When did you learn to read"?

Derek said, "In pre-school".

Now, it's not that unusual for four-year-olds to learn to read, or even three-year-olds, with or without ICBM. But still, I was pretty impressed.

Vanessa chimed in, "I can read, too." She pointed to the bottom of the page in her coloring book and said, "A Pretty Ballerina". Now, admittedly there were a lot of contextual clues—the "tutu" was kind of a give-a-way, but nevertheless "ballerina" is not the easiest word for a four-year-old to recognize.

Unfortunately, I got swept up in the moment and couldn't contain myself—"I can read, too". In my exuberance to prove it, I turned to another page in my coloring book, which happened to be at the beginning. And before I could stop myself, I read out loud "Houghton-Mifflin Publishing; Copyright 1991; all rights reserved." (So much for Guarded Mode.)

I'm sure I looked like a real show-off, exactly what I was trying to avoid. But you know what I discovered? Toddlers are a lot less judgmental than many other age groups. (It probably comes from wearing pull-ups and having other people change you—tends to make you humble.) Anyway, all Vanessa said was "That's good. We can all read."

Mom and Mrs. Davis were sitting on a sofa, not very far from us. I wasn't sure if Mom had heard any of the previous exchange, but obviously Mrs. Davis had.

She came over to the table and looked over my shoulder at the page I had just read from. "That was very good, Benny; those are hard words". I just managed, "Thanks".

Mrs. Davis returned to the sofa and said to Mom, "He's very bright. How did he learn to read?"

"We're not sure. It's just something we discovered a few months ago. I mean, Joe and I read to him a lot, especially when he was younger. And he'd repeat some of the sentences, but we thought he just memorized them".

"When we met in the supermarket I remember you told me that Benny didn't go to pre-school. That's pretty remarkable."

"Funny you should mention about pre-school. We have an appointment at the elementary school on Friday to see what the options might be. Benny's grandfather, my dad, suggested we call the school to see if they would take him a year early. But that still wouldn't be until a year from September; he's only three. However, I saw an article in the paper that the school was doing kindergarten screening this week, and next. So when I called, they said to bring him in on Friday. Evidently, the school is looking into starting a 'gifted' kindergarten class, and they might be accepting three-year-olds."

Mom continued. "But, I'm not sure I like that idea. Benny's bright, but to skip him two years ahead … he just got potty-trained a few months ago." (I thought Mom was doing really great up until then. Shouldn't potty-training information be on a need-to-know basis? That was way above Mrs. Davis' "family security clearance level".)

I glanced at Vanessa and Derek. They didn't appear to have overheard anything, so I thought my public humiliation was kept to a minimum. However, I did get up and go look in the mirror on the far wall. Unfortunately, as I looked at my reflection, it was just as I suspected. Note to Crayola: Another new color—"Total Embarrassment Red".

I returned to my seat and I could hear the conversation between Mrs. Davis and Mom continuing. Mrs. Davis said, "We're very pleased with the pre-school Vanessa goes to. And Derek goes there as well. It's for toddlers up to five, and as young as two-and-a-half, as long as they're potty trained. So, Benny would qualify."

There we go again with the potty training. I mean I know it's important. But it's not as if there's an elite group of children who are the only ones to ever achieve this level of bowel and bladder control—**everybody** eventually gets there. Some parents make it sound like their kid is in some sort of "Special Forces Unit" for gosh sake. "Yeah, my son Bobby's in the '183rd Diaper Brigade'—that's the number of times he's gone on the potty." (How about we just change the subject, please?)

Anyway, I decided to go back over to the mirror and look at my face to make sure I had the shading just right for the new color. I figured I'd select a new page in the coloring book and test out "Total Embarrassment Red". But then I realized that there was no way to explain any of that to Vanessa. So the fine-tuning of the new color was going to have to wait. Sorry, Crayola.

Back to Mom and Mrs. Davis—Mom said, "Are they still accepting students for September?"

"I'm not sure."

"If you could give me the phone number, then after we meet with the school people on Friday, I probably will give them a call."

"One of the things we like about the pre-school is that they really individualize. Vanessa and Derek were ready to read, so they gently moved them in that direction. It seems with Benny's abilities, they would challenge him, but I've never seen them push too hard."

"Thanks, Janet. I think I'm going to look into it."

Back to the coloring table—Derek asked me, "Why were you looking in the mirror?"

"Uh, I thought I might have some Alphabits caught in my teeth." (While this wasn't the real reason, it wasn't totally out of the question. At breakfast that morning, a few of the letters just seemed to disappear while I was trying to spell "quintessential". It was part of an essay on how I thought the play date was going to work out.)

Derek looked more closely at my mouth. "No, I don't see anything."

"Thanks."

Vanessa then spoke up. "You're a slow colorer."

I'm usually not. But with the trips to the mirror, and trying to listen to the adult conversation, "Balloon Boy" didn't get my full attention. Vanessa had already finished coloring three pictures—two ballerinas, and "Androgynous Person". (That wasn't the actual title of the picture in Vanessa's coloring book, but it should have been—male/female? I couldn't tell. And from the puzzled look on her face, I don't think Vanessa could either.)

One of the other reasons Vanessa was able to finish three pictures so quickly is that she's a "feather" colorer. Vanessa outlines the thing she's going to color, like the ballerina's dress, by pressing hard on the pink crayon all the way around the black border of the dress. Then on the inside of the dress itself, she just uses the side of the crayon and "feathers" the color inside the dark border. I think girls do this more than boys. (Maybe I could have given a coloring book to "Androgynous Person" to see what would have happened. I know it wouldn't have been conclusive evidence, but it was probably the next best option, since a DNA sample wasn't available.)

Derek is not a "feather" colorer. He uses the point of the crayon and darkens each area to the maximum. Derek goes through about two boxes of crayons a week. (Crayola much prefers Derek's method.)

Do you think the way Vanessa colors could be considered a new art "movement"? I mean we have "Impressionism", "Cubism", and a lot of other "isms". Why not "Featherism", or possibly "Benjaminism", for that matter? Actually, I kind of like the "Benjaminism" idea; especially since the prospects for discovering a new element are probably pretty slim (unless there's some new concoction of molecules hiding in the Alphabits box).

Vanessa said to me, "Do you wanna watch a video?" And then she looked toward her mom—"Is it okay?"

Mrs. Davis and I both said "Sure" at the same time.

Vanessa took me by the hand over to "Station 2" of the play date, where there was a TV and video case. "Which one do you want to watch?" (To Vanessa's credit as hostess, none of the videos were totally girl-oriented—no Barbie; no Cinderella; no Little Mermaid. Now I think I'm just as enlightened as the next three-year-old, but I was still glad that we were going to be watching something we could all enjoy.

Derek joined us and said, "I like the Charlie Brown and Snoopy ones."

And sure enough, there were a lot of old "Peanuts" videos. Most of them had a holiday theme of some sort—*The Great Pumpkin*, for Halloween; *A Charlie Brown Christmas*; as well as, *Happy New Year, Charlie Brown*—Since it was almost September, I started searching for—*Join a Union, It's Labor Day, Charlie Brown*. But that video was missing from the collection. (Note to AFL-CIO: This might be an untapped public relations opportunity. I know toddlers aren't your target demographic group. But it doesn't hurt to start early.)

Anyway, I was about to suggest—*You're In Love, Charlie Brown*, but I thought that might be too obvious. Instead, in keeping with the circus motif of my "Balloon Boy" picture, I asked for *Life's a Circus, Charlie Brown*.

Derek said, "Good, I like the circus one." He took it out of the case, and put it in the built-in VCR in the TV. He pressed the appropriate buttons, and I thought we were all set for the next thirty minutes.

But before we saw Charlie Brown, Lucy, Snoopy, or "Pig Pen"—there it was—**The FBI Warning**. Was that really necessary before a cartoon video? We now have an entire generation that associates the FBI with Daffy Duck and SpongeBob. Is that the image the FBI is really trying to cultivate?

It did occur to me, however, that in the case of the "Peanuts" characters there were some unusual situations. For example, we don't even know "Pig Pen's" real name. Why the secrecy? Also, he does seem to keep to himself a lot. Could it be that "Pig Pen" is in the "cartoon witness protection program"? Or maybe he's a former "wiseguy" turned informant—Vinnie "Pig Pen" Gambruzzo, formerly *of* Staten Island. (That's the fourth preposition that seems to work in that phrase. I give up.)

I know video piracy is a serious problem, but when you put the warning on a **cartoon video**, doesn't it put it in the same category as "pillow tag removal"?

Can you picture the scene at the maximum-security prison?—Three guys are standing around. The first one asks—"What are you in for"?

"Armed robbery."

"How about you?"

"Pillow tag removal."

"And you?"

"Cartoon video copying."

The guy who's in for armed robbery says, "Can I buy some protection from you guys? There seems to be a lot of you in here."

"Yeah, sure. That's true; there are a lot of us in here. Vinnie "Pig Pen" Gambruzzo rolled on us."

Anyway, despite the FBI warning, the three of us enjoyed watching the circus video. It also gave us a chance to talk to each other. Vanessa said, "We went to the circus."

I said, "Me too. I went with my grandma and grandpa a few weeks ago."

Derek: "Do you go to pre-school?"

Me: "No, not yet."

Derek again: "I like our school. Vanessa goes too."

Okay, not exactly the Lincoln-Douglas debates, but we did start to get to know one another. Then, shortly before the video was over, Mrs. Davis asked, "How about some lunch, guys?"

Have you noticed that "guys" no longer refers to just males? It now refers to any group of two or more people regardless of gender. When did this happen? Was there a notice in the paper? As you well know, I'm already struggling with certain other parts of speech. If things like this are going to change, and there's no notification, I don't know how I can be expected to keep up?

Back to the family room, where the three of us "guys" (I'm nothing, if not flexible) said "Yeah" in response to the lunch question. Mrs. Davis and Mom went off to the kitchen, as we finished watching the video. When it was over, Derek started to rewind the tape, and Vanessa turned to me. "We need to clean up the coloring books". I was about to ask why, when I realized that we were going to eat at the table where we had been coloring.

Vanessa picked up Derek's coloring book as well as her own, and put them neatly on the shelf behind the table. I wasn't sure what to do with my coloring book. I mean, was it mine to keep, or was I just being allowed to use it? I really hoped it was mine to keep, because even though "Balloon Boy" needed some work, I thought he was only about five minutes away from being "refrigerator-door ready". But for the time being at least, I just put my coloring book on top of Vanessa and Derek's.

My back was turned as Mom and Mrs. Davis re-entered with the food. Vanessa and Derek sat in their chairs at the table, and I did the same. Mrs. Davis put a fresh vegetable platter in the middle of the table. There were carrots, celery, cucumbers etc. Then she put a paper plate with chicken nuggets in front of each of us. Derek and Vanessa each got a juice box of fruit punch. As I was waiting for my drink, Mrs. Davis said, "Someone told me that this is your favorite, Benny".

And there it was—a glass full of grape juice—no juice box, no paper cup—a real glass full of grape juice. (It's nice to see that Mrs. Davis adheres to the social graces—company gets the good stuff.)

I looked over at Mom, and she winked at me. I got a big smile on my face, and said, "Thank you very much, Mrs. Davis."

"You're very welcome, Benny."

I looked at Mom again to see if I could read her face. It appeared that all was forgiven. Now, the cynics among you might be thinking—why would my Mom care? After all, it's not her rug. But I prefer to take the high road.

Vanessa, Derek, and I ate our lunch and talked some more. I found out that Derek lived two doors down. His mom had a part-time job, and that was why his "Auntie Janet" was taking care of him. Derek's dad worked for Gillette. (I'm going to keep that in mind when I start shaving.) And Vanessa told me that her dad worked at the airport (Logan), and that they used to live in Chicago. (Okay, we're not ready for prime time on "The Biography Channel", but it was a start.)

I thought to myself, I'm really having a good time; this is fun. I liked both Derek and Vanessa. And while I didn't think either one of them had ICBM (technically, ICVM and ICDM), they were both smart, and most importantly they were both nice.

After lunch was finished, Vanessa asked in her best hostess voice, "What do you wanna do now? We can play Uno or we can use the computer." I assumed this question was directed at me. "The computer sounds good." (Although we had a computer at home, I rarely got a chance to use it. And then only with Mom and Dad helping me.)

This time Vanessa did the "mechanical stuff" and booted up the computer, while Derek and I cleaned up from lunch. We were waiting quite awhile for the dial-up access to kick in. Finally, the AOL screen came up, and Vanessa typed in the address she wanted. We waited some more, and then a Disney website appeared. There were a few games to play, but not too many. (Remember this was nine years ago, so the choices were much more limited.) We tried a couple of the games, but it was really hard with three people and all those fingers, even small ones. Vanessa, ever the problem-solver, said, "Let's print out some pictures to color, instead."

Derek agreed, "Yeah".

And I did too, "Okay." Not being mechanically inclined, I didn't have a clue about how Vanessa was going to do that. But I did like the idea of coloring again. As I mentioned earlier, "Balloon Boy" was not ready for the refrigerator door, but maybe this new picture would be.

After a few minutes the printer spit out three pictures; Vanessa printed Minnie Mouse for herself, Donald Duck for Derek, and Goofy for me. (I didn't take it personally; I mean, it's not like—"You are what you color.")

There was one thing that did bother me though—exactly what kind of animal is Goofy? I really wish I could have gotten some clarification before I began to color; it might have influenced my crayon choices. (Now I know how Vanessa must have felt about "Androgynous Person".)

As I was trying to decide what to do, I studied Goofy closely. He kind of looked like a dog, but that didn't make any sense. I mean, Mickey Mouse already has a dog—Pluto. So then, what are we supposed to believe, that one member of the canine species is Mickey's dog and the other one is his friend? That can't be right, unless there's some sort of Disney cartoon "caste system" that we don't know about.

I didn't share any of these concerns with my two new friends. Instead, I just picked out the black crayon and colored Goofy's nose. That was a safe choice, and then I just let the spirit move me as I colored in the rest of the picture.

I employed the "Featherism/Benjaminism" method Vanessa was using earlier. (I had decided to still keep my naming options open.) At first she didn't notice, but then she said, "I like your picture."

"I like yours, too."

Derek chimed in, "Let's start a club."

Now in most situations, that would be considered the mother of all non-sequitors, like something Robin Williams would say after he was fed caffeine intravenously. But in "toddler-speak", it made perfect sense.

I said "Okay", which actually kind of surprised me, because I'm usually not much of a joiner.

Vanessa said "Sure."

Derek again: "We should call it "The Underwear Club."

Vanessa and I both looked at Derek. This latest remark really stretched the acceptable "non-sequitor boundaries", even for "toddler-speak".

I managed the ever intelligent and insightful—"What?" And Vanessa didn't say anything. She just looked at Derek with a strange expression on her face.

Derek said, "See", as he pointed to something on each of the pictures we were coloring. But he must have been able to tell by the looks on our faces that we still weren't getting it. (Frankly, I was just hoping that there was actually something to "get".)

Derek then pulled out the top band of the back of his underpants and said, "Look". (I still had no idea where this was going, but can you see why I'm not a "joiner"? I was also thinking that I might have been too rash in my judgment of Johnny Buckley as a play date.)

Finally, Derek spelled it out—literally. "B-V-D—that's what it says on the label of my underpants". And then he pointed to the first letter of each of our names that we had printed on our pictures. "'B' for Benny, 'V' for Vanessa, and 'D' for Derek."

Once he said that, I was able to see the connection. And with all the adult vocabulary and articulate speech patterns that ICBM afforded me, I said, "Oh".

Vanessa's response was also a little tentative, but I did sense that the connection had registered with her as well. She simply said, "Okay".

After a few minutes, it began to sink in—I was a founding member of "The Underwear Club". Then a couple of other things started to sink in as well.—I was relieved that nobody wanted to check out the band on my "underwear", which was actually a pull-up. (Hey, accidents happen!) If they had, we could have been known as the "This is the Back Club" (probably preferable to the "This End Up Club" though).

I was also thankful that Derek wasn't wearing "Fruit of the Loom" underwear. In that case the club would have had fourteen founding members. And since the letters "B", "V", and "D" aren't present in the words "Fruit of the Loom", the three of us wouldn't have even been in the club, and it was Derek's idea.

The "Fruit of the Loom" club possibility was fraught with a lot of other problems as well. I remember thinking—what about the "U"? I don't even know anybody named Ursala. And although I thought there was a major league baseball player named Ugueth Urbina, I had no idea how to even begin to get in touch with him.

After all of these ideas had pinballed in my head for a minute or so, I finally spoke up. "I like the club idea, Derek. But why don't we make it a secret club, at least the name anyway?"

Derek and Vanessa both gave the response "du jour"—"Okay."

And so, The Underwear Club was born in the middle of August nine years ago, and it's still going strong. As a matter of fact, if it weren't for The Underwear Club none of the amazing things that happened to me in seventh grade would have come about. And, as far as I know, none of the charter members—"B", "V", or "D", who are still the **only** members (We're not big on recruiting), has ever told anyone else about its existence, until now.

On the way home Mom drove down a street that we usually don't go on. "How come we're going this way?" I asked.

"I thought I'd show you the school where we're having the meeting on Friday. It's up here on the right."

"What about the school that Vanessa and Derek go to?"

"I think that's a real possibility, Benny. But we're still going to keep the appointment on Friday."

"Mom, can we put this on the refrigerator door?'

Mom glanced over at "Goofy" done in the "Featherism/Benjaminism" style. (I think from now on I'm just going to call it "Featherism". It really does describe the coloring process much better than "Benjaminism" ever could. Plus, this way I can still hold on to my "element" dream.)

"Sure."

"Thanks". And I really was thankful—it's tough to start an art movement without a public showing.

CHAPTER 6
▼

It was Friday morning at about 8:15. Since the appointment at the school was scheduled for 9:00, Mom came into my room to make sure I was awake.

"Hi, Sweetie. You slept kind of late today; everything all right?"

"Yeah, Mom—no DL."

Because she's an avid baseball fan, she knew that DL referred to the "disabled list" She then felt my forehead. "You don't feel warm."

"I'm fine Mom, really."

Just then Dad came into my room. "Hi, Pal. Are you ready for today?"

"Hi, Dad. I didn't know you were going with us too."

"Yup, I was able to take the day off. I think whatever we decide should involve all of us."

Dad seemed at a loss as to where to sit. As I mentioned before, Mom usually woke me up in the morning, and Dad usually put me to bed at night. Both of them being there at the same time had thrown them way off. One side of my bed was against the wall, so it wasn't available for "parent edge-of-bed sitting" and the other side was occupied by Mom. You know, where it was printed on my sheets "Parents sit here".

"Parents" is plural, but there was only room for one of them. If they both wanted to sit—then to paraphrase Robert Shaw in *Jaws*—"We need a bigger bed." And I didn't think that was going to happen anytime soon, because I just got my "big boy's bed" not that long ago. Dad kept looking around, but his only option was standing.

I spoke up. "You know, I think in the future when I'm not feeling well, I'm not going to say DL. I'm going to say 'PUP'."

Mom looked puzzled. I could see that she was trying to figure out what "PUP" meant. She waited a moment and then said, "I have no idea, Benny."

Dad looked equally puzzled, but then he got a smile on his face. "I think I know this one—'physically unable to perform'."

"Right, Dad. I thought you'd …"

Dad shook his head back and forth, which was my cue not to offer an explanation. Evidently, there was a bit of competition between Mom and Dad around the anagram game, and Dad had just racked up some big points.

Mom looked back over her shoulder at Dad, and she appeared to be mildly surprised and impressed at the same time. Dad shrugged his shoulders as if to say, "Hey, what can I tell you; it's a gift"; and then he gave me a wink.

Mom looked back and forth at the both of us, becoming suspicious. She paused for a moment and then said, "Okay, you two—'NAPI'".

"'NAPI', huh? Is that N-A-P-P-Y or …?" asked Dad.

Mom interjected. "N-A-P-I".

"What does it have to do with, Mom? Is it the appointment? Or is it something to do with 'PUP', or breakfast?"

Mom shook her head "no" to each question, but she definitely hesitated at the word "breakfast".

"My lips are sealed," she offered, but it was too late; I already knew from the hesitation that "N-A-P-I" was about breakfast. (I really hope Mom never gets into a high-stakes poker game—we could lose the house.)

Mom said, "I'll give you until I count to ten to figure it out." And then she began, "One, two, three …"

When she hit eight I said, "**No A**lphabits."

Mom smiled. "Good, Benny, but what about the P-I?"

There was silence for a few seconds, and then Dad asked very tentatively, "Pancakes, instead?"

The expression on Mom's face was just like when a "Texas Hold 'em" poker player is bluffing, and his opponent says, "All in." She was more than a little surprised. (Just to be on the safe side, I'm going to see if the house is in both my parents' names. I don't want Mom doing anything foolish.)

Mom decided to give credit where credit was due. "That was pretty impressive, you two. I'm going to start calling you the 'Dynamic Duo' after Batman and Robin."

I have to admit that my guess of "No Alphabits" wasn't that hard to figure out. Whenever we have to be someplace early in the morning, I'm not allowed to have Alphabits. Even if I abide by the rules, it still takes me much too long to eat and "write" my breakfast. I tried using shorthand, but that actually took longer. I had to break up the letters and try to re-form them into shorthand symbols. And if you remember the rules, I was only allowed to do that with my spoon in the milk. (Shorthand was not only more time consuming, it was way messier.)

As I thought about it, I realized that Dad's "pancakes, instead" guess wasn't all that difficult either. I'll bet he must have seen the pancake batter already made when he walked into the kitchen before coming into my room. Still, it was pretty good.

Mom continued. "I'm going to finish making the pancakes. What would you like on them? I have blueberries or strawberries."

I started to say, "No BS", but I realized how that would sound, so I just said, "Either one's okay, Mom." Dad echoed me. "Either one's fine. Thanks, honey."

"Okay, I'll put them both out. See you in the kitchen". She nodded her head once at each of us—"Batman, Robin."

Mom vacated the designated parent sitting area, and Dad immediately filled in.

"Are you nervous about today?"

"No, not really. Mom told me a little bit about it, but I was wondering how come they have to do this?"

"In general, I think the school is just trying to find out if kids are ready for kindergarten. In your case, since you're only three, I think that it might be a bit more …"

Dad was searching for the right word, when I supplied it, "Extensive?"

Dad laughed. "Yeah, extensive. I think if the school had just heard this conversation, you wouldn't have to go for the screening."

"What happens after today is finished?"

"I think we'll get the results in a couple of days. If you're accepted, then we'll decide what to do."

"So, I don't have to go, even if I'm accepted?"

"No, you don't. We're all going to talk this over, okay?"

"SG."

"Sounds good?"

"Yeah."

Dad gave me a hug. "Let's get some of those pancakes—Robin."

"Wait a minute," I said. "I thought you were Robin, and I was Batman."

"Nah, you're not old enough. You can't even drive the Batmobile. Supermarket shopping carts don't count."

I started to protest, but the logic of Dad's argument was pretty compelling.

On the drive over to the school Mom said, "We're scheduled to meet with the principal, Mrs. Stanton, right at nine, but I don't think she'll do the actual screening. I think that's done by one of the kindergarten teachers."

Dad's mind was obviously somewhere else, because he didn't acknowledge Mom's comment at all. Mom tried again, "Joe, did you …" She didn't get a chance to finish because Dad interjected.

"You know when Benny said 'PUP' when we were in his room, and I said 'physically unable to perform'? Well, that's actually a term from the NFL … That's the only reason I knew it."

Mom started to say, "I was wondering how …" Then she paused. "You know what, telling me that was a really sweet thing to do … I knew there was a reason I married you." And with that Mom gave Dad a kiss on the cheek.

The non-sequitor that Dad had just come up with would probably not raise an eyebrow among the toddler set, because of the level of acceptance of "toddler-speak". But I was kind of surprised that Mom took it in stride. I mean, going from talking about kindergarten screening to the NFL PUP list was a dandy. (By the way, when a coach says that a player is "physically unable to perform", does that mean that the player is injured, or could it be an assessment of his talent?)

Since Mom did take the non-sequitor in stride, it got me thinking that there must be different non-sequitor acceptance levels for various groups of people. For example, I'll bet that couples like Mom and Dad readily accept non-sequitors all the time, and it's no big deal. You probably don't even need to be married. I mean, if you've been going out with someone for a while, it probably wouldn't faze you if your partner comes up with some statement or idea that has nothing to do with what you've been talking about. (I'm hoping this also applies to the reader and author relationship. Although technically, I don't employ non-sequitors, I just go off on tangents. Regardless, I do appreciate your patience.)

I think *Cosmopolitan* should do a survey in their next issue to determine if couples are compatible based on their acceptance levels of non-sequitors. (Tell me this isn't just as good a measurement as anything else *Cosmo's* used in the past.)

Okay, so here's my idea, *Cosmo*:

See If You're Compatible:—Imagine that you and your boyfriend are having a conversation about where your relationship is going, and you say, "Honey, I think we should take our relationship to the next level. I'm ready to make a life-long commitment. How about you?" *Listed below are a number of possible responses your boyfriend might offer. Circle any response that doesn't seem to follow.*

A. "Is it illegal to remove the tag from a pillow?"

B. "Are any superheroes gay?"

C. "Look, a duck!"

D. "Is 'Mount Rushmore' a natural formation?"

E. "Why did Prince change his name to an unpronounceable glyph?"

If you didn't circle **any** of the non-sequitors, then you're probably very compatible … or incredibly understanding. (However, I do feel like I have to ask—Did you really consider "Look, a duck!" carefully? And are you still all right with it?)

I guess there's only one other thing I would ask you to do. Since the non-sequitors are for illustration purposes only, if your boyfriend has actually **used** any of the choices listed above, please consider the implications of having children with this individual and perpetuating that particular trait in the "gene pool".

Anyway, back to the kindergarten screening—We parked in the school's parking lot, and then headed into the building. I glanced at the name over the door—*Franklin E. Clark Elementary School*—the initials were FECES (Not a good omen). I decided to keep that observation to myself, what with the importance of first impressions and all.

The main office of the school was near the front door. If school were in session, we would have been required to sign in and wear visitors' badges, but since it was the summer—"We don't need no stinkin' badges." (Sorry, I couldn't resist.) There was a very friendly secretary who greeted us and escorted us to a waiting area outside the principal's office. "Mrs. Stanton will be right with you."

Mom and Dad both said, "Thank you."

I looked around the waiting area and saw a bookcase. "Mom, can I go look at the books?" (This question is in the same category as "Can I have some more broccoli?" Is there a parent alive anywhere who has said no to either request?)

Mom followed suit. "Of course, Benny."

I walked over to the bookcase. There were a number of reading series, some books on educational practices, and some individual titles. I selected one of the *Goosebumps* books. (After I heard rumors about their legal troubles with the copyright infringement, I had been reading every one of them I could get my hands on. You never know when they could be pulled from the shelves.)

I brought the book back to my seat and started to read. Mom and Dad were speaking quietly to each other, so I couldn't make out what they were saying. After about five minutes, the door to the principal's office opened, and a woman came out and introduced herself. "Good morning, I'm Claire Stanton." And she offered her hand.

"Hello, I'm Lillian Curtis and this is my husband, Joe, and our son, Benjamin." There were handshakes and "Pleased-to-meet-you's" all around. I said, "Excuse me" as I walked back over to the bookcase to return the book I had been reading. On my way back I heard Mrs. Stanton say, "Please come into my office."

There were three chairs lined up in front of Mrs. Stanton's desk, one for each of us. I took the middle seat, with Mom on my left and Dad on my right.

Mrs. Stanton began. "I thought we should meet briefly so that I could outline the procedures for today. This will be a little different from our usual kindergarten screening because of Benjamin's age and the new program we're initiating. While Benjamin … By the way, what do you prefer to be called … Benjamin, Ben, Benny?"

"Benny is fine."

"… While Benny sees the nurse for vision and hearing testing, I thought we could remain here so I can tell you more about the new program, and answer any questions you may have. After Benny finishes with the nurse, he'll meet with one of our kindergarten teachers who will assess his readiness for school. After that Benny will have a break. We have some snacks and drinks for the children and some coffee for the adults. Following the break, Benny will meet briefly with Dr. Foster, our school psychologist. Dr. Foster won't be conducting any tests or assessments. He'll just have a conversation with Benny to give us a clearer picture of his social readiness."

Mom said, "That seems very thorough".

"For the most part, it is. We've found that if we do any more testing than what I've just described, it's too taxing on the children."

Dad asked, "Who makes the final decision?"

"I do," said Mrs. Stanton, "with input from the other professionals".

It has always struck me that schools are one of the few organizations where you are able to talk directly to the person in charge—you know, the actual decision-maker. If your child's bus arrives five minutes late, the principal of the school will take your call and try to fix the problem; or if there's some policy at the school that you have concerns about, you can arrange to talk with the principal directly—no problem. But if your can opener breaks, do you really think you'll be able to get an appointment to speak to the president of General Electric?

Actually, the situation with the kindergarten acceptance was even more impressive. Not only was Mrs. Stanton accessible, but she was also willing to take full responsibility for the decision. Who does that anymore? That's easy—**Nobody**!

Let me give you an example. Remember I mentioned about how the word "guys" is no longer gender-specific? Well, we still don't know whose decision that was. I mean, I haven't heard of anybody coming forward to accept responsibility. See what I mean? There's no one to complain to. You can't even write a letter. Well, I guess you could, but then who do you address it to—"Dear Guys"? (And doesn't that create a vicious circle?)

There are other things like the "guys" issue that are also bothering me, like who's responsible for the decision that Pluto is no longer a planet? Seriously, who are these people? I know one thing; whoever they are, they missed a golden opportunity. What a great reality show that would have made—*Survivor-The Solar System.* Instead of being voted off the island, a planet would have gotten voted out of the solar system.

I really wish they had created that show. At least that way we'd know who made the decision. And you know what? If there was such a show, there's no way Pluto would have been voted out. Tell me it wouldn't have been **Uranus**. I mean, since most people pronounce it "your anus", it's already a huge embarrassment, as it is. I think maybe we should vote it out anyway—show or no show. We could start a bumper sticker campaign "Get Rid of Uranus". (Maybe not)

I just realized that the last few chapters have included a lot of talk about potty training, feces, and now Uranus. Is that what they mean by the phrase "anal-retentive"? (Sigmund, what do you think?) Anyway, I am sorry. I'll try to keep those references to a minimum, unless they're really integral. And then … well, you know the rest.

There's another thing I read about Pluto. It's now being called a "**dwarf** planet". Do you think Snow White knows? Is Disney involved? I have to tell you, I'm a little suspicious. It seems that Disney has something against the name Pluto. First there's the cartoon "caste system", and now this.

I know we've been spending a lot of time in Tangent City, but if you can just bear with me for another few moments, I'd appreciate it. I mean, I think I'd really be remiss if I didn't bring up a few more related points.

Have you ever seen those ads that urge you to pay $54 to have a star named after you? I ask again, who are these people? (I did ask my dad, and thank goodness his ad agency doesn't handle that account.)

You know, it's one thing to have an art movement or an element named after you, but a star—that's way too much. And it's fraught with all sorts of problems—what if there's intelligent life in other parts of the universe, and they're doing the same thing? Who decides what to call this star that at least four "life forms" have named? Talk about a "turf war", (well, actually a "gaseous nebulae war").

You know, even if nobody else in the universe is naming stars, doesn't it just seem silly? I mean picture this scenario: An astronomy professor is teaching a class and he's showing slides of the heavens. He uses a laser pointer to show the students the location of various stars. "Notice this bright star—that's 'Alpha Centauri', and this is 'Polaris'; this one is 'Procyon B'; this is 'Torcularis Septentrioinalis', and this new one is ... 'Fred'."

How about the name of that star before "Fred"? Not exactly nursery rhyme material—"Twinkle, twinkle little Torcularis Septentrionalis ..."

Anyway, back to Mrs. Stanton's office.

"Benny, I noticed you were looking at a *Goosebumps* book."

I think Mrs. Stanton probably chose her words very carefully. She said "looking" rather than "reading". I'm sure she didn't want to presume that I could read. I was about to respond to her statement when Dad beat me to it.

"Actually, Benny's read a number of them."

"Really, at age three, that's pretty special."

I then followed up. "I like the *Goosebumps* series. And with their legal problems, I'm just trying to read them all before anything happens."

I'm sure Mrs. Stanton had been around a lot of precocious children in her time, but I could tell that my comments had thrown her a bit. Her mouth started to form the letter "W". So I was expecting a "what", "why", or "where", but no sound emerged. Her surprised expression wasn't quite as dramatic as Mom's jaw-dropping or Grandpa's eyebrow-raising, but it was close.

Dad and Mom both shrugged their shoulders as if to say, "We don't know what to make of it either."

Mrs. Stanton struggled to compose herself. She finally said to me, "Make sure you tell Dr. Foster about that."

I didn't say anything, but I was wondering why he would want to know. Was he a lawyer or something? Well, no matter; I figured, why not? Maybe he knew somebody in the publishing field who could help.

Mrs. Stanton continued. "Benny, why don't I take you to the nurse to begin the screening process? Mr. and Mrs. Curtis, I'll be right back."

I went with Mrs. Stanton to the nurse's office, which was on the other side of the main office. I was introduced to the nurse, and she tested me for about fifteen minutes. When we were finished, she brought me to a small classroom for the academic screening.

As we entered the classroom, an older woman got up from behind a table and greeted us. "Hello, Benny. I'm Mrs. Jarvis. Please come over to the table and have a seat."

I did that while she talked briefly at the door with the nurse. After a few minutes Mrs. Jarvis sat back down at the table across from me. She smiled and said, "I was just speaking with your parents. They told me you already know how to read, so maybe some of the questions I'm going to ask you won't be very hard, especially the first few. Are you ready to begin?"

"Okay."

Mrs. Jarvis reached for some charts that were on the left side of the table. She opened up to the first page or so, and said, "Benny, I'm going to point to a letter. See if you can tell me its name."

She then pointed, and I said, "B".

"Correct. How about this one?"

"M"

"Good. And this one?"

"G"

"Excellent. And this …"

I interrupted at this juncture. "This font looks familiar. Do you know if it's the same one they use in Alphabits?"

"Excuse me?"

"I think this is the same font that Post Cereal uses in Alphabits. Do you by any chance have any letters in the Cheerios font? There are some subtle differences between the two that you can't really distinguish when they're floating in milk."

Mrs. Jarvis started to purse her lips, so I was anticipating a "W" word. And she didn't disappoint. "What …" But she was unable to finish the question. She stared at me for another few seconds and then said. "I'm not sure I know very much about … what did you call them … Alphabits? This is the only chart of letters we have, so maybe we should go on to something else, okay?"

I was somewhat disappointed, because I'd never seen the Alphabits font outside of the cereal mode. This screening chart looked like it had some real potential. On the other hand, without the Cheerios, it was all speculation anyway, not very empirical. So, I figured we might as well move on to the next thing, and I indicated that to Mrs. Jarvis.

"Okay, we can do something different."

"Benny, do you know your shapes and colors?"

I wasn't sure how specific the questions about these topics were going to be, so I was a bit tentative in my response—"I think so."

"Good, let's start with your colors."

Mrs. Jarvis reached for another chart from the corner of the table, opened it up and pointed to a color on the first page. "What color is this?"

I stared at it for about ten seconds. "This is harder than I thought."

"It's all right, Benny, take your time."

"I can't decide between two."

"Which two are you thinking about?"

"Well, it's either 'periwinkle blue' or 'robin's egg blue'; I'm not sure which ... but if you add just a feather stroke of pink to it, I think it would become 'temper-tantrum blue'. That's a new color I'm hoping Crayola picks up in time for the next school year."

I looked at Mrs. Jarvis. This time there was no "W" word about to be formed. Instead her mouth was wide open in an oval shape. It appeared that she was either really surprised, or was about to sing an aria.

A few moments passed without any operatic notes filling the room, so I assumed it was the former.

"Did you say 'periwinkle'?"

"Darn it; it's 'robin's egg', isn't it?"

"I don't know. I was just looking for 'blue'."

"I'm sorry, I didn't know how specific I was supposed to be."

"It seems that we probably don't need to spend any more time on colors. We can probably move on to shapes."

"Mrs. Jarvis, how specific should I be about the shapes?"

"Just general information will be fine."

Mrs. Jarvis then took another chart and opened it up. She pointed to a shape and said, "What's this, Benny?"

I paused for a moment, thinking—okay, 'general' not 'specific'. And then I said, with a knowing smile on my face, "That's a quadrilateral."

Mrs. Jarvis started to shake her head, so I thought I had gotten it wrong. But then I realized Mrs. Jarvis was just showing surprise again. And since she had already pursed her lips and opened her mouth in the shape of an oval, she probably didn't want to repeat herself.

She stopped shaking her head and said, "You know Benny, technically you're correct, but usually most people are a little more specific. Could you do that?" (I didn't want to be rude, so I didn't say anything. But, I wish she would make up her mind.)

"Well, depending on how strict your definition is ... it's a form of rhombus called a square."

"Did you say 'a form of rhombus'? There's not even a place on the screening assessment sheet to put in that response."

"Well there probably should be, don't you think? I mean, technically a square is a rhombus. But we usually think of a rhombus as more of a diamond shape. What exactly do you think they were looking for, Mrs. Jarvis?"

"Probably, 'square'."

I sensed from her tone of voice that maybe I was starting to win her over to my point of view. I think she was just as exasperated as I was that the assessment sheet didn't have all the necessary choices listed.

Mrs. Jarvis stared at me for a moment and then said, "I think I probably have a good sense of your knowledge of shapes, Benny. I think we can move on to something that's more 'hands-on'."

She reached under the table and got a box of wooden blocks in various shapes and sizes. "Benny, I'd like you to build a tower using these blocks. You don't have to use all of them, and there's no time limit." I sensed that she was trying to anticipate if there were any other parameters she should mention, but she didn't come up with any. But, I did.

Since I was only three, my eye-hand coordination was not as developed as it would be later on. So, I wanted to make sure that I gave myself every possible advantage to do this tower-building correctly.

"Excuse me, Mrs. Jarvis. Is there any particular architectural style I should use? My dad works at The John Hancock Building in Boston, which I think was designed by I.M. Pei. But I don't see any windows in this box, so it's going to be difficult to replicate that."

Mrs. Jarvis was now shaking her head. (While this is a "showing surprise repeat", she was running out of body parts, so I understood.) She was also chuckling. "No, Benny, you can make up your own style." (Hmph—my own architectural style—once I do that, can *Benjaminium* be far behind? But, no matter what, I'm still not naming a star after myself. Although, don't you think that 'Benny' sounds better than 'Fred'?)

I spent about five minutes building the tower. It took a little longer than I anticipated, because it fell once. (I was never very good at Jenga.) I also should have remembered to use more arches; they distribute the weight more effectively.

Despite the one failed attempt, Mrs. Jarvis praised my efforts. And then we went on to the next part of the screening. "Benny, I want you to draw a person and a tree on this paper. And no, you don't have to imitate any particular artist, or follow any particular art movement."

"I was just curious, Mrs. Jarvis, have you ever heard of Featherism?" (I knew this was pushing it. After all, my rendition of Goofy had only been on the refrigerator door for two days. Still, word-of-mouth in the art world travels at lightning speed.)

"Featherism, no, I don't think so."

I began to draw. The finished product was much more 'Picasso' than 'Whistler', but all the requisite body parts were there, and in approximately the right places. The tree, however, was another story. (If New England foliage excursions were dependent on trees that looked like the one I drew, the tourist trade would take a huge hit.)

When I finished, Mrs. Jarvis asked me to make up a story about the person and the tree. (Since *A Tree Grows in Brooklyn* was taken, I had to head in another direction.) I didn't say anything for about fifteen seconds.

"Benny, you look puzzled."

"Does it just have to be about the person and the tree, or can I add other characters?"

"Sure, you can add other characters."

"I mean, the boy in the picture will still be the main character, you know—the protagonist, but …"

Mrs. Jarvis interrupted, "Did you just say 'protagonist'?"

"Yes, I …"

"You can add whatever you like."

I've always believed in the age-old adage "write what you know". So, I told Mrs. Jarvis a story I was familiar with. "The boy in the picture is named Timmy. He's out in the north forty looking for the well that Mrs. Wilson has fallen into …"

After I finished Mrs. Jarvis said, "That was very good, Benny. It did sound kind of familiar though."

"Well actually, it was based on an episode of *Lassie* that I watched with my grandpa. Was it all right to use that?"

"It's fine … but I'm curious … why wasn't Lassie in the story?"

I explained to Mrs. Jarvis that while I liked Lassie, I thought she got too much credit. My story gave Timmy his 'fifteen minutes'—long overdue in my judgment.

(I know it was unrealistic to think that not even **one** of the thirteen Lassies would have been available on the day that my story took place, but as the author, that's what I decided to go with.)

Mrs. Jarvis must have accepted my explanation of Lassie's absence from my story, because she started to prepare for the next part of the screening. "Okay, Benny, one more task, and then we're done. Let's go over to the area on the other side of the room where the mats are."

I wasn't sure what was going to happen now. What's with the mats? Do they have interscholastic wrestling in kindergarten? Mrs. Jarvis wasn't expecting me to wrestle her, was she? I mean, she was an older woman, but she seemed pretty solid. I might win one match, if I was lucky. But two out of three was out of the question. If we were going to wrestle to see if I was going to be accepted, why didn't we do that at the beginning? Was all that academic stuff just a ploy to get me overconfident before the real "test"?

"Benny, I want you to hop on one foot for about ten or fifteen seconds. Do you think you can do that?"

I was still suspicious that she was just trying to tire me out. "Is that all?"

"Yes, this is the last thing."

While I certainly was relieved that it wasn't going to be a wrestling match, I still had some concerns about the hopping. Three-year-olds are not all that coordinated. But here's where my ICBM helped me compensate.

As I started to hop, I grabbed my right leg and hopped on my left. I started to describe to myself what I was doing—"I hop, I hop …" which made me think of **I**nternational **H**ouse **of P**ancakes, which made me think of breakfast. And then I was "in the zone". I probably could have hopped for at least a full minute, no problem.

However, after about twenty seconds, Mrs. Jarvis said, "You can stop now. That was very good."

As I was catching my breath she continued. "I'm going to take you into the classroom next door to wait for your parents. There are some snacks and drinks available." She then extended her hand and said, "Benny, it has been a real pleasure meeting you. I think you're a very special young man."

"Thanks, me too." Then I thought how that sounded, so I tried to clarify. "When I said 'me too' I didn't mean that I thought I was a special young man. I probably should have said 'you too'. Oh, but that would have seemed like I thought you were a special young man. What I really meant was …"

She smiled. "I know what you meant, Benny. And, thank you."

Mrs. Jarvis brought me into the next room. Mrs. Stanton was there, but my parents hadn't arrived yet. Mrs. Stanton said, "Your parents will be right back, Benny. Would you like something to eat? Help yourself."

Mrs. Stanton and Mrs. Jarvis went just outside the door of the classroom for a moment, as I walked over to the sink to wash my hands before eating. I was close enough to the door to overhear their conversation.

Mrs. Stanton: "What were your initial impressions?"

Mrs. Jarvis: "Well, he's not like any other three-year-old I've ever met. It's not just that he's bright. It's something else, entirely. He certainly qualifies for the new program. He could probably **teach** it!"

They both laughed, and I headed back to the goodies.

Mrs. Stanton came back into the room a short time later. Mom and Dad were not far behind. Mom came over to me and said, "Hi honey, how did everything go?"

"Fine."

Mrs. Stanton interjected. "Mrs. Jarvis was very impressed with Benny. He's quite mature for his age." (I don't take compliments well, so I started to blush, nowhere near "total embarrassment red", but blushing, nonetheless.) Mrs. Stanton continued. "Please help yourselves to some refreshments. I'm going to check on Dr. Foster's availability."

She was gone about five minutes. When she returned, she indicated that something had come up and Dr. Foster would be tied up until the afternoon. "Would it be possible for you to come back at two or two-thirty today? I'm sorry to ask you to do that, but Dr. Foster had an unexpected conflict."

Dad looked at Mom and she nodded. Dad said, "That's fine. We understand. We'll be back around two."

That was actually good news for me. I didn't necessarily take a nap every day, but on that day I definitely needed one. (Hey, you try building towers and hopping on one foot for twenty seconds, and see if you're not tired—"in the zone", or not.)

At home I watched some videos, had lunch, and then took a nap. We left the house a few minutes before two o'clock and headed back to the school. As we entered, I glanced up at the name of the school again. I thought maybe I'd mention my concern about the name of the school to the psychologist. He of all people should realize the implications. (Although I had no way of knowing if he followed Freud or not.)

Mrs. Stanton greeted us again as we walked in. "Thanks for being so flexible, Mr. and Mrs. Curtis, and you too, Benny. The two of you can wait in the classroom with the refreshments while I take Benny to Dr. Foster's office. It shouldn't take very long."

As we walked down the hall, Mrs. Stanton said, "Mrs. Jarvis talked with me about the time you spent together this morning. She said that she thought you were a very bright young man."

I said, "Thank you", and left it at that. I wasn't going to get caught up in the 'me too' and 'you too' problem again.

Mrs. Stanton continued. "Dr. Foster is just going to have a conversation with you. There won't be any tests or additional screening to worry about."

"Okay."

"Here we are."

Mrs. Stanton knocked on the doorjamb because the door was already open. "Dr. Foster?"

"Hi, Mrs. Stanton."

"Dr. Foster, this is Benny Curtis, the young man I told you about earlier."

"Hi, Benny. I'm Dr. Foster." He offered his hand, and I shook it. "Come in, please. Thank you, Mrs. Stanton."

Mrs. Stanton exited and closed the door behind her.

Dr. Foster said, "Benny, let's sit at the table over here."

As we both sat down, Dr. Foster continued. "So Benny, I guess you had quite a morning, huh?"

"It was fine."

"Mrs. Stanton told me that you already know how to read. She mentioned something about *Goosebumps*."

"Yeah, I like those books. Do you know anything about their legal problems?"

Dr. Foster chuckled. "As a matter of fact, I don't."

"I think it's about copyright infringement."

"Really. Do you know what that means?"

"I'm not sure. Is it like plagiarism?"

He was still chuckling. "Pretty close. Does that bother you?"

"Well, I kind of like those books, and I haven't read them all. So, if they can't publish them anymore, I might not get the chance."

"You know what, Benny? I'm pretty sure we have copies of the whole series at the school here. I'm sure I can arrange for you to borrow them."

"Really? That would be great. Thanks a lot."

"Of course, we'll have to check with your parents to make sure it's all right. Aren't those books a little scary for you?"

"A little bit. And actually, some of them are pretty formulaic, but they're still fun to read."

"Formulaic, huh? I don't think I ever used that word until I was in college, maybe graduate school." This was said more to himself than to me.

"Sorry, it just seemed to fit."

Dr. Foster was smiling. "Benny, there's no need to apologize. You used the word perfectly." He paused and then said, "Tell me about some of the other things you like."

"I like grape juice—a lot."

Smiling more broadly, he said, "I guess I meant other things that you like to do."

"I like to watch videos, and I like reading, and coloring with my friends."

"Who are your friends?"

"Derek and Vanessa."

"Do they live near you?"

"Pretty close, but Mom has to drive me."

"Do they go to school?"

"Yeah, but not here. They go to pre-school."

Remember the connection I felt with Derek and Vanessa? Well, I was feeling a similar connection with Dr. Foster.

Note to American Psychiatric Society: Instead of the long drawn-out process that patients have to go through in trying to select a mental health professional, what about **"Speed Referral"** based on the "Speed Dating" model? If you can feel a connection with a potential date in five minutes, shouldn't you be able to do the same thing with a potential therapist, just as easily?

I've taken the liberty (I tend to do that a lot) of recommending a few modifications to the "Speed Dating" model, prior to piloting "Speed Referral":

- In Speed Dating they use chairs, in Speed Referral they should use couches.

- In Speed Dating they use a bell or gong to end the session; in Speed Referral they should use a blinking red light, and then the potential therapist should play a few notes on the triangle. (Quite soothing, don't you think?)

- In Speed Dating each session lasts five minutes; in Speed Referral each session should only last four minutes. (After all, a therapist's "hour" is only fifty minutes, not sixty.)

- In both Speed Dating and the Speed Play Date, I discouraged bringing stuffed animals and action figures, but in Speed Referral, I would actually **encourage** it—at least for the patients, not so much for the doctors.

Anyway, since I felt this connection with Dr. Foster, and we had just been talking about where Derek and Vanessa went to school, I decided to bring up the issue of the school's name. "Dr. Foster, are you aware that the initials for the school spell out 'feces'?"

Dr. Foster started to laugh. "Benny, I think you're the only other person besides me that's ever noticed that." He paused. "I've been debating whether to bring that to anyone's attention. But how about, for the time being, we just keep it to ourselves?"

As I got to thinking about it, it occurred to me that Dr. Foster had a real dilemma. I mean, as the school psychologist, if he pointed out the connection between "feces" and the name of the school, wouldn't it tend to raise some eyebrows? And you know that I have more than a passing familiarity with that particular non-verbal expression.

After Dr. Foster's last rhetorical question, I just nodded my head and he changed the subject. "Benny, tell me about your family … and your friends too."

For the next twenty minutes or so I told Dr. Foster all about Mom and Dad, and Grandma and Grandpa, but I didn't bring up my Aunt Mona or my Uncle John; that would require a lot more than my allotted twenty minutes, for all sorts of reasons. After I finished with our family, I moved on to my last two play dates—the one with Johnny Buckley, although, I don't use his real name (Hey, Johnny could become Dr. Foster's patient.), and the one with Derek and Vanessa. I made Dr. Foster laugh a few times, but mainly he smiled a lot and asked me some follow-up questions. (If this is what psychoanalysis is like, I may owe Freud an apology.)

"Benny, before I take you back to your parents, is there anything else you'd like to say, or any questions you have?"

"Well, I was kind of wondering … am I normal?"

Dr. Foster totally broke up at that one. "Yes, Benny, you are definitely normal. You certainly have above average intelligence, and I suspect you have what's called an eidetic memory—which is a good thing. It means that if you see something once, you can usually remember it."

"Yeah, that does happen to me." I paused. "Can I ask you something else?"

"Of course."

"Could you tell all that by just talking to me?"

He smiled. "No, Benny, I'm not that smart. I also spoke with Mrs. Jarvis and Mrs. Stanton; and from what they told me I was able to come to some conclusions."

"So, it's not a formal diagnosis?"

He started laughing again. "No, it's not a formal diagnosis."

"Can I ask one more question?"

"You can ask ten more if you want."

"Did I qualify?"

"That's up to Mrs. Stanton, but I'd be very surprised if she said no." He watched me for a moment. "You don't look very excited about that."

"Well, I really would like to go to the school that Derek and Vanessa go to."

"I see. Have you told that to your parents?'

"Yeah, sort of. And they seem to understand."

"Well, assuming that you're accepted, the decision is up to them whether you come here or not." He studied my expression briefly. "I'll tell you what. I never interfere in these kinds of decisions, but I will tell your parents what you told me. How about that?"

"That would be great. Thanks."

I finally caught up with my parents. We thanked everyone and said goodbye. Mrs. Stanton indicated that she would call Monday or Tuesday of next week with her decision.

In the car on the way home Mom asked, "So, Benny, what did you think?"

"Everyone was very nice. I especially liked Dr. Foster."

"Yes, he seems very nice."

Obviously, Dr. Foster hadn't spoken to my parents yet, but I decided to lay some groundwork. "Can we still think about the pre-school where Derek and Vanessa go?"

"Honey, nothing's been decided yet."

"You know how when kids apply to college—they apply to one school that they're sure they can get into? Well, maybe Clark Elementary could be my 'safe school', if I don't get into the pre-school." (I decided not to call the elementary school by its full name. I was nervous that Dad, who went to 'Archie Bills' after all, might shorten the elementary school name, and figure out what the initials spelled.)

After the "safe school" remark, my parents looked at each other and simultaneously said, "We'll see."

Note to kids: In the old days, parents would just say "no" (even before Nancy Reagan made it popular). Then the word "maybe" became the new "no". And now, "we'll see" has become the new "maybe". In short, when your parents say, "we'll see", the chances of it actually happening are about as good as my Aunt Mona winning an Academy Award; or even less likely—Paris Hilton winning an Academy Award.

Speaking of Paris Hilton—I just realized that her initials are PH. Doesn't that have something to do with science? Isn't there a PH scale that measures acidity or something like that? If that's true—exactly what is Paris Hilton the "litmus test" for?

Actually, if I'm not mistaken, she was named Paris because that's where she was **conceived**—Paris, France. I'm kind of glad all parents don't follow that particular name selection process. Imagine the possibilities:

- "Backseat of my Chevy" Fitzmaurice

- "Sperm Bank and Test Tube" Peterson (Twins)

- "In a Rented Row Boat on Lake Winnipesaukee" Cunningham

I realize that I've been kind of picking on Paris Hilton. So, to make things right, I'm instituting a new policy—I'm going to treat her the same way I treat grape juice. I'm only going to bring up her name if it's integral to the story, or if I'm trying to make a point, or if it really seems like it fits, or … okay, actually there is no change in policy.

Anyway, back to the selection of my school—When we got back home, I went to my room to play, and Mom and Dad went into the kitchen. After about fifteen minutes I headed toward the kitchen also, to ask if I could have a snack. Just before I got there, I heard Mom say something to Dad about calling the pre-school. I was stunned. It appeared that against tremendous odds, the aforementioned "We'll see" that Mom and Dad had uttered, had actually become "Let's seriously look into it." (If something like that can happen, then there may be real hope for my Aunt Mona, and Paris Hilton as far as the Academy Awards are concerned. Well, at least Aunt Mona, let's not go crazy.)

I continued listening as Mom dialed the phone and started to talk. Obviously, I could only hear Mom's side of the conversation.

"Hello, yes. My name is Lillian Curtis and I have a son Benjamin who is three. I was wondering if you have any openings for the upcoming year.

"Oh, you do."

"Uh-huh, uh-huh."

"Well, we're waiting to find out about the screening he had at the elementary school this morning."

"Yes, I'm sure we can do that. Yes, three. Yes, they're starting a new program."

"Actually, he does. Vanessa and Derek Davis. That's how we found out about your school."

"Right. Yes. I think we'll hear early next week. Would it be okay to talk with you after that?"

"Okay, thank you."

And then she hung up.

I waited an appropriate amount of time and then walked into the kitchen. "Hi, Mom. Can I have something to eat?"

"Sure, Benny, how about some fruit?"

"That would be good."

As Mom opened up the refrigerator to get a fruit cup, she said, "Your father and I have a surprise for you."

Of course I knew what was coming, so I had to decide how I was going to play this out. I wanted to appear surprised, but which facial expression should I use? As you well know, I've got a lot to choose from—jaw-dropping, eyebrow-raising, the "pursed-lips 'W' formation", etc. I was strongly considering "the Pollyanna Frist semi-jaw drop", but at the last minute, I decided to go with Grandpa's partial eyebrow raise. (Blood is thicker than water.)

Mom continued. "We called the pre-school that Derek and Vanessa attend. There are some openings, but we still have to wait until next week when we get the screening results. Then we'll decide."

My eyebrows reached the midway point, which triggered my verbal response. "Really? Oh, thank you, thank you!"

Dad spoke up. "Again, Benny, remember, nothing's been decided, but your Mom and I are willing to look at all the options."

Finally, Monday came, and around 10:30 Mom got a phone call from Mrs. Stanton. When she hung up, she told me that we would be going to the school in the afternoon to meet with Dr. Foster to discuss the results of the kindergarten screening.

We arrived at the school around 1:00 and the secretary in the main office brought us to Dr. Foster's office. As soon as he saw us, he got up from behind his desk, and with a genuine smile on his face said, "Hello again, Mrs. Curtis. And how are you doing, Benny?"

"I'm fine. How are you?"

"Fine, as well. Please sit down."

Mom and I sat down, and Dr. Foster began to speak to us, although for the most part he addressed his remarks to Mom. "Well, Mrs. Curtis, as you already know, Benny is quite intelligent. In fact, although most of our results are qualitative and anecdotal, frankly, he's off the charts. Again, I'm probably not telling you something you don't already know. And, although Benny's only three, our assessment team believes he would more than hold his own in our new gifted kindergarten program." He paused. "However, I'm going to suggest to you that you seriously consider waiting a year."

Mom: "Really, why is that?"

"When I met with Benny he spoke a lot about his two new friends." He checked his notes—"Derek and Vanessa. And if I'm not mistaken, they attend one of the local pre-schools. Frankly, it sounds to me that Benny would be happier there. This is probably not what you were expecting to hear from me, but that's the way I see it."

(Forget "Batman"—Dr. Foster was now my new favorite superhero. I tried to think of a good name for him.—"Psychologistman"?—"Therapyman"?—"Shrinkman"?—I know; none of them came trippingly off my tongue either. I figured I'd have to revisit the naming process later on.)

Mom: "This is a little surprising."

"I'm sure it is. I do want to emphasize that the decision is strictly up to you. Benny is accepted for the upcoming school year, and if you and your husband want him to come here beginning in a few weeks, then he's all set. I will tell you something that Benny told me that certainly influenced my thinking. Evidently, Benny was talking to his grandfather about schools a few weeks ago, and his grandfather said to him 'What's the rush'? I obviously don't know Benny's grandfather, but I think I'd definitely like him."

Mom looked a little stunned. "That certainly is a lot to digest, Dr. Foster, but thanks for being so candid. I certainly need to discuss all this with my husband". Then she looked my way and added, "And of course, with Benny."

Mom paused, still looking at me, "So, young man, what do you think about all this?"

With my most serious face, I said, "Well, Mom, he **is** the doctor."

Both Dr. Foster and Mom broke up laughing.

Dr. Foster was still chuckling when he said, "Maybe I need to re-evaluate my position. I'd love to have Benny's sense of humor around here next year." There was a short pause and then he spoke up again. "One other thing, I have a copy of the assessment team's report. If you decide to pursue enrolling him in the pre-school, you might want to give them a copy."

Mom said, "Thank you", as she accepted the folder from Dr. Foster.

I spoke up. "Dr. Foster, about the report, would it be okay if I added some disclaimers? There were a few times when the level of specificity wasn't really clear to me."

Dr. Foster started laughing again. "Benny, Benny, trust me. That won't be necessary." He paused. "So, when do you think you'll be ready to take over my job—third grade?"

I joined in the merriment. "Nah … maybe fourth."

Mom chuckled and started to get up. "Thank you, Dr. Foster. We'll call you in the next couple of days to let you know what we decide."

Both Mom and I started to leave when Dr. Foster said, "Benny can I see you for a second?"

Mom waited at the door as I went over to where Dr. Foster was standing. He said very quietly, "If you don't end up coming here until next year, it will give me some time to work on changing the school's name."

I smiled at him and said, "Thanks for everything, Dr. Foster."

As we headed out to the car, Mom said, "What did Dr. Foster want to talk with you about?"

"Oh, just to wish me luck."

(I've always subscribed to the notion that doctor-patient confidentiality is a two-way street.)

Chapter 7

During the two weeks leading up to Labor Day, there were a number of times when Mom had to run some errands, and she left me in the care of Mr. and Mrs. Witkowski, our next door neighbors. (He, of the tools. She, of the cookies.)

On one of those days, Mr. Witkowski asked me if I wanted to help him make a bird feeder. I jumped at the chance, and in just a couple of hours we were able to build the feeder, paint it, and put it up on the border of our two properties.

(I'm not sure if the use of the word "border" in that last sentence is appropriate. The word "border" probably connotes something more formal—like the boundary between the United States and Mexico? I mean, I don't want to give you the impression that there were thousands of Witkowskis trying to get on to our property each day. Suffice to say, the bird feeder was midway between our houses. I hope that clarifies the situation.)

Oh, one more thing—when I started to talk about "our property", it reminded me that I had checked out the deed to our house, and it was in **both** my parents' names. That was a huge relief, but I still hoped that Mom steered clear of the poker tables. I mean, it's still possible that she had "power of attorney" for my dad, so I didn't think we were out of the woods yet. (With so much litigation going on in this country, isn't the phrase "**power** of attorney" redundant?)

I do have to say, regardless of whose property it was on, the bird feeder was pretty cool. I could easily see it from my bedroom window, and even with my three-year-old attention span, I was pretty captivated.

All sorts of birds came to feast. It got so that the feeder had to be filled up three or four times a week. Usually, Mr. and Mrs. Witkowski took care of doing that, although sometimes Mom and Dad did it too. (Especially if they were on "border patrol"—just kidding.)

On a couple of occasions, I think Mrs. Witkowski put some of her chocolate chip cookie dough in the feeder. The birds seemed to like that even better than the seeds. (If Mrs. Witkowski decides to go into the cookie business in competition with Mrs. Field, wouldn't that be a great marketing slogan—"Cookies enjoyed by every species"? I think I'll offer that to my dad in case his agency gets the account.)

While I was building the bird feeder and eating cookies (from Mrs. Witkowski's oven, not the bird feeder), Mom was visiting the pre-school that Vanessa and Derek attended. She evidently liked what she saw, because a few days before Labor Day she sat me down and announced that I could attend the "Little Guys Pre-School". (Yeah, that was the name of it. Since the school had been in existence for about five years, it's probable that the memo indicating that "guys" was no longer gender-specific was sent out long before I was even born. So, obviously I couldn't have been notified at that time, but shouldn't there be periodic updates?)

At age three I hadn't read a whole lot of Shakespeare, but I was familiar with one of the Bard's lines that seemed to fit the occasion—"What's in a name?" I decided to adopt that attitude in regards to the school I would be attending. After all, why should I care what they called it? The most important thing was that I would be going to the same school as Derek and Vanessa.

In the few days before the school year began I was in "happy anticipation mode". Remember how I indicated that I love anticipation? Well, this was it in spades. Every school day from now on was going to be like a three-hour play date with my two best friends—what a deal!

I also realized that since the three of us would be together everyday, there were implications and possibilities for "The Underwear Club". So, in the next few days I put my euphoric anticipation aside and did some planning for our club.

Although at age three I didn't know very much about organizational theory, it seemed only logical that "The Underwear Club" should have a mission statement and a set of goals. Unfortunately, our board of directors (that would be Vanessa, Derek and I) had not discussed what our club was going to do. We were in such a hurry to create the organization that we didn't think everything through. (Sound familiar to any of you former ".com entrepreneurs"?)

With no immediate opportunity to communicate with my fellow board members to get clarification, I struck out on my own. I decided to downplay the mission statement and goals, and instead I concentrated on creating a slogan for the club, as well as thinking up some activities we could undertake.

The mistake I made was to think that the slogan and the activities had to pertain to underwear. I think it was an honest mistake. I mean, wouldn't you assume that since the name of the organization was "The Underwear Club", that it had something to do with undergarments? (Of course I should have realized that a club's name doesn't necessarily describe what it's about. There's a fraternal organization in a nearby town called "The Independent Order of **Oddfellows**". What the heck do you think they do?)

Anyway, with the best of intentions, albeit misguided ones, I tried to come up with a meaningful slogan for "The Underwear Club" that had to do with undergarments and their functions. I wanted something easily recognizable, but with a slight twist. (Not in the underwear, in the slogan.)

Here's what I came up with:

- "The Underwear Club—Serve and Protect"

- "The Underwear Club—You deserve a potty-break today"

- "The Underwear Club—Just **Don't** Do It"

When I presented the slogans to Vanessa and Derek on the first day of pre-school, they seemed pretty confused. In my exuberance, and with my ICBM working overtime, I had just assumed that they would know all about mission statements and goals. (I don't know what I was thinking—as if that would be an integral part of the pre-school curriculum.) Plus, I had broken the cardinal rule of business presentations—know your audience.

I was going to try to explain about mission statements and goals, but decided to leave it alone. I figured I'd look like a show-off—again, the last thing I wanted them to think about me. Interestingly, without any business background, they were still able to point out that even if any of the slogans were good, we had agreed to keep the name of the club, if not the **club** itself, a secret. Why did we need a slogan? (Sometimes common sense trumps ICBM.)

I didn't fare much better with my suggestion for an activity, either. Derek and Vanessa said they just liked being in a club. They didn't feel like they needed to be involved in activities, at least to begin with. Since I just wanted to be their friend, scrapping my idea was a no-brainer.

But I still feel like I don't want the idea to go to waste, even today. So I'm going to offer it to anyone out there who would like to pursue it. (Oddfellows?) I haven't registered my idea, so there are no copyright issues. (*Goosebumps?*)

So, anyway here it is:

Since we were "The Underwear Club", I thought an appropriate first activity would be to conduct a survey to try to answer the eternal pop-culture question—Boxers or Briefs? I decided to expand the options slightly, so the question would read:

What type of underwear do you prefer?

A. Boxers

B. Briefs

C. Pull-ups

D. Clean

You know, I think Derek and Vanessa felt bad that I had done all this work and that they had rejected it. So Derek came up with the idea that we should use the initials of the club and refer to it as TUC. Being an anagram aficionado, I suggested that our official name be "The Underwear Club for Kids"—TUCK. I'm not sure if it was a "pity vote" or not, but the extra letter was unanimously approved.

Since the club now had a new official name, I once again proposed a club slogan—"The Underwear Club for Kids—We're not just charter members; we also wear them." That was voted down 2 to 1.

I guess since TUCK was really just about three toddlers becoming friends, it didn't require a slogan. And to this day, we still don't have one. But, in its first year of existence, TUCK met every Friday during free time at the pre-school. The minutes are available upon request.

Let me backtrack a little to tell you about the set-up at the "Little Guys Pre-school". The school consisted of a very large central room with five different learning centers—a dramatic play area, a library, an art center, a games and puzzle area, and a manipulatives table.

When I realized that there was an area for manipulatives, it occurred to me that three- and four-year-olds probably don't need a whole lot of practice in manipulation. If you ask any parents of toddlers, they'll tell you that their children pretty much have the manipulation thing down pat.

Attached to the central room at "Little Guys" were a number of small offices, a kitchen area, adult and kid bathrooms, and a hallway that led outside. There were swings, a slide, and other playground equipment in the backyard, as well as a sand box, and a large rubberized play area. (The whole school was just about the same size as Johnny Buckley's family room.)

The routine each day was pretty similar. We would start with free play—coloring, reading or looking at picture books, playing with blocks, etc. Then we would have our morning meeting called "circle time". It was designed to expand our language development opportunities by both speaking and listening. We would share any "news" we had, and take turns with "show and tell".

I have to admit that my first experience with circle time did not go very well. When the teacher asked about any news, I guess I really didn't understand the parameters. I brought up the legal problems of *Goosebumps,* but evidently that story had lost its "legs", and was now relegated to the back pages of "The Toddler Gazette". Nobody knew what I was talking about.

After being burned once, I was reluctant to bring up any other news. I thought about announcing the formation of TUCK, but Derek and Vanessa reminded me of our secrecy pledge. Still, I wanted to contribute something.

Finally, I came up with what I thought was a real good show and tell. I brought in the bird feeder that Mr. Witkowski and I had made. What a hit that was! As a matter of fact, one of the teachers asked if we could make one for the school. When I got home that afternoon, I asked Mr. Witkowski, and he seemed just as excited as I was. "Sure, let's do it."

That weekend we built two feeders, and when Mom drove me to school on Monday, Mr. Witkowski came with us. We carefully put the bird feeders in the back seat of Mom's car, and Mr. Witkowski put his tools and some lumber in the trunk. He had to attach a red flag to the end of the lumber because it stuck out the back.

When we arrived at school, the teachers had already arranged to move up circle time ahead of free play. Mr. Witkowski told the class all about the bird feeders, but I think he gave me way too much credit, considering the small amount of help I had actually provided.

After he finished telling us about building the feeders, he said he had brought the necessary lumber and tools (what a surprise) and we could watch out the window while he put them up. Since Mom was right there to give permission, I was able to go outside to assist Mr. Witkowski while the other kids looked on through the window.

Although I was thrilled to be helping, I was also concerned that the other kids would see me for the charlatan that I was—I wasn't really an assistant; I was more like a "carpenter groupie".

As always, however, Mr. Witkowski came through. (I've got to believe that he and my grandpa are related—they're so much alike.) Mr. Witkowski asked me to get him a certain tool, which I did. Then he asked me at what height the feeders should be, which I showed him. Then he asked me what kinds of seeds would attract which kinds of birds. I told him that as well. (I left out any mention of the chocolate chip cookie dough.)

Since all of these were the exact same things I had done when we put up the feeder outside my window, I knew precisely what to do and say. I suspect a lot of the kids were jealous of me that day, and honestly, I felt badly about that. But I was really glad I didn't look foolish. I should have had more faith in Mr. Witkowski though; he would never have let that happen.

The bird feeders were a huge hit. Throughout the year, students watched for the birds during free time or before the school day began. Initially, the kids were only able to group the birds by color, but after the teachers got us a couple of books, most of the students could identify the birds by type—like finches and blue jays and sparrows and wild parakeets, and even cardinals.

The Witkowskis must have donated all of the bird seed, because Mr. Witkowski would come twice each week with plastic milk bottles filled with the food, and all of the students would take turns helping him fill up the feeders. Of all the classroom chores, that was everyone's favorite. It made us feel very important, although it wasn't exactly the same as the real chores that kids who live on a farm have to do, like milking cows, plowing the north forty, or rescuing Mrs. Wilson from the well. (The woman's either really clumsy or she's got a death wish.)

Not to be outdone, approximately once a month Mrs. Witkowski would come with chocolate chip cookies for the whole class. Now **I** was the one starting to feel jealous. At one point, I had Mr. and Mrs. Witkowski all to myself, but now I was sharing them.

It's funny—I don't know if it was because of the ICBM and thinking like an adult, at least a **mature** adult, but that feeling of jealousy I was experiencing was not something I liked about myself very much. So I was really glad that I was eventually able to get past those feelings, and just be happy that all of the other kids were sharing the Witkowskis with me.

Do you think jealousy is an immature emotion? Is it something we can control? I didn't have those answers at three; I don't have them at twelve; and I probably won't have them at a hundred and twelve. Maybe I could ask whoever answered that classified ad for the philosopher's position, although I suspect that person wouldn't know either. In fact, if you could post answers to those kinds of questions to a website called "I've_ got_ it_ all_ figured_ out.com", I'll bet you wouldn't get any hits.

Sometime in early October, a few minutes before we were scheduled to leave "Little Guys" for the day, I looked up and there was Dr. Foster. I saw him talking to one of the teachers by the front door. She had him sign in and then pointed him in my direction. I kind of half-waved, and he headed over toward me.

"Hi, Benny, how are you?"

"Hi, Dr. Foster. I'm fine. How come you're here?"

"Well, I made a promise to you about the *Goosebumps* books, and I brought you some."

"You did?" I reached for the bag he was offering, and said, "That's great, thanks."

"By the way, Benny, I checked into those legal issues you had heard about, but I think it was just a rumor, or some kind of misunderstanding."

"Really?"

"Yes, I couldn't find anything about it anywhere. I even called the publisher's corporate offices. I couldn't get through to anyone really high up"—(I'll bet he could have gotten right through to the principal, though, if it had been a school)—"but the person I spoke with said there wasn't anything to it."

"Thanks for doing that." I paused briefly, "Is it possible that they aren't allowed to comment on litigation that's still pending?"

Dr. Foster started laughing. "I hadn't thought of that, Benny. I guess you could be right." He paused. "I'll tell you what. I'll drop by every few weeks or so to bring you some new books, just in case."

"That's very nice of you. I'll make a list of the ones I've already read, and give it to you next time." I paused again. "Dr. Foster, how did you know that I went to school here?"

"I called your Mom to get permission to lend you the books, and she told me. I also know some of the teachers here at 'Little Guys'. And most of the students that go here end up at Clark Elementary." He lowered his voice to a whisper, "Notice, I said Clark Elementary. I'm still working on that name change." (Talk about follow-through—first the books, and then the name. When this guy says something, he means it.)

While I was talking to Dr. Foster, Vanessa and Derek were at their "cubbies" getting ready to leave for the day. I brought him over to meet them. "Dr. Foster, these are my friends that I told you about—Vanessa and Derek."

He shook their hands and said, "It's nice to meet both of you."

Vanessa: "Are you Benny's doctor?"

"No, no, I work for the school department. I met Benny last summer."

Out of the corner of my eye I could see that Mom had just arrived to pick me up. She came over to join us. "Hello, Dr. Foster. It's nice to see you again."

"Hi, Mrs. Curtis. I was just dropping off the books to Benny—and meeting his friends."

Mom acknowledged us. "Hi, guys."

(Okay, I officially surrender. The pre-school was co-ed, but it was called "Little **Guys**"; my mom greeted us—two boys and a girl and said, "Hi, **guys**"; and I had just found out that The Independent Order of Odd**fellows** had started to admit female members. I knew when I was licked. I just had to accept it, and move on. In Bob Dylan's words—"The times, they are a-changin'.")

Mom and Dr. Foster exchanged some more pleasantries. I packed up my stuff, and then we all went our separate ways.

As it turned out, Dr. Foster would make four or five more visits during the school year to bring me the books he promised. Each time, he made it a point to spend a few minutes talking not only with me, but also with Derek and Vanessa too.

I've always felt that toddlers have exceptional "sincerity radar". Toddlers can tell if a person is genuine almost immediately, and Dr. Foster was the real deal. It also seems, however, that toddlers either outgrow or somehow lose this "sincerity radar" as they get older. I suspect the ability to detect phoniness and lack of sincerity has pretty much disappeared right around our eighteenth birthdays—just about the time we're getting ready to vote in our first election. (Too cynical? I guess I'm still smarting from the whole "guys" and "Oddfellows" official surrender.)

I have to say that I really enjoyed pre-school. Of course, as I said before—why wouldn't I? Each day was a three-hour play date with my best friends, and for the most part we got to do a lot of fun things. My literary needs were being met by Dr. Foster, and I was on the board of directors of The Underwear Club for Kids. Life was sweet!

I was still cautious where ICBM was concerned, however—Guarded Mode was almost becoming a lifestyle for me. I mean, sometimes I would blurt out something that would have the teachers looking at me wide-eyed and the other kids scrunching up their faces in a "huh" expression. But for the most part I kept myself in check. If I had said everything that I was thinking, it would have made me look like a know-it-all, and as I've already told you, that's not the image I wanted to project. And besides, ICBM is not like those mall gift cards—"Use it, or lose it".

During the course of the year however, there were a couple of situations that threatened to breach my guarded mode lifestyle. The first one occurred on a snowy day in January during circle time.

The teachers called us together so that we could listen to a story. The first few times they had done that, I had come close to hip-checking two of my classmates into the "manipulatives table", trying to get a front row seat. (Remember how far back I was during the story hour at the library.)

Oh by the way, in case you're interested, Ticketmaster does not handle story hours or circle times at pre-schools for that matter. While I had them on the phone, I asked if they handled reserved seats for "parents sitting on the edge of toddlers' beds". The answer was "no" to that one as well. (I'm hoping they'll expand their offerings in the future. It shouldn't just be about tickets for rock concerts or Cher's **ninth** farewell tour.)

Anyway, back to circle time—Being right up front to hear a story in pre-school was not as critical as it had been at the library. There were only twelve of us in the class, and no matter where you sat, you could see fine. This gave me a great sense of relief. But probably nowhere near the sense of relief felt by the two kids who could have been "drowning in building blocks and Legos".

So on this particular day, I was sitting in the middle of the rug eagerly waiting for the story to begin. The teacher started to tell us about the selection. "It's called *Where the Wild Things Are.*"

As soon as I heard those words, I gasped and my face turned pale. (Note to Crayola: "Blood-drained-from-the-face-white"?—I guess the name probably wouldn't fit on the crayon, never mind.) When I recovered, and before the teacher began to read, I raised my hand.

"Yes, Benny."

"Excuse me, is that book from the library?"

"No, I don't think so."

"Could you just check to see if the last two pages are missing?"

(Even if it wasn't the same book from the library, there could have been a printing malfunction. Maybe it wasn't library vandalism after all.)

"Benny, I think all the pages are here. Would you like to see?"

"No, but do the last two pages read …?" And then I started to recite them word for word, just like I did at the library.

After I had read a few sentences, the teacher interrupted me and said, "Benny, the pages are all here; let's not ruin the end of the story for the rest of the class."

But it was too late; I had already breached Guarded Mode. Even Derek and Vanessa were looking at me funny.

The teacher who was about to read us the story addressed me again. "Benny, was that you at the library this past summer? Miss Frist is a friend of mine, and she was telling me about a little boy who was able to recite one of the books she was reading. Was that you?"

I couldn't lie. "Yeah, it was."

"It's so funny—I've told that story to so many of my friends. Wait 'till I tell them that you're in my class. Is this the only book you've memorized, or are there others?"

I was thinking to myself that this was fast approaching "circus sideshow territory". If I had only stayed in Guarded Mode, none of this would have happened.

I started to downplay what had happened at the library. "I … actually … only recited the last two pages, not the whole …" At that point the teacher interrupted me. I think she began to realize how uncomfortable this was making me.

"You know what, Benny—why don't I just read the story, and if I get stuck, I'll call on you for help? Would that be okay?"

"Yes, it would. Thank you."

I think you can see that this potential exposure of my ICBM wasn't completely my fault. I was just trying to protect my classmates from impending disappointment. But to make matters worse, the library incident was now being embellished upon, and taking on a life of its own—It was becoming an "urban legend" (well, actually more of a "suburban legend").

The other "letting down my guard" incident occurred a few months later. This one, I have to say, was totally my fault. In my defense, however, I did have the best of intentions. I know—the road to Hell is paved with good intentions. (Would that be Route 666? Does the road to Hell pass through Purgatory? What about Limbo? I still can't get a straight answer as to whether Limbo's operational.)

Anyway, sometime in May, our teachers sent a note home announcing that kindergarten screening would be taking place at a number of elementary schools in the area. I was pretty sure that I wouldn't have to go through the screening process again, but I was also pretty sure that Derek and Vanessa would.

So over the weekend, I developed a series of charts similar to the ones Mrs. Jarvis had used when she tested me during the past summer. I also made up some practice exercises about colors, shapes, and letter recognition. (Not to brag, but I think the level of specificity in **my** screening charts was very clear. There was no ambiguity at all.)

My idea was to use the charts to help prepare Derek and Vanessa for the kindergarten screening. I certainly didn't see anything wrong with this at the time. I mean, I wasn't going to be giving them the answers. I just wanted to be sure my friends had every possible advantage in terms of being familiar with the test format—especially when to give general answers and when to give specific answers.

Although TUCK met every Friday during free time, I called an emergency meeting (any charter member could do that) on the Monday morning right after the weekend that I had developed the screening charts.

I made a motion that we suspend the current limited meeting schedule, and meet every day that week in order to practice for the kindergarten screening. The vote was unanimous in favor of the motion. (Actually Derek and Vanessa just shrugged. They were kind of use to my motions by now, and kind of just went along.)

The first two days of the practice went very well. But by the time Wednesday and Thursday rolled around, there were some problems.

For example:

- Derek's tower fell three times. He claimed the table wasn't level, but I'll tell you what I think—"a poor craftsman blames his tools". I heard that one from Mr. Witkowski. (Derek may be the only person on the planet that I can beat at Jenga.)

- Vanessa insisted on building Barbie's Dream House instead of "some dumb tower".

- Derek didn't want to just draw the outline of a person and a tree; he wanted to color them in, as well. And as you know, he doesn't favor the featherism method. So, he used up all of the crayons in the new box he was given before we even got the opportunity to discuss his story.

- Vanessa refused to hop on one leg while holding the other. She pointed out that the only animals she knew of that hopped were bunny rabbits, and they hopped on both feet. So that's what she was going to do. (I wanted to point out that kangaroos also hop, but that was just extraneous information that didn't bolster my argument any.)

This last situation sort of brought things to a head. There were no mats at the pre-school, so Vanessa was trying to do the hopping in a small area away from everything else. Well, if you hop on one foot, you tend to go up and down, and stay in a small area. But if you hop on two feet, you tend to propel yourself forward. (I knew this from personal experience, but you know, it might not be a bad idea to introduce some more advanced subjects into the pre-school curriculum—like physics.) Anyway, after about four hops, Vanessa was halfway across the room. The two students that I had almost "assaulted" when I was trying to get a good seat at circle time were able to get out of her way, but the manipulatives table, being a stationary object, was not. Legos, dominoes, and blocks were everywhere. (Note to Curriculum Director: Please consider adding physics; it could really be a safety issue.)

I'm sure that the two students who almost got hit by Vanessa (and earlier in the year by me) were beginning to think that there was some sort of **conspiracy** going on. If they had known that Vanessa and I were both charter members of TUCK, I think that would have cinched it for them. They probably would have put Oliver Stone on speed dial.

As you can imagine, this commotion didn't go unnoticed by our teachers. As Derek and I rushed over to Vanessa, the teachers did also. Vanessa was fine, but the manipulatives table was a different story. Derek's earlier contention that the table wasn't level may not have been true then, but it surely was now.

Coincidentally, as the teachers were trying to sort everything out, and make sure everybody was okay, in walked Dr. Foster. He put down the books that he was carrying and asked if he could be of any assistance.

The two teachers and Dr. Foster talked briefly among themselves, and then one of the teachers asked Derek, Vanessa, and me to join Dr. Foster and her on the other side of the room. We all sat down at a trapezoid table. (the shape of which Derek and Vanessa were able to easily identify, I might add).

Anyway, I explained what the three of us had been doing for the past week. I brought over the copies of the screening charts I had developed, as well as the assessment sheets I had completed on Derek and Vanessa. (I probably should have had Derek and Vanessa sign a waiver before I released their assessment forms to Dr. Foster, but frankly, it didn't occur to me.)

Our teacher and Dr. Foster looked at the charts that I gave them, and then excused themselves to go to the other side of the room. While they were over there, I couldn't help but think that any chance of keeping my ICBM under wraps was about to come crashing down like one of Derek's towers. (Is that a mixed metaphor?) My main concern was that the teachers would tell the "screening chart story" to their friends and then "Suburban Legend II" would be born.

After a few minutes, Dr. Foster came back over to where the three of us were sitting. "Excuse me, Derek and Vanessa, could I speak with Benny for a moment?"

"Sure." And they get up from the table.

Dr. Foster turned to me. "I brought you some more books."

"Thanks."

"You know, that was a nice thing you were trying to do for Derek and Vanessa."

I was kind of surprised by his comment, but I just said "Really?'

"Yes, you were trying to help your friends. There's nothing wrong with that. In this case though, Benny, I don't think it was necessary. In the last few months I've gotten to know Derek and Vanessa, and they're going to do fine on the screening. And besides, it's not like other tests. It's just to find out how ready incoming students are for kindergarten. In fact, we sometimes use the screening to adjust what we emphasize in the kindergarten curriculum, and when to teach certain things. Derek and Vanessa don't need to prepare for it; the school just wants to find out what they already know."

I paused for a moment, mulling over what Dr. Foster had said. "Can I ask you a question?"

"Of course."

"How is studying for the kindergarten screening different from high school students taking a course to prepare them for the SAT's? Don't the colleges just want to find out how much they already know?"

Dr. Foster started to laugh. "Wow, Benny, that's a good question. As always, you're two steps ahead of me. I'll tell you what. I have an appointment in a little while, so I don't have time right now to continue this discussion, but I promise we will. Okay?"

"Sure."

"Good. Oh, one more thing, Benny. I didn't think you wanted the story about the screening charts to leave this room. So, I asked your teachers to just keep it among us. I hope that was all right."

"Thank you. You have no idea."

He smiled. "Sorry, I have to run to my appointment. I'll see you in a few weeks."

You know what? Instead of making screening charts during that weekend, my time would have been much better spent coming up with an appropriate superhero name for Dr. Foster—he kept coming to my rescue.

The school year ended in the middle of June. Mom and Dad spoke with Mrs. Stanton, the elementary school principal, to ask if it would be all right for me to enter the gifted kindergarten program in the fall. According to my parents, Mrs. Stanton said, "We are very much looking forward to it."

At the end of June, I went for my second annual extended visit with Grandma and Grandpa. I think each year the visits got better and better.

Around the first of August, Grandma and Grandpa brought me back home to Massachusetts. I really enjoyed the trip back because we took the ferry across Long Island Sound to Connecticut.

Believe it or not, the ferry we rode on was a former U.S. Naval vessel that had actually been at the invasion of Normandy in World War II. Once Grandpa found out about that, the whole hour and twenty minute trip was about that battle. I loved every minute of it. The man can tell a story!

My grandma and grandpa stayed with us for a week after they brought me home. On the day before they were scheduled to go back to Long Island, we had a big cookout in our backyard. Derek and Vanessa and their parents came. The Witkowskis also came, and I asked Mom to invite Dr. Foster, and he came.

It was great to see how everybody enjoyed themselves. Mr. Witkowski and Grandpa hit it off immediately, and so did Mrs. Witkowski and Grandma. Mr. Witkowski showed everyone the bird feeder we had made, and Grandpa took a special interest. Grandma complimented Mrs. Witkowski on the chocolate chip cookies she had baked. I think Mrs. Witkowski actually gave Grandma her recipe—she must have **really** liked Grandma. I'm sure that in Dr. Foster's job he was used to just listening, so it didn't surprise me that I didn't hear him say very much, but nevertheless, he seemed to be enjoying the goings-on.

I know it was just a cookout, but the people I cared about most in the world were all together. And you know how people often say, "We should do this again", and then never do? Well, the other people in my backyard that day must have felt the same way I did, because that cookout has become a tradition that we've maintained every August since then.

Just before Dr. Foster had to leave, he asked to see me.

"Thanks for coming, Dr. Foster."

"Benny, this was terrific. I really enjoyed myself." (The sincerity meter registered a solid ten.) "Before I left, I just wanted to tell you that all three of you—Derek, Vanessa, and you will be in the same kindergarten class next year."

"Really? Wow! Do they know?"

"Not yet. But I told their parents, and they said you can tell them."

He then knelt down so he could speak more softly. "Oh, and a couple of more things, I haven't forgotten about the kindergarten screening and the SAT debate. We'll pick that up in September, okay?" And then with a big smile on his face, he said, "And check out the new name of the school over the door!" And with that he winked at me, and went off to say goodbye to the adults.

"Genius-man"? "Fix-it-man"? "Get-it-done-man"?

Okay, I agree; they still weren't very good.

Chapter 8

▼

Prior to entering kindergarten in September, I was required to have a physical exam, as well as various booster shots and vaccinations. (Nice way to spend the last few days of summer vacation, huh?)

My trip to the pediatrician was uneventful (no rashes on the groin). The doctor and one of the nurses filled out the required forms and returned them to Mom. The forms indicated that I had blue eyes, brown hair, weighed 40 pounds, and was three feet six inches tall. My weight put me in the seventy-first percentile for boys my age, and my height put me in the seventy-second percentile (I like consistency).

By the way, at what age do they stop using percentiles to describe height and weight categories? I mean, you never hear of a thirty-five-year-old woman who has dropped a few pounds, declaring—"Yes, I went from the fifty-eighth percentile to the fifty-sixth percentile." Although maybe that's not such a bad idea, especially for people who are obese. Statistically there is no "hundredth percentile" so, unless you're in the *Guinness Book of World Records*, theoretically, there's always going to be someone heavier than you are.

Along with the forms for the doctor to fill out, the school sent us a packet of information about kindergarten. It contained a list of supplies I would need, the announcement of an Open House before school started, and a detailed outline of the kindergarten curricula.

Speaking of that—What's with the word "curricula? I mean, I know it comes from the Latin, so the plural form of "curriculum" is supposed to end in "a" rather than "s". But, why is that? I mean, it's an **English** word now; we've added it to our language. Let's just add the "s". Trust me, Julius Caesar's not going to care.

This whole situation probably wouldn't bother me so much if the English language were a bit more consistent. (I've already told you what a big fan I am of consistency—just check out the height and weight percentiles again.) The problem is that sometimes when a word ends in "um" we add an "s", and sometimes we get rid of the "um" and add an "a". For example, if we have more than one "Hoover" in the house, we don't say, "I think I'll use both of the 'vacua' today"; we say "vacuums".

To be fair though, maybe the word "vacuum" doesn't come from Latin, so that's why the plural is "vacuums". But if that's the case, then in order to spell the plural of some words correctly, you're going to have to know from what language they're derived. Doesn't that seem like a lot of pressure to put on little kids, just learning to talk? (I mean they already have the potty-training pressure. This just seems like piling on.)

Note to parents of toddlers: I guess you could always combine the two. For instance, you could make up a list of English words derived from Latin that take on a various plural endings. Then review the list with your toddlers while they're sitting on the toilet. Talk about "two birds with one stone".

Here's another example of the "plural issue" to illustrate my point—Say you're in the produce department at the local supermarket and the manager is helping you. If you didn't know from what language the word "plum" was derived, you might be tempted to ask for two apples, two pears, and a couple of "**pla**". Purchasing fruit shouldn't be that hard.

The information we received about the kindergarten curricula (if I can accept "guys" and "Oddfellows", I can accept curricul**a**) was actually quite interesting. Since the kindergarten class was a pilot program for "gifted" students, there was a greater emphasis on creative thinking and problem-solving skills. The guide also indicated that there would be a focus on communication, personal growth, and leadership.

I understand the communication, and to some degree the personal growth part, but I had a hard time imagining how the typical kindergarten activities would prepare me to be a leader. I've never heard of anyone at the U.N. General Assembly playing Duck, Duck Goose or using blunted scissors to cut out circles from construction paper. (Okay, maybe once, when Fidel Castro spoke for five straight hours.) But to tell the truth, I wasn't that concerned about the leadership component. After all, I was on the Board of Directors of TUCK.

There were two additional pieces of interesting news in the packet that was sent to us from the school. The first one was that Mrs. Jarvis (she, of the screening charts) was going to be my kindergarten teacher. The second piece of news was that there would be monthly "group guidance" sessions with Dr. Foster.

I looked upon both of these developments as very positive. Certainly, spending more time with Dr. Foster was a real plus, and since Mrs. Jarvis already knew me, that was a plus as well. I also suspected that Mrs. Jarvis had some suspicion about my ICBM; and that meant I probably didn't have to be in Guarded Mode all the time. She would be more understanding.

After I found out that Mrs. Jarvis was going to be my teacher, I decided that one of the first things I needed to do was to apologize to her for the way I acted during the screening. I mean, I hadn't really done anything wrong, but I think my responses definitely made her uncomfortable. And, as I've told you before, I really don't like doing that to people. I considered giving Mrs. Jarvis the kindergarten screening charts I had made up as a peace offering, but then I decided to just "let sleeping charts lie".

On the day of the kindergarten Open House, Mom and I arrived at the same time as Derek and Vanessa and their moms, so we all walked in together. There was some remodeling going on at the front door, so we couldn't go in through the main entrance. That meant I couldn't view the new name of the school that Dr. Foster had told me about. (Postponement of gratification is not exactly my strong suit, so I was hoping we'd take up that particular issue when we focused on "personal growth".)

As the kids and their parents entered the classroom, Mrs. Jarvis was there to greet us. In most instances she just said "Good morning", but when Mom and I approached, she said, "Hi, Benny. Hi, Mrs. Curtis." It had been over a year since the kindergarten screening, but I suspect that when Mrs. Jarvis looked at the class roster, my name might have rung a bell—probably a cacophony of bells. (I was hoping to find a legitimate place to use the word "cacophony"—I just like it! Do you think it was too forced?)

Anyway, Mrs. Jarvis reviewed some of the material we had previously received at home, and answered all the questions we had. Dr. Foster made a brief appearance to introduce himself and to talk about the group guidance sessions. For the remainder of the time at the school, the students and their parents familiarized themselves with the classroom and its surroundings. Then everyone took a tour of the building to see where the main office was located, as well as the nurse's office, and the special areas, like art and music.

When most of the students and their parents had left the classroom to look at the rest of the school, I asked Mom if I could go speak to Mrs. Jarvis privately. Mom looked a little surprised but said, "Yes."

"Excuse me, Mrs. Jarvis, may I speak with you?"

She turned toward me and smiled. "Why of course, Benny. How are you?"

"I'm fine." And then I hesitated.

Mrs. Jarvis must have realized that I had something else on my mind, because she said, "Was there something else you wanted to ask me, Benny?"

"No, I don't have any other questions. You did a very thorough job explaining everything."

She smiled more broadly. "Well, thank you, Benny; that was nice of you to say."

"Mrs. Jarvis?"

"Yes."

"I think I owe you an apology because of last summer."

"Why would you think that?"

"Well, I kind of think I sounded like a wiseguy during the screening."

"A wiseguy?"

"Yeah, I mean not like a wiseguy from Staten Island ..."

"Staten Island?"

"Yeah, **in** New York. Well, it's a part **of** New York. Sorry, I'm never sure what preposition to use."

She was smiling, but there was also some puzzlement in her expression as well. "Yes, Benny, I know where Staten Island is, but I'm not sure I see the connection."

I figured I would just drop the whole "Staten Island thing"; it was just confusing the issue, so I said, "I guess I just meant that looking back on it, I think maybe I was rude to you."

"Benny, it's very sweet of you to want to apologize, but I don't think it's necessary." She paused. "If I had to describe you, words like bright, intelligent, and creative would come to mind—certainly not rude." And then she smiled an even bigger smile.

"Really?"

"Really!"

Mrs. Jarvis was registering a 9.5 on the "sincerity meter". (The only reason it wasn't a solid 10 was because of the changes to the international "toddler sincerity scale", as dictated by the 1988 "East German toddler amendment".)

"Benny, I'm really looking forward to having you in this class, and I think you know how much Dr. Foster thinks of you."

"Thanks, Mrs. Jarvis. I feel a lot better." I shook her hand and went back over to Mom.

"Is everything all right, honey?"

"Yes, Mom, everything's fine. I think it's going to be a great year."

We toured the school for about a half hour, and then went home.

The first day of kindergarten was scheduled for the Wednesday after Labor Day. A week or so before that, I had asked Mom and Dad to check all the video stores to see if there was a new "Peanuts" movie about Labor Day, but none of the store personnel knew what my parents were talking about. Mom and Dad did, however, find a "Peanuts" video for **Arbor Day**. (Who would have thought that the Sierra Club had more clout than the AFL-CIO?)

I was also disappointed that I hadn't heard from Crayola. It had been over a year since my suggestion about temper-tantrum blue, but still not a nibble. I guess that's the way the crayon crumbles. (After observing the intense pressure Derek employs whenever he colors, this cliché seems much more appropriate.)

Despite no "Peanuts" Labor Day video, and no contract, or even **contact** with Crayola, I was still upbeat about school beginning. The regularly scheduled meetings of TUCK could resume, and just like last year, I'd be with Vanessa and Derek each day.

So, on the morning of the first day of kindergarten, Mom didn't have to wake me up; I got up on my own, got dressed, and went into the kitchen for breakfast.

"Good morning, Sweetie."

"Good morning, Mom."

"What would you like for breakfast, as if I didn't know?"

"Actually, now that I'm in kindergarten, I've decided to cut back on the Alphabits." Mom looked at me strangely as I continued. "When I was listening to Mrs. Jarvis at the Open House, it sounded like we're going to be doing a lot of writing, so I probably can get my 'creative liquids' flowing in school rather than at breakfast."

Mom was smiling. "Wow, that's a surprise ... but I think you mean "creative **juices**".

"I thought about that, but since our rules about Alphabits are very strict—they have to be in **milk**—shouldn't it be more generalized to '**liquids**'?"

Mom started shaking her head. "Okay, you got me. So then, what are you going to have for breakfast?"

"How about Cheerios? At least that way, I don't have to go cold turkey."

Mom completely broke up. "All right, I'll get the Cheerios."

Using Cheerios instead of Alphabits severely limited my writing options. The only sentence I was able to create was a line of dialogue showing a **tremendous** amount of surprise.

After breakfast, Mom drove me to school. She started to go toward the parking lot, but I asked her if she could just go in the drop-off lane in front of the school. "I would kind of like to walk in by myself." Since the drop-off lane is very close to the main entrance, and Mom could watch me the whole way, she agreed.

The reason I wanted to go in by myself was so I could look at the new school name over the door. As I got closer, I could see the name very clearly—"Franklin Clark Elementary School"—the middle initial had been removed. But it wasn't just that; the entire name had been replaced with new metallic letters.

I stopped just in front of the door and stared up for a few moments. I wasn't absolutely positive, but believe it or not, I thought the new letters were in the **Alphabits font**. (Just when I thought I was out, they kept pulling me back in!)

I considered asking Mr. Witkowski if I could borrow one of his ladders, just to satisfy my curiosity. But I really felt like I was over the Alphabits thing. It was so pre-school.

Later that day we had our initial group guidance session with Dr. Foster. Our group consisted of Derek, Vanessa and me. (I'm guessing that the grouping was not done by lottery.) These guidance sessions were intended to gauge how well students were adjusting socially. But since all of us knew each other so well, I suspected that our sessions might be a little different. I mean, we already had our own built-in support system.

When we arrived at Dr. Foster's office, he greeted us, and invited us to sit at a table on the far side of the room. And, as you would expect, we all were immediately comfortable with each other. (It's tough to be in awe of someone who you witnessed spitting out watermelon pits at a cookout a few weeks before.) After about ten minutes of discussion, Dr. Foster gave passes to Derek and Vanessa to return to class, but he asked me to stay back for a moment.

"So, Benny, did you see the new name over the door?"

"Yes, just this morning. How did all that happen?"

"I really can't take any credit. When they decided to redo the front entrance, the building committee recommended eliminating the 'E', primarily because it was standing by itself, and not very secure. It actually had broken off and fallen a few times in the past."

"So, you didn't have to bring up … the other thing"?

"No, I didn't, but I probably would have, if they had decided to keep the 'E'.
"I'm glad."
"I am too."
"Dr. Foster, who is Franklin Clark, anyway"?
"He was the first superintendent of schools in this community, sometime in the 1800's. And his full name was Franklin **Excelsior** Clark.
"Excelsior?"
"Yes, it's Latin for 'ever higher'."
"I know it was in the 1800's, but why would anyone name their child Excelsior, even as a middle name?"

Dr. Foster shrugged. "Who knows? But it sounds like his parents had very high expectations for their son from the moment he was born."

I've since looked up the word "excelsior" in the dictionary, and it has an additional definition. It also means "wood shavings used for packing breakable things". So, it's worse than I thought. If Franklin Clark had been born more recently, and his parents used the modern equivalent of "Excelsior", he would have been named "Bubble Wrap". (I think the building committee did us all a favor by removing the "E".)

Since Dr. Foster had mentioned that "Excelsior" was from Latin, I asked him if he knew much about Latin derivations.

"Some. Why do you ask?"

I was thinking about the whole "curriculum, vacuum, plum business". But since I already had enough "balls in the air" having to do with language, I decided to drop it.

"Just curious."

"Benny, before you go back, I thought we could finish our discussion about the SAT's and the kindergarten screening."

"Okay." I paused. "You know, I was thinking about that some more, and I actually do see a difference. Colleges use the SAT's to help decide whether to admit students, but the screening doesn't have anything to do with accepting or rejecting kids."

"That's exactly right, Benny. That was pretty … uh, sophisticated."

As you know, I'm not very good at accepting compliments so I just nodded my head. But I wasn't quite done. "Dr. Foster, there's still something else bothering me about this though."

Dr. Foster was smiling. "What's that, Benny?'

"When you're in college, don't you have to write a lot?"

"Certainly—term papers, essays, research papers, yes."

"So, how come if the colleges use the SAT's to decide who gets accepted, the SAT's don't have a writing section?"

Dr. Foster started chuckling. "I don't have an answer for that one, Benny. But, the good news is that you don't have to worry about any of this for quite a few years."

"Yeah, that is kind of a relief." (It should be noted, by the way, that in the last couple of years, the SAT's have added a writing section, but they eliminated all the analogies—go figure.)

I decided to shift the topic. "Do you think I should give Mrs. Jarvis the screening charts I made up for Derek and Vanessa?"

Dr. Foster paused. "I'm not sure that's a good idea, Benny."

"Yeah, I think you're probably right." I hesitated. "What about if I give them to you? You could keep them on file—sort of like an 'alternative assessment'."

"Where did you come up with that phrase?"

"I don't know. I guess I read it somewhere when I was gathering information about the SAT's."

"Actually, if you want to give them to me, that would be fine. I'll just put them in **your** folder, and when you're famous, people can look at what you were doing as a four-year-old."

I knew he was only half-joking. But again, I can't take a compliment very well. So I just smiled and said, "That would be good. Thanks." (I did hope that the "personal growth" stuff was going to start soon.)

Besides Vanessa, Derek, and me, there were two other students in the kindergarten class that had been at "Little Guys" last year. One of them was a girl named Jill, who kind of had a sour disposition. I don't know what her parents were thinking by naming her **Jill**, since their last name was **Koy**. I mean, look what happens when you transpose the first letters of her two names. (Is it possible for the naming of a child to become a self-fulfilling prophecy? First, "Excelsior", and now this.)

The other student from our pre-school class was a girl named Megan Sullivan. After only a few weeks of school, she started being absent a lot. Finally, Mrs. Jarvis announced that Megan would be out of school for an extended period of time. She assured us that Megan was going to be fine, but that she would have to be taught at home for several months. When a number of kids asked Mrs. Jarvis what was the matter, she just said, "Megan's sick, but she's going to be okay."

Mrs. Jarvis had everyone in the class make cards for Megan each week, which was a very nice gesture, but it somehow didn't seem like enough. So on Friday at the weekly TUCK meeting, I asked Derek and Vanessa if they could think of anything else we could do. (We kept the TUCK meetings on Fridays to avoid having to post "change of meeting" notices in the newspaper.)

Vanessa: "I feel bad for Megan. Do you know what's the matter with her?"

Me: "No, I don't. But Mrs. Jarvis said she's going to be okay. Maybe we can ask Dr. Foster."

Derek: "Last year, I think Megan enjoyed watching the birds eating at the bird feeder, more than anyone else."

Me: "Yeah, I think you're right." I paused for a moment. "What about that?"

Vanessa: "What do you mean?"

Me: "I could ask Mr. Witkowski to build another bird feeder, and we could give it to Megan!"

Vanessa: "Yeah, that's a great idea."

Derek: "Yeah."

Me: "We're going to need some money. I wish we had thought of creating a treasury for TUCK."

Derek: "Treasury? What are you talking about?"

Me: "Well, we have to buy the wood and stuff like that. We can't expect Mr. Witkowski to pay for it. He doesn't even know Megan."

Vanessa: "If we tell Mrs. Jarvis about it, maybe she can help."

Vanessa went and told Mrs. Jarvis about our idea. Vanessa said that Mrs. Jarvis really liked it, but she had to talk with Megan's parents before we could do anything. Mrs. Jarvis also said that she could reimburse Mr. Witkowski from money the PTA had given her.

After reporting all this, Vanessa said, "We should do this again. This should be what TUCK does."

I was thinking to myself—I really hope we **don't** have to do this again. I certainly don't want any more of our classmates getting sick, but then I realized what Vanessa meant. And so, the first real activity of TUCK was to come up with an idea that helped one of our friends feel better. (I must admit, it was a much better activity than the "underwear survey" I had originally proposed.)

Maybe we're destined to be "idea people". If so, we may have to consider expanding our name—**TUCK-TT**—"The Underwear Club for Kids Think Tank".

The whole bird feeder suggestion came together in a hurry—from idea to reality in less than two weeks. A group of us from the kindergarten class, Mrs. Jarvis, and Mr. Witkowski went to Megan's house right after school got out one afternoon.

Megan and her mom watched from the window as Mr. Witkowski put up the feeder, and we filled it with birdseed. To this day, I'm not sure I've ever seen two bigger smiles in my life. I could also see that Mrs. Sullivan had started to cry. I looked over, and Mrs. Jarvis had to brush away a tear as well. Anybody watching the scene unfolding in the Sullivans' backyard would certainly have a greater understanding of the phrase "tears of joy".

I suppose there are some people who might suggest that even **little** boys shouldn't cry. But, I did cry that day. I didn't try to hide my tears, and I didn't care who saw me. I'm not sure why I was crying, but I don't think genuine emotions are supposed to be analyzed anyway. Let's just say that my heart told my brain that crying was the best way to express what I was feeling. (The "heart-brain connection" makes a lot of sense to me; I've always been a big fan of "The Tin Man" and "The Scarecrow".)

A few weeks after we had delivered the bird feeder to Megan, I was over at the Witkowskis' house. Mr. Witkowski told me that he had decided to start building and selling bird feeders. It wasn't really to make money he told me; he just enjoyed making them, and people seemed to enjoy having them in their yards. (Imagine that, Mr. Witkowski was going to be his own "cottage industry". If I could have only persuaded Mrs. Witkowski to get moving on the "chocolate chip cookie front", the Witkowskis could have become a conglomerate.)

At the next group guidance session, I thought about asking Dr. Foster what was wrong with Megan, but I figured it was none of my business, so I dropped it. Dr. Foster did bring up Megan, however, but that was to praise the three of us for our idea about the bird feeder. I really had to bite my tongue not to mention TUCK and what might become its unwritten mission statement of helping people. But, despite my hemorrhaging tongue, I didn't divulge our secret.

Megan returned to school in April—somewhat later in the year than we expected, but the whole class was glad to see here. She was allowed to do a couple of "show-and-tells" in a row, sort of to catch up. They were both about the bird feeder, and some drawings she had done of the birds that visited. I think she has some real artistic talent. Of course, this is coming from a person who during the kindergarten screening could not draw a tree that anyone could recognize. You can bet that if I can't draw a tree, I'd be hard pressed to draw anything that lives in one.

In May, right around my birthday, a letter was mailed home to all the parents indicating that Mrs. Jarvis was going to continue as our teacher in first grade. In education circles this arrangement is known as "**looping**". (Don't you think that the educational establishment could have come up with a better term than "looping" when you have the same teacher two years in a row? I mean, this is the same profession that gave us "pedagogy", "taxonomy of educational objectives", and "authentic assessment". What's with "looping"?)

But, if educators insist on using a word that sounds so informal for teaching the same kids in back-to-back years, I've got some other suggestions. How about:

- Two-Timer

- Knockout—KO—Kindergarten/One

- KFC—Kindergarten/First/Continuum (If Mrs. Jarvis teaches the same kids three years in a row, would that be "Continu**a**"?)

- Jarvis^2 (Jarvis Squared)

Anyway, you can think about it and get back to me.

CHAPTER 9

Summer came to an end, and September took its place. It was time for first grade. Have you noticed that the structure of the last few chapters has closely resembled the time structure of the typical school year? (Yes!—"Art imitates life". That's probably a little pretentious. How about—"Faux art imitates life"?) The reason I used the phrase "imitates life" is because school-age kids and their families go by a different calendar than everyone else. For school-age kids, the calendar year begins in September and ends in June. We don't really pay much attention to the conventional January to December parameters.

And as far as the months of July and August are concerned (I was going to say that they're "in Limbo", but I'm still not sure if it's in operation), suffice to say that July and August get lumped together as "summer". They don't get a lot of **individual** attention. Since most kids are just happy that school's not in session, no one cares what anybody calls them. I do find it interesting how July and August got their names, however.

Historians tell us that July was named for Julius Caesar, and August for Caesar Augustus. If they were still around, I imagine they'd be none too pleased that those months get such short shrift, although I think they're exacting some revenge by giving us all those "um" words. (Did you know that technically the plural of "stadium" is "stadia"? Who the heck says "stadia"? The only way "stadia" could become acceptable in everyday usage is if one of the networks started a reality TV show featuring gladiators.—"Yes Jim, we're all very excited that Russell Crowe has agreed to be in our new reality series—*Celebrity Gladiators*. We'll be filming at various **stadia** around the country."

Anyway, if Julius and Augustus are monitoring things from the hereafter, they may in fact resent the lack of attention paid to their namesake months, especially considering all the trouble they had to go through—Supposedly, they stole two days from February to make sure both July and August would have thirty-one days.

Do you know if that's a true story or not? I mean, it kind of makes sense. It's pretty easy to picture a couple of self-absorbed Roman emperors (Is "self-absorbed" and "Roman emperors" redundant?) altering the calendar to try to ensure that their names lived on. Anyway, here's how that whole thing reportedly came about:

Once upon a time there was a little known emperor named "Februus". His parents had thought of naming him "Excelsior", but even during the short time between his birth and the naming ceremony, his parents could see that he **wasn't** "an Excelsior". The only other name they considered, which seemed to match his personality, was "Flaccidus". But they decided to go with the more ethnic "Februus".

Februus was the emperor just prior to Julius Caesar and long before Caesar Augustus. Around the time of Februus' reign, however, the Roman calendar was being reworked, and the months were all being renamed. To be honest, Februus was not all that well liked. He was seen as wishy-washy, and there was a substantial amount of graffiti on the aqueducts questioning his manhood; the bumper stickers on the chariots weren't all that much better.

The Calendar Commission had a real dilemma. They wanted to rename all the months after gods, celestial bodies, or prominent Roman citizens; and certainly, the emperor had to be considered a prominent citizen. But he was viewed as so ineffectual, that they couldn't bring themselves to do it. Then one of the commissioners had a brainstorm. "You know how much we've debated about what to call the second month? Well, why don't we just bite the bullet (he probably didn't say 'bullet' since they hadn't been invented yet), and go with something at least close to 'Februus'? By doing that, we get to keep our jobs, and probably our heads. And even though many of us were pushing to name the second month 'Uranus', this seems like a good compromise. Plus, I'm sure everyone will be thinking—'Uranus' … 'Februus' … 'six of one, half a dozen of another'." And that's how February got its name. But that's not quite the end of the story.

Julius and Augustus were able to procure an advanced copy of the Calendar Commission's report. A servant for Julius Caesar, named Whoopsus, (who became a eunuch after a tragic circumcision accident) was able to smuggle the report out of the Senate. Both Julius and Augustus were very pleased to see that they each had a month named after them. But they were **not** pleased to see that their months had only thirty days in them. Julius told Augustus that he had an idea. "I'm going to go see that wimp emperor of ours, and get him to give us some of his days". (Historians have debated for centuries whether Julius knew that Februus' **actual** nickname **was** "Wimpus".)

Julius visited Februus as soon as the Calendar Commission report came out of committee, but before it was officially voted upon.

"Februus, thank you so much for seeing me."

"Hello, Julius. What can I do for you?"

"Actually, I think I can do something for you."

"Really? Do tell. I love surprises."

"I went to a soothsayer yesterday, and he told me that the emperor should beware the '**double** Ides of February'."

"Really? And what are the Ides again ... I think I was absent that day?"

"The Ides are the fifteenth, but the soothsayer said to beware the '**double Ides**'."

"Ah, so the twenty-eighth then."

"Uh, no—actually, the thirtieth."

"Yes, right, right. What do you think it means?"

"I think you'll be in danger on February thirtieth every year."

"Oh my."

"I think I have a solution."

"Really. What's that?"

"If you were willing to give up two of the days in February, say one to July and one to August, then there would never be a February thirtieth ever, and you'd be safe."

"Julius, you are a dear. Have your people messenger my people. Let's get this baby done."

This has probably been our longest visit to Tangent City in some time. Thanks for your patience. I just figured that by including this last section in the book, we might be able to market it as "historical fiction".

So, now you know that the "de facto" calendar for kids is exactly the same as the school calendar. But do you know why the school year begins in September and ends in June? It's because we used to be an "agrarian society", and we needed the kids to help out on the farms during the summer months, particularly for harvesting. Actually, it wasn't just the kids that helped out; the whole family pitched in. (Well, everybody except Mrs. Wilson—nobody could ever find her.)

I'm kind of glad, though, that we're no longer an agrarian society. I mean, most people now-a-days can't even maintain their lawns; how the heck would they grow something you could actually eat?

It's kind of interesting that once "September through June" schools were established, even after we became more industrialized, most communities just left the school year the way it was. There are some places, however, that have switched to year-round schools.

It seems to me, though, that the teachers who work in year-round schools lose one of their key motivational tools. I mean, not too many students are going to respond positively to the following: "If you don't buckle down, you're going to have to go to summer school. Of course, if you **do** buckle down, you're going to have to go to school during the summer anyway." (Not much inspiration there)

The same week that first grade started, Dad enrolled me in a five- and six-year-old soccer league. If you remember, Dad was a pretty good baseball player in high school and college, but he hadn't played that much soccer. Nevertheless, he signed on to be the assistant coach of my team.

As it turned out, head coaches, never mind assistant coaches, don't really have to know very much about the game, because peewee soccer has only a distant relationship to real soccer (sort of like a cousin three times removed).

If I may use an analogy—The rules of regular soccer are similar to the laws that govern driving on the Massachusetts Turnpike ("The Pike"—to those of us who live in Mass. and shorten everything). Anyway, according to the laws on The Pike—you should obey the speed limit, never pass on the right, stay in your designated lane unless passing, etc. Basically, the rules for regular soccer and the laws on The Pike are written down and intended to ensure that order is maintained.

Peewee soccer, on the other hand, is analogous to the way people **actually** drive on The Pike. The rules are just simply ignored. And, just like the drivers on The Pike, peewee soccer players are rarely where they're supposed to be. There is no order. Everybody goes as fast as they can in ten different directions. Interestingly, however, I have noticed that some of the drivers on The Pike have decided to adopt the most important rule of soccer—**They don't use their hands.**

There are so many **unintended** differences between regular soccer and peewee soccer that it's hard to know where to begin. But let's just start with the positions. In regular soccer there are designated positions—fullback, midfielder, forward, goalie, etc. In peewee soccer, for all practical purposes, there's a goalie and everybody else. And sometimes the goalie is optional.

The reason for the discrepancy between regular soccer positioning and peewee soccer positioning is that the peewee players just run to wherever the ball is. They never stay where they're supposed to be. In fact, the only reason you can recognize the goalie is because he's allowed to wear something to distinguish himself from his teammates.

Our team was co-ed, and our goalie was a girl. She decided that to distinguish herself from her teammates she would wear a dress. I mean, she called it a "smock", but it wasn't—smocks don't have frilly stuff on the bottom. Anyway, since there's no rule against wearing a smock, or a dress for that matter, she was allowed to wear it. Of course, instead of looking like an athlete, she looked like she was about to roll eggs on The White House lawn.

The back-up goalie, who was a male, was not too thrilled with the first-string goalie's choice of attire, because whenever he entered the game, he had to put on the dress. As a matter of fact, the only reason he was selected as back-up goalie was because he could fit into a size 6X. (Is it any surprise that we don't do well in The World Cup?)

I once saw a series of aerial shots of a peewee soccer match. The images looked like a giant moveable daisy. The ball was in the center of the flower, and the twenty-two kids who surrounded the ball looked like petals. Occasionally, the "daisy" looked as if some gigantic being had been playing "she loves me; she loves me not", because a couple of the twenty-two "petals" would stray away from where the ball was. This was not done in order to assume their appropriate position on the field, but rather because they didn't feel like playing anymore. In metaphysical terms, and keeping with the flower motif, they wanted to "stop and smell the roses". In reality, they "stopped and picked the dandelions"—literally.

Most peewee soccer games end in a 0–0 tie. On occasion, however, if a few of the "petals" go off in search of dandelions, an opening in the flower may occur, and an accidental kick may find its way to the goalmouth. We actually lost two games that way—the ball was headed toward our back-up goalie and he tripped over the lace that had come loose on the bottom of his dress. (I repeat—no way that was a smock.)

If you think peewee soccer games are interesting, you should see the practices. For most peewee teams it was unnecessary to actually work on kicking. As I said before, certain things are pretty intuitive for little kids. They don't need to practice manipulation, and they don't need to practice kicking, although one clever coach in our league put pictures of his players' siblings on the soccer balls. They were the highest scoring team in the history of the league.

Without question, the most difficult part of soccer for little kids to learn is the idea that you can't use your hands. Our head coach originally thought about tying our hands behind our backs but decided against it when my dad pointed out that five-and six-year-olds have enough trouble keeping their balance, and the hand-tying technique could actually lead to a lot more falling down—not the position you want your players to be in. The head coach did insist, however, that we clasp our hands behind our backs. During the first few practices we looked like Irish step dancers. Anybody watching this ritual, especially with the way we were lined up, might have assumed it was an off-Broadway production of *Lord of the Dance*.

Despite all of these issues, I really did look forward to soccer. This was primarily due to the fact that Vanessa was on my team. Derek, however, didn't sign up to play. Since Derek's mom and dad both worked during the week, I think they figured that the weekends were the only time the whole family got an opportunity to spend any time with each other.

Vanessa is a pretty talented athlete, but more importantly, she was one of the few players that understood soccer strategy. Because she was so fast, she often got to the ball before anyone else. Then she would signal to the other ten "petals" on our team to run in the other direction. The other team's "petals" would follow, including the goalie, and Vanessa would have an open shot at the net.

Vanessa was easily the high scorer on our team, but that wasn't her only contribution. She also was responsible for naming our team. Initially, the head coach had notified the league that our team was tentatively going to be called "The Avengers" (Do you think our coach was a tad too intense? I mean this was **peewee** soccer—so what's with the name "The Avengers"? What, were "The Pillagers" and "The Visigoths" already taken?)

Anyway, Vanessa, even as a six-year-old, was pretty sensitive about violence, so she offered a number of alternative names. The coach let us vote for the name we wanted, although he lobbied hard for his initial choice. But the name garnering the most votes was "JFK". Our team wasn't named after the former president, however, but rather it was an abbreviation for "Just for Kicks". Vanessa had done some lobbying of her own.

There was one write-in vote for "Barbie and Ken's Dream Team". I think our goalie might have written in that choice, although I guess it could have been the back-up goalie. I mean, wearing a dress everyday in practice might change your perspective on things.

Anyway, from early September until the middle of November, it was peewee soccer season. Even though I told you that I'm not much of a joiner, soccer was actually fun. I found that I did like being part of a team; I got to spend more time with my dad, and I discovered that I enjoyed the running I did in the game as much as I enjoyed the game itself.

Since I was now in school for a full day, Mom was able to increase the number of hours she did volunteer work. There was a women's shelter in a community not far from where we lived. Mom started putting in a lot of time there. She said that the hospital, where she had volunteered previously had plenty of people helping out, but the women's shelter was often short-handed.

Mom juggled so many things; it was amazing. She ran the household, drove and picked me up everyday from school, volunteered at the women's shelter, chaperoned a number of school field trips, and did it all with a smile on her face. Of course, Dad was no slouch in the work ethic department either. He had a full-time job, helped coach a peewee soccer team, also chaperoned some of my field trips, and one Saturday a month volunteered at Habitat for Humanity. (I began to think that when I figured out a superhero name for Dr. Foster, I should do the same for Mom and Dad.)

A few weeks before Thanksgiving, Mom picked me up from school, and she looked like she had been crying. "Is something the matter, Mom? Did something happen?"

"No sweetie, nothing happened. I mean, nothing to do with us." She paused and glanced over at me. I'm sure she was trying to decide if she should tell me anything. After about a minute she said, "I was just at the shelter and a woman with three small children came in. She had to leave her house because her husband was hurting her, and she was afraid he might start to hurt the children."

I sat quietly for a few moments, and then said, "Where are they going to live?"

"There's some space at the shelter, at least through Christmas."

"Then where will they go?"

"I'm not sure, but we'll work something out."

"Are they safe?"

"Yes, for now they are". Mom paused. "You're pretty curious today."

"Yeah, I guess so. How old are the kids?"

"Three, five, and seven—all boys."

"Is their father going to get in trouble?"

"He has to go to court."

There was silence in the car for another minute.

"Mom?"

"Yes, honey."

"Couldn't I give them some of my toys—you know like the ones we used to give to the hospital?"

"That's a great idea. Let's take a look when we get home." She looked over at me. "You're a pretty terrific kid, you know that?"

I find that because I don't take compliments well, even from my family, I often make a joke about things. "Mom, can I build up credit, so that when I do something wrong, I won't get in trouble?"

She smiled. "You've already got plenty of credit built up, but okay, we'll add some more, why not?"

When we got home, we started to look through my toy chest and closets. We filled a large plastic bag with toys that still worked and games that had all their parts. Mom also found some toys in the attic that would be appropriate for the three-year-old. Most of my old videos had already been donated to the hospital, so there weren't too many of those. Mom said that was just as well, because there were a lot of other people at the shelter and it wouldn't be fair for the kids to monopolize the TV by watching videos all the time.

"So, there's only one TV?"

"Yes, honey, there is."

I sat quietly for a moment and then said, "Couldn't we get the kids a small TV with a built-in VCR? They're not that expensive, are they?"

She shook her head, and started to chuckle. "No, Benny, they're not. Okay, let's go out and get a TV … and some videos too. We'll bring these toys with us and drop off everything later this afternoon."

"SG, Mom."

"Actually—'ST'. It doesn't 'sound good'. It 'sounds terrific'."

The next day I told Derek and Vanessa about the kids at the shelter. We had an emergency meeting of TUCK and voted to ask Mrs. Jarvis if the class could help out. She said, "Yes", and TUCK went into action organizing a food drive for Thanksgiving and a toy drive for Christmas. Every one of our classmates contributed to both of the holiday drives. In fact, we received so much food, and so many toys that we donated the overflow to a local food pantry and "Toys for Tots".

Derek, Vanessa, and I also asked our parents to buy an extra gift for each of the three boys. It was Derek's idea—"Just in case Santa doesn't know where the shelter is."

I guess this is as good a time as any to bring up the topic of Santa Claus. With my ICBM and the whole "thinking like an adult thing", I never really had the traditional kid's view of Santa Claus. Well, at least I didn't believe he brought gifts to two billion children around the world (talk about a logistical nightmare).

Instead, I kind of put Santa Claus in the same category as superheroes. I knew that characters like Batman and Superman didn't really exist, but that didn't stop me from enjoying their adventures. So that's what I did with Santa Claus. That way, I still got to enjoy all the great kid things about Christmas and Santa because it was all part of "superhero world". And therefore, I could talk about it with my friends and classmates and not spoil anything for them.

Before I came up with this "Santa as superhero" idea, I kind of thought Santa was like "Area 51". That's the place where the government supposedly keeps aliens. (The kind from outer space, not the undocumented kind, although in this climate of concern about immigration, who knows?) Anyway, I went through a period of time when I wasn't sure if "Area 51" existed, just like I wasn't sure if Santa Claus existed.

As I mentioned, I've since decided that Santa doesn't exist, at least not in the traditional sense. But, I do think it's possible that "Area 51" exists, but probably not in New Mexico; more likely in The Bermuda Triangle. (Okay, now I'm just messin' with you.)

So, Christmas morning finally arrived. I rushed to Mom and Dad's room, and knocked on the door, and Mom called out, "Come in."

"Is it okay to get up now, and look at my presents?"

"Sure, Honey. We'll be right there."

I ran to the living room where the tree and all the presents were. I just started to open the first one, when Mom and Dad came in. They watched me open my gifts, and they opened some of their own as well. When I was almost finished, for some reason I thought about the three boys in the shelter. I remember feeling the same way I did when we put up the bird feeder in Megan Sullivan's backyard.

Maybe because the three boys weren't right there in front of me, I didn't start crying like I had done at Megan's, but I felt like I was going to. Mom sensed that something was wrong. "What's the matter, Benny?"

"I don't know. I was just thinking about the boys in the shelter. I mean, I know they're going to have a nice Christmas and all, so I don't know why I'm feeling so sad."

Mom had a soft smile on her face, but there were some tears in her eyes as well. "Sometimes, even when we're happy, or feeling good about things, our emotions can kind of rise up. And the only way they can escape is through our tears."

"Sometimes I feel like I'm too sensitive."

Mom continued to smile. "I don't think so. I'd say you're 'just-right' sensitive."

One day in early May, Mrs. Jarvis announced that we would be taking a field trip as part of our social studies unit on Community Helpers.

"Next Friday, boys and girls, we'll be visiting the Pet-Pals Animal Clinic in the morning. Then we'll have lunch and visit the library in the afternoon."

One of our classmates raised her hand, and Mrs. Jarvis acknowledged her. "Yes, Sarah."

"My dog, Petey, got 'fixed' at the Pet-Pals Clinic."

Needless to say, Mrs. Jarvis blanched. (It wasn't "all-the-blood-drained-from-your-face-white", but it was close.) All she could manage to say was, "Really?"

Then a couple of other students spoke up.

"Was your dog broken?"

"How did they fix him?"

I don't think too many five-or six-year-olds know what "getting fixed" means, but evidently Sarah's parents tried to explain it to her, because she said, "He wasn't broken, silly; it just means Petey can't have puppies." (I may be going out on a limb here, but since Petey was a male, I don't think that was an option before the "fixing".)

Since Petey can't really speak for himself, I'm going to do a little projecting. I would imagine Petey would take issue with the use of the term "fixing". Whatever happened to the old adage—"If it ain't broke, don't fix it"? And evidently, that part of Petey's anatomy was working just fine, otherwise why would they have to "fix" it?

Anyway, Mrs. Jarvis recovered enough to say, "Thank you for sharing that, Sarah." (That barely registered a three on the "sincerity meter", even using the scale **prior** to the "East German toddler amendment".)

Doesn't this whole "dog neutering issue" seem like it would make a good Country-Western song? How about this?

<u>My Dog—He is A Changin'</u>

Music and Lyrics by Snipp Doggy Dogg (Crossover Artist)
My heart is heavy, but I'm on a mission.
I'm fixin' to give my dog a fixin'.
There's gonna be a major switch.
Cause we're changin' him from a guy to a …

Well, you get the idea.
When are the Country Music Awards, anyway?

You know, maybe I'm being a bit callous about this issue. I mean it's undoubtedly a very traumatic experience. (I dare say, much more so for the dog, than for the owner.) On the other hand, I think most Country-Western songs are fair game, don't you? To cover myself however, I think I'll pick up a belated "Good luck on your 'fixing'" card for Petey.

Anyway, the day of our field trip finally arrived. Mom had volunteered to be a chaperone, as had three other parents. We arrived at Pet-Pals at about 11:00 in the morning and began the tour.

Either there were none scheduled for that day, or more likely, the tour didn't include getting "up close and personal" with the canines, because we didn't get to see any "fixings" that day. Instead we were led into the kennel area and heard from one of the veterinarians about the "mission" of the clinic. (I gave a quick glance over to Derek and Vanessa. They evidently could read my mind, because they both shook their heads indicating we weren't going to revisit a mission statement for TUCK.)

After we visited the main kennel area, we went to another section of the clinic that had additional cages and terrariums (terraria?—who knows?). This area housed more exotic animals—like iguanas, and lizards, and snakes. (Oh, my!)

Does anyone really enjoy having these kinds of animals for pets? I mean, sometimes even taking care of a cat or dog can be taxing, but at least cats and dogs don't look at you like they want to have you for lunch. I'm not so sure that's true with boa constrictors or Gila monsters. Of course, to be fair, once Petey realized what had been done to him, he might have been looking for some payback too.

While we were still in the "exotic pet area", I raised my hand to ask a question. The veterinarian acknowledged me, "Yes, the boy in the **back**." (Ticketmaster doesn't handle "exotic pet areas" at Pet-Pals, either.)

"Where did the snakes come from? Are any of them local, like from neighborhoods around here?" (I still believed our house was in a "snake-free zone", but with global warming and all, you can't be too careful.)

"No, son, they're not from around here. All of these animals are pets. In some cases the owners couldn't take care of them anymore. We take them in and try to place them with new owners, or pet stores, or sometimes, zoos."

"Thank you." (One less thing to worry about.)

There were a few more questions, and then we finished up the tour and went to a local park for lunch. After we finished lunch, and played at the park for a while, we boarded the school bus and headed for the library.

I hadn't been back to the library very often since the "two-pages-missing" incident. I wasn't purposefully avoiding the library. It was just that between the books Mom picked up for me, and the books Dr. Foster lent me, I was pretty much all set. Even on the few occasions that I had visited the library, I hadn't seen Miss Frist. I didn't think she still worked there. But as soon as we walked in, I spotted her behind the circulation desk.

When she saw our class come in, she immediately came over to greet us. "Welcome, everyone. Please follow me to the reading area."

Being back in that area of the library was like "déjà vu". (Although, I think it's kind of rare for little kids to have "déjà vu"; it's much easier for adults. I mean, when you've only been alive for a few years, how many events are really going to repeat themselves?)

Isn't "déjà vu" like those other things I mentioned earlier—dreaming, hypnotism, Tourette syndrome? If you haven't experienced it, wouldn't you find it hard to believe?

Remember that movie *Groundhog Day*? That was about Bill Murray's character experiencing "déjà vu" over and over again. In one repeated scene, he was trying to impress Andie McDowell's character. But each day he would say something even more stupid than the day before.

Once again—"Art imitates life." For some people, saying stupid things day after day isn't really "déjà vu"; it's their **real** life. You know, like certain radio talk show hosts, and okay ... Paris Hilton. (Too easy?)

Anyway, back to the library. Miss Frist showed us how the library computers could be used to locate a book or research a topic. I thought that the research idea might be a little too advanced for first graders, but Miss Frist just asked us for some general topics, typed the key words into a search engine, and the results were projected onto a large screen connected to the computer. Pretty simple.

There were a few anxious moments for Mrs. Jarvis, however, because when Miss Frist asked for topics to research, Sarah (owner of Petey) offered, "Dogs".

Miss Frist: "What about dogs? Can you be more specific?"

Sarah: "Dogs that have been ... No, dogs that are big."

(I think I actually heard the sound "whew" when Mrs. Jarvis exhaled.)

Miss Frist: "Okay, I'll type in 'large dogs'."

I almost suggested the topic "library vandalism". After all, there could have been a databank on the Internet that could have pointed us in the right direction.

And as far as I knew, they hadn't yet found the culprit who tore out those last two pages. At least it hadn't been reported in the police log. I checked.

After telling us about the computers and the research possibilities, Miss Frist read us two *Curious George* books. We all applauded when she was done, and then Mrs. Jarvis told us to get ready to leave.

As we were lining up with our chaperones, Miss Frist came over to see me. "Hi, Benny."

"Oh, hi, Miss Frist."

"I thought that was you when the class came in, but you've gotten so big, I wasn't sure, so I asked Mrs. Jarvis."

Deflecting the growth compliment, I said, "How did you remember my name?"

She smiled. "You're pretty unforgettable, you know?"

"You mean the memory thing from *Where the Wild Things Are*?"

"Yes."

I think she sensed my discomfort, so she changed the subject. "So Benny, how are you? How's your mom?"

"Fine. My mom's over there."

"Oh yes, I see her. I think I'll say hello. Excuse me, Benny. It was nice seeing you again."

As she turned to go, I said, "Miss Frist".

"Yes."

"You did a real good job reading the *Curious George* books."

"Well thank you, Benny."

If Miss Frist had access to a "toddler sincerity meter" she would have seen that my comment was in the 9–10 range. She **actually** had done an excellent job with the books. I think her high-pitched voice is much more suited to comedy, rather than the "sturm und drang" of *Where the Wild Things Are*.

The next few months were relatively uneventful, except for two things. We found out that Derek's mom was going to have a baby. She was due sometime in October, and Derek seemed very excited about it. The other interesting occurrence happened on the last day of school, when we got our report cards.

Usually, every student's report card indicates the name of next year's teacher. But for everyone in our class, it didn't. In the space for the teacher's name was typed the words "To be announced". There was also a note attached to everyone's report card that indicated the school would be contacting the parents over the summer with more details about next year's program. So, our status for next year was "in Limbo". (It's so much easier talking about "Limbo" in the abstract. But when it involves you, it seems more real. I'm thinking maybe it **is** in operation.)

About two weeks later, over the Fourth of July weekend, Mom and Dad drove me to Grandma and Grandpa's house for my annual month-long stay. I usually talked to my parents three or four times a week from my grandparents' house, and every time I talked with them there was still no word about next year from the school.

Our annual cookout was held the first weekend in August in our backyard in Massachusetts. All of my family was there, as well as the Witkowskis. Dr. Foster also came; and so did Vanessa and her mom and dad; they also brought Derek. Derek's parents weren't there because Derek's mom had gone into labor on Friday, and Derek's baby sister, Samantha, had been born early Saturday morning. Despite the fact that the baby was two months premature, she was doing fine. And so was Derek's mom.

About a half hour into the cookout, while Vanessa, Derek, and I were playing a game, I saw Dr. Foster talking to Mom and Dad, as well as to Vanessa's parents. After a few more minutes he came over to see the three of us kids. "Hi, **guys**." (Forget it! I'm not discussing it.)

We all responded, "Hi."

"So Derek, you're a big brother now. And Vanessa, you have a brand new cousin. Congratulations."

They both said, "Thanks."

"I wanted to talk to the three of you about next year."

We all looked up at him, eager to hear what he had to say.

"I'm afraid there isn't going to be a gifted program next year, because of budget cuts. So, we're not sure exactly what's going to happen." He quickly added, "But I'm strongly recommending that the three of you be in the same class. After all, we can't break up this little club, can we?"

The three of us just looked at each other. Being together again next year in second grade was great news, but how had Dr. Foster found out about TUCK? Did we have a "mole"?

I spoke up. "What club?"

"Well, I didn't mean an actual club. I just meant that the three of you are like … Can I say 'The Three Musketeers', Vanessa?" (I still don't get it. You have to ask permission to use "The Three Musketeers", but "guys" is a given?)

Anyway, Vanessa said, "Sure, that's fine."

"Good. And since all the second graders are going to have group guidance next year, that also means that 'The Three Musketeers' can have their sessions together. How about that for good news?" (It really wasn't a question, so there was no need to answer, but it certainly was good news.)

Once I got over the shock of the possibility that TUCK had been exposed, I realized that Dr. Foster had come through yet again. So I finally decided—Dr. Foster's superhero name was going to be "Lookoutman"—because that's what he always did for us.

Remember that I said I also wanted to give superhero names to Mom and Dad? Well, I changed my mind about that. I kind of liked calling them by the names they already had. "Mom and Dad" worked just fine.

Chapter 10

With the cancellation of the gifted program, all the students going into second grade were placed in heterogeneously grouped classes. (I still don't get it. The field of education gives us words like "heterogeneous" and "homogeneous", but can't come up with anything better than "looping". Actually, I'm not all that enamored with the word "homogeneous" either. Doesn't it sound like some sort of dairy product, or an adjective for something you'd spread on your toast?)

If the truth be told, however, I was kind of glad that there was no more gifted program in the second grade. I mean, I was happy that I got to start school a year early back when I was in kindergarten, but as I've mentioned before, elementary gifted programs strike me as elitist, and they take away resources from other things, so I'm not a big fan. Besides, just as Dr. Foster had recommended, Vanessa, Derek, and I were all in the same heterogeneously grouped class. That was kind of all that mattered to me.

Last year in the first grade there was no need to have separate reading groups because the reading ability spectrum was so narrow; we were all reading at about the same level. This year, however, there was a much broader range, so the teacher decided we should have reading groups based on ability.

In some ways, the toughest thing about creating reading groups is not deciding who is in which group, but rather selecting names for each group. Teachers try to be careful to keep the names of the groups "ability-designation neutral". Their intention is to name the groups in such a way that nobody can figure out which is the top reading group and which group is comprised of students who are struggling.

So for example, teachers stay away from names like "Feudal Lords" for the top reading group, and "Serfs" for the lower reading groups, or "Top of the Heap" and "Bottom Rung of the Ladder", or "The Evelyn Wood Group" and "The Paris Hilton Group". (I really am trying to cut down, but it's not easy; there are just so many opportunities.)

What's interesting about this whole naming process is that teachers go through this painstaking effort to try to ensure that students don't feel labeled (and rightly so), but the kids know 2.8 seconds after the groups are formed which is the top reading group and which is the lowest. But you know what really matters? Does the teacher treat **all** the groups the same; and does she have high expectations for each of the students, regardless of which group they're in? And you know what? Kids figure out if they're being treated fairly in even **less** than 2.8 seconds.

Anyway, our second grade teacher decided that even before the reading groups were formed, the students could vote for five names that would be randomly attached to the five reading groups. (I love the democratic process.)

Our second grade class had about six other students that had been at "The Little Guys" pre-school with us. So it wasn't a big surprise when one of the students suggested that we name all of the reading groups after birds. If you remember, Mr. Witkowski's bird feeders had been a huge hit in pre-school, and undoubtedly most of the kids still remembered the names of the different kinds of birds that frequented the feeders.

After some spirited debate, the class voted that the five reading groups should be called "Blue Jays", "Cardinals", "Robins", "Finches", and "Eagles". The first four selections were birds that we had actually seen in the area. (The only way we could have seen an eagle in person is if we went to a Boston College football game and sought out the mascot.) Nevertheless, "Eagles" was the fifth selection.

During the nominating process for the reading group names, there were a few interesting moments. One of the boys in the class actually nominated "Pigeons". He had recently moved to the suburbs from Boston. (By the way, is the pigeon the official bird of Boston?) Anyway, unlike most former urban dwellers, this student actually **liked** pigeons and wanted a reading group named after them. The vote was surprisingly close, but "Pigeons" lost out when its supporters couldn't change the minds of the "statue sympathizers".

Another girl in our class nominated "Crows". Our teacher asked the girl to elaborate on her nomination.

"Well actually, can it be 'Crows' with initials?"

Our teacher responded. "I'm not familiar with that particular term; is that a special kind of crow?"

"I'm not sure, but we have a garden, and every time my father sees the birds eating the vegetables, he runs outside and yells at them, 'G' ... 'D' ... 'F-in' crows'."

I looked over and saw that one of the teacher aides was smiling, and our teacher was trying not to. She recovered enough to say, "Why don't we just put 'Crows' on the ballot?" (You think teaching second grade is easy?)

Anyway, after the dust settled and the reading groups were formed, Derek, Vanessa, and I ended up in the Cardinals. If the name of our group had been the Blue Jays, I probably would have filed a formal protest. After all, the Blue Jays are in the same division as the Red Sox. Although I wasn't thrilled with the Cardinals, at least they're in the National League, so I could live with it.

Actually, I really wanted to be in the Finch group. I had just finished reading *To Kill a Mockingbird,* and then I watched the movie at Grandma and Grandpa's house during the summer. Atticus Finch quickly became one of my favorite literary characters. In fact when Halloween rolled around, I asked Mom and Dad if I could dress up as Atticus Finch.

Dad spoke to me about it, "Benny, I love the idea that Atticus Finch is someone that you admire, but I'm not sure it's a good Halloween costume."

"Yeah, you're probably right—nobody would know who I was supposed to be; I'd look like a CEO from a Fortune 500 company."

Dad chuckled. "Maybe some of the more traditional CEO's, but not one of those CEO's who runs an Internet company—no suit and tie for them."

"But with the 'Atticus Finch big thick glasses', I **would** look like one of those new CEO's, don't you think? I mean, geeks are in, right?"

Dad was still chuckling. "Yes they are."

"Dad, do you think Atticus Finch and those CEO's with the thick glasses graduated from Princeton at age sixteen?"

"Why would you ask that?"

"Just curious."

Mom then entered the room. "Did I overhear a costume discussion?"

"Yeah, Dad and I were just talking about it."

"So, did you come up with anything?"

"Well, Atticus Finch is out."

Mom looked over at Dad and got a look in return that said, "Don't ask," so she dropped it. "Any other ideas, Benny? What about a superhero?"

"Hmm, that's a possibility, I guess. You know, it's probably too soon, Mom, but could you check to see if any of the stores carry a 'Lookoutman' costume?"

"Lookoutman? I've never heard of him. Is he a superhero? I mean with a name like 'Lookoutman', he almost sounds like a criminal."

"Oh, he's definitely not a criminal. But … Oh, I just had an idea. If you're going to call some costume places, could you try some on Staten Island?"

I have to admit that Halloween is something of a mystery to me. It seems like it's full of paradoxes—from the time you're little, your parents tell you over and over again, "Don't take candy from strangers". But isn't that exactly what they encourage you to do on Halloween? Very confusing!

And isn't "trick-or-treating" a form of extortion? You're asking for something of value, or you'll do something mean. I obviously use the phrase "something of value" quite loosely. A mini-box of stale raisins, a half a licorice stick, and two Milk Duds hardly qualify as "something of value". (Of course if I went out trick-or-treating earlier in the evening, maybe I wouldn't be stuck with all the leftovers.) Regardless, I think it's extortion.

Speaking of Milk Duds, did you see that the company that makes them has decided not to use **real chocolate** in them anymore? So, what the heck are they going to be made of them? I'm telling you, before I put another Milk Dud in my mouth, I'm going to scrutinize the "nutrition facts and ingredients label" very carefully. If I see anything suspicious, I'm switching to Raisinets or Goobers. Of course, I'm not sure switching is going to make any difference. Evidently, almost everything we eat contains some weird ingredient. You think I'm kidding? A Snickers bar contains "Partially Hydrogenated Soybean and Hydrogenated Palm Kernel Oil." What the heck is that stuff? (By the way, does the company that makes Snickers also make Chuckles? And if so, I wonder why they didn't continue with that theme. You know—Snickers, Chuckles, Yuk-Yuks, Belly Laughs, Smirks, Mildly Amusing Bars, I Laughed So Hard I Wet My Pants Mints.)

Anyway, after checking the labels on a bunch of candy bars, I discovered that almost all of them contained the exact same ingredients I just mentioned. That makes me nervous, and a little suspicious—I mean, why is the soybean only **partially** hydrogenated, but the palm kernel oil gets the full treatment?

I've come to a decision. I'm not eating any food that has ingredients spelled with more than nineteen letters. (Note to candy manufacturers: If you want my business, you're going to have to go the whole route with the soybean. If you just **partially** hydrogenate it, it's way over nineteen letters. And as far as the palm kernel oil is concerned, whatever you're going to do to it, make sure that the process only has six letters in it. It can be mashed; it can be boiled; it can be dyed, but pureeing and whipping are out.)

By the way, in case you're curious as to why I decided on nineteen letters, it's because that's the number of letters in "monosodiumglutomate". I'm not giving up Chinese food. Let's not get ridiculous.

I also have some other issues with the "nutrition facts and ingredients" label law.

Haven't we gone too far with it? Can't we just use some common sense? The law requires that we put these labels on everything, but shouldn't there be some exceptions? Do we really need the ingredients label on **bottled water**? Surprise, surprise!! It says 100% water. (What reading group were these geniuses in during the three years they spent in second grade?) How about fruit? Oddly, the ingredients in an apple are 100% apple. Good to know.

If there's any chance we're going to make modifications to the label law, I have a few more suggestions, especially for more exotic foods. For example, when you head down the "Snake and Lizard" aisle of the local supermarket, and you pick up a box of "boa constrictor burgers", wouldn't it be helpful if the label included the following: "100% boa constrictor—but it tastes like chicken! Best served just before a nuclear holocaust when you really don't care what happens to your digestive tract. (Too long for the label?)

You know what the label law also reminds me of? Handicapped parking. I mean, I'm all for handicapped parking in 99.9% of the situations. But again, can't we use some common sense? For example, why do we need handicapped parking at a racquetball club, that doesn't allow spectators, or at a rock-climbing location? Who are those spaces for? Okay, I know what you're thinking—what if those places have employees that need handicapped parking? Well, I thought of that; just paint "reserved" on as many parking spots as you need. As a matter of fact, sociologists tell us that people are less likely to park in reserved parking spaces, than handicapped ones. Problem solved.

You know, I just read over the last few pages, and even considering all the connections that I tend to make with my ICBM, we did travel pretty far into Tangent City. Not to worry, however; we still have a long way to go before we reach "No-Connection-Whatsoever-ville", or "Huh? Township". In fact, there's nothing to be really concerned about, as long as we don't find ourselves in "Dissociative Behavior Village". It's tough to get back from there, even using Mapquest or a GPS system.

Anyway, the last main topic I was talking about was Halloween and trick-or-treating. So, let's leave Tangent City and get back to that.

When you think about it, is there any real difference between a kid trick-or-treating and a guy robbing a bank?

- They both wear disguises.

- They both threaten harm if they don't get what they want.

- They both get their pictures taken while in disguise—the kid by his parents, the robber by the security camera.

Too many similarities for my taste. Should we really have a holiday that encourages kids to mimic criminal behavior?

Anyway, the only way I was able to reconcile my feelings about Halloween and still go out trick-or-treating was to set up a few rules: I only visit houses of people I know, and I only dress up as a character from history or literature. (Although there's a lot of latitude with this last rule. For example, I count comic books as literature. That allows me to dress up like a superhero, even a superhero that hasn't appeared in any comics yet, like "Lookoutman".)

Despite my machinations to create this giant loophole (I may have a future in writing tax law), Mom was not able to find a "Lookoutman" costume. She even tried a store on Staten Island called "Disguises 'R' Us", but to no avail. The store-owner did indicate he had a very large supply of "Fugeddabout-it-man", if we were interested. We weren't.

So after much deliberation, I decided to be Caesar Augustus for Halloween. I know it probably seems like an odd choice, but I did feel kind of sorry for him. Did you realize that August is the only month that doesn't have a holiday in it? I mean, I know Augustus was involved in stealing the days from February, but it was really Julius' idea. Plus, I figured if I dressed up as Augustus, whenever I used the wrong plural of those "um" words, we could call it even.

Obviously, the Augustus costume was pretty easy for Mom to make, except for the wreath of bay leaves for my head. But finally we were able to locate some at a specialty produce store. (Surprise—the ingredients label read 100% bay leaves.) When I went out trick-or-treating in my Augustus costume, however, most people thought I was supposed to be John Belushi from *Animal House*. I thought it might help if I spoke Latin, but it didn't. Besides, there was nothing in the English to Latin dictionary that easily translated into, "I'd prefer the Milk Duds". However, people did seem to understand me when I said, "Amo Reeseus Pieceus".

Anyway, to paraphrase Augustus' great uncle, Julius, on that particular Halloween—"Veni, Vidi, Vici, Vane"—"I came, I saw, I conquered … and I went with Vanessa".

Despite getting all that candy, as I guess I've made pretty clear, Halloween's not one of my favorite holidays. Actually, it's not even in the top ten. The only reason it's ahead of Labor Day is that at least Halloween has a "Peanuts" video. As you know, we're still waiting on the Labor Day video release.

In case you're interested, here's a list of my top ten holidays:

1. Christmas—for obvious reasons.

2. Thanksgiving—family, and I love turkey.

3. July 4th—the start of summer, and I go to my grandparents' house.

4. Patriot's Day—this holiday is only celebrated in Massachusetts, but it's the day of the Boston Marathon.

5. Groundhog Day—moved up on the list after I saw the movie.

6. New Year's Day—I like noisemakers.

7. Columbus Day—I love the jingle—"In fourteen hundred ninety-two Columbus sailed the ocean blue."

8. Arbor Day—pays homage to something I can't draw.

9. St Patrick's Day—I love saying, "Top o' the mornin' to ya".

10. Valentine's Day—I suspect this will move up on my list, as I get older. It used to be after Halloween; until I met Vanessa, that is.

Okay, it's not as clever as Letterman's top ten, but the primary goal of my list is information, not humor. (I sound pretty defensive, don't I? Sorry.)

Of course, about a month after Halloween comes Thanksgiving—number two on my hit parade. On this particular Thanksgiving we had two additional guests at our dinner table—Mr. and Mrs. Witkowski.

On most Thanksgivings the Witkowskis traveled to the home of one of their children or grandchildren, or sometimes their family would come to them, but this year, for whatever reason, things didn't work out. I suspect that since they were both approaching eighty, they didn't want to travel very far. I mean, they both seemed pretty energetic, but long distance air travel takes its toll on young people, never mind people in their seventies.

Anyway, when Mom found out the Witkowskis were going to be by themselves for Thanksgiving, she insisted they come to our house. There was a mild protest, but once they found out that Grandma and Grandpa were coming, and Mom suggested that Mrs. Witkowski make her famous chocolate chip cookies to go along with the more traditional desserts, it was a done deal.

That year, with our added guests, Thanksgiving resembled a mini-version of our annual August cookout, only moved indoors. (Hey, Augustus, do you think we could count our annual cookout as a holiday?) The whole scene was about as "Norman Rockwell" as you could get—family, friends, and football; turkey, stuffing, cranberry sauce, sweet potatoes, and pumpkin pie; and although chocolate chip cookies aren't traditionally associated with Thanksgiving, no one cared, and they were great. After we finished eating, there was one more tradition—the tryptophan-induced nap.

Note to pharmaceutical companies: Have you considered using tryptophan in your sleep-aid medications? I've seen first-hand how it affects my dad and grandpa. If you decide to go in that direction, I've come up with a few ideas you might be interested in.

If tryptophan were to be produced in tablet form, here are some suggested product names and slogans:

- "Turkey Snooze"—Take two giblets just before bed.

- "Poultry Pellets"—No, no it's not what you think. Swallow a pellet and into sleep you will sink.

- "Turkey in a Bottle"—The tablets could be shaped like turkeys.

  When I'm trying to get to sleep,

  But I'm feeling much too perky,

  I don't count little white sheep,

  I just swallow a tablet of turkey.

As you know, my dad works in advertising. When I showed him these ideas, he suggested that the advertising industry might not be ready for me just yet. I don't think it was a compliment.

One last thought before I leave the memories of that Thanksgiving from six years ago—As I looked all around me that day, I remember thinking how lucky I was to have such a great extended family. And you know what? The phrase "extended family" doesn't just apply to people you're related to. The Witkowskis are my extended family also.

As you might remember, at the beginning of this chapter I talked about the formation of our reading groups at school. Well, as the year progressed I noticed some interesting things about the reading program. As you might expect, the emphasis was on reading comprehension. But as I listened to some of my classmates trying to read, I began to realize that there is no such thing as **reading** comprehension.

I mean, there are students who have trouble understanding what they read, but that's not a problem with **decoding** the words. It's a problem with understanding what the words mean and how they relate to one another. That's not an issue with **reading** comprehension; it's an issue with comprehension period.

Let me give you an example of what I mean—If I were to give you a paragraph to read that was written in Latin, would you understand what it said? (Other than the "um" words of course) Probably not; so, does that mean you have a reading problem? No, it means you have a comprehension problem; you can decode the words fine, but you don't know what they mean or how they fit together.

This whole reading comprehension thing reminds me of something that happened a few years ago. My dad and I were talking to a neighbor one day, and he related to us that he had recently been in Boston and was traveling down Hemenway St.

My dad said, "Hemenway St.? I don't think I know where that is." Our neighbor raised his voice slightly, and said, "You know, Hemenway St."

My dad shook his head. "No, I'm not sure."

Our neighbor repeated himself two more times, raising his voice even more each time. "You know, Hemenway St., Hemenway St.!!!!"

My dad didn't lose his patience. He just said, "You know what? No matter how loudly you say it, I still don't know where it is."

So what's the point of the story? If children have comprehension problems, you can have them read a story to themselves; you can read it to them; you can use a bull horn; or you can try it in Chinese, but they're still not going to be able to locate Hemenway St.

So, what do you do? Well, you do exactly what our second grade teacher did. She often read to the Blue Jays reading group, but she paused after every few sentences and asked them what was happening in the story and how they knew that. She used various strategies to help them build their vocabularies. She talked about idioms, although she never used that word. She taught them Latin and Greek prefixes, suffixes, and root words. Sometimes she would also have members of the Blue Jays group read to each other, and have them pause after each paragraph to talk about what they had just read.

By the spring, three members of the Blue Jays "left their nest" and joined the Finches. It wasn't a biological mutation, but rather a talented educator helping her students "spread their wings", and then allowing birds of a feather to flock together.

While the reading curriculum took up the largest percentage of our academic time in second grade, the math curriculum was not far behind. But, unlike reading, we weren't placed in ability groups for math. I was a little disappointed though, because I had already come up with some names for our math groups— "The Euclids", "The Pythagoreans", "The Lois D. Nominators".

When I was thinking about potential names for our math groups, it occurred to me that in the case of Euclid, it was pretty cool to have a branch of geometry named after you. And how about Pythagoras? He had a theorem named after him. I still don't think those things are quite up there with having an element named after you—like Benjaminium, but it's close.

You know, on reflection, it was probably for the best that we didn't have math groups. I mean, I really started to get interested in some of the higher math I was reading about, but I was still in Guarded Mode about my ICBM. I could have blown everything by asking questions about parabolas and quadratic equations. Especially since our first math lesson dealt with "what time is it when the big hand is on the nine and the little hand is on the three?"

Although telling time was part of the second grade math curriculum, I really wonder how long that will continue. I mean, almost everything is digital now. Do we really need to know how to tell time the old-fashioned way? I know the Rolex people will have a fit, and it is breaking with tradition, but maybe its 'time' has come. (That last sentence is like a pun and a paradox "Rolexed" into one. Hey, no groaning!!!—How about one more? Is telling time with an analog timepiece an anachronism?)

This whole issue also reminds me of cursive writing. Won't that soon be eliminated from the curriculum too? It seems to me that in the future we'll either print everything or use a computer. No more practicing the Palmer method. (Who invented the Palmer method anyway? Bud? Betsey? Arnold? Some of you might not know the first two, but my grandpa told me about them.)

So, if analog time-telling and cursive writing go the way of the eight-track, I think that doctors will be the most affected. Their patients will probably be more aware of how long they've been kept waiting, and doctors will have to practice making their **printing** undecipherable.

Besides telling time, the math curriculum focused on addition, subtraction, word problems, and understanding about money. Probably when many of you learned subtraction, one of the steps was called "borrowing". It's not called that anymore; it's now called "trading". Who made that decision? It's like "guys" and Pluto all over again.

Could there be a conspiracy at work here? I mean, "borrowing" connotes debt, whereas "trading" connotes stocks and bonds and investing. I don't know if "Big Brother" is watching, but it sure seems like "Big Business" is involved somehow.

Anyway, it was quite interesting to me that right after we finished studying "trading", the next unit was about money. (Coincidence? I think not.) Speaking about the unit on money, why not teach the four standard math operations—addition, subtraction, multiplication, and division—using money? Tell me that's not an excellent motivational tool.

Even kids who have difficulty learning math, understand about money. It's almost instinctive. For example, if the Tooth Fairy leaves 50 cents under a little boy's pillow (a half dollar, not the rap star), the little boy immediately understands that the Tooth Fairy is cheap, and should have left at least double that amount to even approach the going rate for a tooth. (Bicuspids are commanding even more.)

What kid hasn't sold lemonade in front of his house? So, we already understand about profit and overhead—that's addition and subtraction; and if you franchise your lemonade stand—that's multiplication; and if business is slow and you have to downsize—that's division. I really think this would work. (Note to Houghton-Mifflin: How about—"Learning Second Grade Math Through Mergers and Acquisitions"?)

Money might also be a good way to teach word problem strategy. Although if we insist on using the same old subject matter for word problems, I doubt that we'll be able to make very much headway. Talk about anachronisms. I mean, whether you're just about to take the SAT's for the first time, or you're already collecting Social Security, I know you've heard some variation of this word problem: A train leaves Boston at 4:00 traveling west. It arrives in Worcester an hour later, but the smoke takes thirty minutes to drift back to Boston, because the wind is blowing east at 30 miles per hour. How long ...?

(Don't you want to scream—we use diesel trains now. **There is no smoke!**)

In talking about the heterogeneously grouped class and the math curriculum earlier in the chapter, I hope I didn't give you the impression that I didn't like second grade, because I really did. In fact, at our last group guidance session with Dr. Foster in June, that was the topic of conversation.

"So, Vanessa, Derek, and Benny, how are you doing?"

"Fine."

"Good."

"Good."

"Derek, how's your baby sister—Samantha, right?"

"She's fine. She just started walking, and she says 'duh'. My mom thinks it's for Dada, but I think it's for Derek."

Dr. Foster laughed. "And how are your parents?"

"They're great too."

"How about you, Vanessa? How are your mom and dad?"

"Everybody's terrific. Sometimes my mom takes care of Samantha, and I help her."

"That's great. And what about you, Benny?"

"Mom and Dad are fine, and so are my grandma and grandpa. I'm going to see them in about three weeks."

"That's right. And then they bring you back in August for the cookout."

"Yup."

"How are Mr. and Mrs. Witkowski?"

"They're okay too."

"It's funny, I was over at Little Guys Pre-school last week. Those bird feeders are still there; the kids love them. Could you mention that to Mr. Witkowski the next time you see him?"

I nodded. "Yeah. I'm sure he'll like that."

"So, guys, (The use of "guys" doesn't even faze me anymore.) I know we talked about this last time, but tell me about how second grade is finishing up, and what you're looking forward to for next year."

Derek spoke up first. "I really liked all the computer time we got at the end of this year. And next year, don't we get to go to the computer lab a lot, instead of just using the computers in our classroom?"

"Yes, Derek, I believe that's right."

Vanessa was next. "I liked the computers too, but I really liked having more art and music and gym."

My turn. "I think it was a good year. I liked the fact that our teacher let us read different books than just the ones that were in the classroom."

"Well, let me tell you guys, from what I can see on your report cards, and in talking with your teachers, you all had a **great** year."

We all smiled. "Am I right that you would like to be together in the same class again next year?"

We all responded at the same time with an enthusiastic "Yes!"

"Okay, I'll take care of it."

We talked for about ten more minutes and then Dr. Foster gave Vanessa and Derek passes to go back to class. He asked me to stay behind for a moment. "I wanted to talk with you privately, Benny, just to make sure everything's okay."

"Everything's fine." I paused. "Is there something I don't know about?"

"No, no, not at all. It's just that in speaking with your teachers, they tell me you're right at the top of the class in everything, but you don't necessarily speak up in class as much as you could."

"That's probably a fair assessment."

Dr. Foster smiled as I continued. "Dr. Foster, you know that I really don't like the spotlight. I mean, I'm already a year ahead. I just want to fit in with everyone. If I say some of the things that I'm thinking, the other kids and my teachers are gonna think I'm strange. I know you put the three of us in the same class, mainly for my benefit. Vanessa and Derek are good friends and they like me no matter what, but some of the other kids might not."

Dr. Foster continued to smile throughout my "speech". When I finished he said, "Remember a few years ago when I thought you were ready to take over my job? Well, if I had any doubts whether you could do it or not, I don't anymore."

As usual, I deflected the compliment. "Well, if I do take over, I'm redecorating the office. I know they're supposed to be soothing, but … way too many earth tones."

CHAPTER 11

▼

A couple of weeks before the start of third grade, my parents got a letter from the school indicating that the teacher I was scheduled to have was taking a position in another town. My new teacher would be Mrs. Jarvis. Yes, that Mrs. Jarvis!

Okay, those of you in the education field, so what the heck do we call this arrangement? I mean, if teaching the same kids in back-to-back years is called "looping", what do you call it when you skip a year, and then teach most of those same kids the following year?—"Out of the loop"; "I'm just plain loopy"; "Loop, loop, skipping a loop, skipping a loop my darling"?

Actually, this might make a good math word problem (and there wouldn't be any trains involved).—Write an equation that represents the following situation: A teacher teaches the same class in back-to-back years, skips a year, and then teaches those same students again the next year. The answer would be "Jarvis + Jarvis - 1 = 3rd grade". Anyway, whatever you decide to call it, please keep me informed. (I was going to say, "keep me in the **loop**", but that would be pretty hypocritical, don't you think?)

When Mom told me that Mrs. Jarvis was going to be my teacher again, I was actually very happy about it. I liked Mrs. Jarvis, and she'd known me for a few years. So I viewed this as a positive development.

I overheard Mom and Dad talking about it, and they seemed to think it was a good thing as well. "You know, Lillian, I like the idea that Benny's going to have Mrs. Jarvis again."

"Yeah, I agree. I think she's a very good teacher."

"Well, it's not just that. I think they may have assigned her to the third grade because of MCAS."

"Does MCAS start in the third grade now?"

"Yeah, it's part of 'No Child Left Behind'."

"You know what? You're probably right; I'll bet that's why Mrs. Jarvis is going to be teaching the third grade."

After all those references to MCAS and "No Child Left Behind", I'm going to assume that some of you have no idea what my parents were talking about. And maybe, if you were speaking with me directly, you might even want to use Ricky Ricardo's famous line—"Benny, you got some 'splaining to do." Okay, fair enough, here goes.

MCAS stands for Massachusetts Comprehensive Assessment System. It was a major component of educational reform in our state during the early and mid 1990's. The state created curriculum frameworks and standards at all grade levels and in all academic disciplines. The goal was to have all the school districts in the state align their instruction with the standards, and then through the state-generated tests measure how well students were achieving.

Public schools are required to administer tests to all students in grades 3–8 in both math and language arts. (We don't call it "English" anymore, by the way; just like we don't have "libraries" anymore; we have "media centers".) I'm really not being judgmental here; I'm just trying to keep you updated. In case you're curious, my official source for all this name change information is *Educational Jargon Monthly*. I've had two letters to the editor published in that journal—both about "looping", but as yet nobody's given me any feedback on what to call Mrs. Jarvis' current situation.

As I was saying, before I interrupted myself, students are tested in math and language arts in grades 3–8. Most recently, tests in other subjects have been added at various grade levels as well—for example, science and technology in grade eight, American history in grades nine and ten, etc. Individual states can decide for themselves if they want to do this. But, all fifty states are required to test in grades 3–8 under the federal statute known as "No Child Left Behind".

You know what? I don't think anybody can really argue with the notion of raising standards, but this whole thing seems like overkill to me. In some states eighth graders take 25–30 hours of mandated state exams during the last month of school. If students are sitting for that long taking tests, the name of the law should be changed to "No Child Left **With** A Behind". (*Educational Jargon Monthly* has not weighed-in on the name switch.)

Don't you think that all this testing has to substantially reduce instructional time? Instead of focusing on learning, we seem to be focusing on test taking. There's a common sense quote that kind of sums up what I'm getting at—"You don't fatten a sow by weighing it." I'm not sure who said that, but wouldn't you suspect it was a farmer?

I wonder if it was a farmer from Iowa? I mean, up until a few years ago, all students used to take the "Iowa" tests. But, we didn't take them every single year; we took them every other year at the most. It seems to me that those tests gave us all the information we needed. I think it's pretty evident that those Iowa people know what they're doing. I just thought of something else. Isn't Iowa the place where presidential campaigns begin? Isn't that where the first caucuses are held? How about this idea? Why not make all the presidential candidates take the "Iowa" tests, and if they don't get a "passing" score, they can't run?

I know that sounds quite punitive. But actually, it's pretty similar to what almost every state in the country is doing concerning high school graduation. In most states there are now a series of exams you **must** pass in order to graduate. (Pretty high stakes, wouldn't you say?) Okay, I understand the rationale for this, but I still think the idea is flawed. There are many learning disabled kids who can compensate for their disability and pass all their subjects, but who might have real difficulty passing some of these high-stakes exams.

The proponents of this "no pass—no graduate" policy would tell you that the exams represent the **minimum** that students should know when they leave high school, and that learning disabled kids can, in some instances, take an alternative assessment. But kids that are learning disabled may already be "stigmatized" by pull-out programs and the like. Don't alternative assessments perpetuate the notion that they're not like everyone else?

So here's my idea. (You knew I'd have one, didn't you?) Have everyone take these high-stakes tests and record the scores on each student's permanent record, but don't deny them a diploma because they "failed" any of the exams. As long as they've passed their courses and met all other requirements, they should graduate. College admissions counselors and potential employers can get access to students' permanent records. Let them make the judgment whether to accept these students into their colleges or their companies.

It's conceivable that a very talented high school artist, or singer, or computer phenom might not know that the plural of "symposium" is "symposia", but does that mean he shouldn't be allowed to graduate? (Okay, probably an oversimplification) The point is, however, that there are going to be some students with a number of admirable talents and attributes, who will not be able to pass a high-stakes exam.

I wonder how the "powers that be" at the Department of Education would feel if we created a law that would require all of them to break a hundred on a regulation golf course; and failure to do so would result in them losing their jobs. And to make it even more similar to the MCAS exams, it wouldn't matter if they had arthritis, gout, scurvy, a torn rotator cuff, or just a bad day; they would still have to shoot a 99 or better.

I can hear the protestations now. "The MCAS is a mental exercise and this golf thing is physical. Plus, what does playing golf have to do with my job at the Department of Education?" My answer to that is—probably nothing. But if you practice something for hours and hours, regardless of whether it's physical or mental, and you still can't do it, but you have other traits that more than compensate for this one deficiency, I don't think you should be so severely penalized—as in no diploma or no job.

In the interest of compromise however, how about this idea? You people at the Department of Education can keep your positions by "passing" an alternative assessment. Just go to the local miniature golf course and get a three or better on the "windmill hole". (Look at it this way; at least you're trying to avoid windmills, instead of **"tilting"** at them like I'm doing—If you didn't get the literary reference, add one stroke to your score.)

That last sentence got me thinking—maybe I could be Don Quixote next Halloween; and Vanessa and Derek could be Dulcinea and Sancho Panza. Where's the phone number for "Disguises 'R' Us"? (Of course, even if they both agreed, we'd still have to decide on a "Quest". My preference would be either MCAS reform or finding Milk Duds that contain real chocolate—both noble pursuits, I might add.)

As I mentioned before, some states are actually expanding the number of tests required for graduation. In many places students will soon have to pass a science exam. I think we really need to be careful here. Science changes so rapidly that two weeks after a test is created, it could be invalid. For example—What's the right answer to these true-false questions?

A. Pluto is a planet.

B. Uranus is pronounced "your" "anus".

C. Milk Duds contain chocolate.

See what I mean?

You know what else is under consideration in some states? An art exam. If it's not about art history, which they claim it isn't, how the heck do you create an art exam? What's it going to measure? If any of the questions involve drawing a tree, then my high school transcript is in the toilet. (How did I go from Princeton at sixteen to "would you like fries with your Big Mac" so quickly?)

If, on the other hand, the exam asks questions about current art movements and trends, I might be all right. I mean one of my closest friends, Vanessa, is a strict "featherism" devotee. And although I'm still not sure what you call Derek's method of coloring, with the number of crayons he goes through, he's the honorary poster boy for Crayola. That ought to count for something.

I suppose, if worse came to worse, I could always develop a portfolio as an alternative assessment. I could create a mixture of crayons to illustrate the three colors I invented—"temper-tantrum blue", "total embarrassment red", and "all-the-blood-drained-from-my-face white". And as the final part of the portfolio, I could write a research paper on that picture that was in Vanessa's coloring book—"Androgynous Person". I mean, **volumes** have been written about Mona Lisa's enigmatic expression, so what's wrong with a paper entitled "Gender Bending and Identity Issues in the Coloring Book Genre—The Case for Androgynous Person"?

Don't you think that seems like a really good backup plan? I'm feeling much better about this whole art exam thing. Where did I put that Princeton brochure anyway?

As I told you earlier in this chapter, Massachusetts has created curriculum frameworks and standards in all the academic disciplines at each grade level. So, during third grade we were introduced to the study of various sciences. We learned some things about geology, mainly rocks and minerals, although we also saw a "fascinating" video entitled "The Life of Sand". (Forget that "tryptophan idea" I had. If the pharmaceutical companies can figure out a way to "bottle" this video, they'd make a ton of money, and no one would ever have insomnia again.)

We also studied some astronomy and found out that there were nine planets. (But as you're aware—"Pluto, we hardly knew ye".) Mrs. Jarvis taught us that the earth revolved around the sun, and the moon revolved around the earth. (I hope **that** hasn't changed. If it has, I sure didn't get the memo.) She also told us that some people used to think that the earth was at the center of the universe, but that was proven false. (There are certain Hollywood personalities that seem to know that fact instinctively, without having learned it in school—"How could the earth be the center of the universe, when I am?")

Another one of the science topics we studied was biology, more specifically, animals. One of the units was about snakes. As you know, they're not among my top ten favorite creatures. In fact, on my favorite animals list they're actually 624th, sandwiched between "rabid mountain lions" and the velociraptors from

Jurassic Park (and they've been extinct for a few hundred million years). Despite this, for my required project about animals, I decided to do a report on snakes that inhabit Eastern Massachusetts. (Know thy enemy)

My report was pretty extensive, and I thought it was well done; but Mrs. Jarvis found a few inconsistencies. It seems that I had included boa constrictors and pythons in my report, but she pointed out that snakes that live at Pet-Pals didn't count as inhabiting Eastern Massachusetts.

I mean, I understand the logic behind Mrs. Jarvis' criticism of my report, but from a public safety standpoint, shouldn't we know where all these snakes are located? So I was thinking—you know how some criminals have to wear ankle bracelets? Couldn't we put body bracelets on all the snakes in the area? It seems to me that if we have this technology and don't use it, shame on us!

As I've already told you, I'm concerned about science "facts" changing all the time—Pluto, Milk Duds, etc. Well, I just remembered another example from third grade. Mrs. Jarvis told us that there were only three kinds of animals that could recognize themselves in a mirror—humans, chimpanzees, and dolphins. All the other species think that their reflections are other animals, so they often make noises to try to scare them off, or they prepare to fight them.

But recently, scientists have discovered that elephants can recognize themselves in a mirror also. It's interesting to me that humans, chimps, and dolphins all have a fairly sophisticated communication system, but elephants don't. On the other hand, scientists tell us that there **is** something that links these four species to each other. Since they can all recognize themselves in a mirror, the members of these four species are considered to be "self-aware", which means they're capable of caring about other animals and creating complex social structures like families and communities.

Anyway, besides being interesting, I thought that there might be a real practical application for this new scientific discovery. I was thinking that this information could be incorporated into the new MCAS science exam. I mean, it's so recent that there's no chance it could be proven inaccurate before the exam is completed. Plus, it's certainly "on the cutting edge" of scientific inquiry. So I came up with this essay question:

Scientists recently conducted an experiment involving three adult female elephants. Each of them had an "X" made of adhesive tape secured to one side of their heads, and a clear, invisible "X" secured to the other side of their heads. The invisible "X" was of the same consistency and texture as the adhesive tape "X". The elephants were then placed in an enclosed pen with a huge mirror that allowed them to see their full reflections. After looking at themselves in the mirror and walking away, all of the elephants *attempted to remove the **visible** "X" with their trunks, but never touched the invisible "X". Scientists concluded that the elephants recognized the reflection in the mirror as their own image.*

Write an essay explaining which of the following statements most likely represents what the female elephants were thinking when they first looked at their reflection.

1. "Holy crap! Does anyone have the number for Jenny Craig?"

2. "What's with the "X"?—Martha, did you put that there? I thought we agreed no more practical jokes after the 'kick me sign' incident."

3. "Are you talkin' to me? Are you talkin' to me?

4. "Oh my heavens, I've never seen so many wrinkles. Does anyone know if Botox injections are covered by our health plan?"

5. "Well, other than the stretch marks from delivering junior, I think I look pretty good. Hmph, those human mothers complain about nine months, try carrying a 300 pound baby elephant around for **two years**."

6. "I wonder if changing my hair style will make my ears look smaller. Boy, they're huge. Maybe that 'Dumbo' story is true."

7. "Will you look at the size of me? How is that possible? I thought peanuts didn't have trans fat."

8. "I've got to do something to make my trunk look smaller; it just dominates my face. Maybe a little pancake make-up …"

9. "Just my luck; elephants never forget. I'm going to be stuck with this image in my head for the rest of my life"

10. "I have **round feet**! Who the heck has round feet? How am I ever going to find shoes?"

Anyway, back to third grade. Besides the expansion of the academic curricula, we also got a chance to do more in the "special" areas as well. There was more time for art, music, media center, physical education, and computer.

I liked all of my "non-academic" subjects, although as you might imagine, art was a bit of a challenge. Vanessa was good at everything in school, but she particularly liked gym. She was probably the best athlete in the third grade—male or female. (If you score that many goals in peewee soccer, you've gotta be good.) Derek was pretty good at everything as well, but he really excelled at computers. Derek took to computers like an elephant takes to a mirror. (Periodically, I figure I'll try out some new clichés. Let me know what you think.)

Derek became so knowledgeable, that he almost knew as much about computers as the lab supervisor. In fact, Derek was so excited about his new computer skills that he suggested we create a website for TUCK, and post the minutes of our meetings on-line. This was now role reversal. **I** had to remind **him** that TUCK continued to be a secret club, and having a website was not conducive to maintaining our anonymity.

What I actually said, however, was that we should be more like chameleons and blend into our surroundings, rather than peacocks that everyone noticed. As I mentioned before, I really am attempting to upgrade my cliché and simile usage. Here are some more:

1. Instead of "Every dog has his day", how about "Every emperor has his day"? (Especially if he steals it from February)

2. Instead of "You can't judge a book by its cover", how about "You can't judge a politician by his cover-up"?

3. "Talk is cheap"—I'm not going to change this one; let's just add some clarification—"unless you go over your allotted minutes".

In the springtime, a young man's fancy, or at least the fancies of seven-and-eight year-old boys, turn to baseball. Dad signed me up for Little League, but in our community if you hadn't yet turned eight, you had to play T-Ball.

T-Ball is much closer to baseball than peewee soccer is to regular soccer. Other than the players hitting the ball off a tee, rather than having it pitched to them; and making sure that everyone puts the ball in play, and not permitting strike-outs or walks, or bunting; and ... Okay, T-Ball is nothing like baseball. I mean Abner Doubleday might be able to see the connection, but supposedly, he invented baseball, so you'd kind of expect that.

By the way, where do you think the name "Doubleday" comes from? I mean, the derivation of some names is obvious—"Smith" and "Cooper" come from occupations. And certainly, Native American names like "Flowing Brook" or

"Desert Flower" make sense. But where the heck did "Doubleday" come from? Here are some possibilities:

- The original "Doubleday" was the first person to experience déjà vu; it occurred on February 2nd—Groundhog Day.

- He was a storeowner who confused a half-off sale with a "charge twice as much sale".

- He was related to Julius Caesar, and assisted in the "stealing two days from February" scandal.

- He was the first doctor to alter standard medical advice—He suggested to his patients that they take a couple of aspirins and call him **two** days from now.

I don't know if any of those are real, but regardless, don't you think "Doubleday" is a strange name? Although something just occurred to me—if by any chance this book is **published** by Doubleday, then as Gilda Radner's character, Emily Litella, used to say, "Never mind".

Okay, back to T-Ball. Unlike peewee soccer we didn't get to vote for the name of our team. In T-Ball, local merchants sponsor all the teams; and the name of the business becomes your team's name. My team was sponsored by a window treatment store called Empire Blinds. As you might imagine, we didn't get the benefit of too many close calls. When our fans yelled out "Empire Blinds", it sounded way too much like "umpire blind".

As a matter of fact, we managed to win only one game all season. It was against a team sponsored by a company that cleaned out and drained cesspools. Their workers all wore blue uniforms (just like umpires do), and the company was called—Men in Blue. On more than one occasion, people in the stands equated the action performed by the cesspool vacuums with the job being done by the umpires. Men in Blue didn't win a game.

The toughest part about T-Ball for most seven-year-olds is being in the field—not the positioning like in peewee soccer, but rather the actual "fielding" itself. Most seven-year-olds don't have the dexterity or hand-eye coordination to place their baseball mitt in even close proximity to the ball. Most T-Ballers struggle to catch a ground ball, or a fly ball, or a line drive, or a pop-up, or a bunt—pretty much anything where the ball is actually in motion.

My team was no different. Well actually, if I'm being objective, we were very different; we were much worse. My grandpa once told me about a comparison made by a sports announcer on TV. He was discussing the particularly poor defensive performance of a professional team. I think his comparison kind of sums up the fielding ineptitude of our team as well. "What do Michael Jackson and the Empire Blind team have in common? They both wear gloves on one hand for no apparent reason."

I suspect a large part of our fielding woes had to do with the fact that, like most kids our age, we were afraid of the ball. I mean, we weren't afraid of it when it was sitting on the tee ready to be hit. But put that sphere in motion and send it toward us, and it was like a cobra ready to pounce. (I know I was going to suggest some **new** similes, but not so much when they refer to snakes—those still work for me.)

One of our coaches spent a lot of time trying to help us out with our fielding. He was more cerebral in his approach, however, and although he meant well, his words of encouragement really didn't improve the situation.

Little kids may hear the phrase "Don't be afraid of the ball", and process it intellectually; but it doesn't change how they feel emotionally. Again, I know the coach meant well, but sometimes I couldn't even accept what he said on an intellectual basis—"There's nothing to be afraid of". Sure there is. "The ball won't hurt you". Yeah, it will.

I didn't think that the Little League field was a totally appropriate forum to discuss my philosophical concerns, so I made an appointment to see Dr. Foster.

"Hi, Benny, come on in. Is everything all right? When I saw the note that you wanted to see me, I got a little concerned."

"No, everything's fine. I probably could have waited until our group guidance session next week, but since I had recess now, I figured I'd see if you were available."

"So, what did you want to see me about?"

"Well, it seems kind of silly now."

"I doubt that. Why don't you just tell me?"

"Well, I'm playing T-Ball this year, and one of the coaches who was helping us with our fielding said, 'You shouldn't be afraid of the ball.' I know he was just trying to encourage us, but when I was thinking about what he said … well he made it sound like we had a choice. I mean, it's like when someone says to you, 'Don't be embarrassed' or 'You shouldn't feel that way'. You don't really have a choice, do you? I mean I can't **decide** not to be embarrassed; and I can't **choose** to feel a certain way, right?"

Dr. Foster smiled. "I think you're right, Benny; we can't choose those things. But I think people who care about us, or are trying to help us, say the words they think will make us feel better."

"Yeah, I get that, and I know we all do it. I guess I just wanted to make sure that I wasn't missing something. I mean, if it were possible to choose not to feel a certain way, I wanted somebody to show me how to do that."

Dr. Foster was now chuckling. "If somebody figures out how to do that, they're going to be very rich."

I started to smile. "I was also thinking that it goes beyond those things, like being afraid of the ball, or being embarrassed. I mean, for example, you can't choose to like certain foods; you either do or you don't. And you can't decide to like a team that you don't really like. I can't wake up tomorrow and **choose** to like the Yankees, can I?"

"No, Benny, you can't. Of course if you did, I think your grandpa would be thrilled. On the other hand, you might have to move out of your parents' house." Now it was my turn to laugh as Dr. Foster continued. "And, as far as food is concerned, I don't believe we can choose what tastes good to us. It may be possible to 'acquire' a taste for certain things, however."

"You mean like wine or … sushi?"

"Yes."

I hesitated. "I guess I can understand wine, maybe. But why, if you don't care for sushi, would you make the effort to try to like it?"

Dr. Foster was still smiling broadly. "Benny, there is absolutely nothing in all of my professional experience that I can call upon to answer most of the questions you ask me. And you know what? I love that." He leaned forward in his chair and lowered his voice. "Between you and me, I don't think sushi's worth the effort."

"Me neither; or snakes—I don't mean to eat, I mean just to even be around." I was quiet for a moment, and then I asked, "If what we've been talking about is true for food and snakes, isn't it true for more important things?"

"Like what?"

"Well, if you can't choose to like **things**, I don't imagine you can choose to like people either, or … love them, for that matter. I mean, I love my mom and dad, and my grandma and grandpa, but I didn't **choose** to love them; I just do. And what about when you get older and start dating? Does it work the same way?"

"I can't say that I'm an expert, but yeah, I do think it works in a similar way. The difference is that once you're older and have a romantic interest in someone, you eventually may 'fall in love'. But with your family, you're kind of already there. There's not much you have to do, or they have to do. It's much more unconditional."

"That's sort of what I was thinking,"

"So, with all this relationship conversation, does that mean that you're giving up the idea of taking over for me, and now you're setting your sights on Oprah and Dr. Phil?"

I smiled. "It depends. Do you know if their walls are covered in earth tones?"

Dr. Foster laughed out loud. "Are you telling me that my job might be safe?"

"It's possible. And with all the work I'm going to have to do, I just might look into decorating as a possible career."

Dr. Foster put his hands up in front of himself as if he were framing a picture "I can see it now—'Interiors by Benny Curtis'."

Once I stopped laughing, Dr. Foster changed the subject. "Hey, don't you have a birthday coming up soon?"

"Yup, next week. I'm going to be eight."

"That's right. You're a year ahead; I forgot that for a minute. So next week … when we start MCAS testing?"

"Nice birthday present, huh?"

"You're not worried about it, are you?"

"No, not at all. Actually, I think it's a good thing for me."

"Really? Why's that?"

"Well, you know how I kind of hold back during class activities? I don't have to with MCAS."

"It's funny, I wanted to talk with you some more about that. I was a little concerned about you 'holding back'. I think sometimes when we create a pattern of behavior for ourselves, it's difficult to change it."

"There's really nothing to worry about. When I know something's important, then I don't hold back."

"Okay, that's good." He looked at his watch. "Well, as much as I'm enjoying our conversation, I think recess is over, and you need to get back to class."

As Dr. Foster started writing out a pass for me, he said, "So, what did you ask your parents to get you for your birthday?"

"My own computer. I know they're pretty expensive, but it's hard for me to use the one we have, because Dad needs it when he does work at home."

"So, if you do get your own computer, what kinds of things will you use it for?"

I paused, considering the question. "A lot of the usual stuff, but there's one new program I think I'd like to try."

"What's that?"

"C-A-I-D."

"I've heard of CAD—Computer Assisted Design, but not C-A-I-D. What does that stand for?"

"Computer Assisted Interior Decorating."

Dr. Foster shook his head and began to laugh. He handed over the pass he had written for me. "Get outta here."

Chapter 12

▼

As you know, I'm not much of a joiner. But on my eighth birthday, when Mom and Dad bought me a computer, I officially became a member of the "Information Age". I don't mean to imply that there was any kind of formal ceremony involved. Actually, I didn't even get a membership card to prove that I belonged. In fact, this "Information Age" group seemed to be just about as informal as TUCK. (Although TUCK actually does have membership cards—they entitle us to 15% discounts at Hertz and Domino's Pizza.)

Anyway, Dad set up the computer and printer in my room, and I was ready to roll. Nearly everything I used the computer for was related to school, although periodically I would research various topics for my own purposes. (I mean, I felt like I was entitled. After all, I was a card-carrying member of the "Information Age"; or at least I would have been, if they had actually had cards.)

It probably would come as no surprise to you that if you had clicked on the "My Favorites" icon on my computer that addresses dealing with the following topics would show up: snakes, Julius Caesar, word derivations, and acquiring a taste for sushi.

About a week after my birthday, Dad came into my room and said he wanted to talk to me.

"So, are you enjoying your computer?"

"Yeah, Dad, it's great."

"What kinds of things are you doing with it?"

"Mainly stuff for school. But there are also some cool games and things."

"That's good." He paused. "I probably should have spoken to you about this when we first set up the computer, but I didn't think it was necessary ... actually, I still don't. But, I'll feel more comfortable if I just say it."

"What, Dad?"

"Well, you know, Benny, you have full Internet access, and your mom and I didn't feel like we had to install any filters or block anything. I think you know that we trust you, but I still wanted to let you know that you should use good judgment about the sites you visit and what you do with the computer."

"That's not a problem, Dad. I don't visit chat rooms, and I don't go to any sites that I would be embarrassed to show you."

"That's kind of what I expected to hear." With that, he gave me a kiss on the top of my head and left the room.

While I was really excited about getting my own computer, Derek was positively euphoric. He was like a religious missionary. But instead of spreading "**The Word**", he was spreading "**Microsoft** Word", and I was one of the first "pagans" to be enlightened. He showed me how to do spreadsheets, and how to create Power Point presentations. He set up an e-mail account for me, and he would have created the Benny Curtis website, if I had let him. It was really hard to get him to curb his "religious" fervor. But finally, after I agreed to conduct some of our TUCK meetings electronically, he calmed down.

There was one thing about having an e-mail account that I hadn't anticipated. Since there were no filters on my computer, I received a lot of unsolicited advertisements. (I was glad to see that none of them came from any of my Dad's clients.) And given the nature of these unsolicited ads, I suspected that eight-year-olds were not really the targeted audience for these companies.

At least once every day, and sometimes more frequently, I received the exact same advertisements about the exact same products and services—refinancing your mortgage, the benefits of Viagra, and having your "organ" enhanced. (And no, it wasn't about adding pipes to your Wurlitzer.)

I made sure to tell Dad about the last two ads. I mean, even though I didn't seek out any of that information, I had decided to alert him whenever anything inappropriate showed up on my computer. However, I didn't bother to tell Dad about the refinancing advertisements, and I most certainly didn't tell **Mom**. I just deleted those ads as quickly as possible. I hadn't seen any evidence that Mom was playing in any of those high-stakes poker games, but why put temptation in the way?

As usual, over Fourth of July weekend (my third favorite holiday, by the way), Mom and Dad drove me to Grandma and Grandpa's for my annual summer stay. As always, I had a terrific time. The second week I was there, Grandpa suggested that we watch a golf tournament on TV.

"Grandpa, how come you want to watch the golf; you don't even play, do you?"

"No, I don't. But if Tiger Woods is in the tournament, I watch."

"How come?"

"Well, I suppose it's because he's probably going to turn out to be the best golfer that's ever played the game. Watching him is like watching something you'll probably never see again. Plus, I like that he's got such a sense of the history of golf and of all the great players that came before him. And you know how I feel about the history of things. I guess I never thought I'd say this, but Tiger's probably even more special than Mickey Mantle." He then paused and smiled. "Don't you dare tell your father I said that."

Prior to that time, I had never really paid much attention to golf. (Hey, when you're involved in elite sports like peewee soccer and T-ball, why look elsewhere?) But watching Tiger Woods that weekend made me a huge fan. Now, anytime he's in a tournament on TV, I try to tune in also. My grandpa was right—Tiger is special. In fact Mom and Dad have become fans as well, and they don't even play golf either.

As you might have guessed, once I got interested in Tiger, I started to do some research about him on the computer. It also got me thinking about his name. As you've no doubt noticed, word derivations and name derivations kind of fascinate me.

For those of you who don't know much about golf, the clubs that the players use are primarily divided into two categories—"irons" and "woods". So, isn't it funny that Tiger's last name is identical to the name of the equipment he actually uses in his occupation?

After doing some additional research, I discovered that there were some specialized clubs that golfers used in the past, but that aren't manufactured any more. These clubs had wooden shafts and were called "spoons" and "niblicks". It occurred to me that since Tiger's real first name is Eldrick, if he had been born a few decades earlier, his name could easily have been Eldrick Niblick. (And I thought the name "Abner Doubleday" was strange.) I know I've already told you that I subscribe to Shakespeare's philosophy of "What's in a name?", but I gotta say, it's hard to imagine anybody named Eldrick Niblick putting on a green jacket at Augusta.

Okay, I need you to indulge me for just a little bit longer. Don't you think it's interesting that Tiger's last name is **also** the place where he almost never finds himself on a golf course—**woods**? I mean, if we use that as the criteria, he could just as easily be known as Tiger Water Hazard, or Tiger Unplayable Lie, or Tiger Out of Bounds, or even Tiger Buried in a Sand Trap. (Feel free to substitute "Eldrick", if you think the name flows better.)

You know how I mentioned that I was going to try to come up with some new clichés and similes? Well, the one about "time flies when you're having fun" is off-limits. Every summer, the month or so that I spend with Grandma and Grandpa, goes by in a blink. (That off-limits thing didn't last all that long, did it?) Anyway, you get the idea—before I knew it, it was the first week in August, and we were headed back to Massachusetts for the annual cookout.

Everybody was able to attend this year, including Derek's little sister, Samantha, who just turned two. Samantha stuck to Derek like orange on an orange. I was going to say, "like white on rice", but don't you think the orange simile works better? I mean, the name of the fruit is the same as its color; that's pretty unique. You don't hear people say, "I'm going out to the vineyard to pick a bunch of 'purples'. I think it's also interesting that nothing rhymes with "orange". Of course, come to think of it, nothing rhymes with "purple" either. Do you think it's a "color thing"? Maybe I'll ask Derek to find out; as you know, he's pretty tight with Crayola. (I just realized that I'm able to see the outskirts of "No-Connection-Whatsoever-ville". I think we better head back.)

So, as I was saying, Samantha didn't leave Derek's side at the cookout. As far as she was concerned—forget what Copernicus and those Hollywood types might have thought—Derek was the center of the universe. I have to say; Derek was very patient with her. And Vanessa and I tried to help out also; we included her in whatever we were doing, as much as possible.

Finally however, Samantha went in for a nap, and Derek announced that he had a surprise for everyone. (Vanessa and I were the only two people who knew what was coming.) Derek had created an e-mail account for everyone at the cookout who didn't have one. That included my grandma and grandpa, the Witkowskis, and Vanessa's parents.

When Derek first told me about his idea, I thought it was great, but I wasn't sure my grandparents, never mind the Witkowskis, would like it. Boy, was I wrong! And there was no way for me to know at the time how important all of this would be in a few years.

As I mentioned before, the Witkowskis and my grandparents had become very good friends. Now, with their new e-mail accounts, they could communicate even more frequently. And when Derek showed my grandpa how to attach documents to e-mail—well, Grandpa looked at Derek the same way Samantha looked at Derek.

I've been considering putting my e-mail address in this book; it only seems fair. I mean, I keep asking you for feedback on certain issues, or I request that you keep me posted on things, but I haven't provided you with an easy way to do that. Certainly e-mail would do the trick.

Unfortunately, I'm still being inundated with e-mail—at least ten messages each day from Vanessa and Derek, not to mention the Witkowskis, and Grandma and Grandpa. Grandpa's attachments alone use up most of my computer's memory. Given all that, I don't know when I could possibly get to yours.

I asked Derek what he thought I should do about all the messages I was receiving. He suggested (for the second time) that I allow him to create an interactive website. I was about to give him the go-ahead, but then I was watching a golf tournament on TV, and I saw a player with the same name as mine—Ben Curtis. (He's pretty good, by the way.)

So, I told Derek to wait until we found out if there was already a "Ben Curtis website". I mean, I don't want to confuse people. Imagine fans going to a website looking for golf tips, and ending up having to read my report on "Snakes of Eastern Massachusetts". Of course if those fans are not very good at golf, they probably spend a lot of time in the woods with the snakes anyway. So, maybe that report could actually provide a public service. At the very least, my report could be linked to the other Ben Curtis' website—if he has one, that is. You know, all this could be resolved if we just required those full body snake bracelets I mentioned before.

I have to admit that there was another thing that made me hesitate about having an interactive website—the Spam issue. Wouldn't an interactive website open the floodgates?

For those of you who don't know—Spam is "unsolicited bulk electronic messages". (Shouldn't that be "Ubem" instead of Spam?) Anyway, the comedy troupe "Monty Python" (I like them a lot, by the way, despite the snake reference) is generally credited with originating the use of the term "spam" to define "unwanted things in large quantities". It came from a skit they did in the 1970's, and then someone applied it to Internet messages.

The original SPAM is a meat product made by Hormel. And what you might not realize is that SPAM has become a huge part of pop culture. There's a SPAM website, a musical—*Spamalot*, and even a **museum** in Minnesota. After I found out about all of this, I figured I needed to do a little more research.

I had eaten SPAM a few times, but not recently, and since we didn't have any cans of it in the house, the next time Mom and I went to the supermarket, I decided to check out the ingredients and nutrition label. After all, with my new rule about not consuming anything that had any ingredient spelled with more than nineteen letters, I figured, whether I liked the taste of SPAM or not, there was a good chance that I was never going to be able to eat it again.

Guess what? The first ingredient listed was "chopped pork shoulder"—**exactly** nineteen letters. What are the odds? (I heard a rumor that Hormel was considering listing the first ingredient as "**granulated** pork shoulder", but when they found out about my new rule, they changed it to "chopped".)

In case you're interested, the other ingredients in SPAM are salt, water, ham meat, sodium nitrate, and sugar. **Sugar?** How is it possible that SPAM contains sugar? Maybe they should emphasize that in their advertising.—Picture this TV ad:

A mother is talking to her little girl, "Honey, would you like a lollipop?"

"No thanks, Mom, but could I have a slice of SPAM, and could you put it on a stick?"

And then a voiceover is heard—"It's almost Halloween. What better treat for all those ghosts and goblins than SPAM on a stick? Time to stock up now."

The name SPAM actually comes from "**S**houlder of **P**ork and **H**am. Notice, the product was named **before** the shoulder was chopped. If they had included the chopping, the product would have been called C-SPAM. They probably didn't use C-SPAM because it sounded too similar to the name of that cable network. Do you think some people might suggest that the similarity doesn't end with the names?

A number of jokes have arisen as to what SPAM actually stands for:

- Spare Parts Already Minced

- Specially Processed Artificial Meat

- Something Posing As Meat

I think, regardless of whether it's the SPAM you eat or the Spam you get on your computer, for the time being, I'm going to try to cut down. So as far as my e-mail address or a website is concerned, I'm going to put that on hold for a while.

About three weeks after our annual cookout, school was back in session. It was really hard to believe that we were going into the fourth grade. As usual, Dr. Foster (aka "Lookoutman") had arranged for Vanessa, Derek, and me to be in the same class.

During the second week of school, we had a slight change in our class schedule that gave us a double period of music. This additional time allowed students to sign up for the elementary school band and to fill out applications to rent instruments. It also afforded the music teacher a chance to hold mini-auditions for those students who were taking private lessons.

Derek had been taking piano for two years, and Vanessa had taken up the flute. (Talk about a Renaissance woman—she was very smart, a star athlete, and a talented musician. I think she was capable of reading a book, playing the flute, and scoring a goal in soccer—simultaneously.)

I decided to try the clarinet, the same instrument my mom used to play. Evidently however, musical ability is an acquired talent, not an inherited one. I wasn't very good. However, I made up my mind to stick with it for a number of reasons.

In the first place, although I'm not a joiner, I'm also not a quitter. In the second place, the band met every Tuesday and Thursday morning before school, and Derek and Vanessa were part of the band, so I wanted to be there too. And in the third place, Mom had spent a couple of hundred dollars for me to take lessons, and she said I had to give it more time. (I probably should have offered that last piece of information first, huh?)

A month or so into the school year, during early morning band, our music teacher decided that we should hear a series of selections by some of the world's best musicians. One of the first pieces was by cellist Yo-Yo Ma.

I may be going out on a limb here, but I suspect most of the selections we heard that day, including the cello piece, have not been downloaded on to too many kids' iPods. In fact, if you asked most kids the question "Who is Yo-Yo Ma?", I'm guessing the reply might be—"Isn't he like a new rapper?"

I've already mentioned that I don't have much musical talent, but I could certainly appreciate it in others. So when I heard Yo-Yo Ma, I was sort of mesmerized. I felt like, what Tiger Woods was to golf, Yo-Yo Ma was to the cello. (I'm really getting better at this "cliché, simile, and analogy thing", don't you think?)

Of course, you know that I'm not capable of just leaving that comparison alone. With my ICBM, I always make other connections. And bingo, there it was—their names. I've already talked about Tiger's name, so now it's Mr. Ma's turn.

Although his name is a combination of a child's toy and a shortened version of a relative's name, I didn't see it that way initially. I mean, I did see the child's toy part, but his last name is also the same as the postal abbreviation for Massachusetts, and that's the connection I made first. Okay, so you kind of know how my mind works on these sorts of things, but I thought I'd recap anyway.

If other parents followed the lead of Mr. and Mrs. Ma, then their children's full names would be a combination of a child's toy or game, and a state. As a little added bonus, I've included the instrument each of them might play:

- Pick-up-Sticks Pennsylvania—the snare drum

- Hula-Hoop Hawaii—the tambourine

- Whack-a-Mole Wisconsin—the bass drum

- Uno Utah—a vocalist—sort of a Johnny-one-note

- Tickle-Me-Elmo Tennessee—the piano

On the last day of February (in pre-Roman times it would have been two days later), our classroom teacher announced that we would be putting on a class play in early May. She said she was going to give us a letter to bring home, explaining all about it. And even though the play wasn't scheduled to be performed for two more months, she wanted to give our parents plenty of notice; she was hoping that they could assist with making costumes, building sets, and painting scenery. She also indicated that no decision had yet been made as to which play we would be performing.

One of my classmates asked if it was going to be a musical. Our teacher said that was a possibility. That didn't thrill me. With my musical ability, I'd probably end up playing a tree. But, better to play one than to draw one. (Even though I just made that up, it probably has pretty limited usage potential. The "like orange on an orange" saying was much better, don't you think?)

When I went home that night, I tried to think of some plays we could put on. I even included some musicals. Hey, I'm a team player. If one of the roles was a tree, and I was assigned that role, then I intended to be a stand up guy. (Of course in what other position would you find a tree?) Anyway, this was my list of possibilities:

- *The Birdman of Alcatraz*—I figured Mr. Witkowski could be our technical advisor.

- *Man of La Mancha*—I knew where there might be some leftover Halloween costumes for Don Quixote, Dulcinea, and Sanch Panza.

- *The Elephant Man*—Even though no real elephants ever appear on stage, I still didn't think we should allow any mirrors—too distracting.

- *Inherit the Wind*—If Mom entered any of those high-stakes poker games, **wind** was about all I was going to inherit!

- *Seven Brides for Seven Brothers*—Since we probably didn't have enough boys with strong voices, I thought we could put on "the state of Utah version"—*Seven Brides for **One** Brother*.

As it turned out, our teacher didn't take any of my suggestions. Instead, she decided to write the play herself. We had been studying the Middle Ages, so she wrote a comedy set during that time. It was called *King Arthur and the Knights of the Trapezoid Table*. (I think she borrowed that last part from the kindergarten screening.)

The play was actually very funny. I particularly liked the names of the main characters:

- Queen Gwena-veer-to-the-left—she wasn't making a political statement; she just had a lazy eye.

- King Arthur Andersen—he was dethroned after the royal auditor looked at the royal books and told him he was royally screwed. He did resurface in another kingdom, however, where his new legend flourished—*King Arthur Andersen and the Knights of the Actuarial Tables*.

- Marlin the Magician—he was the former manager of the Florida Marlins who beat the Yankees in the World Series.

- Friar Perdue—actually, he preferred to be called **Fryer** Perdue—things may be coming home to roost.

- Sir Lanced-a-Lot—he had many medical procedures because of hemorrhoids.

Our teacher created enough characters in the play so that everyone had a speaking role. But instead of tryouts, she just assigned the parts. I was assigned the role of "The Reader". It called for me to read a bedtime story out loud to myself. And then once I fell asleep, my dream turned into the play.

I think our teacher chose me for that particular part because I could read pretty well, especially out loud. Of course, it could have been that she thought my lack of musical ability might extend to anything connected to the stage.

Regardless, I did prepare for my role very seriously. Although I only had to read a few paragraphs and then pretend to be asleep for the next sixty minutes, I still wanted to be believable. I even studied up on method acting, and various other techniques. But when push came to shove, just prior to going on the stage each night, I ate two turkey sandwiches. Once the tryptophan kicked in, I was dead to the world. I received a lot of compliments on the realism of my performance. As usual, I deflected the praise.

I actually had no doubt that the play was going to be a huge success, regardless of my performance. I thought our teacher was a very gifted playwright. See what you think. Here's the description and dialogue of the first scene in the dream sequence: A maiden is trapped in a tower, and Sir Lanced-a-Lot happens by. His opening line is, "Fair maiden, why do you shed your tears into the already well-filled moat?" Right then and there, I was thinking—"Tony Award".

With only two weeks of school left, a new student joined our class. Our teacher introduced him as Jimmy Fenton from California. She explained that school in California finished up a few weeks earlier than we did, and since Jimmy was going to be at our school next year, his parents thought that coming for a few weeks now would help him get adjusted.

As soon as I got the chance, I told Derek and Vanessa that I thought we should invite Jimmy to eat lunch with us, since he didn't know anyone.

Vanessa said, "Sure, great idea."

Derek also agreed, although he pointed out that we had scheduled a TUCK meeting during lunch. "But, not to worry; we can e-mail each other." (I think he preferred that anyway.)

We had a short break in our classroom activities, so I went over to Jimmy and introduced myself. "Hi, I'm Benny."

"Hi, I'm Jimmy."

"Do you want to sit with us at lunch?", and then I pointed to Derek and Vanessa.

"Yeah, that would be great."

"Okay, when it's lunchtime, I'll take you down to the cafeteria, and show you where we sit."

"Thanks, Benny."

Sometimes I brought my lunch, and sometimes I bought it. On that particular day I had planned on buying it, so Jimmy and I went through the lunch line together. We were so involved in our conversation that we didn't pay attention to what we were putting on our trays.

When we sat down at the table where Derek and Vanessa were already sitting, we all started talking to each other between gulps of food. After about ten minutes of eating and talking, I glanced over at Derek's tray and Vanessa's tray, and spotted a brownie on each. But when I looked at my tray and Jimmy's tray, I realized that neither of us had picked up a dessert when we went through the lunch line.

"Jimmy, I'm going up to get a brownie; I forgot to get one when we got our lunch. Do you want one too?"

"Yeah, I really like brownies, but I can get it."

"No, don't worry about it, I'll get them."

I went back up to the front of the cafeteria, and into the serving area. There was no one else in line at that point, but one of the cafeteria ladies that I knew was behind the counter.

"Hi, Benny. Can I help you?"

"Hi, Mrs. Dawkins. When I was in line before with my friend … uh, we forgot to pick up dessert."

"Are you sure you're not just trying to get seconds?"

"No, really we …"

"I know, I'm just teasing you. But the problem is that we only have one brownie left. I could cut it in half, if you'd like."

"No, that's okay. I'll just give it to my friend."

"Well, then what are you going to do for dessert?"

"Do you have any SPAM?"

Chapter 13

The summer before Derek, Vanessa, and I were to enter the fifth grade, Derek's little sister, Samantha, turned three years old. She still worshipped Derek, and followed him around like the paparazzi pursue a celebrity. Well, not exactly like the paparazzi. I mean, she didn't camp outside Derek's room with a telephoto lens. Actually, I'm not sure that she even owns a camera. And as far as I know, Derek's picture has never been sold to *The National Enquirer*, at least not by Samantha. Also, there's never been a story in the tabloids about him being abducted by aliens—the outer space kind, not the undocumented kind. But just to be clear, he's never been abducted by undocumented aliens either.

Anyway, as you probably remember, Samantha was born during the weekend of our annual summer cookout three years earlier. Therefore, it seemed only logical to celebrate her birthday each year at that time. Her parents always had a "regular party" for her earlier in the week, so our celebration was more like a mini-party. But nevertheless, we had a cake, decorations and presents.

But like most little kids, Samantha didn't always appreciate the presents she received. Last year when she got some really nice new clothes, she seemed somewhat disappointed that the box didn't contain a toy, or a game, … or a pony. (I'm not sure toddlers have that whole "spatial relationship thing" down yet.) Still, I was a little surprised that Samantha couldn't figure out that there was clothing in the box. I mean, once she saw the Gap Kids printing, I thought she would have realized it wasn't a pony—After all, Gap Kids had discontinued selling horses quite a while ago.

Everyone at the cookout must have remembered Samantha's disappointment last year, because they all made sure to bring **two** gifts this time. One was clothing, and one was a toy or game (still no ponies). I suggested to Mom that we get Candy Land for Samantha. The game didn't require any reading or counting, although Samantha did both of those things pretty well. Instead, the only thing the players had to do was move their game pieces around the game board to the space that corresponded to the color on the card they drew.

By the way, I decided to recommend Candy Land rather than Chutes and Ladders because of what happened at **my** third birthday party. If you remember, the Chutes and Ladders tournament got pretty intense. Another reason I asked Mom to get Candy Land for Samantha was because it was a "classic". In fact, it's in the National Toy Hall of Fame. (I think the manufacturer of Candy Land should use that information in their advertising. What about this for a slogan?— "Ponies may come and go, but Candy Land is a national treasure.")

Did you even know that there was a National Toy Hall of Fame? I just found out when I went with Mom to pick out Samantha's present. There was a poster in the toy section of Target. Currently, there are thirty-six "classic" toys and games in the Hall of Fame, including checkers, Lincoln Logs, the Erector Set, Monopoly, the Duncan Yo-Yo (I'll bet Mr. Ma is happy), and Crayola crayons (I **know** Derek is happy).

This Hall of Fame thing really piqued my interest, so I did some additional research on the toys and games that are already enshrined. Evidently, toys and games get "enshrined", but people get "inducted". So what do you think they did for Barbie and G.I. Joe? Did they get enshrined or inducted? I was also curious as to whether Ken went to the ceremony. I mean, I'm sure that he was happy for his girlfriend, but think about it—Ken didn't get in, and yet he has to sit there with a smile that looks like it was painted on his face. (Well, actually it was.) And then, to make matters worse, his chief rival, G.I. Joe, gets inducted/enshrined—tough day for Ken.

I'm sure the headlines in the toy celebrity section of *The National Enquirer* were pretty scathing:

"There's trouble in the Malibu dream house."

"Is Ken spending too much time with Skipper?"

"Read why Ken's upset with Barbie's plastic surgery." (I'm not sure Ken should be all that upset. Isn't **plastic** surgery the only kind Barbie can have?)

Anyway, as I was saying, besides the thirty-six toys and games that are in the National Toy Hall of Fame, my research uncovered some other toys that are fighting to be recognized. Here's what I found out:

- While Candy Land is already in, most people don't expect the newly created SPAM Land to have much of a chance. But a spokesperson for SPAM Land was quoted as saying, "Hey, it's not that big a deal; after all, we have our own museum."

- Silly Putty was enshrined in 1998 when the Hall of Fame was established. But conventional wisdom suggests that the new toy, Goofy Grout, doesn't have much of a shot, especially considering that you can't really play with it. It was actually created to trick kids into retiling the bathroom. (It's only sold at Home Depot.)

- During my research, I was a little surprised to discover that the game of Clue isn't in the National Toy Hall of Fame. I'm sure you remember that game. You have to solve a mystery, and the game ends when one of the players figures out that "Colonel Mustard did it with the candlestick in the library." So, I'm guessing if Clue didn't meet the standard, then there's not much hope for the new game "Clueless". The latest edition features celebrities that have **no clue**, and ends when someone finally figures out that "Paris Hilton did it with her boyfriend on the Internet."

- There's one toy among the thirty-six that really puzzles me (puzzles are in there, by the way), and that's—Cardboard Box. I know you think I'm making that up, but I'm not; it's really in there. Please, somebody tell me how a cardboard box qualifies as a toy. And even if it does, how do you package it to give it as a gift? Put it in another box? Eventually, it would get to look like those Russian dolls—one inside the other, inside the other, etc. If we thought Samantha was disappointed when she got clothing, how was she going to feel if she just got a box, and that was the **good** present? I gotta tell you, since Cardboard Box got in, there's hope for Goofy Grout.

Anyway, back to the cookout and Samantha's third birthday party. Samantha wasn't terribly impressed that Candy Land was in the National Toy Hall of Fame, but she was thrilled that Derek, Vanessa, and I said that we would play it with her. I think we finished about ten games, and Samantha won eight of them. She wasn't necessarily more skillful than we were, but every time we forgot whose turn it was, she would say, "It's mine." If you get five extra turns in Candy Land, you're pretty much going to win eight out of ten times.

There was a good reason that we often forgot whose turn it was—Derek, Vanessa, and I were talking all the time we were playing. Samantha didn't like that very much, although I don't think she realized it was probably the key to her success. Nevertheless, she let us know how she felt about it, "You guys talk too much.", "Stop talking.", or "Shh, no more talking."

During our final game of Candy Land, Derek, Vanessa, and I started discussing the upcoming school year. Samantha tried to silence us a few times with those same comments, but when that didn't work, she raised her voice slightly and said, "Red light".

Vanessa asked, "What did you say?"

"Red light."

Derek joined in, "Why did you say that?"

"Well, red light means stop, and I wanted you to stop."

We all started laughing, and then Vanessa spoke up, "I like that, Samantha. I think I'm going to use that."

And so she did. Even though our TUCK meetings were not very contentious (certainly, nothing like a game of Chutes and Ladders), on occasion we would disagree over something. And then if the discussion bogged down, Vanessa would invariably say, "Red light". Some of you purists who know *Robert's Rules of Order* might suggest that a motion to suspend debate would have been more appropriate. But I gotta tell you, that "red light" phrase really did the trick. Once we heard it, the debate was over, and we took a vote.

Without question, "red light" has made TUCK a much more efficient organization. "Out of the mouths of babes", huh?—I meant Samantha, who originally said it, not Vanessa. I mean, Vanessa's very attractive and all, so some people might refer to her as a "babe". But, I'm not sure it would be wise for me to do that. That would probably result in another kind of a "red light" moment, which undoubtedly would include **flashing** "red lights", sirens, and emergency vehicles.

The annual cookout also provided Derek with an opportunity to show everyone some additional things to do with the computer. And I have to say, I was surprised at how quickly Grandpa and Mr. Witkowski picked up on everything. I know sometimes older people don't take to technology very easily, but that wasn't the case with those two. And it went way beyond e-mail.

They both knew how to post information and opinions on electronic bulletin boards; they ordered products on-line; they renewed their driver's licenses and paid their taxes on-line. Mr. Witkowski even sold his bird feeders on-line. (Since he built them himself, it took him quite a while to fill the orders. And since he kept the price way down, he didn't make much of a profit. But as he said, "I don't care, that's not why I'm doing this.")

As I know I've mentioned, Derek loves everything electronic. The previous Christmas his parents had gotten him a BlackBerry PDA. I'm not sure a ten-year-old needs a PDA, but in all honesty, I don't know enough about them to make that judgment. What I do know is that at all our TUCK meetings his thumb moved over that device at lightning speed.

However, on more than one occasion, Derek complained of severe pain in his thumb from pressing the buttons so much. This condition has come to be known as "BlackBerry Thumb." I have to tell you, I don't have a whole lot of sympathy for anyone who has "BlackBerry Thumb".

You know the old joke about the guy who goes to the doctor, raises his arm above his head and says, "Doc, it hurts when I do this"? And then the doctor says, "Well, don't do that." I think it's the same thing with "BlackBerry Thumb"—Don't spend so much time pushing those little buttons with your thumb. You certainly don't need a medical degree to figure that one out.

If people are going to the doctor to be treated for "BlackBerry Thumb", is it any wonder why medical costs are skyrocketing? I mean, I don't think "BlackBerry Thumb" even rises to the seriousness of a paper cut. At least in the case of a paper cut, it's usually accidental and unavoidable. With "BlackBerry Thumb", the individual purposefully continues to do the very thing that's causing him the pain.

So, what do you think will be the next technology-induced medical condition—"Flip-phone Finger"?—that's caused by closing your cell phone without removing one of your digits. (Hey Jerry, if you can squeeze us in, we might need a new telethon for this one.)

Anyway, the three weeks after the cookout seemed to go by very quickly, as they always did, and fifth grade beckoned. Well, it didn't actually beckon. Maybe you could say, "It was there for the taking". But actually, we didn't really take anything. This transition paragraph is a lot more difficult to write than I anticipated. Note to editor: I know it's not very stylistic, but I'm just going to state what happened, okay?

Derek, Vanessa, and I were now in fifth grade. Being a fifth-grader was actually pretty cool. The sixth-graders still ruled, but we were the heirs apparent. As usual the three of us were in the same class, and the class schedule was very similar to our fourth grade schedule—the same amount of time for academics and art and music etc. Our group guidance sessions with Dr. Foster continued, but only once a month. Of course I sometimes went to see him more frequently, if I needed to talk about something

There was, however, a major addition to the program of studies in grade five, actually in grades 5–8. The school district decided to add "character education" to the curriculum in those grades. It was a new initiative, that if proven successful, would be expanded K-12.

The program was primarily literature-based. We read a number of books that dealt with themes like respect, justice, and loyalty. And while I enjoyed reading about those topics, I have my doubts that you can actually teach character. I mean, I think your parents and other family members can **instill** character in you, and they can model how you should act, but I'm not sure fifth-graders really alter their behavior because of classroom discussions. I suspect it's a much more complex and extended process. So, as is often the case, I brought my concerns to Dr. Foster.

"You know how much I love *To Kill a Mockingbird*, Dr. Foster, but I don't think reading that book made me a different person."

"I don't know about that, Benny. I'm sure you already had formed beliefs about right and wrong, and the book probably just reaffirmed them, and made you feel even better about who you are. But in some cases, I think people's lives can be changed by what they read or study. I'm sure you've heard the expression, 'That book changed my life.' Well, I think that can happen."

"Do you think it can happen to nine-and ten-year-olds?"

"Probably not immediately, especially since the program only exists in a few grades. But that's why eventually it's going to be offered K-12. I think that if we create an atmosphere of respect and caring in each building and in each classroom, it'll have a major impact on kids, especially if they don't have that at home."

"That makes sense. But I kind of think there's a lot of respect in our class already."

"I think you're right, but not all classrooms are like yours."

"How will you know if it's working?"

"That, young Mr. Curtis, is the $64,000 question."

"I saw reruns of that show with my grandpa." I paused for a moment. "So, are you saying that there's no way to tell if it's working?"

"Well, it's probably going to be about impressions, more than hard facts. For example, at the high school level we teach units in health class about the dangers of drug and alcohol abuse. And, whenever we give an exam about the facts related to those topics, the students do extremely well. But that knowledge doesn't necessarily result in a change in their behavior. So, we can't really use the test scores to proclaim that the health course is making a difference. Instead, we try to get a sense about what does change behavior, and implement that. You know, Benny, it's the same with people who smoke. They certainly know all about the dangers of smoking; they have all the information, but they don't quit. Sometimes education alone doesn't make a difference. So, you try something else … Isn't 'Hope' one of the themes you guys are studying in the character education program?"

"Yeah, it is."

Dr. Foster started to shake his head. "Too much philosophical talk so early in the morning, don't you think, Benny?"

I smiled. "Maybe, but it was interesting. I like what you said."

"Well, thank you." He paused. "Speaking of philosophy; I was thinking about you the other day. I was reading an article about John Stuart Mill—do you know who that is?"

"I think he was a philosopher, but I don't know much about him."

"You're right—an English philosopher. The reason I thought about you was because you seem to have the same kind of memory as John Stuart Mill had. It's claimed that he memorized entire books, and that at the age of three, he read Plato and Socrates **in the original Greek**."

"Really? Wow, that's pretty impressive. I don't think I even know any Greek words, unless … Do Telly Savalas and George Stephanopoulos count?"

Dr. Foster busted out laughing. "I'm not sure why I even try. I just can't keep up with you."

I was also laughing when I said, "You should come to our classroom this week. I'm pretty sure we're starting that unit on 'Hope'."

"Okay, enough. I'm changing the subject. So, did you go out trick-or-treating last week?"

"Yeah, but I stayed close to home."

"Oh right, I remember about your rules for Halloween. Did Derek and Vanessa go with you? What did you guys dress up as?"

"Yeah, we all went together. Vanessa went as Mia Hamm, the soccer player, and Derek went as Bill Gates."

"That figures. How about you?"

"Well, in keeping with the character education theme, I went as Atticus Finch. Even though I was carrying a thick law book, nobody knew who I was supposed to be. Actually, nobody knew who Derek was supposed to be either. When most people came to the door, they saw the two of us wearing glasses with black frames, and said, 'Look, two Harry Potters'."

Dr. Foster started laughing again, and he nodded his head as I continued. "I wish Derek had stuck with his original idea. He was going to go as Mark Schwab."

"Who's that?"

"The CEO of Crayola."

At the end of December, a few days after Christmas, I sat at the desk in my room and began my annual ritual leading up to January first. Unlike most people who make New Year's resolutions, I simply update my "Favorites Lists". You remember, I told you about some of them—my list of favorite holidays and my list of favorite animals etc.

Anyway, as I was working on my favorite holidays list, I made a significant change. After that past year's Thanksgiving, it got moved up to number one, even ahead of Christmas. So, let me tell you about the reason for the shift in rankings.

The Witkowskis joined us again that year, and Grandma and Grandpa were there as well. For some reason, almost everything we did on Thanksgiving struck us as funny. I don't ever remember laughing as hard as I did on that day. If I didn't know better, I would have thought that the Butterball people had taken the tryptophan out of the turkey and replaced it with nitrous oxide. (I actually checked the ingredients label—100% turkey, no laughing gas added.)

I think it all started because Grandpa kept insisting all morning that he needed to check his e-mail, and Grandma kept saying to him, "No, it's rude. And besides, who's going to be sending you e-mail on Thanksgiving? Almost everyone who sends you e-mail is right here in this house." But finally, she relented. "Oh, go ahead."

Grandpa went over to the alcove in the living room where Mom and Dad's computer was located and logged on. And sure enough after about twenty seconds, we all heard the familiar "You've Got Mail".

"See that," said Grandpa. "Oh, ye of little faith."

As he opened up the five messages, he started to laugh. All the messages had been sent within the last five minutes by Mr. Witkowski, who used his laptop in the other room. Mr. Witkowski stuck his head around the corner and said to Grandpa, "I didn't want you to feel like nobody cared."

It was all downhill from there—or uphill, depending on how you look at it.

Besides the Thanksgiving and Christmas switch, there weren't a lot of changes to my favorite holidays list, except for one addition. I don't know if it technically counts as a holiday, but hey, it's my list, right? Anyway, "Take Your Child to

Work Day" debuted at number twelve. Actually, I had been to Dad's office a few times in the past, but never for the whole day. I really enjoyed myself.

It took me about three hours to update all my other lists—favorite cars, favorite singers, favorite stores, etc. I should also tell you that SPAM moved up on my favorite food list, primarily because of the sugar. And miraculously, snakes moved up one notch to 623 on my favorite animals list. (It wasn't so much a change of heart, as it was that I had counted warthogs twice.)

Note to scientists: I really would like to get over my aversion to snakes. Do you think you could try that "mirror experiment" with them? I mean, if they became more self-aware, they might be able to work on their image. It's entirely possible they just don't know how they come across.

I was trying to imagine what the "mirror experiment" might be like if they did try it with snakes. I was picturing a giant cobra looking at himself:

"Boy I'm glad I don't look like those other snakes with the different colored patterns—they look like argyle tube socks. Of course, being all coiled up like this, I guess I kind of look like a black Slinky. But hey, if this snake thing doesn't work out, at least I can take comfort in the fact that I'm in the National Toy Hall of Fame."

During the early spring, our class started making plans for the annual fifth grade trip to New York City. Mom volunteered to be a chaperone, and at Grandpa's suggestion, Mom asked my teacher if it would be possible for Grandpa to be a chaperone too. Mom explained that Grandpa was a retired humanities professor who had lived in New York his entire life and could act as our own personal tour guide. She also mentioned that Dr. Foster knew Grandpa and would surely vouch for him.

My teacher thought it was a great idea, and she said he was welcome to be part of the trip. But she reminded Mom that all chaperones had to submit to a CORI check. (CORI stands for Criminal Offender Record Information. It's designed to find out if someone supervising children, even volunteers, has a criminal record.) The CORI checks are valid for a few years, so Mom's was still up-to-date. (Evidently, nothing about high-stakes Texas Hold 'em poker showed up.)

When I heard about the CORI check for Grandpa, I got a little concerned. I mean, I know my grandpa is a model citizen and all, but I thought it might be likely that a school in Massachusetts would consider being a Yankee fan criminal behavior.

As it turned out, Grandpa was cleared to chaperone, although there was a clause in his volunteer contract that prohibited any public displays of favoritism or taunting of students when we passed Yankee Stadium. (The contract was silent on the **students'** use of the "Bronx Cheer", however.)

We left Massachusetts on a Wednesday morning in the middle of May and headed for the Big Apple. Since the hotels were so expensive in New York City, we ended up staying in Connecticut. So technically, we weren't in the Big Apple, we were more like—out on a limb near the Big Apple.

I kind of know how the New York Giants and the New York Jets must feel. We were visiting New York, but we weren't staying there. Both of those teams have "New York" in front of their names, but they actually play in New Jersey. So why aren't they called the New Jersey Giants and the New Jersey Jets? I sent a letter to the NFL, but nobody's gotten back to me yet.

Anyway, on Thursday, Friday, and Saturday morning before we headed out, Grandpa drove up to Connecticut from Long Island and met us. The four fifth grade classes and the chaperones fit onto two coach buses, and Grandpa took turns riding on each bus following the sightseeing stops we made.

On our way to the Statue of Liberty on Friday morning, as we crossed into New York from Connecticut, Grandpa stood up and asked if anyone knew the state nickname of New York. Several students raised their hands and Grandpa called on one of them.

"The Empire State."

"Very good. Does anyone know the New York state motto?"

Usually, I wouldn't raise my hand in these situations, but nobody else seemed to know it, and my grandpa was looking directly at me. So, my hand went up.

"Yes, Benny."

"Excelsior—it means 'ever higher'."

"That's correct."

I decided not to bring up the fact that "Excelsior" was also the middle name of the man our school was named after. I glanced over at Dr. Foster, who was one of the chaperones on our bus, and he was shaking his head. I took that as an indication that he didn't think we should revisit the whole "FECES" situation either.

As I've told you before, my grandpa is a great storyteller. It doesn't matter whether it's a made-up story or actual history. He's pretty captivating. So, no matter where we went—the Statue of Liberty, the Empire State Building, the United Nations, or Central Park, Grandpa knew everything you could possibly want to know about it.

I think all of the other kids on the trip got a glimpse of what I experience every summer. In fact all the kids, and even the adults, started calling him "Grandpa Evans".

Saturday was the last day of our visit, and our final destination was the Bronx Zoo. I had been there a number of times before with Grandma and Grandpa. But it didn't matter; I always enjoyed the zoo. (It gave me some empirical data when I was revising my favorite animals list.)

The entire fifth grade was divided into smaller groups with one chaperone for each. Grandpa was the chaperone for my group, which consisted of me and seven other students. We got a chance to visit almost all the exhibits, although we didn't spend much time at the snake house. That was actually at the insistence of a number of the other students in my group. (See, it's not just me!)

Our last stop was the elephant pen. Since my last visit to the zoo, they had installed a huge reflecting pool in that area. Of course I didn't think much of it at the time, but it almost seemed like the elephants were looking at themselves in the water. I remember saying to Grandpa that it was as if the elephants were primping as they stared into the reflecting pool. As I look back on it, just as I made that remark to my grandpa, I remember one of the female elephants glancing over, and I swear she winked at me.

Chapter 14

As you've seen, each of the intermediate grades at the Clark Elementary School has some long-standing traditions. In grade four we have the class play, and in grade five we have the trip to New York City. Ironically, the traditions in grade six primarily focus on **leaving** the school. We select courses for next year; we visit the middle school on Moving-up Day; and then the year culminates with the sixth grade dinner dance. But there's one exception to the grade six traditions that have to do with leaving the school—the "maturation movie".

Each year, shortly after the school year begins, all sixth-graders are brought into the auditorium to see the maturation movie; it's the kick-off for the school district's sex education program. Most of us actually had begun to hear about this movie from other students when we were in the third grade. But nobody who has ever seen it talks specifics. So I kind of figured that maybe some of the kids didn't fully understand it and didn't want to look foolish in front of other kids by talking about it. Either that, or the movie had a surprise ending, sort of like *The Crying Game*. (That was a pretty appropriate comparison, don't you think? I really am pleased with my progress with this analogy business.)

Unfortunately, the maturation movie was a major disappointment. I would have thought that the school's experts in the field of sex education would have realized some obvious truths. When kids are approaching puberty and are beginning to be curious about sex, they're anticipating that this movie is going to answer some fundamental questions, like how everything works, or is supposed to work. Instead, the focus of the movie was on **secondary** sex characteristics. I gotta tell you, we were pretty much looking forward to learning about the ones that **came in first**.

For the boys, the movie primarily talked about facial hair, voice changes, and the fact that we have more prominent Adam's apples—Whoopee ding! At least for the girls, there was some discussion in the movie about breast development. Of course, it also mentioned that girls develop "subcutaneous fat" just beneath their skin. (Vanessa wasn't thrilled with certain parts of the movie either.)

As I reflected back on the information contained in the film, it occurred to me that a more prominent Adam's apple shouldn't even be a **tertiary** sex characteristic, never mind a **secondary** one. I mean, big deal—I have a large Adam's apple. So … What, now I am a man?

You know how much I enjoy making lists. Well, after seeing the movie I decided to start a new one—my favorite sex characteristics. However, instead of a strict numerical ranking, I decided to lump the characteristics together in categories—primary, secondary, tertiary, etc. (Maybe "lump" is a poor choice of words; you know with that whole "subcutaneous fat" thing. I don't want to get Vanessa upset.)

So anyway, I decided that a prominent Adam's apple belonged in the fourth category, but I couldn't figure out what that level was called. I thought of "quadrilateral", but then your Adam's apple would have to have four sides. I thought of "quadricentennial", but then it would have to be four hundred years old. Finally, I had to look it up. The word I was looking for was "quaternary". (I double-checked the spelling, but doesn't it look like that word should have an "r" between the "a" and the "t"?)

I originally created eleven levels of sex characteristics. My least favorite ones were placed in the higher categories. One of the characteristics at the eleventh level was "fat deposits around the abdomen and waist, creating an apple-shaped physique". (Yeah, that's the look I'm shooting for.)

When I was checking on the names for the numbering sequence, I discovered that the twelfth level is called "duodenary". (Try to fit that into your daily conversation sometime.) Anyway, it made me think of the word "duodenum", which is part of the small intestine. Now, I don't really think the small intestine plays any role in the reproductive process (the maturation movie was silent on that point), but I decided to add a twelfth level anyway, just in case. So just to be clear, the duodenum has been tentatively placed in my duodenary level of sex characteristics. (This grouping of sex characteristics has proven to be a lot of work for something most people seem to enjoy.)

I decided to leave facial hair in the secondary category, although I suspect once I start shaving, I'll be moving it further on down. Neither my grandpa nor my dad likes to shave, and why would they? It's not just that it's time consuming; it's also become very expensive. The companies that manufacture razors keep making "improvements", and then they raise their prices higher and higher.

Some historians believe that South Pacific natives and possibly Native Americans used sharpened clamshells as the first razors. I'm imagining two rival tribes, the "Schicks" and the "Gillettes", in fierce sartorial competition. Initially, one tribe comes up with the lubricated clamshell. Then the other tribe develops the tempered clamshell. Next we're told that a single clamshell won't do; we'll need double clamshells. And then we'll need a third; and a fourth, and now a fifth.

So let's fast-forward. I really thought that once Schick created the Quattro with four blades that would be it. (By the way, why do you think they spelled "Quattro" with two "t"'s?) But no, Gillette now manufactures Fusion with **five** blades. (Isn't fusion the process used to make hydrogen bombs explode? Yeah, that's exactly what I want close to my face.)

Where does this notion of adding blades stop? Why not eight blades, or ten, or fifteen? I think it's possible that in the near future, there will be a separate shaving room in each home. In the center of the room will be a six-foot tall razor with 150 blades. It'll look like a cat's scratching pole. Men will rub their faces up and down until all their whiskers are gone. (Purring will be optional.)

If you remember, Derek's father works for Gillette. I'm going to have him check with their research and development department to see how far away this cat pole razor is from the marketplace. Of course, once this becomes a reality, men using the six-foot razor are going to require really large mirrors. (Note to interior decorators: Check with your local zoo, there might be a good deal on large mirrors that the elephants aren't using anymore.)

Did you notice that I didn't bring up my namesake company—BIC? As you might recall, my initials are also B-I-C. Well, to be fair, I should acknowledge that besides pens, BIC also makes razors. But, to this point, they have resisted manufacturing four-or five-blade models. I do understand, however, that they're considering making a very long-handled razor with a pen on the bottom. That way, the busy executive can write a memo and shave at the same time. Plus, if he cuts himself shaving, he can write out the swear words, rather than yelling them aloud and traumatizing his whole family.

In my research about shaving I discovered some other interesting information. Were you aware that a long time ago, besides cutting hair and shaving people, the local barber served as the town dentist, and also performed surgery? Boy, I'm really glad that somebody put a stop to that practice. I mean, I really like Angelo, our barber, but I wouldn't want him filling any of my cavities, or worse, messing with my duodenum. (I know it's been relegated to category twelve, but still.)

Even though the school showed us the maturation movie at the beginning of sixth grade, none of the boys in my class looked like they were going to be shaving any time soon, except Demetrious Christopolous. Actually, he had been shaving since the third grade, although only twice a week. The reason I know all this is because, when he was in my class that year, he brought in his shaving kit for show-and-tell. (Do you think I can add Demetrious' name to my list of Greek words?)

A few months into the school year, we had a unit in our English class that dealt with "propaganda techniques". We studied strategies like "bandwagon" and "celebrity endorsement". We read political speeches, editorials, and advertisements, and analyzed how the writer tried to persuade the reader to take some action. I really enjoyed that unit, probably because so much of it had to do with word choice and connotative language.

Instead of a final exam at the end of the unit, our assignment was to create a magazine advertisement for a fictitious product. We were allowed to use artwork or computer graphics, but the bulk of the ad had to be text. We were permitted to make up claims about the product, but they had to be realistic. As soon as I found out about the project, I went right to my dad to get as much information as possible.

"Sure, Benny, besides any current stuff, I think I have a book that shows some magazine ads from twenty-five or thirty years ago. That should give you some good ideas."

Dad went to locate the book and came back in about ten minutes. He had put Post-It notes on a couple of the pages, and then opened up the book to one of them. "Here, take a look at this ad. Why don't you read it, and then we'll talk about what you've read."

The top of the advertisement looked like an engraved invitation: "You are cordially invited to a personal showing of a totally new car." The lower portion of the page had a picture of a Chrysler Cordoba. In the background was a photo of what looked like a Spanish castle. The text read as follows:

This is Cordoba. The new small Chrysler. With the warm colors of wood in a finely detailed instrument panel ... and the rich colors of earth in the deep shag carpeting. The soft warmth of glowing lamps in five separate locations ...

When I finished reading, Dad said, "What do you think?'

"Well, aside from all the punctuation errors, it looks like they're trying to make you feel like you're special, like it's a personal invitation."

"Good, that's right."

"And with the name of the car, and the background, it looks like it's from Europe."

Dad grinned. "It does, doesn't it?"

"But thirty years ago, wasn't that car made in Detroit?"

"Right … What about the text?"

I was thinking for a moment and then I said, "Well, wouldn't the phrase 'with the warm colors of wood in a finely detailed instrument panel' mean that the car had a brown dashboard?"

Dad started to laugh. "Exactly. But do you see how 'brown dashboard' is not the image the company probably wants to promote?"

"Yeah, that makes sense."

"What else?"

"Maybe, the description of the 'soft warmth of glowing lamps in five separate locations'. Is that the light in the glove compartment, and the overhead light that goes on when you open the door?"

"You got it."

"Wow, do most people even pay attention to those kind of things in an ad?"

"Probably not."

"When I went to work with you, I didn't see you doing stuff like this."

"No, that's not what I do. I used to do a lot of the writing, but now I'm the Projects Director."

"What's that?"

"Well, we have teams of people who create marketing campaigns for various products. Sometimes I give the teams ideas, or sometimes they come up with them on their own. The teams then work up some preliminary ads and present them to me. Usually, after some minor changes, we're ready to show the campaign to Mr. Jenkins, and if he likes it, then to the client."

"So, do you consider yourself more of a 'big idea' man than …"

Dad started chuckling. "No, actually I like the small details. If you get those right, the other stuff usually takes care of itself."

"Do you ever have to make up an ad for a product you don't like?"

"No, actually we don't. You've met my boss, Mr. Jenkins. Well, he owns the agency, and he won't do ad campaigns for anything questionable."

"Like what?"

"Cigarettes, for example."

"That's good. Anything else?"

"Nothing specific. But, I think we have pretty high standards in terms of what we're willing to use in an ad."

"Is that the same for most ad agencies?"

"No comment. I don't want to be quoted in your report for school."

Dad started turning the pages in the book he had in front of him. "Let me show you another ad that may help clarify what you were asking about." He flipped through some pages and then said, "Here it is. This ad is from many years ago also, but I always refer to it when we hire new people. It's cleverly written, but it's not the kind of advertisement we want coming out of our agency."

I began to read the ad, which was for a "self-improvement" pamphlet entitled *Say Goodbye to Cellulite*. Part of it read as follows:

What exactly is cellulite? It's that doughy, flabby mass of flesh that afflicts almost 90% of the women in the world, distorting the feminine curves of ladies from 15 to 90 … Yes, recently uncovered facts now confirm that these women are not "just fat"! They are the victims of the "Cellulite Scourge"! And cellulite is not ordinary fat. It's lumpy, bubbly globules of toxic material which has become trapped in small pockets just underneath the surface of what used to be flawlessly smooth skin.

… All you need to know is … contained in these three all-important methods of self treatment.

First …'Anti-Cellulite Self-Massage Treatments'

Second …'Anti-Cellulite Food Program'

Third …'Anti-Cellulite Relaxers'—a new kind of condensed, effortless exercise …

(How about that last phrase?—"effortless exercise"—Talk about an oxymoron. What the heck would constitute "effortless exercise"?)

Although there was a lot more to the advertisement, I stopped reading at that point. But I have to say, whoever wrote it certainly had a way with words. I mean I wasn't in the target-age demographic, or even the gender one, for that matter, but **I wanted** to buy the pamphlet. However, when push came to shove (maybe all this mental pushing and shoving is what they mean by "effortless exercise"), I was able to resist. But I did ask my dad to make a copy of the ad for Vanessa. It occurred to me that the description of cellulite sounded suspiciously like the girls' secondary sex characteristic—"subcutaneous fat". Maybe they're not the same thing, but I figured that Vanessa would want to know, and sort that out for herself.

After talking to Dad, I came up with a number of ideas for my advertising project. Finally, I settled on one of them. But I was a little concerned, because technically the product I wanted to use in my ad wasn't a fictitious one. But after I explained what I wanted to do to my teacher, she told me to go ahead.

Here are some excerpts, see what you think:

Moms and Dads—Christmas is just around the corner. Get your kids the "imagination toy of the future"—**The Cardboard Box**—(Jimmy and Suzy will **have** to use their imaginations, because this toy doesn't actually do anything!)

Don't think **outside** the box. Think about **buying** the box.

- No assembly required

- No batteries necessary

- No colors to choose from—See what brown can do for you!

- No backordering. We have plenty!

- Easy storage—Either fold it up, or put it inside another box.

Here's what a couple of lucky kids had to say last Christmas:

"The Cardboard Box is in the Hall of Fame. Hey, it's not Cooperstown, but if I cut it up and use it for bases, maybe it will help **me** get there."

"It's the biggest present I ever got; it's what our refrigerator came in."

(Note to cardboard box manufacturers: Are you happy with your current advertising agency? If not, give me a call.)

Right after the April school vacation, our class began to have meetings with Dr. Foster to discuss next year's course selections. Actually, in many ways, the schedule for seventh grade at the middle school was not all that different from the sixth grade schedule.

All seventh graders had English, math, social studies, and science every day; and art, phys. ed., computer, health, and home and career two or three times each week. The last two courses that completed the schedule were music and world languages. Music classes met three times per week, and we had the option of choosing band, chorus, or general music. The world language classes met every day, and we could choose from among Spanish, French, and Latin.

I'm not sure how Latin qualifies as a world language. I mean, very few people use it anymore. Even priests have to get special permission to say the Mass in Latin. Still, I suppose you could argue that Latin helps in vocabulary development. But I decided that with all those "um" words, it might prove to be a real struggle for me.

It wasn't an easy decision though. When I was doing my research about the calendar and Julius Caesar, I did learn a lot of Latin words and phrases, as well as some Latin grammar, like the principal parts of verbs. For example, the principal parts of the verb "amo" are amo, amare, amavi, amatus—I love; to love; I have loved; having been loved. I also learned some irregular verbs as well, like the Latin equivalent of—I am; to be; I have been; and having been, which translate—sum, esse, fui, futurus.

Still, I figured there was no "futurus" in me taking Latin. If I did, I was worried that I was going to—flunko, failare, bomb-it, no passus. So when I saw Dr. Foster, our conversation kind of went like this:

"So Benny, have you decided which music class and which language you're going to take next year?"

"I think I'm going to stick with the clarinet, so I'd like to take band."

"Okay. How's that going, by the way?"

"Well, I'm getting better, but any similarity between me and Benny Goodman is strictly our first names."

Dr. Foster started laughing as I kept going. "My grandpa told me that they used to call the clarinet the 'licorice stick'. I was thinking that maybe I'd play better if I got a **red** clarinet. I really like cherry Twizzlers."

Dr. Foster continued laughing and shook his head in mock disgust. "Okay wiseguy, I bubbled in band for next year; what about your language?"

"Probably Spanish, although I was considering French, because Derek and Vanessa are going to take French. But I think I'll stay with Spanish, even though it'll be the first time since pre-school that we won't all be together."

"Well actually, there's a good chance you won't be together for a lot of your classes next year. You'll probably all be in the same homeroom though. Since the homerooms are alphabetical, "Curtis" and "Davis" should be together."

"Will you be at the middle school at all next year?"

"Some. I'm going to teach a few of the character education classes in seventh grade. Those are scheduled every Friday afternoon. So I'll probably see you at least a couple of times a month. Plus, you know if you need to talk, you can just e-mail me, and I'll make arrangements to come up to the middle school to see you."

"Thanks."

Neither one of us said anything for a few moments, but then Dr. Foster broke the silence. "Things change, Benny."

"I know."

"But don't think you're getting rid of me that easily."

There were some additional silent moments before I said anything again. "I was just thinking that maybe I should switch my language choice. Does the middle school offer Greek? I mean, I know I'm way behind; but maybe I could start to catch up to that John Stuart Mill guy."

Dr. Foster started to grin, and after a brief pause he said, "Sorry Benny, we can't really add Greek." His grin turned into a huge smile just before he offered the punch line. "It's kind of like professional soccer and ordering at a Chinese restaurant—no substitutions."

Now, it was my turn to laugh.

About three weeks after the scheduling meetings were all completed, the entire sixth grade boarded buses for our visit to O'Rourke Middle School. This particular activity was referred to as "Moving-up Day". I'm not sure why it's called that. I mean we're not actually moving anything. There were no huge vans outside the school. There were no large men carrying cardboard boxes that read, "This contains schoolbooks; this is not a toy."

Shouldn't this excursion be called "Visitation Day"? Isn't that what we're really doing? To be fair, however, that sort of sounds like a scheduled trip to the penitentiary. But still, we should find a new name. What about "Orientation Day"? I kind of like that. I'm going to speak to Dr. Foster. I mean, it doesn't help **our** grade any, but we should always be looking out for future generations, don't you think?

By the way, is it possible that when kids in Asia visit their new school, it's called "Occidentation Day"? And, while we're on the subject of Asia, do you think American restaurants in China allow substitutions? You know, like instead of beef teriyaki, can you get SPAM teriyaki, or is that just for dessert?

Anyway, once we arrived at the middle school, we were escorted toward the auditorium where our new principal was going to speak to us. On the way, I noticed a plaque on the wall dedicated to the man for whom the school was named—Walter O'Rourke. It was a little disconcerting to realize that the school's full name was Walter O'Rourke Middle School—W-O-R-M-S.

I know that worms aren't even in the same genus as snakes, but they must at least be distant cousins or something. It was only a momentary concern, however, because I'm not really afraid of worms. It's not just that they're smaller then snakes; it's more that worms aren't interested in attacking people or in biting them like snakes want to do.

In fact, one of our teachers told us that worms eat dirt. Once I learned that piece of information, worms moved up about 20 places on my favorite animals list. I just don't view an animal that thinks eating dirt is a good idea as something to be feared. When I was two years old, Mom arranged a play date for me with a kid named Bobby Mortenson. He ate dirt. I never saw him as much of a threat either.

Once all the sixth-graders were in the auditorium, we were introduced to Mr. Martin, the principal of the middle school. He outlined what the day was going to be like, and he told us a little bit about what we could expect next year. And although I was interested in all those things, I have to say that it was the last few minutes of his talk that really impressed me.

"The rules and regulations at O'Rourke are based on three things—respecting yourself, respecting others, and respecting property. Here at the middle school we live those ideas everyday ... The worst thing you can do at this school is to be mean to someone else, to embarrass them, to belittle them, to hurt them in any way. We're very tolerant at O'Rourke, but not for that ... I think you're all going to have the opportunity for a great seventh- and eighth-grade experience here, especially if what I just said guides your behavior."

I hadn't used my "sincerity meter" in quite awhile, but I still think it was functioning pretty well. Mr. Martin's speech was a solid ten.

After we finished in the auditorium, all the sixth-graders got a tour of the school. We visited a number of classrooms and were shown the gym, the nurse's office, the main office, and the library. When we visited the guidance office, one of the counselors explained that next year the seventh grade would be divided into teams of students. There would be two teams of approximately 100 students each, and a group of four teachers—one each for English, math, social studies, and science—who would teach those 100 students.

See now, I don't have a problem with anyone calling this particular grouping method "teaming". It describes it accurately, and there's no negative connotation. I mean, it's not like that "looping" thing Mrs. Jarvis was involved in. By the way, even though I never heard back from *Educational Jargon Monthly* about my "looping" concerns, I did send them a letter about getting it right with the "teaming" nomenclature.

On the bus ride back to the elementary school, I asked Dr. Foster if I could sit with him for a minute.

"Sure, Benny, What's up?"

"Nothing special. I was just wondering if you knew Mr. Martin very well. I really liked what he had to say."

"Actually, I do know him pretty well. He's a very nice guy, and a good administrator. And that speech about respect, it's not just talk. I'll tell him you liked it; he'll be pleased."

We were both silent for a moment, and then I spoke up again. "Isn't it unusual for a middle school to only have two grades?"

"Yes, it is. Most of the time there are at least three—usually a six, seven, eight configuration."

"How come O'Rourke's only seven and eight?"

"Sometimes we have to do things because of space limitations, not because it makes the most sense educationally. We just can't fit three grades at O'Rourke, so it's only seventh and eighth. Mr. Martin does a great job, but it's kind of difficult for kids to feel a strong connection to the school, because every student is either just coming in or just going out."

"I never thought of that. But I still think I'm going to like it, especially with all the new things we'll get to do."

He smiled. "I have no doubt."

The sixth grade dinner dance was held about a week before school got out for the summer. I should point out that the school never officially called it a dinner dance. The kids and the parents are actually the ones who tend to push the social agenda, so for as long as anyone can remember, it's been "unofficially" referred to as the dinner dance. Of course, social mores aside, "dinner dance" is a much better name than the school's official title—"The Sixth Grade End-of-the-Year Get-Together".

And while most parents didn't encourage "dates" for twelve-year-olds (eleven, in my case), the majority of kids arrived as couples. I didn't really ask Vanessa to go with me; it just kind of happened. Derek went with a girl who had recently transferred into our computer class and who actually understood most of what Derek said about computers. The rest of us had no clue. (I later found out that Derek had asked Dr. Foster if the middle school language choices included "Technospeak".)

The night of the dinner dance, my dad drove the four of us to the school. Derek sat up front so he could plug his iPod into the car's sound system. Dad didn't seem to mind, especially since it was only a seven-minute ride to the school. Dad asked Derek who it was we were listening to.

"Pink."

"I don't think I've ever heard of her, but she has a good voice. What else do you have on your iPod?"

"Blue Suede Shoes, Yellow Submarine, A Whiter Shade of Pale … It's my Crayola mix."

It's funny; the ride seemed a lot longer than seven minutes.

The Monday after the dinner dance I went to see Dr. Foster.

"Are you coming to the cookout in August?"

"Benny, you know I've made it every year; I wouldn't miss it."

"I know. I guess even though I'm going to see you then, I just felt like I wanted to say goodbye and thank you, now that I won't be at Clark anymore."

"I appreciate that, Benny, and thank you, but it's not really goodbye. I told you, I'm going to be around next year."

"I know. But, it's not going to be the same as seeing you everyday, and being able to …"

"Do you want to talk about that?"

I hesitated, but finally said,"No, I'm all right."

"You sure?"

I just nodded, and I think Dr. Foster could see that I was starting to fill up, because he changed the subject. "So tell me about the dinner dance. I was hoping to stop by, but I didn't get the chance."

I was able to get my composure back. "It was good."

"You went with Vanessa, right?"

"Yeah, but it's not supposed to be like a date."

"I know; I meant that you went together as friends."

"Yeah, we did, but it seemed a little different. I mean, we were all dressed up, and we danced … so … I don't know, it seemed different."

"You know how to dance, huh?"

"Sort of. Mom showed me."

"That's good."

We were both quiet for a few moments and then Dr. Foster said, "It seems like you've got something else on your mind, Benny. Is there something else you want to talk about?"

I smiled at him and shifted my position in the chair. "Well … I think I'm starting to feel different about Vanessa. I mean, we've been friends since I was three, but now …"

Dr. Foster smiled back. "Benny, the next few years are going to bring a lot of changes, and I don't know what's going to happen with you and Vanessa, but I have to tell you, the best grown-up relationships come from being friends first."

"Really?"

"Yes."

"But how am I going to know if it's becoming something else? I mean, I think I'm feeling something different towards her, but how am I going to know for sure?"

Dr. Foster's smile became broader. "I wish I could tell you that there was some kind of test you could take, but I'm afraid there isn't." He paused. "It's probably going to be just like seventh and eighth graders at O'Rourke Middle School."

"What do you mean?"

"For quite a while, you won't know whether you're coming or going."

I thought Dr. Foster was getting pretty good at the whole analogy thing also.

Chapter 15

As had been the case for the past eight years, Mom, Dad, and I headed for Long Island over the Fourth of July weekend. We always left very early in the morning and drove the whole distance, or we took the ferry across Long Island Sound to avoid the traffic around New York City. Either way, the trip took almost five hours.

Actually, I've never really minded riding in the car for that long, provided I didn't take it upon myself to read anything while the car was moving. I found out the hard way (actually, Dad's upholstery found out the hard way) that reading in the car makes me nauseous. In fact, I even get a queasy stomach if **someone else** reads in the car. Mom knows this, so she never brings any reading material with her. Since Dad usually drives, reading is not much of an option for him, although I remember one trip to Long Island when we got stuck in a huge traffic jam on I-95. Dad could have read *Crime and Punishment* before we even got to New Haven! (I would have been willing to wear a blindfold if it had been that important to him.)

So, since reading is out, we pass the time on our long trips by just talking, playing travel games, or listening to music. Because of my time with Grandma and Grandpa, I've been exposed to all types of music, so usually whatever Mom and Dad want to listen to is fine with me. Nevertheless, I was a little surprised when the first three songs emanating from the CD were *Crimson and Clover, Mellow Yellow,* and *Purple-People Eater.* Evidently, Dad had made his own Crayola mix.

During the last hour of the trip, we talked about a number of different things, including my impending move up to the middle school. Dad raised the topic first.

"So, are you nervous at all about seventh grade?"

"No, not really. I think I'm more excited about it than anything else."

Mom jumped in. "Why's that?"

"Well, even though a lot of the subjects will be the same as we had in elementary school—you know, like computer and art. We're going to have them more frequently, and we'll probably get to do more. Plus, one of the new classes sounds kind of interesting—Home and Career."

Mom again. "Is that the same as Home Economics and Shop?"

"That wasn't very politically correct, Mom."

"Well, that's what we called them when I was in the seventh grade."

Before I spoke up again, I reconsidered my previous statement. "Actually, 'politically correct' is probably not the right phrase, is it?"

Dad took a moment to think about that, and then he said, "How about 'domestically correct' and 'industrially correct'?"

With some good-natured sarcasm in my voice, I responded, "Yeah, Dad, that's way better."

Mom chimed in. "What a way with words. It's hard to believe you don't still write advertising copy."

"Okay, knock it off, you two. I only said that because I think they used to be called 'Domestic Arts' and 'Industrial Arts'."

"Is that what they were called when you took them, Dad?"

"No, don't forget, I went to parochial school; we didn't have those subjects. In fact, if we hadn't lived next door to Mr. Witkowski, I still wouldn't know what a 'left-handed Palumbo wrench' is."

In my best straight-man voice I offered, "But Dad, there's no such thing as a 'left-handed Palumbo wrench'."

"I know—they only come in the right-handed model."

Unfortunately, there was no drum set in the back seat for me to do a rim shot, so I just looked skyward and thought of Henny Youngman.

Mom had heard that joke about a hundred times. Nevertheless, she chuckled and shook her head. "Boy, it doesn't get any better than this—first *Purple-People Eater* and now Abbott and Costello."

"You want Benny and me to attempt 'Who's on First'?"

Mom was still shaking her head. "Wasn't there a movie a few years ago called *Drive, She Said*; why don't you try that?"

Dad chuckled too. "Yes, dear."

After about twenty seconds of silence, I started a new conversation. "You know, there are sports in seventh grade next year."

Dad said, "That's right, I forgot about that."

Mom asked, "Which sports?"

"Well, I think it's mostly intramurals, but there are two sports each season where we get to play other schools. In the fall season it's soccer and cross-country."

Dad said, "So, are you going to try out for the soccer team?"

"Actually, there are no tryouts; everybody makes the team. But I think I'm going to join cross-country instead of soccer."

Both Mom and Dad said "Really?" at the same time.

"Yeah, I like running. It was actually what I liked best when I was playing soccer."

Dad was nodding his head. "Well, you always had a lot of endurance. I remember when everybody else was ready to collapse, you didn't even seem to be winded."

"Dad, that was when I was playing goalie."

"No it wasn't, you wiseguy."

All three of us were smiling, and then Dad spoke up again. "Listen Benny, we're about twenty miles away from your grandma and grandpa's house. You could run alongside the car to get some practice in."

For just a second, before she realized Dad was kidding, Mom had the same expression on her face as she did when I spilled the grape juice at my third birthday party.

I responded to Dad. "I don't think that's such a good idea. We're almost on the Long Island Expressway. With the usual traffic and all, I'd probably get to Grandma and Grandpa's way before you did."

"Good point."

Actually, the traffic was pretty light, so it only took us about half an hour to go the twenty miles. A few minutes before we arrived, Mom called Grandma to let her know we were almost there.

It's funny in this day and age that neither of my parents carries a cell phone with them. They both have cell phones, but they leave them in their cars most of the time in case of emergencies. So Mom had to use Dad's phone to call Grandma. Actually, in New York, it would have been illegal for Dad to make the call while he was driving, unless he had a hands-free device.

I think that's a pretty good law, don't you? I think talking on the phone and trying to drive is really dangerous. Actually, I wish they'd pass a law that would restrict cell phone use in a lot of other situations. People are just plain rude and inconsiderate when it comes to cell phones. Don't you love sitting in a restaurant trying to enjoy a nice meal, while the person at the next table is giving the details about Uncle Harold's colonoscopy?

Or how about this scenario:

"Bless me Father for I have sinned. It's been two weeks since my last confession, and I've committed adultery four times."

Brrring, brrring.

"Oh, just a minute, Father; I need to take this, it might be important."

When I think about how rude people can be, I'm kind of glad that my parents don't carry cell phones. Of course, I guess it's possible they don't carry them because they're afraid of getting "flip-phone finger".

Grandma and Grandpa were waiting for us on the front lawn when we arrived. There were hugs all around, and we gave as good as we got. It was almost lunchtime, so shortly after we put our luggage in the rooms where we would be sleeping, we sat down in the kitchen to eat. After we finished, Grandpa indicated he wanted to talk to all of us about something.

"Have you ever heard of a 529 plan?"

Dad responded. "Isn't that some sort of college account?"

"Yes, that's right. Well, we're starting one for Benny."

Mom spoke first. "Oh, Dad, that's terrific." She then turned to me. "How about that, Benny?"

"That's really nice. Thank you, Grandpa and Grandma."

Dad re-entered the conversation. "That's very generous of you, Marc."

"Well, Ellen and I both get a pension, and we're eligible for Social Security this year. The house will be paid off soon. Property taxes are a bit high, but all in all, we're fine. Plus, isn't that what families are supposed do for each other?"

"No matter, it's still very generous."

Grandpa turned in my direction. "I wanted to tell you about this, Benny ... uh ... before you went downstairs."

I got a puzzled look on my face. "I don't understand."

"Well, to give your college fund an initial boost, I sold some of my old records."

I was almost in shock. "You didn't really, Grandpa, did you?"

"Now, don't get upset. All the music I still want to listen to, I had transferred onto CD's, or I downloaded. So, I still have everything I want ... just in a different format."

"But, you love those records."

"No, I **love** the music; it doesn't matter how it gets to my ears."

Mom asked, "How did all this come about?"

Grandpa filled us in. "I picked up a memorabilia book out of curiosity, and discovered that some of my old records were pretty valuable. Even the album jackets and sleeves that were used to protect the records are worth money. Anyway, I put a few items on ebay. Actually, Benny, your friend Derek helped me with that. I got a very high level of interest on those first items. Then one of the buyers asked me to catalog everything I was willing to sell, and he said he would make me an offer for the whole collection. Two weeks ago, we made the deal ... I got a check for almost $60,000."

Dad: "What?"

Mom: "Are you serious?"

Me: "$60,000?"

Grandma said, "Tell them about the Elvis Presley record."

Dad interrupted. "You said $60,000, right?"

"I know; I was surprised too. But one of the Elvis records I had was on the Sun label and was in mint condition. It was worth over $5000 by itself."

Mom: "That's amazing!"

Grandpa talked to us for ten more minutes about the ebay transactions and the record collection sale. Then he started to explain how the college fund worked.

"Ellen and I opened an account in Benny's name with an initial deposit of $10,000. With that amount, there's no gift tax, and we can claim a deduction on our state taxes. We'll do the same thing each year for the next five years. All of the interest earned is tax-free. So, when Benny's ready to go to college, we can withdraw as much money as he needs, and we don't have to pay taxes on any of it. I'm also checking on something else; since we're his grandparents and not his parents, I don't know if the 529 account is figured into any financial aid he may be eligible for."

Mom was shaking her head. "This is really something, Dad."

Grandpa just smiled.

Dad asked, "What happens if Benny gets a scholarship?"

"Then the money can be used for anything. You just have to pay taxes on the interest earned. It's a very flexible plan. For example, if you do need the money for college expenses, you can use it for tuition, room, board, books, even a computer."

I asked, "What about a car?"

Everybody laughed.

I got up from my chair and went over to hug my grandparents.

"Thank you, Grandpa; thank you, Grandma."

It's funny, just a moment ago everyone was laughing, but now everybody had tears in their eyes, including me. We all took a moment to compose ourselves, and then I asked, "Am I correct that the plan is still for me to finish high school and then go on to college? That hasn't changed, right?"

Everyone was looking at me strangely. Dad said, "What do you mean?"

"Well, it occurred to me that once I finish seventh grade, I'll be twelve, and if I went right off to New Jersey after that, then I'd graduate from Princeton at sixteen. And, I thought we had already scrapped that idea."

Everybody was back to laughing.

As you know, I love the anticipation of things almost as much as I love the things themselves. It was a little different, however, with the upcoming start of middle school. Although I was really excited, as I had told Mom and Dad, there was a part of me that was still a bit nervous. Without question, one of the biggest adjustments was trying to get to know so many different teachers, all of them with their own personalities, and their own ways of doing things.

It's funny, during all the orientation programs (occidentation, if you come from Asia) the adults kept saying that the biggest challenges in seventh grade would be the extra homework, the longer school day, and remembering your locker combination. Nope.—It's the people. In new situations, it's always the people.

But as it turned out, any anxiety I had quickly disappeared. Right from the first day, I could sense a real positive tone in the school. I'm sure a lot of it was due to Mr. Martin, because the notion of respect was evident everywhere. It was obvious that this was a place where people felt comfortable, and that idea fed upon itself, and spread to everyone in the building.

What also struck me was the informality of the school. Nobody seemed uptight. People went about their business and were very friendly and courteous. (It certainly didn't hurt that the staff never used their cell phones in the building.) Let me tell you about an incident that occurred during the first few days of school that helped form this positive impression.

My homeroom teacher asked me to bring our attendance form down to the main office. I said sure, picked up the sheet of paper, and headed in that direction. Just before I arrived at the office, I noticed Mr. Martin near the front entrance; he was encouraging some students who were just coming in to hurry along.

There was a short line in the main office, primarily comprised of students who were tardy, or students who were dropping off something, just like me. When I got to the front of the line, I handed the attendance form to the secretary behind the counter. She said, "Thank you ... uh, just a minute. You're from homeroom 107, right? I need to give you something to bring back to your teacher. Can you wait a moment, please?"

Just then the phone rang, and the secretary picked it up. It sounded like it was going to take a while, and I didn't want to appear to be eavesdropping, so I moved away from the counter and looked out into the corridor in front of the main office. Mr. Martin was about fifteen feet away, with his back to me. It appeared that he was waiting for the bell to ring to end homeroom, so he could assist with the traffic flow. (They could have really used him on the Long Island Expressway.)

As I glanced down the hallway, I saw one of the girls from my homeroom who had been marked absent, heading toward Mr. Martin. She started running, and she had her head down, so she didn't see him. As she got closer, Mr. Martin put out his right hand, sort of like a traffic cop. He moved it forward and back as an indication that she should take it easy and slow down. He still hadn't said anything out loud; I'm sure he was afraid if he did, it might startle her.

Just before the girl reached Mr. Martin she finally looked up, and evidently saw his extended hand with the open palm facing her. The next thing I knew, she gave Mr. Martin a **high-five**, kept on running, and disappeared around the corner in the direction of our homeroom.

Mr. Martin appeared momentarily stunned, but then he burst out laughing, and put his hands on his hips. There was nobody else in the corridor, so no one else observed what happened, except me. I smiled and headed back to the counter in the main office.

Now, I don't want to overanalyze this little scene, but I have to say it made me feel good about being in a school where the principal's reaction to what happened was laughter and not detention.

Although I enjoyed all of my courses in seventh grade, I'd have to say that health class and "advisory" were probably the most interesting. Health class met twice a week, and the topics ran the gamut from "nutrition and exercise" to "smoking and drugs" to "relationships and sex education". The advisory class met once each week on Fridays and was part of the district's character education program. The topics in advisory included "respect", "tolerance", "understanding differences", "bullying", etc.

Most middle schools have the two courses I just mentioned, although they're often called something else. Some schools call the advisory course "Advisor/Advisee Time". (Do you think that the same person who came up with "looping", came up with that one? Come on, people; who uses the term "advisee" unless they have a cup of tea in their hand and a pinky extended?)

Actually, I'm not a big fan of a lot of those words that end in "ee". You know, like the ones that denote a person in a less prestigious position. I mean we're all used to words like "employer/**employee**", so that's not so bad, but what about ones like "counselor/**counselee**", "auditor/**auditee**", or "mentor/**mentee**"? Doesn't that last one sound like the person's a very large marine animal? I know that's actually a manatee, but I still think the words sound too similar. (Just so you know, this has nothing to do with how I feel about manatees. I actually kind of like them; they're 127th on my favorite animals list. Compared to snakes in 623rd place, manatees are practically family.) Anyway, I'm just glad our school simply called the program "advisory".

Before we talk any more about the advisory course, I need to tell you about the health class. Toward the end of September, we started a six-session unit on sex education. For the third and fourth sessions, the boys and girls were separated. Schools generally don't like to separate students by gender, but in this case, with the sensitivity of the subject matter, it was probably a good idea.

The two sessions when the boys and girls were separated were very specific and very informative. I was also pleased to see that most of the primary sex characteristics for males were placed in the same category level that I had placed them in. (Affirmation is a wonderful thing.)

It might surprise you, however, to find out that I actually hadn't done a lot of in-depth research on the topic of sex. I mean, I was naturally curious like everyone else my age, but I kind of viewed sex in the same way I viewed 401(k) plans—eventually I would be paying a lot of attention to both of them, but right now there was no likelihood of any activity on either front.

I also found it interesting that as you reach the age when your interest in sex starts to decline, your interest in 401(k) plans increases. (Ah, the synergy of nature and finance) I also think that sex and 401(k) plans are similar in another way. I mean, it's conceivable that in the future both my 401(k) plan and a certain primary sex characteristic might not be performing well. If that turned out to be the case, then I would certainly look into taking care of those things at that time, but why look for trouble now? (By the way, if you want some advice about your 401(k), and you consult a stockbroker, does that make you the "brokee"? Actually, **that** particular double "ee" word seems appropriate in that situation.)

Before I made the final decision to postpone any in-depth research about sex, I did look up a few things; but those were in the philosophical realm, rather than the physical one. I know what you're thinking—that's like claiming you buy *Playboy* for the articles. But actually, I do like to know the philosophical foundation of things. Although, to be honest, I never did look into what John Stuart Mill had to say on the subject.

Anyway, during my **semi**-philosophical pursuit (happy?), I did discover one theory that didn't make a lot of sense to me. It seems that ancient Chinese philosophers believed that sex was 90% **mental.** When I first read that, I remember actually speaking out loud—**"Not if you're doing it right!"** Upon reflection however, since there are nearly 1.4 billion Chinese, you'd have to think that they probably have this whole sex thing down pat. On the other hand, if sex **is** 90% mental, how do you explain that Paris Hilton is able to do it?

Around the same time we started the sex education unit, our health teacher, who was also a coach, reminded us that the deadline for the fall sign-up for soccer and cross-country was October first. My dad signed all the requisite forms, giving permission for me to be on the cross-country team.

I had actually started getting in shape over the summer. I ran four or five times a week when I stayed at Grandma and Grandpa's house, and I continued to practice in August and September at home. It's kind of hard to explain, but even when I was feeling totally exhausted, there was an exhilaration that came over me when I ran three or four miles without stopping. And although I really didn't have any way to judge, I thought that distance running was something that I might be good at. Plus—worst-case scenario—it improved my wind and made me a better clarinet player.

As you might have guessed, the name cross-country bothered me; but I really didn't dwell on it. (Okay, maybe a little.) Let me just bring up a couple of points, and then I'll move on. Why is it called cross-country? Nobody's going to be running from Boston to Los Angeles, at least nobody on the O'Rourke Middle School team. I mean, I have heard of adult runners doing that, but usually only for charity. Actually, I guess I wouldn't mind running across the country when I get older, but I'd only do it for something really important, you know, some worthwhile cause, certainly not "Blackberry Thumb". (I don't think that this paragraph constituted "dwelling", do you?)

Anyway, there were fourteen of us on the O'Rourke cross-country team, and as you might expect, I was the youngest runner at eleven and a half. Some of the eighth-graders had actually already turned thirteen. But unlike a lot of other sports, in cross-country physical maturity didn't matter as much. In fact, extra bulk and muscle development usually doesn't help distance runners. (But big muscles were not something I had to concern myself with anyway, at least not now; they were sort of in the same category as sex and 401(k) plans.)

You already know that I have difficulty accepting compliments, and I don't like to blow my own horn (clarinets don't count). But … well, I'm actually a pretty good runner. Our team was undefeated in October, and I came in first place all three times. Our cross-country course is only 1.6 miles, but still, for 11–13 year-olds, it's a pretty good challenge.

In case you don't know, in cross-country the team with the lowest score wins, just like golf. But, other than those two, I can't think of any other sport where that's true, can you? In fact, there are probably not too many things in life where less "wins". Well okay, getting stitches after you cut yourself, and maybe the number of times you throw up when you get a stomach bug, and … All right, I'll stop; I'm starting to dwell.

Anyway, back to the scoring in cross-country. The score for each team is calculated by adding up the numerical value of the place finish of each of the team's first five runners. Then you compare that total with the other team's total, and lowest score wins. (There is another wrinkle to the scoring system called "displacement", but since the explanation is only slightly less complicated than the D-Day invasion plans, if you're interested, you'll have to check it out yourself.)

As I've told you before, all this running was very exhilarating. Of course, the fact that I was having some success didn't hurt either. But there was a downside. I was usually up at 6:00 in the morning to get ready for school, and I didn't get home from practice until around 5:00 in the afternoon. By 8:00 most nights, I was ready for bed. And it seemed that on the days when I was most tired, I'd have nightmares, and they always involved running. But it wasn't the typical kind of running we've all experienced in our dreams, like when someone's chasing you. My nightmares were much more elaborate than that.

Have you ever seen *Marathon Man* with Dustin Hoffman and Sir Laurence Olivier? Well, my dream was like that. I was Dustin Hoffman's character, who was a distance runner that participated in marathons—hence the name of the movie. I was abducted by the Laurence Olivier character, who thought I could provide him with some information he needed. The Olivier character performed some unnecessary dental work on me without Novocain, all the time asking, "Is it safe? Is it safe?" And, as if that weren't bad enough, what really made the nightmare scary was that instead of Sir Laurence Olivier doing the dental work on me, it was Angelo, my barber.

There was one additional downside to distance running besides the nightmares. I began to notice the rapid development of one of the sex characteristics we had learned about in the maturation movie—active sweat glands. In my initial list, I had placed active sweat glands in the ninth level (are you listening, Dante?), but after I became aware of the odor that I was generating, I created a brand new level thirteen category. And I moved active sweat glands in there, away from everything else. Finally, Mom bought me some deodorant, and what a difference that made. I think my teammates appreciated it also. Prior to that, I was beginning to ascribe new meaning to the book title *Loneliness of the Long-Distance Runner*.

But you know, it's funny—once I started using deodorant, my nightmares disappeared too. Here I was blaming being tired as the cause of my nightmares, when it may simply have been lack of social interaction.

As I mentioned before, I came in first in all the meets we had in October. What made that even more special was that Mom and Dad were able to come and watch me run. They also brought Mr. and Mrs. Witkowski.

Now, cross-country isn't really much of a spectator sport, but that's why it meant so much to me that they were all there cheering me on, especially when I saw how their faces lit up when I crossed the finish line.

Chapter 16

On a Friday in late October, Derek, Vanessa, and I held an emergency TUCK meeting during lunchtime. With Halloween fast approaching, we had to make up our minds if we were going to participate or not. Given our lofty new status as seventh-graders, we had to decide whether we were above all this "trick-or-treating business", or whether our "sweet tooth" would win out. (By the way, just to keep you updated, "sweet tooth" is number 17 on my list of favorite metaphorical body parts.)

Anyway, we debated the trick-or-treating issue for a few minutes, with Derek punching in the notes on his BlackBerry. He was slower than usual because he could only use his left thumb; his right one had suffered a relapse. (I hope he doesn't have to use a Palumbo wrench any time soon.) We finally came to the conclusion that trick-or-treating was just "retro" enough to be cool, and therefore we were "in".

The second item on the agenda was also related to Halloween. Once we decided we were going to participate, we had to figure out what costumes we were going to wear.

Derek opted to go as Steve Jobs, the co-founder of Apple Computer. Since he had gone as Bill Gates in the past, Derek figured this would satisfy all FCC regulations regarding equal time. I tried to tell him that I didn't think FCC regulations applied to Halloween, but he said he just wanted to be on the safe side. Derek reminded me that the FCC had really tightened up after the "wardrobe malfunction" incident at the Super Bowl. (I never really understood that whole thing. What "malfunction"? I have no doubt that Janet Jackson exposed herself on purpose; how is that the blouse's fault?)

Vanessa decided to go as Nomar Garciaparra; that's Mia Hamm's husband. When Vanessa dressed up as Mia Hamm, not that many people knew who she was supposed to be. But she figured if she went as Nomar, despite the trans-gender issue, she would be much more recognizable. Even though Nomar doesn't play for the Red Sox anymore, people around Boston still know who he is. Of course, since Vanessa had the name Nomar embroidered on the back of her shirt in six-inch letters, it might have enhanced the identification process.

My costume choice was much less involved; I decided to go as a cross-country runner. I know it wasn't much of a stretch, but at least I didn't have to go searching for something to wear. And besides, dressed like that, there was a chance that some people might give me deodorant instead of candy. (I was still very sensitive about the "active sweat glands" issue.)

Oh by the way, speaking of candy, remember I mentioned that the manufacturer of Milk Duds wasn't going to use real chocolate in them anymore? Well, guess what I found out? **Hershey's** makes Milk Duds! Doesn't that make the situation even more bizarre? I mean, why would one of the world's largest producers of chocolate decide not to use it in one of their products? Have I uncovered a conspiracy here? Is Hershey's creating an artificial shortage, like OPEC does with oil? Do they have a large domestic supply of chocolate in Alaska that they can tap into whenever they want? I don't know what's going on here, but I'd appreciate some answers.

Despite all the lists I have generated, like favorite animals, favorite foods, favorite sex characteristics, etc., I don't yet have a list of favorite classes in school. I don't mean favorite courses like English or computer; I mean favorite individual lessons. If I finally do decide to create that list, without any doubt, the lesson we had in our advisory class following the TUCK meeting last November will be number one.

As Derek, Vanessa, and I approached the classroom after lunch, I noticed that Mr. Martin, our principal, was standing next to the doorway. As we entered, we all said, "Hello". I was a few steps behind Derek and Vanessa, and as I made eye contact with Mr. Martin, he said, "Nice running yesterday. Was that your fastest time?"

I stopped short, more than a little surprised. I didn't think Mr. Martin even knew who I was, never mind that I ran cross-country. But I managed to say, "Thanks ... Yes, it was my best time ... How did you know?"

"I just got there at the very end of the meet, but I did see the finish. You've come in first in all three of the races, haven't you?"

Now, I was even more surprised. "Yeah, but I didn't see you …"

Mr. Martin smiled. "I have my spies, Benny."

I smiled back. "Thanks, Mr. Martin. I'll see you later."

"Actually, you'll see me in just a minute. I'm going to be teaching this class today."

"Really, our advisory class? What's it going to be about?"

"You'll see in just a minute."

I went into the classroom and took my seat. After a few more minutes, all the students were where they were supposed to be, and Mr. Martin began.

"How is everybody today?"

There was a smattering of "Fine", "Good", "Excellent", and one "Awesome".

"Well, that sounds pretty positive. I hope you still feel that way when I tell you that I'm going to be teaching this class today."

There was a lot of head nodding and smiling.

"Well, that's a good sign too—no booing, no fruit or vegetables being thrown, especially since you just came from lunch. Okay then, let's get started."

"I know that recently you've been talking about 'understanding differences'. So today we're going to continue with that topic, but I want to start out by doing something a little different. We're going to do some brainstorming. I want you to think of words or phrases that describe 'things that aren't cool'. Please raise your hand, and wait to be called on, don't just shout out your ideas. Okay, so how about some words that describe 'things that aren't cool'?"

A number of students were called on, and Mr. Martin wrote the responses on the board—"stupid", "gross", "dumb", "bogus", etc.

"Okay, that's a pretty complete list. Now I need for you to give me some words that describe **people** that aren't cool."

That elicited "nerd", "loser", "retard", "jerk", etc. I had my hand raised to offer the word "dweeb", but then I figured that anyone who actually used the word "dweeb" might be perceived as being one, so I lowered my hand. (Did you realize that including "dweeb", there are only four words in modern English that begin with the letters "dw"? The others are "dwarf", "dwell", and "dwindle". In my list of favorite words that begin with "dw", "dwell" is first.—no big surprise there, huh?)

Anyway, Mr. Martin had written all of the responses about people on the board and then he said, "Okay, I think that's enough for now." He paused for a moment, still looking at the list and then continued. "Let me ask you a question. What do you think happens when we refer to people by using these terms, or when we put people in these kinds of categories?"

A number of students raised their hands and offered some ideas. One student said, "We don't show people respect if we call them names." Another student suggested that when we refer to people with those words "we're putting a label on them".

Mr. Martin encouraged the students to elaborate on some of their answers, and then he said, "That was very good; it's just what I was looking for. So, let's consider the idea of labeling. What if I suggest to you that labeling people is a lazy thing to do? What do you think I mean by that?"

Nobody put up their hands immediately, but after a few moments, Vanessa raised hers, and offered that "Labeling doesn't treat people as individuals; it's like stereotyping."

"That's excellent."

For the next few minutes, Mr. Martin explained further about stereotyping and labeling. He gave additional examples that illustrated, as one of the students had suggested, how labeling gets in the way of showing respect to people; and then Mr. Martin began the part of the lesson that made such an impression on me.

"I want to share with you a personal situation that I think will help you further understand what we've been discussing. It's about my son Michael. Michael is twenty-two years old, and just graduated from a special high school. For those of you who don't know, students with special needs, often attend school well beyond age eighteen to help them develop as many skills as possible."

"When we first realized that Michael had some problems, we brought him to be evaluated. Unfortunately, no one was able to specifically diagnose his condition. So the doctors and educators didn't know where to 'place' Michael, what category to put him in. Eventually, he was labeled as 'mentally retarded'." As he finished this last sentence, Mr. Martin underlined the word "retard" on the board, and then continued.

"Like most labels, 'retarded' doesn't tell you very much about the individual person—what he's capable of doing, or what limitations he has. So even though Michael had the 'official' label of 'mentally retarded', it didn't really describe him. My wife and I decided that we had to look past that particular label, if we were going to help our son. What we discovered was that Michael had a lot of **autistic** characteristics. Does anyone know what autism is?"

A couple of students raised their hands, and Mr. Martin called on one of them. "Yes, Katie."

"My cousin is autistic. He's thirteen and he doesn't talk very much, and he likes to be by himself. Sometimes he kind of rocks back and forth, and oh yeah, he likes to watch the same shows over and over."

"Thank you Katie, that was very helpful." He paused for a moment. "A lot of people with autism do those things that Katie mentioned; my son Michael even does some of them. But what doctors and scientists are finding out is that almost nobody has **all** of the characteristics of autism. So, instead of labeling people as autistic, doctors have created an 'autism spectrum'." As he said this, Mr. Martin drew a line on the board. On one end he wrote "non-verbal", and on the other end he wrote "high-functioning".

"You should know that the terms I've written up here aren't official or medical terms, but they should help illustrate what I'm trying to get at. People that have autistic characteristics usually have trouble in the areas of communication, social interactions, and understanding the world around them. If I were to place Michael somewhere on this spectrum, it would probably be about ¾ of the way toward 'high-functioning'."

"Scientists don't know what causes autism. There are some newer theories out there that suggest that **mercury** might have something to do with it—the element mercury, not the planet ... or the car, for that matter."

Most of the class started to laugh as Mr. Martin continued. "Even though there's no proven cause of autism, many doctors believe that most people on the autism spectrum receive 'information' through their senses in a very exaggerated way. For example, if someone drops a glass, an individual with autism might hear that sound as being twice as loud as other people. If someone taps an autistic person on the shoulder, it might feel to the autistic person like he was being slapped."

"So according to this theory, guess what occurs when things like I just described happen to autistic people? Their brains figure out a way to shut out all the things that hurt their senses, and they kind of go inside themselves; they close themselves off to the rest of the world. And that's exactly what we observed in Michael when he was very little."

"Michael has always loved watching television, videos, and DVD's. When he was very small he would watch *Sesame Street* for hours on end. He would become so engrossed in it that even when we were right next to him, and tried to get his attention, we couldn't. We actually started to believe he had a hearing problem. In fact, one day when Michael was fixated on the TV, I got the tops of two pans and struck them together like cymbals. Michael didn't budge. That's when we had him evaluated again."

"The doctors said he definitely wasn't deaf. In fact, he had a heightened sense of hearing. When we related other stories about Michael's behavior, and they ran some additional tests, the doctors concluded that Michael had some autistic behaviors, but was not 'classically autistic'. So that's how the label 'mentally retarded' was given to him."

"When we were speaking to the doctors, they told us that some autistic people are able to do amazing things. Some of them have what's called 'savant-like abilities'." He wrote that phrase on the board. "Now don't get the wrong idea; they're not like superheroes—none of them can fly, and they don't have x-ray vision, but what they can do is still pretty unbelievable. And Michael has some of these 'savant-like abilities'."

A lot of the students started to look at each other across the rows of desks with wide-eyed expressions on their faces, in anticipation of what was to come. And Mr. Martin didn't disappoint us. For the next thirty minutes he told us one amazing story after another about what Michael was able to do.

The first story he told us occurred when Michael was around six months old. Mr. Martin said that Michael never liked to be held as a baby. (It was probably due to his exaggerated response to being touched.) So it was very hard to comfort him when he started crying, particularly at night when he was supposed to be sleeping. Mr. Martin and his wife decided that maybe taking Michael for a ride in the car would settle him down. And it did. But what they began to realize was that after he stopped crying and they were on their way home, as soon as they turned onto their street, Michael would start crying again. Originally, they thought it was just a coincidence. There was no way that a six-month-old baby knew where his house was located. But the next time they took Michael into the car, they decided to go home a different way, just to see what happened. Sure enough, when they turned onto their street, Michael started crying immediately. And it happened **every time** after that! Mr. Martin said that if that had been the only thing that Michael did that was unexplainable, he and his wife would not have thought that much of it. But there was much more to come.

Mr. Martin told us that Michael didn't begin talking until he was about eighteen months old. And even then, it was hard to understand him. His vocabulary was limited to things he could see or touch, things that were right in front of him. When Mr. Martin came home from work, he would greet his son by saying, "Hi, Mike"; and Michael would respond back, "Hi, Mike". Michael didn't even understand that "Hi" was a greeting, and "Mike" was his name. During the next year of Michael's life, at an age when most children were showing an interest in books, Michael didn't want any part of them. He just wanted to watch TV or videos.

However, just before Michael's third birthday, something amazing happened—Michael started to read. It seems that one day Mr. Martin went out to the mailbox to retrieve the mail. One of the pieces of mail was *Newsweek* magazine. Mr. Martin said he put it on the coffee table in the living room and went into the kitchen to get a glass of water. When he returned to the living room, Michael had the magazine in his hand, and read the headlines out loud—"Crisis in the Middle East". (As a side note, while Mr. Martin said that he was sure of when this specific incident took place, he couldn't verify it by that particular headline, because unfortunately, that same headline appeared about every two weeks, no matter what year it was.)

Although Mr. Martin was stunned by what it appeared his son was able to do, he still thought it was possible that Michael had seen the cover of *Newsweek* on a commercial; and that all he did was repeat what the person on TV had said. So Mr. Martin decided to sit with Michael and ask him to read some more. It was very unusual for Michael to be willing to sit still to do anything. But on that particular day, Michael did sit with his father for about ten minutes. And, while Michael's willingness to sit still for that length of time was surprising, it paled in comparison to hearing Michael read out loud **every paragraph** Mr. Martin asked him to.

Mr. Martin said that Michael mispronounced a few words, but overall he read every sentence like someone who was in the fifth or sixth grade. Mr. Martin said he remembered thinking. "How is this possible? Michael can't understand the difference between a greeting and his own name. And yet he's able to read, and nobody taught him how." After Mr. Martin told his wife what had happened, they both came to the conclusion that Michael must have learned how to read from watching *Sesame Street*, but they couldn't be sure.

Mr. Martin said that since Michael didn't actually comprehend what he was reading, technically he was just decoding words, not reading them. But, regardless of what it was called, you could see by the expressions on the faces of the kids in the advisory class that they were totally awestruck by the story they had just heard.

Mr. Martin went on to say that one of the reasons Michael couldn't comprehend what he was reading was because he could only understand about concrete things, things he could touch. There was no way for him to understand that a word on a page was a symbol for the real object.

Another problem Michael had was that he couldn't generalize. For example, Mr. Martin told us that Michael would know enough to throw away an empty candy wrapper, but wouldn't know what to do with a banana peel. So he had to be taught about all of the potential pieces of trash, individually.

Despite some of these challenges, Michael began to make progress in a lot of areas, particularly once he started at the special school he attended. However, in some other areas, Michael was a complete mystery, especially concerning the savant-type abilities he continued to display.

It was evident very early on that Michael had an incredible memory. His primary grade teachers indicated that Michael could spell any word correctly after he had seen it just once.

And one day when Michael was bowling at the Special Olympics, the automatic scoring machine broke down and Michael kept a running score of all five players who were bowling with him, **in his head.** He didn't make one mistake.

Michael could tell you the record of every professional sports team in the four major sports for the last twenty years. He could tell you all of the college basketball teams that qualified for the NCAA tournament for the past two decades, and where they were seeded, how far they went in the tournament, and the scores of all the "Final Four" games. (Mr. Martin said that his son probably didn't inherit that amazing memory from him. "I have trouble remembering what I had for breakfast.")

Although Mr. Martin said he wasn't sure if the story he was about to relate to us had anything to do with Michael's incredible memory, it was, in his opinion, the most amazing thing Michael had ever done.

Mr. Martin explained that Michael has the ability to tell you what day of the week any date from the 20th century or the 21st century has fallen on, or will fall on. He has what's called a "perpetual calendar" in his head. (I didn't get the chance to ask Mr. Martin why Michael could only figure out the dates for the current century, and the last one. I hoped it had nothing to do with Julius and Augustus messing with the calendar.) Anyway, here's Mr. Martin's description of how he found out about Michael's ability.

Back in November of 1999, the Martin family was having Thanksgiving dinner. Mr. Martin's sister, who was visiting from out of state, was also celebrating her 40th birthday. Someone at the dinner table mentioned that Mr. Martin's sister had actually been born on Thanksgiving day exactly forty years ago. Michael spoke up and said, "No she wasn't. November 25th was a Wednesday in 1959, not a Thursday." When they checked, Michael was right.

Mr. Martin then asked Michael about some other dates in the past, like December 7th, 1941, the attack on Pearl Harbor. Michael didn't even hesitate; he just responded, "Sunday", which of course was correct also. Finally, after a few more calendar questions, which were followed by all correct responses, Mr. Martin said to Michael, "How did you do that?"

According to Mr. Martin, whenever he had posed this question to Michael in the past, following something incredible he had done, Michael had looked at his father as if to say, "What do you mean, how did I do that? Why can't you do that?" But this time Michael responded, "I used the 'twenty-eight-year differential'."

Mr. Martin said he was totally stunned by Michael's response, and he tried to prod him for more information about this 'twenty-eight-year differential', but Michael couldn't explain it any further. Mr. Martin was able to find out from Michael however, that he hadn't learned about it in school, and nobody in the Martin family had taught it to him. In fact, in checking with all of them, nobody had ever heard of it.

In the next several days after Thanksgiving, Mr. Martin said he talked to math teachers at O'Rourke Middle School and at the local high school. He called math professors at colleges in the area. He tried the library and the Internet—**Nothing**!

Then about two weeks later, Mr. Martin was watching a news program on TV, and the reporter was interviewing a professor from MIT. The professor was talking about the so-called "Y2K glitch"—the concern that when the year changed from 1999 to 2000, computers would crash. But the professor said there was nothing to worry about because he and some of his colleagues had run a test. They had "tricked" the computers into thinking it was going to be 1972, and the results were fine. The interviewer asked the professor why they chose 1972, and he answered, "Because the calendar repeats itself every 28 years."

All the students in the class sat in stunned silence for a few moments, and then Derek asked, "Is that true; does the calendar repeat itself every 28 years?"

Mr. Martin responded, "It appears that it does, but I have no idea how Michael figured that out, or how he came up with that name."

During the last few minutes of the class, Mr. Martin told us some additional things about another side of Michael. It seems that Michael has never told a lie in his life. He's not capable of doing that. He can't even shade the truth. (Looks like a career in politics is out.) Evidently, because Michael's such a concrete thinker, he sees everything in "black and white"; there are no "gray areas". When he was growing up, Mr. and Mrs. Martin told him to always tell the truth, and he always has. He is the ultimate "tell it like it is" person.

Mr. Martin related a funny incident concerning Michael's penchant for truth-telling. Three years ago, when Michael had just turned nineteen, the Martin family was flying somewhere on vacation. Of course, all adults had to show a photo I.D. at the ticket counter in order to be able to board the plane. The woman behind the ticket counter said, "I need to see your photo identification please, unless you're under eighteen?" Now, Mr. Martin hadn't thought to get Michael a photo I.D., so he just said, "My son's only seventeen." Of course Michael overheard this, and said very loudly, "No I'm not, Dad; I'm nineteen. Don't you remember; I was born on Thursday, July twenty-first …?"

Fortunately, Michael had a school photo I.D. with him, which after a bit of haggling was finally accepted. (I'll bet nobody in Michael's family ever asks him questions like, "What do you think of my haircut?", or "Does this outfit make me look fat?".)

Mr. Martin finished up telling us about Michael by indicating that his son had never uttered a swear word in his life and had never intentionally hurt anyone's feelings. And then he posed this question to the class. "If there's someone that can do all the amazing things Michael can do, who never tells a lie, who never uses bad language, who always treats other people with respect, should that person be labeled with this word?" And he pointed to the word "retard" on the board.

Nobody said anything for a few moments, and then Vanessa raised her hand.

"Yes, Vanessa."

"Well, I kind of think it's unfair. I mean wouldn't we be a lot better off, if people were more like Michael?"

Mr. Martin smiled. "Yes, I think in many ways we would." He then checked the clock on the wall and said, "I wish we had more time, but the bell is about to ring. I want to thank you for paying attention … and I want to ask you a favor. I hope you come away from today's class understanding how labels can be misleading and can even hurt people … I'd like to begin to eliminate some of them, at least at our school … So, I'm going to ask you not to use the word 'retard' anymore when talking about other people, even if it's just kidding around. Let's not ever hear that word again at O'Rourke. And this isn't really about Michael; it's about treating everybody with respect, and not putting labels on people that can hurt them. Okay? Can we try to do that?" Just then the bell rang, and the class was over.

I didn't think about anything else besides Michael and Mr. Martin for the rest of the school day. And I suspect most of the other kids in that advisory class didn't either. Even when school ended, as I headed down to the locker room to change for cross-country practice, I was still thinking about it.

As I turned the corner near the gym, I noticed Mr. Martin about twenty feet in front of me. He was talking with two girls who had also been in the advisory class earlier in the day. As I got closer, I stopped at a water fountain to get a drink, and I couldn't help but overhear the conversation. One of the girls said, "That was really interesting today, Mr. Martin, but if your son's not autistic, and he's not really retarded, then what would you call him?"

Even though I didn't think the girl meant anything bad by her question, as I passed by the three of them, I said the first thing that came into my head, "You'd call him Michael." And I disappeared into the locker room.

Over the weekend, I was still thinking about the advisory class. I even told Mom and Dad about it. When I finished relating what Mr. Martin had told us, Mom was the first one to say something. "That's truly amazing. I give Mr. Martin a lot of credit; it must have been difficult for him to talk about."

"I don't know, Mom. It didn't seem to bother him. It was more like … he thought that by telling us, it would make the school better."

"You mean, because of the way kids will treat each other?"

"Yeah, I think so."

Dad joined in. "What does Mr. Martin's son do, now that he's out of school?"

"I don't know."

"Can he work?"

"I'm not sure. There really wasn't much time to ask questions."

Mom spoke up again. "When you were telling us about all this, Benny, you seemed kind of sad."

"I guess a little bit."

"Why would you be sad?"

"I'm not exactly sure. Mr. Martin didn't seem sad, and he told us that Michael liked watching sports on TV and playing video games. You know, stuff like that, so it doesn't seem like Michael is unhappy. Maybe it's just that it seems Michael is missing out on some things. I don't know."

Actually, I did know a little bit more about why I was feeling the way I was, but it hadn't crystallized in my brain yet, and so I wasn't really ready to discuss it. Somewhat to my surprise however, I did get the opportunity to do just that on the following Monday.

As I was walking to Spanish class, the last period before lunch, I spotted Dr. Foster. I often saw him in the building on Fridays, but I'd never seen him there on a Monday before. "Hi, Dr. Foster."

He turned at the mention of his name. "Well, hi, Benny; good to see you."

"How come you're here today?"

"I was just dropping off the MCAS results from last spring."

"Oh, are those for our grade, the ones we took in May?"

"Yes, they're going to be mailed out next week sometime." He paused for a moment, and got a curious expression on his face. "Since when are you interested in MCAS?"

"I don't know; I was just wondering ..."

He continued to watch me, as the sentence trailed off. "Benny, I've known you since you were three. I can usually tell when something's on your mind. And I'm sure it's not MCAS. You've gotten a perfect score every single year. So, what's going on?"

I kind of gave him a half smile. "Maybe I just wanted to see if I kept my record intact."

"Not buying it."

My smile got bigger. "Well, there is something I wouldn't mind talking about, but I've got Spanish class, and you're probably ..."

"When do you have lunch?"

"After Spanish."

"How about then?"

"Don't you have to get back to the elementary school?"

"You know, Benny, Mrs. Stanton is a real taskmaster, but she does allow me to eat lunch ... at least on Mondays."

I chuckled. "Are you sure you don't mind?"

"Of course not. After Spanish, why don't you go and get your lunch in the cafeteria, and bring it to the guidance office? I'm sure I'll be able to find an empty conference room there."

"That'd be great. Thanks."

"Oh and by the way, congratulations on all your wins in cross-country."

"How do you know about that?"

"Sometimes we spies share information."

The classroom where I have Spanish is very close to the cafeteria, so I was able to get in and out of there quickly. Dr. Foster was waiting for me in one of the small conference rooms usually used for speech therapy or special testing.

"Come on in, Benny. Sit down."

"Thanks." I paused. "So really, how did you know about my running?"

"Mr. Martin told me. He keeps tabs on everything at the school." He paused. "I hope you weren't thinking about that all through Spanish class. Were you?"

"No ... well, maybe a little."

Dr. Foster smiled. "You keep forgetting how well I know you."

"True, but I'm getting better at not dwelling on things. I'm certainly not doing it as much as I used to, but it's tough to go cold turkey."

Dr. Foster continued to smile, as I kept talking. "Maybe, since I was just in Spanish class, I should say, 'it's tough to give up the whole enchilada'." (I don't have a list for my favorite metaphorical food phrases, but I'm considering it.)

Now Dr. Foster started to laugh. "I gotta tell you, Benny, I miss this."

"Yeah, me too."

We were both silent for a moment, and then Dr. Foster spoke up. "So tell me, does this have anything to do with last Friday's advisory?"

"How did you know about that? I think you really do have spies."

"I ran into Mr. Martin as I was leaving the building after school on Friday. He told me about the class and what you said outside the locker room. He was very touched by that. He said he was going to speak with you about it, but he probably hasn't had a chance yet."

"He didn't think I was being a smart aleck?"

"No, not at all; why would you think that?"

"Well, I don't think that girl meant anything by her question, and then what I said just kind of came out of my mouth. It was sort of a flip remark."

Dr. Foster scrunched up his face and began shaking his head. "I certainly didn't get that impression from Mr. Martin. And, I'll tell you something, Benny, it's not always the case, but I think most of the time, the first things that come out of our mouths are what we really believe or feel, otherwise they wouldn't be right there in the front of our brains for us to grab hold of."

"I guess that's probably true."

Dr. Foster studied me for a moment, and then he tilted his head and asked, "But that's not all you wanted to talk about, is it?"

"No, not quite."

"Okay, you're going to have to pick up the pace here, we only have ten more minutes of lunch."

I started to smile. "How much did Mr. Martin tell you about the class? Do you know all about his son, Michael?"

"Yes, I've met Michael a few times. I really enjoy him."

"So, do you think he's happy?"

"Yes, I think he is; although since his mother died, things have been difficult."

"Mr. Martin's wife died? When?"

"Oh, it was probably a year and a half ago. He didn't mention it when he talked to your class?"

"No, I had no idea."

"Maybe he'd prefer that students didn't know. Please don't say anything."

"I won't."

There were a few moments of silence, and then Dr. Foster said, "It seems like you've been doing a lot of thinking about Michael. How come?"

I had my head down and didn't answer right away. When I finally made eye contact again I said, "When Mr. Martin was talking in class, I kept thinking about how similar I am to Michael."

"What do you mean?"

"Well, Mr. Martin talked about Michael's memory, and I know I can't do those things with the calendar, but I can do a lot of the other stuff. It just got me thinking ... How come Michael turned out the way he did, and I turned out the way I did? Is there some chemical in my brain that Michael doesn't have, or some circuit that got connected in my head, but not in his?"

"I hope those questions are meant to be rhetorical, Benny. Because I don't think there's a medical person, or a philosopher, or even a clergyman for that matter, who can answer them. Is that why you asked whether Michael was happy? Because you think you could have been like Michael?"

"I guess so."

"It almost sounds like you feel guilty because you have some of the same abilities as Michael, but you don't have any of the limitations."

"No, I don't exactly feel guilty. I just wish somebody could do something to make Michael better. I don't know, 'better' isn't the right word ..."

"I think I know what you mean though. But I'm afraid nobody has that power, Benny."

"I guess I know that in my head, but somehow it felt better to say it out loud. But I think I probably need to sort all this out for myself."

"This is pretty heavy stuff."

"Yeah, I know."

"If you want to talk some more, just let me know."

"Thanks, but I think I have to do this on my own."

"Okay." He paused briefly. "So, what happened to that guy who didn't like to analyze things?"

"It's funny you should say that. I actually do think about things much more than I used to, especially when I'm running."

"That's interesting. Maybe that's why you're so good; all that thinking takes your mind off how exhausted you are."

"I never thought of that. Maybe I should skip the rest of my classes today and go out and run a few miles, so I can properly analyze whether that's true or not."

As it turned out, for the next several months, there would be something else occupying my mind whenever I was running.

Two weeks after my conversation with Dr. Foster, around Veterans Day, I got off the school bus at about 4:45 after practice and walked home. Mom was sitting at the kitchen table when I came in.

"Hi, sweetie."

"Hi, Mom."

"Benny, could you put your things in your room, and then come back into the kitchen; I need to talk to you about something."

There was obvious concern in Mom's voice, so all sorts of things were going through my head as I deposited my backpack in my room and headed back toward the kitchen. Once I sat down, Mom didn't pull any punches; she just said, "Mr. Witkowski's in the hospital; he had a stroke."

Chapter 17

It's a funny thing about the word "stroke". When it's part of a phrase, it seems to suggest something very positive, like "a stroke of good fortune", or "a stroke of genius", or even Tiger Woods' favorite, "a stroke under par". But when the word "stroke" is all by itself, with no other words around, well that's a different story. When it's all by itself, it seems to take the form of an invisible arrow that comes in through your ears, registers in your brain, and then heads straight for your heart.

Maybe there are some other words that do the same thing, but I couldn't think of any, although I didn't try very hard. Having one word that acts like that and can cause that much pain is probably enough anyway.

Once I was finally able to process what Mom had told me, I blurted out, "Oh no! What happened?" And Mom went on to explain as much as she knew at that point.

Mrs. Witkowski told Mom that Mr. Witkowski was complaining of a headache after eating breakfast and had gone back to bed to try to get rid of it. He got up about a half hour later and said it wasn't much better. Mrs. Witkowski then called the doctor and said she was bringing her husband into the office. On the way over, his symptoms got worse, and Mrs. Witkowski decided to drive straight to the hospital. Mr. Witkowski evidently collapsed just as they were checking in.

"How bad is it, Mom?"

"Well, they don't think it's life-threatening at this point, but with stroke victims, what happens during the first forty-eight hours usually gives you a good indication of what's to come."

"Is he paralyzed?"

Mom hesitated. "Yes, completely on his right side." She hesitated again. "And he can't speak." She saw the expression on my face and quickly added, "But those things may be temporary. Sometimes people who have had a stroke can't talk because they've lost the use of the muscles that help them form words, or sometimes they can't talk because their brain forgets **how** to form words."

"I know Mr. Witkowski's about eighty years old, but he's so active; it seems like he's in really good shape."

Mom smiled. "Yes, he is Benny. And I think that will really help him overcome this."

"So, you think he'll be okay?"

"There's no way to know for sure." Mom paused. "Remember when I used to volunteer at the hospital?"

"Yeah."

"One of the things I did was to read to the patients, and some of them were stroke victims. It's more difficult for older people to recover very quickly, but because of the fact that Mr. Witkowski takes such good care of himself, and he'll push himself to get better, I have a good feeling about this."

Sometimes when people say things like that, they're just trying to make **you** feel better, and they don't believe it themselves. But in this case, I think Mom believed everything she said to me. So after the initial shock, deep down, I began to think that things were going to be all right.

I was also feeling optimistic because of the hospital where Mr. Witkowski was a patient. It wasn't just that Mom had volunteered there; it was because the hospital was rated among the top 100 hospitals in the country. (I don't have a list of favorite hospitals, but if Mr. Witkowski gets better, I'm going to start one. No question which hospital will be number one on that list.)

Mom and I continued talking for a few more minutes, and then Dad came home from work. Although Mom had called him earlier, she didn't have much information until just before I walked in the door. She repeated some of the things she had told me, and answered some of Dad's questions. When she finished, Dad looked over at me and said, "Well, if I were going to bet, I'd bet on Mr. Witkowski; he's a fighter."

Mom smiled at me and nodded her head. "That's just what I told Benny, too."

"Do you think I can go see him?" I said.

Mom responded. "Not yet, Benny. Technically, you're supposed to be at least twelve before you're allowed to visit. But you probably shouldn't go right away anyhow. Like I said, the first forty-eight hours or so ... Let's see how things develop. I still know a lot of people at the hospital, so I don't think your age will be a problem, but we have to see what the doctors advise about visitors. Okay?"

"Okay." I paused. "Do Grandma and Grandpa know?"

"Yes, I already called them. Later on I'm going to call Vanessa's parents and Derek's parents and also Dr. Foster."

Dad agreed. "That's a good idea. Is there anything else we can do to help out?"

"Mrs. Witkowski told me that her children and some of her grandchildren are coming in the next couple of days. So, I offered in the meantime to drive her back and forth to the hospital. She said she doesn't mind driving during the day, but if I could drive her at night, she would really appreciate it. I'm taking her tonight at about seven. I'm just dropping her off and then picking her up when visiting hours are over. As I said before, they don't want anyone in to see him except for immediate family at this point."

That night I suspected I was going to have trouble sleeping because of Mr. Witkowski, but I didn't. I think I was so emotionally exhausted that my brain decided to shut everything down for a while and let me regroup. Just before I did fall asleep, however, I remember thinking how lucky I was. No really bad things have ever happened to me, or to people I care about, until now. I mean, my biggest challenges in life have to do with updating my list of favorite animals and checking whether the Milk Duds I got for Halloween contain real chocolate. (By the way, nobody gave me deodorant when I was trick-or-treating. I'm taking that as a compliment.)

A week later as I headed to the cafeteria for lunch, I heard Dr. Foster's voice from behind me. "Benny, Benny, can I see you for a second?"

"Hi, Dr. Foster." I tilted my head and got a questioning look on my face. "Two Mondays in a row?"

"Yeah, I'm here for one of your health classes. You have it later on today, right?"

"Last period. Are you teaching the class?"

"Part of it. I'm going to talk about the decision-making process related to the unit you just finished on smoking. So anyway, that's why I'm here today. But then when I saw you, I thought you might know more about how Mr. Witkowski's doing. I spoke to your mom last Thursday, but I was wondering if there was anything new."

"Mom said that there's been some improvement; and it looks like he's understanding what people are saying, but he still can't respond. The real good news is that the doctors don't think there's any immediate risk that he'll have another one."

"That is good news. Have you been able to visit him?"

"No, but I think Mom's making arrangements for Vanessa, Derek, and me to go this Thursday. Most of his family was here last week, but they've gone home, although some of them are coming back at Thanksgiving."

"I think I'm going over to see him tonight." He paused. "Oh, congratulations by the way, on coming in first again. When was it, last Wednesday?"

"Yeah, it was. Thanks." I got a puzzled expression on my face.

"No spies this time. Your mom told me when she called."

I nodded my head and smiled. "Remember when I told you that sometimes when I'm running, I analyze things in my head?"

"Yeah, I remember you saying that."

"Well, now I don't really analyze things, I just think about Mr. Witkowski. Whenever I'm really tired or I feel like slowing down, I think about what he's going through, and it kind of spurs me on. It's like, if I run faster, then he'll get better. I guess it sounds pretty silly, huh?"

"No, I don't think so. It actually sounds uh ... almost spiritual, almost like praying."

"Well, I do say prayers for him, but this feels like I'm doing something ... I don't know ... more tangible."

Dr. Foster smiled at me and said, "I think that's great, Benny", and then he patted me on the shoulder. "You'd better grab some lunch; I'll see you later."

So, did you notice the sequence of the units in my health class?—Dr. Foster was going to talk to our class about the decision—making process related to **smoking.** And that immediately followed the unit on **sex.** Smoking after sex—talk about a cliché. Either whoever sequenced the curriculum has a good sense of humor, or they know nothing about symbolism.

To be fair, it was probably just a coincidence. I think the real reason we were studying smoking in November was because of The Great American Smokeout. Now obviously, there aren't too many seventh-graders who smoke, and none that I knew of at O'Rourke. But there were still a lot of parents and grandparents that did, so students could get extra credit on their health grade if they could get adults to sign up for the Smokeout. I wasn't eligible because I actually didn't know anyone who smoked. Come to think of it, that's probably extra credit enough.

During each of the four marking periods in the school year, all seventh-graders were required to do a project for our health and advisory classes. Since we didn't have tests or quizzes in those courses, the projects served as the primary means of assessing how much we had learned. Most of the projects had to be approved by the teacher beforehand, and they had to relate to one of the topics we had studied.

Many of the students chose to do reports, posters, or research papers about the unit we had on sex. (I think they were hoping that "life would imitate art".) One student actually did a diorama. (Don't ask.)

I decided to do a report on smoking for my project. (I was going to say that I know that smoking is not quite as sexy as sex, but I don't like redundancy.) Actually, the main reason I wanted to do my project about smoking was because I thought it might give me some insight into why people take up smoking, but it didn't. I gotta tell you, I just don't get it; I don't see the attraction, and I'm not sure I ever will.

Most historians believe that the first people to use tobacco were from the Mayan Civilization. (I thought the Mayan Civilization was supposed to be pretty advanced—maybe not as much as we believed.) I mean, what were they thinking? How did anyone even come up with the idea of smoking?

I'm picturing something like this—"Hey Apocalypto, you see these dried up leaves on the ground? Well, I'm gonna roll them up and put them in my mouth, but I'm not gonna eat them. Get this. I'm gonna set them on fire, right next to my face, and then I'm gonna breathe in the smoke. Whatta you think?"

I can imagine Apocalypto shaking his head back and forth, and replying. "Hey Dudeo, why would you do that? It sounds like maybe you've already been smoking something." (Actually, he probably didn't say those exact words; I don't think Apocalypto liked redundancy either.)

It's also believed that Sir Walter Raleigh was the first Englishman to smoke. (Now there's a distinction I wish I had as part of my biography.) He's also credited with laying his coat across a puddle so that Queen Elizabeth wouldn't get her shoes muddied. I know that what he did was viewed as the ultimate act of chivalry, but I'm not so sure. I actually think his coat reeked of cigarette smoke; the public washing of clothes was quite common in Elizabethan times, and the puddle was handy. You do the math.

On Wednesday afternoon we had our final cross-country meet. Our team was 5–0, and I had come in first place each time. But this meet was going to be a really tough one. The school we were competing against was also undefeated; and their best runner was an eighth-grader who hadn't lost in two years.

During the entire race, just like the week before, I thought of Mr. Witkowski. It was like all the strength he had lost was being passed along to me. I know that sounds strange, but that's what it felt like. Anyway, we won the meet 27–28 to finish the season undefeated. I ran my fastest time and won by three seconds.

As I said before, cross-country isn't a big spectator sport, so we rarely have many people watching, other than family. But after I crossed the finish line and looked around, I noticed that the crowd was larger than usual. (Of course, "crowd" is a relative term in this context.) The stalwarts were all there, like Mom and Dad, and Derek and Vanessa, but I wasn't expecting to see Dr. Foster, and definitely not Mrs. Witkowski. On the other hand, I guess I shouldn't have been as surprised as I was because "family" is a relative term also. (No pun intended.)

The next day during homeroom, Derek, Vanessa, and I held a TUCK meeting. We were scheduled to visit Mr. Witkowski that afternoon, and we thought it was probably a good idea to talk about it ahead of time. I started the conversation. "My mom says that Mr. Wikowski can probably hear and understand what people are saying, but he can't really respond. He can move one of his hands just a little bit, but he can't write or use a keyboard, so there's no way for him to communicate what he's thinking."

Vanessa spoke up next. "It's so sad; I mean, he's such a nice man. Is he going to get better?"

"Nobody knows for sure, but my mom says there are some good signs, like with his hands."

Derek entered the conversation. "He'll recognize us and everything, right?"

"Yeah, everybody thinks so. It's just that he doesn't have any way of acknowledging it. But the doctors believe the more familiar faces he sees, the better. Anyway, my mom will pick you up at four o'clock, okay?"

On the ride over to the hospital that afternoon, Mom tried to prepare us some more for how Mr. Witkowski would look, but I think the three of us were still surprised. We didn't stay very long because there wasn't much we could say or do, but I was glad we went.

Twice during our visit, I thought I saw the very corner of Mr. Witkowski's mouth turn up ever so slightly. The first time was when Derek told him he would clean out and update Mr. Witkowski's e-mail account, so that as soon as he got better, he could use it.

The other attempt at a smile, if that's what it was, occurred when Vanessa held Mr. Witkowski's hand and told him that I had finished the cross-country season undefeated, and that we expected to see him at all the spring track meets.

On the way home in the car, Mom said, "You guys were terrific. I know it wasn't easy seeing him like that, but he is getting better, and you helped just by being there."

Vanessa then asked Mom, "How long will he be in the hospital?"

"That's hard to say. At his age probably longer than most people who have had a stroke. But after he leaves the hospital, it's likely he'll have to go someplace for more intense rehabilitation, you know, for walking and talking. Sometimes people who have had a stroke can go home shortly afterwards and have their rehabilitation at home. But I don't think Mr. Witkowski will be ready to do that any time soon; he needs too much looking after."

Derek asked, "Eventually though, is he going to be all right?"

"No one's sure, Derek. But despite his age, he's got a lot of things in his favor. So, I'm going to say 'yes'." As she finished the sentence, Mom made eye contact with Derek in the rear-view mirror and smiled.

The following night, Mom was later than usual coming back from picking up Mrs. Witkowski at the hospital. When she came in through the back door, Dad was sitting in the kitchen, and I was lying on the couch in the living room reading a running magazine. I heard Dad say, "Is everything all right? You look upset; it's not Mr. Witkowski, is it?"

I started to get up from the couch when I heard Dad's question, but I sat back down when Mom responded. "No, no, not really. I mean it's not about his condition; he's actually doing better." Mom paused. "It's just that when I was driving Mrs. Witkowski home, she told me that the doctors want to move Mr. Witkowski to a skilled nursing facility where he can get additional rehabilitation."

"Well, that's good news, isn't it?"

"Yes, but it's very expensive."

"But he's covered by Medicare, right?"

"Yes, but when Mrs. Witkowski talked to the social worker, she found out that Medicare only provides full coverage for the first twenty days. Then they have to come up with a $100 co-payment each day for the next eighty days ... about $3000 a month. And after that, the family has to pay about **$300** a day."

"You're kidding; I had no idea. Can that be right?"

"Yeah, it is. Mrs. Witkowski doesn't know what to do. She told me that they refinanced their house last year to help out their youngest son and his family. Their son's making the mortgage payment for them, but their other expenses don't leave a lot of extra money, certainly not $3000 a month. She thinks that their other two children might be able to help out, but she hasn't asked them yet. She just found out about all of this." Mom shook her head and then continued.

"Joe, she's actually thinking about selling the house. She said at least that way she could come up with about $40,000–$50,000."

"What about an equity loan?"

"When they refinanced, they were left with only 10% equity in the house, so that's not really an option."

"We could probably help out a little."

"I told her that, but she said she hadn't told me about the situation so that I'd offer them money. I told her I knew that, but nevertheless, we'd do whatever we could. She said she really appreciated the offer, but she wanted to talk with her children first, and then she'd get back to us."

"How soon is he going to be moved to the rehabilitation center?"

"I think they're looking at the Monday after Thanksgiving. But my understanding is that the facility won't accept him until Mrs. Witkowski makes some sort of financial commitment. I don't know if she has to sign a contract, or make a deposit; this is a real mess."

"How was that part left?"

"As I said, she won't do anything until she talks to the rest of her family. And then I guess we'll talk some more, probably sometime Sunday."

"Is there anyone you know at the hospital that could give her some other ideas?"

"I know the social worker Mrs. Witkowski spoke with. She knows what she's doing. If there were any other options, she would have found them." Things were quiet for a moment, and then Mom said, "You know, I think I need to just sleep on this tonight. I'm going to change into my nightgown. Could you make me some hot chocolate?"

"Nothing stronger?"

"No, I need some comfort food."

As she passed through the living room, Mom saw me lying on the couch. "Hi sweetie, I didn't realize you were there. I guess you heard what we were talking about."

"Yeah, it sure doesn't seem fair."

"No, it doesn't."

"Will they really have to move?"

"No, I don't think it's going to come to that, but I'm not sure how this is going to all work out." She gave me a kiss on the top of my head and said, "Dad's making some hot chocolate; let him know if you want some."

"Thanks, Mom."

That night as I was lying in bed, half asleep and half awake, an idea started to percolate in my brain. And just before I finally did go off to sleep, I remember thinking—I really hope that this idea is as good as it seems to be, and that when the morning comes, it doesn't turn out to be some way-out-there dream that doesn't make any sense. Fortunately, it was the first scenario, and not the second.

After I woke up the next morning, I stayed in bed for about fifteen minutes going over my idea, thinking it through, making sure I hadn't missed anything. When I was satisfied that I had all the bases covered, I got out of bed and headed for the kitchen to talk with Mom and Dad. Mom saw me first.

"Hi sweetie, did you have a good sleep?"

"Yeah, I did."

"Good morning, son."

"Good morning, Dad."

I started to head for one of the cabinets to get some cereal. But then I stopped because I didn't want to have to try to explain my idea with a mouthful of Alphabits. (I had tried a lot of other cereals, but I always went back to Alphabits. I haven't been able to find any other cereal that has anywhere near that much literary potential.) I just got myself a glass of orange juice and sat down.

Mom said, "Aren't you going to have some breakfast?"

"Yeah, I'll have some cereal in a minute."

Both Mom and Dad continued to look at me, sensing that something was on my mind. After a few moments I spoke up. "Mom, are you going to see Mrs. Witkowski soon, you know, about the nursing facility?"

"Probably tomorrow; she has to talk with her family first."

I hesitated for a moment. "I kind of have an idea about that; you know about paying for it."

"What do you mean?"

"Well, I heard you and Dad say that you wanted to try to help out."

"We do, honey, but we can only afford a small amount. Plus, I think Mrs. Witkowski's going to be reluctant to even accept that. She'll consider it charity; she's a very proud person."

I had considered that this might be a possibility when I was formulating my idea, so I had an alternative already in mind. "What about if you **loan** her the money, not just part of it, but the whole thing?"

"Benny, you know we would, if we could. But we don't have that kind of money."

"But … Grandma and Grandpa do."

"What are you talking about?"

"My college fund."

There was silence for a few moments, and then Dad spoke up. "Benny, that money's for your education …"

"But I don't need it yet. I won't need it for six more years. Isn't there some way to loan it to the Witkowskis, and then they can pay it back when I'm ready to go to college?"

Dad responded again. "Son, you know how we all feel about Mr. and Mrs. Witkowski, but even they wouldn't want to jeopardize your college education."

"Dad, I really think this will work, and it doesn't jeopardize anything. We don't need the money for six years, and Grandpa said he hadn't put most of it into the college account yet, so it's available. Why can't we loan it to the Witkowskis? We don't need it right now, but they do."

I got the sense that Dad was wavering a little bit when he replied. "I don't know about this, Benny. What do you think, Lillian?"

Neither Dad nor I had looked over at Mom since the conversation had started. When I looked over now, I saw that tears were streaming down her face. It took her a moment before she could say anything. "Benny, I can't tell you how proud I am that you're my son … I mean, I've always been proud when you brought home your report cards, and winning all those races … but those things don't compare to this. For you to be thinking of …" And then she couldn't continue.

Both Dad and I started to get teary-eyed. I finally decided to break the tension. "Mom, when you said how proud you were, how come you didn't mention my clarinet playing?"

Now we started laughing through our tears. As Mom came over to me, I stood up and she gave me a kiss on my forehead and a big hug. She was still semi-holding me when she said, "You know what? I think your idea is terrific, but we need to make sure that we've considered everything very carefully." Mom looked over at Dad, and he nodded in agreement as she continued. "Plus, we have to talk to your grandma and grandpa about all this. After all, even though it's meant for you, it's still their money." Mom paused and smiled at me. "But knowing them, I think they're going to want to help … I know it's hard for you, but we just need to take this slow."

Even though I wanted to argue my case some more, I knew that Mom was right, so I smiled back and just said, "Okay, Mom." But I think she sensed that I was still a little disappointed.

"Listen honey, we're going to be able to talk to your grandma and grandpa tomorrow. They decided to come a few days early to avoid the Thanksgiving traffic. And they figured that coming early would give them a chance to visit Mr. Witkowski." Mom gave me another hug. "I think this is going to all work out, Benny. The more I think about it, the more I like it."

Dad joined in. "I feel the same way." He paused and then looked over toward me. "I'll tell you what, your Mom and I don't have any set plans for today, so in honor of your great idea, what would you like to do?"

"Really?"

"Yes, really."

I didn't have to think very long. "Well, the state high school cross-country championships are in Boston today. Could we go to that?"

"I don't see why not. Sort of a busman's holiday, huh?"

"Yeah. Actually, some of the kids I ran against are competing."

"How can they do that? They're not in high school yet?"

"Eighth-graders can participate if they go to school in the same building as the high school students."

"Hmmph, I didn't know that. So, what time is the meet?"

"I think ten o'clock."

"Well, we better get going then."

I didn't move from where I was for a moment, and then I asked, "Do you think I should bring my clarinet, you know, so I can practice in the car?"

"You're such a wiseguy. Just get something to eat and get dressed."

Grandma and Grandpa arrived early Sunday afternoon. After they got settled in, we presented our case for the loan idea, but they didn't need much convincing. And after a brief discussion, they agreed it was something we should do. Grandpa then suggested that he and Grandma go next door to see Mrs. Witkowki and present it to her.

They were gone about an hour, and when they came back, Mrs. Witkowski was with them. She had obviously been crying. When she saw Mom and Dad, she went over to each of them and gave them a hug.

"I don't know how to thank you. I didn't know what I was going to do. I just couldn't bear the thought of selling the house. Once Jack gets better, he has to have a real home to come back to."

Just after Mrs. Witkowski finished the sentence, she saw me in the kitchen doorway. She came over to me, and before she gave me a hug, she said, "You're a special young man, Benny; and you're as precious to me as my own grandchildren and great-grandchildren." With that she started to cry again. She wasn't alone.

On Thanksgiving Day many of their family came back to Massachusetts to be with Mrs. Witkowski, and to visit Mr. Witkowski in the hospital. Our whole family decided to visit him as well, and we got a chance to meet some of the other Witkowski family members that we hadn't met before. They all thanked us for our generosity and were obviously very appreciative of what we were going to do.

Although some of Mr. Witkowski's family probably didn't realize there was any change in his condition, because they hadn't been there before, I definitely noticed some improvement in what Mr. Witkowski was able to do. Even though it was very limited, I saw him moving his left hand more than he had before, and that gave me another idea.

The Monday after Thanksgiving was the day Mr. Witkowski was to be moved to the rehabilitation center. The facility was about five miles from the hospital in a nice setting, with lots of walking paths and plenty of trees.

We didn't have school that day because it was a professional development day for teachers. Grandma and Grandpa had decided to stay until Tuesday so that they could get all the information they needed to start the loan process. Mrs. Witkowski insisted that everything be drawn up legally, which everyone agreed was a good idea.

Since Grandma and Grandpa were still visiting, we all decided to go see Mr. Witkowski in the rehabilitation center Monday afternoon. On the way over, I asked Dad to stop at Derek's house because I had to pick up something. I had called Derek earlier, so when we pulled up, he met me at the door and handed me a plastic bag.

When I got back in the car, Mom asked me, "What's that?"

"Just something I thought might help Mr. Witkowski." I removed it from the bag and handed it to her. "It used to be Samantha's. It's a magnetic board with lots of plastic letters." As she took the board in her hands, I continued. "I noticed that Mr. Witkowski could move his left hand a little bit, so I thought maybe he could move the letters around and spell some words with this."

Mom looked at the board and then said, "Wow sweetie, what a great idea. I just don't know if he can retrieve words in his head yet, but this is certainly worth trying."

When we arrived at the rehabilitation center, we signed in at the front desk and got directions to Mr. Witkowski's room. Mom had noticed on the sign-in sheet that Mrs. Witkowski was still there. We found Mr. Witkowski in a semi-private room right next to what's called the Day Room; that's a common area with chairs and tables, a large TV, and a sitting area with more comfortable furniture. It had very large windows on one side that looked out onto the wooded area in back of the center.

After visiting for a few minutes, I asked Mom if I could bring out the magnetic board. She went over to Mrs. Witkowski to explain what I wanted to do, and then Mom gave me the go-ahead.

When I took the magnetic board out of the bag and held it in front of Mr. Witkowski, I thought I saw the corner of his mouth go up a little further than it did the last time I was there. I thought he was trying to smile.

I moved the board and letters as close to his left hand as possible. Initially, he wasn't able to move anything, but then he started to push some of the letters with his knuckles. As he did this, I watched his eyes. He moved them in such a way that he seemed to be trying to direct me to move some other letters closer to his hand. It took ten minutes, but he finally separated three of the letters from the rest—"F", "D", "R".

Mrs. Witkowski was the first to say anything. "He's always been a big fan of the former president, but I'm not sure what this could possibly mean. He showed so much persistence; I don't think it was an accident that he separated those letters."

We discussed it for quite awhile, but nobody could figure out what the "FDR" stood for. Finally it was time for our family to leave. We said goodbye to Mrs. Witkowski, and I went over to Mr. Witkowski to say goodbye to him also. As I got closer, he shifted his eyes toward the window that was right next to his bed. Initially, I didn't think too much of it, but then he did it again. I looked out; it was the same view as the large windows in the Day Room, toward the wooded area. I noticed that there were a large number of birds flying around. I watched them swoop toward the window a few times, and then it dawned on me. They had nowhere to land!

I turned to the other people in the room and said, "It's not Franklin Delano Roosevelt. The 'FDR' stands for 'feeder'. He wants us to put one of his bird feeders outside the window!"

If there was any doubt that I was correct, it disappeared when Mr. Witkowski's mouth turned up ever so slightly, and a tear formed in the corner of his eye.

CHAPTER 18

▼

I know that some people believe in the healing power of inanimate objects, like pyramids, or crystals, or even clay and mud. But I've never heard of anyone who suggested that bird feeders are the aviary equivalent of Oral Roberts.

I'm sure if they did a scientific study, the fact that Mr. Witkowski started to improve so dramatically after my dad and I put up the bird feeder outside his window would be chalked up to coincidence. And it probably was. But coincidence or not, it was pretty remarkable.

The therapists at the rehabilitation center said they had almost never seen this much progress in such a short period of time, especially in someone Mr. Witkowski's age. During the month of December, he started to regain the use of his left hand, began to make some sounds, and was able to hold his head more erect. Doctors rarely use hyperbole, so we never heard them utter the word "miracle", but they were clearly amazed, and so were we.

I'm actually glad no one used the word "miracle". Don't you think we toss that term around way too much? I mean, sports announcers claim that something miraculous happens on athletic fields on a daily basis. It seems to me that the word "miracle" should be reserved for something that's really extraordinary—something that won't be replicated for centuries, or at the very least decades—like the Red Sox winning the World Series.

If you have any doubt that we use the term "miracle" to describe relatively mundane things, how do you explain the fact that there's a sandwich spread called **Miracle** Whip? I mean, what's so miraculous about this stuff, that it looks and tastes like mayonnaise? I don't even think it qualifies as "Phenomenon Whip", or "Moderately Interesting Whip", never mind Miracle Whip. I could probably live with "Barely Raised an Eyebrow Whip", but that's about as far as I'm willing to go.

So, were all the strides Mr. Witkowski made just coincidence, or was there some sort of causal relationship at work connected to the bird feeder? Well, I don't think it was directly cause and effect, but I'm not sure it was purely happenstance either.

It's funny that in our society we seem to have such a tough time understanding cause and effect relationships. I mean, a lot of people just assume that if one thing happens before another thing, the first one must cause the second one; and of course, that's not necessarily true.

Evidently, a lot of people in the Roman Empire had a similar problem with sound reasoning, because they even came up with a name for it. Remember when I was considering taking Latin at the beginning of seventh grade? Well, I came across the phrase "Post hoc ergo propter hoc". (I kind of like that phrase—no "um" words.) Anyway, it means "after this, therefore because of this".

Legend has it that some of the Roman citizens believed that when a rooster crowed in the morning, it caused the sun to rise. I know, pretty stupid, huh? And yet, don't many people now a days think in a similar way? Don't we engage in all sorts of superstitious behavior in the belief that it will bring about some positive result—like rubbing rabbit's feet, searching for four-leaf clovers, or wearing the same underwear if your favorite team's on a winning streak? (Yeah, believing that donning filthy undergarments will result in a victory is way more logical than the rooster thing.)

I think this whole cause and effect hang-up we have is related to wanting to be able to place "blame". We have a hard time just accepting that sometimes things happen that are nobody's fault. We even have a lot of states now that have "no-fault" car insurance, and it may be a good idea from a financial perspective, but I think it's unrealistic. Have you ever heard of anyone who had an automobile accident say, "It was nobody's fault"? Even when **they** hit the other car, they somehow try to blame the other driver—"The guy came out of nowhere."

And now we have "no-fault" divorce. Yeah, I'm pretty sure that will put an end to any finger pointing during the depositions.

Anyway, I did all this analysis while I was out running during our Christmas school vacation, getting in shape for spring track. And so, what did I conclude about Mr. Witkowski? I guess what I believe is that your physical well-being is closely tied to your mental outlook on things. So when Mr. Witkowski saw those bird feeders outside his window, it made him feel happy and proud. Maybe that was all he needed to motivate himself to get better. I don't think it was a miracle, but whatever it was, I'm glad it happened.

But I've gotta tell you, just to be on the safe side, whenever Mom makes me a sandwich, I tell her to "hold the **Miracle** Whip". I figure we've already gotten more than our fair share.

On the first Friday in January, our homeroom teacher reminded us that our mid-year advisory/health projects were due in a few weeks. She also indicated that we would have some time during advisory period that afternoon to brainstorm about ideas for our projects. Before she sent us off to first period, she offered one additional caveat. "If you're going to do a project related to any of the topics we studied in the sex education unit, you may **not** do a diorama."

I know you're probably curious about the original diorama. But honestly, there's no way I could possibly describe it and do it justice. You'd really have to see it to appreciate it. But that actually might be a possibility. My understanding is that the diorama was put on ebay by the parents of the student who made it. And evidently, Hugh Hefner now owns it; he was able to outbid Paris Hilton. Mr. Hefner supposedly is going to display it at the Playboy Mansion. I'm kind of glad Mr. Hefner won the bid; I don't think Paris Hilton's intentions toward the diorama were purely decorative in nature.

I realize that I've spent a lot of time talking about the health program, particularly the unit on sex education. So it might seem to you that our school system over emphasizes that part of the curriculum. Although **I** don't really think so, I know there are some parents in the community that do. And they also think that the sex education curriculum starts much too early.

Philosophically, I'm not sure how I feel about that, but personally I think the schools are right on target. I heard a joke once that might help put into perspective how "sophisticated" kids are about sex these days:

There were two four-year-old boys playing with trucks in the backyard. One of the four-year-olds says to the other, "Yesterday, my brother found a condom on the patio." The other four-year-old says, "What's a patio?"

That afternoon during advisory, our teacher handed out a list of guidelines for our upcoming projects. Number one on the list read as follows: **No Dioramas!!!**

Number two on the list indicated that we could do a group project if we wanted. Since Derek, Vanessa, and I were only in the same class for a few subjects, a group project would give us additional time to work together, so we jumped at the chance.

We decided that all of our discussions about the advisory project would technically qualify as TUCK meetings. And, although we never formally adopted a mission statement for TUCK, it had always been about helping people, so we decided that our group project would have to reflect that.

Derek spoke up first. "How about we do a report on decision-making, like what Dr. Foster taught us?"

My turn: "I don't know, Derek, I think it would be hard to do a report on that. I mean, once you've learned the process, don't you just do it? There aren't any real facts we could report on."

The verbal tennis match continued. "Well, maybe we could report on a decision we made, and how it worked out."

"Why do you think doing a report is such a good idea? When we present it, we'll just be reading to the class. I think we should do something else."

"Like what?"

"Well, I'm not sure, but a report seems more like a one-person project."

"It doesn't have to be; it could …"

Vanessa finally had enough. "Red light, red light."

(If you remember, that was the phrase Vanessa borrowed from Derek's sister, Samantha.) As usual, it worked very effectively, stopping both of us in our tracks.

Ever the diplomat, Vanessa continued. "I think you both have a point, but I think we have to find a more interesting topic, or at least a more interesting way to present it. I'm not really comfortable just reading a report to the class."

Derek: "What are you afraid of—they'll get bored, and yell 'Red light'?"

Vanessa: "Only when **you're** reading."

Derek: "Oh yeah …"

The good-natured kidding between Derek and Vanessa continued for a few more moments, but I really didn't hear much of it. I was focusing on something Vanessa had said, and an idea was starting to come together in my head. It centered on the "red light" phrase, and Vanessa saying she wasn't comfortable.

I guess I was staring off into space, because Derek said, "Earth to Benny. Earth to Benny."

"Oh, sorry. I was just thinking about an idea."

Derek: "That's good. That's what we're supposed to do when we're brainstorming. Do you want to share it?"

"Yeah, sure. But, it just started to come to me, so I haven't worked out all the details …"

Vanessa: "That's okay; spill."

Derek: "Did you just say 'spill'?"

Vanessa: "Yeah, you know, tell us about it."

Derek rolled his eyes and shook his head. "Spill. Who says 'spill'?"

Vanessa ignored her cousin and turned toward me as I started to explain. "Well, when you said you weren't comfortable just reading a report to the class, I put that together with 'red light'—you know 'stop'."

Vanessa: "I'm not sure I see the connection."

"Like before, when Derek and I were arguing, you said 'red light' to make us stop."

"Right, but what does that have to do with our project?"

"Well, what if whenever somebody said or did something that made you uncomfortable, you said 'red light'?"

"I do."

Derek: "And how."

Vanessa gave him a look.

Me: "Yeah, you do. But why couldn't we do a project, or a campaign, or something, so everybody did that."

Derek: "I'm still not following."

Vanessa: "I think I see what you're talking about, like if someone said a swear word, another person would say, 'red light'."

Me: "I wasn't thinking about swear words, but yeah, that would work too. I was thinking about the lesson Mr. Martin taught us, about not using the word 'retard'. What about if all the students were told about 'red light', and then if anyone said 'retard', the other person would say 'red light' to let him know that it made him uncomfortable?"

Derek: "Oh, I get it."

Vanessa: "That would work for swear words too …"

Me: "Yeah, you're right; it would. It would work for anything that made you uncomfortable, like …"

And with that, a floodgate of ideas opened up. In fact, we got so excited that we decided to meet at my house after school to finish putting all our ideas together. By the end of the afternoon, we had created "Project Red Light" with an outline of the way it was supposed to work. Here are some examples:

Anytime one student made another student feel embarrassed or uncomfortable, the student on the receiving end could say "red light" and that would be the signal for the first student to stop.

By using the phrase "red light", students didn't have to explain themselves, or try to find the exact words to make the offending student understand. "Red light" simply meant—"that bothers me, please stop it".

Vanessa, Derek, and I figured that the phrase "red light" could be used to help stop swearing, racial or ethnic jokes, put-downs about the way people look or act, offensive words like retard, etc.

Derek volunteered to put together some Power Point slides to present to our homeroom teacher on Monday. The project wasn't due for two more weeks, but we were so excited, we couldn't possibly wait that long.

First thing Monday morning we arranged to meet with our teacher during our health class later that day. During that period the rest of the students were going to do some additional brainstorming for the mid-year project, so we wouldn't be missing any new material.

Derek set up the Power Point presentation that outlined the main ideas of Project Red Light. To say that our teacher loved it is a huge understatement. "This is absolutely terrific. How did you come up with this? I'm going to see if Mr. Martin is available; he needs to see this."

Our teacher called the main office on the intercom, and a few minutes later Mr. Martin joined us. We showed him the Power Point and elaborated on a few of the ideas that were on the screen.

I think he was even more excited than our teacher was. "I can't tell you what an amazing idea this is. It's so simple, but I think it can have a huge impact on the way kids treat each other." He paused for a moment, obviously thinking of something. "Maybe this should be presented to all the students; I'm wondering if we should set up an assembly for the whole school."

I think Mr. Martin noticed the look of surprise on my face. "Don't worry, Benny. If we do that, you three can be as involved as you want to. We're going to give you full credit, and it would be better if you participated, but if being on stage makes you uncomfortable, well then …"

"I guess I could just say 'red light'."

"There you go."

We all started laughing.

Over the next two weeks, we met with Mr. Martin four more times. On two occasions Dr. Foster joined us, and it was finally decided to move forward with the assembly. Since everyone agreed that Project Red Light would be more readily accepted if it was initially introduced by students, it was decided that Derek, Vanessa, and I would start the assembly by putting on a skit that would depict how Project Red Light might work. And then Mr. Martin and Dr. Foster would take it over from there.

The assembly program was held on a Friday afternoon in late January. There was no way to gauge what kind of impact our idea would have, certainly for weeks, and possibly for months. But if our reception at the assembly was any indication, Project Red Light was going to be a huge hit. The skit Derek, Vanessa, and I put on was particularly well received. It had some funny parts to it, but it also made a point.

If I'm being objective, I think I was the weak link during the skit. I was kind of hoping that my acting ability would more closely resemble my running ability. Instead it resembled my clarinet-playing ability. Maybe it has something to do with being on stage. (Thank goodness they don't hold cross-country meets in an auditorium.)

That night I told Mom and Dad how well the assembly had gone and how pleased Mr. Martin was. Mom said, "Well, I'm not surprised; I thought the idea was terrific."

Dad: "Were you nervous on the stage? I know that's not your favorite thing."

"A little bit, but it was okay. It's funny that I get more nervous on stage than I do before a cross-country meet."

Mom: "I'd be petrified before both of them."

I smiled.

Dad: "So what happens next, anything?"

"I think there will be some follow-up in the advisory classes, and then Mr. Martin said something about having a presentation for the parents."

Mom: "I think that's a great idea. When will that be?"

"It's not definite yet, but probably just before February vacation."

"Will you perform the skit again?"

"I don't know. Mr. Martin hasn't decided. It's okay either way. Although, it wouldn't break my heart if we didn't."

Dad and Mom both smiled.

I smiled back. "I think I'll go check my e-mail."

I left the kitchen and headed for my room. I jiggled the computer mouse, and my screen saver disappeared. (My screen saver was a picture from last year's cookout, which I change every year.) I clicked on the AOL icon and then the mailbox. I had seven messages. Six of them were ads, but the seventh one was not. I opened my eyes wide as I reread the sender's name. I double-clicked and read the message. It was very short; it simply said, "Thank you for everything." But it was signed "Mr. Witkowski"!

I went running from my room, calling out, "Mom, Dad, come look at this!"

"What is it, Benny? Are you all right?"

"Yeah, I'm fine. You've got to see this!"

Mom and Dad both got in front of the computer screen and looked more closely. Mom put her hand over her mouth but just moved it aside enough to say, "Oh my gosh. That's really from Mr. Witkowski?"

"Yeah Mom, it is."

"It's only been about a week since I saw him. I know he was making amazing progress. But who thought he'd be able to do this, so soon?"

"I'm going to e-mail him back. Can we go to see him this weekend?"

"Sure."

Dad: "I have to say, Mr. Witkowski sure seems to be defying the odds. I've never heard of anyone his age making a recovery like this."

Mom: "Well, you said it yourself; he's a fighter. But you're right; no one could have anticipated this."

As Mom and Dad were talking, I started to unload my backpack to see how much homework I had for the weekend, so I could plan when to visit Mr. Witkowski, and how long I could stay.

As I finished taking the last book out of my backpack, I realized something was missing. "Oh, darn it."

Mom: "What's the matter?"

"I think I left my science book in my locker, and we have a big test on Monday."

"Is there any way to get into the school over the weekend?"

"I think there's a custodian there on Saturday morning."

"Well, why don't we go tomorrow around ten?"

"Thanks, Mom; sorry."

"It's fine. Come out and say goodnight before you go to bed, okay?"

"Sure."

On Saturday morning Mom drove me to the school to pick up my book. The front doors were locked, so we weren't sure how we were going to get in. But after about two minutes, the head custodian passed by and opened the doors for us.

"Is it okay for my son to get a book from his locker?"

The custodian turned to me. "Where's your locker?"

"On the first floor, down there."

"Okay, that's no problem. We just washed the other corridor, so I couldn't let you go down that one."

"Thanks."

"Just please go out the same way you came in."

"Okay, thanks again."

We headed toward my locker, past the main office. The lights were on so I glanced over, and I saw Mr. Martin sitting at one of the secretary's desks. "Look Mom, it's Mr. Martin."

"Where ... oh, in the office."

"Do you think it would be okay to go in and say hi?"

"I don't know. If he's in here on a Saturday, he's probably pretty busy ... but ... okay, why don't we just say a quick 'hello' and be on our way?"

The door to the main office was unlocked, so we opened it and stepped inside. Mr. Martin heard the door open and looked up.

"Hi, Benny. Hi, Mrs. Curtis."

"Hi, Mr. Martin."

As we said hello, he got up and came over to the counter to shake our hands. He pretended to get a stern look on his face. "You do know that it's Saturday, and you don't have to be here until Monday?"

"I just forgot my science book ... But, isn't it Saturday for you too?"

He smiled. "Yes, but sometimes principals don't have weekends off ... some reports to catch up on. And how are you, Mrs. Curtis? I think the last time I saw you was at the cross-country meet."

"Yes, I think you're right. I'm fine."

"Did Benny tell you about the assembly yesterday? The kids did a great job."

"Yes, he did. Benny said you're thinking about having an evening presentation for the parents."

He started to nod his head. "Probably in about two weeks."

"Well, my husband and I will be there."

"It's all because of Benny, Derek, and Vanessa, you know?"

"I do. But if you didn't create an atmosphere of respect at the school, I don't know if they would have been thinking along those lines."

"That's nice of you to say, but we have a lot of great kids here; it makes my job easier."

"Nevertheless ..."

Mom didn't get a chance to finish her thought because there was some loud music coming from Mr. Martin's office. We all turned that way just as the volume got lower. Mr. Martin looked like he was about to offer an explanation when I asked, "Was that Scooby-Doo that I heard?"

Mr. Martin started to chuckle. "Yes, I think it was. That's my son, Michael." He paused briefly. "You remember the class I taught ..."

I started nodding my head as Mr. Martin continued. "I usually bring him with me when I come in on Saturdays. I set up a VCR or DVD player in my office, so he can watch his videos." He paused again, obviously weighing what to do. "Would you like to meet him?"

"Yeah, sure."

"I'll go get him. Come on around behind the counter."

Mom and I did just that, as Mr. Martin went to get Michael. Mr. Martin opened his office door and poked his head in. "Michael, please put that on pause. I want you to come out here and meet some people."

The sound was muted a few seconds later, and Mr. Martin left the doorway of his office followed by his son. Michael was about six feet tall and had a thin build, similar to his father's. I'm not exactly sure what I was expecting, but Michael had no outward signs that he was disabled in any way.

Mr. Martin said, "Michael, this is Benny, and his mother Mrs. Curtis."

Michael came over to the two of us. He made brief eye contact with me, gave me an exaggerated handshake, and said, "Nice to meet you". He did the same thing with Mom.

Michael's movements and actions seemed learned rather than natural, which of course they probably were. There was an awkward moment of silence before I looked toward Michael and asked, "Was that *Scooby-Doo and the Loch Ness Monster* you were watching?"

Michael turned to me with a bit more eye contact and answered, "Yes, it was." He seemed excited that I recognized what he was watching, and he started to flail his hands, and he got up on his tiptoes.

I continued. "Is that your favorite?"

"Actually, I like them all."

(When Mr. Martin first told our class that Michael was incapable of telling a lie, if you remember, I ruled out a career in politics for him. But with that last response, politics might still be an option.)

Michael kept talking. "Scooby-Doo calls his friend 'Raggy' instead of 'Shaggy' because Scooby's a dog, and dogs can't talk."

"You're right, Michael," I said. "Dogs can't talk."

"Except sometimes they can."

I wasn't sure how to respond to this last remark, so I stayed quiet for a moment, and then Michael said, "If you ask a dog what's on top of a house, he'll say 'roof'."

I started to laugh, and so did Mom. I wasn't just being polite. Even though I had probably first heard that joke when I was about three, in this context, it just struck me funny.

Michael got a huge grin on his face, and I think he figured that he was on a roll, so he said, "If you ask a dog where Dad hits his golf balls, he'll say 'rough'." I laughed even harder at that one.

Michael was really enjoying himself. He got an even bigger grin on his face, and his hands were flapping a mile a minute. He started to say, "If you ask a dog …". Before he could finish, Mr. Martin jumped in, "Okay Shecky, that's probably enough. What were you going to do, go through your whole routine?"

"One more, Dad?"

Mr. Martin got a fake look of exasperation on his face. "If Benny and Mrs. Curtis can stand it, so can I."

Michael didn't even wait for our assent; he just started right in. "If you ask a dog if he wants a lollipop, what will he say?"

I didn't think about the answer right away, because I thought Michael was going to supply the punch line, just like he did the last two times. But this time he didn't. So I began to try to figure out what sound a dog would make that could possibly fit, but nothing came to mind.

Even Mr. Martin looked puzzled. Finally, he said to Michael, "Okay, I give up … unless Benny or Mrs. Curtis have an idea." Both of us shook our heads. "So, what does a dog say when you ask him if he wants a lollipop?"

"Nothing, Dad; dogs can't talk."

With that, everyone totally broke up. But by far, Michael was laughing the loudest. Mr. Martin finally said, "Well, I've never heard that one before; trying out some new material, huh?"

Michael was still laughing, so he just nodded his head as Mr. Martin looked toward us and said, "I think we better let Benny and Mrs. Curtis be on their way …"

I sort of interrupted. "Actually, I was wondering, Michael, do you have any other Scooby-Doo videos?"

He looked over toward me. "I have two more here and six at home."

"Which ones?"

Michael then proceeded to list them for me in alphabetical order.

"Those are good ones."

"When's your birthday?"

The non-sequitor kind of threw me for a moment, but I responded, "May twenty-third."

"That's a Tuesday this year."

Michael then turned toward Mom. "When's your birthday?"

"September ninth."

"That's a Saturday this year.'

I looked around, but there were no calendars in sight. And even if there were, nobody could have flipped the pages that fast. It reminded me of somebody who can manipulate an abacus and get the correct answer to a complex math problem faster than someone who uses a calculator.

Mr. Martin turned toward Mom and me. "I think Michael's trying to get his own HBO special."

I have to say, Michael fascinated me, and I probably could have stayed there for hours. But I also felt strange, as if I were intruding. I began to feel like I was gawking at Michael—that I couldn't wait for him to do his next "trick". I don't think he sensed anything like that, but it bothered me, so I said, "I think I should probably get my science book."

Mom: "Right; yes."

"You can stay here, Mom; I'll be right back."

We all said our goodbyes, and I went to get my book.

In the car on the way home I said to Mom, "Boy, Michael's really something, isn't he?"

Mom looked over at me and smiled. "That's exactly what Mr. Martin said about you, when you went to get your book."

"He did?"

"Yes. He told me what you said when that other student asked what to call his son. You know, when you said 'Call him Michael'? That obviously meant a lot to Mr. Martin. He seems to think the world of you. And then with this Project Red Light …"

I don't know if it's possible to feel yourself blush, but I knew without looking that I was bright red. Mom squeezed my arm. "I think Mr. Martin's a pretty good judge of character."

On Monday at school, Mr. Martin made it a point to thank me for being so nice to Michael. Although I didn't say it, the thought occurred to me—How could you not?

The following Saturday, I asked Mom to drive me to the school again. I hadn't forgotten anything this time. Instead, I had found some old Scooby-Doo videos in my closet that weren't on Michael's list. I wasn't going to be watching them any more, so I figured he might enjoy having them.

Mom made sure that I could get into the school, and that Mr. Martin was there before she dropped me off to run an errand. She said she would be back in about twenty minutes to pick me up.

Michael seemed really excited to get the videos and maybe also to see me again. Mr. Martin was a little reluctant to allow Michael to accept the videos, but when he saw the expression on his son's face, he changed his mind, especially once I explained that I was finished using them.

Mr. Martin went back out into the main office to do some work, so Michael and I spent about fifteen minutes by ourselves, talking intermittently while watching one of the videos I had brought.

It was difficult to carry on any kind of conversation with Michael, because for the most part, he would just throw out random statements:

"I like pizza."

"Last year it snowed on this day."

"My mom's in heaven."

That last statement really took me by surprise, although I recovered enough to say, "I know." But Michael kind of left it hanging there and went on to something else. It was almost like Michael was reciting his autobiography in list form. The only exchange that we had that even remotely resembled a conversation happened just before I left, and had to do with his "job".

"I work at OSC."

"What's that?"

"It's kind of far away. I take a van."

"What do you do there?"

"I put things in boxes."

"What kinds of things?"

"That people need."

Our "conversation" about Michael's job continued for a few more minutes, and then Mom arrived to pick me up.

Over the weekend I Googled OSC and found out it stood for "Organization of Special Citizens", and that it had a facility in Plymouth. Their website had pictures of the facility and described the kind of work that was done there.

I also spent some time on the weekend thinking about my most recent visit with Michael. It's hard to say that we were exactly friends, but I liked Michael, and I think he liked me. During this last visit it felt much more like we were equals. As I said, it hadn't felt like that the first time, which was **my** hang-up, not Michael's.

On Monday Dr. Foster came to the school. The evening presentation for the parents was coming up, and he was going to introduce the program, so he wanted to talk with Derek, Vanessa, and me about our skit.

"So, this is what I'm thinking. I'll give a brief introduction about Project Red Light, and then you three will come on. Mr. Martin and I will then do some follow-up, and answer any questions. Is there anything you need to review as far as your lines are concerned?"

We all shook our heads.

"Good. I know I've already told you this, but your skit is excellent; I love the message that it sends. By the way, we've invited the parents of elementary students to come also. We're going to introduce Project Red Light at the elementary grades, particularly around behavior on the playground, the cafeteria, and the bus. You guys have really started something."

We all smiled.

I changed the subject. "Did you hear about Mr. Witkowski?"

"I did. I actually saw him about two weeks ago."

"The doctors think he may be able to get up and around using a walker soon."

"That's unbelievable."

Derek entered the conversation. "He e-mails me almost every day now."

Vanessa added, "Benny's mom said that he spoke some words the other day. They were hard to understand, but still …"

Dr. Foster looked at me. "Is that right?"

"Yeah, Mom was right there with Mrs. Witkowski."

"That's truly amazing. What great news." He paused. "Okay, before I let you go back to class, is there anything else you need before Thursday night?"

"No, I think we're fine," said Vanessa.

"Okay, that's great. I'll see you at about six-thirty on Thursday then."

We all got up to head back to class. As Derek and Vanessa got to the door, I said, "I'll catch up with you in a minute. Dr. Foster, can I see you for a second?"

"Sure Benny, what's up?"

"I don't know if Mr. Martin mentioned it, but Mom and I met his son, Michael, about a week ago."

Dr. Foster shook his head. "No, he didn't say anything to me. Michael's a nice young man, isn't he?"

"Yeah, I really liked talking with him."

"Just the fact that you were able to talk with him must mean that he likes you. He doesn't say too much sometimes."

"Yeah, I know. The first time we met him he told us some jokes though."

"Even better."

"Anyway, he told me about the work that he does. Do you know anything about OSC?"

"It's like a sheltered workshop. The people that go there do various jobs and earn some money. But they're in an environment that's non-threatening for them. I think Michael goes to the one in Plymouth."

"Yeah, that's what I found out. It's kind of a long ride, isn't it?"

"Yeah, it is." He looked at me with a puzzled expression, before he continued. "Why all the questions?"

"I was just thinking that with Michael's memory and all his other abilities, maybe he could do something else, at least maybe something closer. I mean, he didn't say specifically that he didn't like OSC, but he's not very specific about a lot of things. I definitely got the feeling that he goes there because he's supposed to, but that he really doesn't like it very much … I don't know, maybe it's just the travel."

"You could be right, Benny. I think Mr. Martin struggled with the decision. But he didn't think a regular job was right for Michael yet, because of his limited social skills." He paused briefly. "But this isn't idle curiosity, is it? Knowing you, you must have something in mind, right?"

I smiled. "Well, I was kind of thinking about it over the weekend. Do you think it would be all right to talk to him about it?"

"You mean Mr. Martin, or Michael?"

"Mr. Martin, first."

"I think he'd be fine with it, especially coming from you. Do you want to talk about your idea, or is it private?"

"I think I need to think it through some more before I tell anyone."

"Fair enough. But if you need to talk, just let me know."

"I will. Thanks."

Dr. Foster got a half-smile on his face. "Wait a minute. This doesn't have anything to do with you and Michael taking over **my** job, does it?"

I began to answer him as if he were being serious, but then I shifted gears. "Wow, you're so intuitive."

"Out, out! … Oh, wait this isn't even my office."

We both started to laugh, as Dr. Foster patted me on the shoulder and we left the conference room.

Chapter 19

The evening presentation for the parents went very well, even better than expected, although I think Mr. Martin and Dr. Foster were a little disappointed that the auditorium wasn't completely full, especially since the parents of elementary school students had been invited. Nevertheless, the people that were there seemed very receptive and enthusiastic. They asked some good questions and offered excellent comments after the formal presentation was completed.

The primary focus of the evening was the implementation of Project Red Light at O'Rourke Middle School and the two elementary schools in the district. Interestingly, however, during the question and answer session, a number of parents indicated that they liked the idea so much that they thought it should be expanded into the home and the community at large.

Mr. Martin and Dr. Foster had made some references to those ideas in their part of the presentation, but I know they felt it was tricky to try to "impose" an idea that's being used in school onto the home. It was obvious, however, that a number of parents saw real value in doing just that.

One parent went so far as to say, "Couldn't we instruct our own pre-schoolers to use the 'red light' phrase in a lot of different situations, even—I'm almost reluctant to say it—when we're talking to them about appropriate and inappropriate touching, for example? It seems to me, if children in our community were taught about this even before they entered school, it would become second nature to them. And they'd be more likely to speak up later on with more confidence in uncomfortable situations. I'm going to start this with my own children first thing tomorrow, and I urge all of you to do the same. Thanks for inviting us tonight; this was great."

Another parent followed up. "I agree with the woman who just spoke. I think we need to expand this idea. I have one son here at the middle school and another at Clark Elementary. I really like the idea that when they come home from school, instead of just asking 'how the day went', and getting the typical shrug, if I sense that something's wrong, I can ask if they used the red light phrase in school, or if they felt like they wanted to, but didn't. This will help open up lines of communication. We should make sure that more adults in the community know about this."

Most of the comments were in a similar vein. One of the last people to speak indicated that she taught middle school in another town, and she wanted permission to bring this idea to her school. Mr. Martin said, "Absolutely. We think the more schools that do this, the better. And as I said before, you can get a lot more information about this on the district's website." He started to smile, and then joked, "But you better hurry, before our copyright certificate arrives."

At the very end of the program, Mr. Martin reintroduced Derek, Vanessa, and me. We received a standing ovation. (I'm pretty sure it was for coming up with the Project Red Light idea, and not for my acting performance.)

The next day in school, which was the Friday before February vacation, Mr. Martin called the three of us into his office to thank us for everything. "I've gotten about twenty e-mails this morning about last night. Some of them are from other principals who want more information. I also received a phone call from *The Patriot Ledger*. They want to do a feature article on Project Red Light. This is really taking off; you three should be very proud."

We all said, "Thank you."

Mr. Martin got a little smile on his face. "Oh, and by the way, the mid-year advisory projects haven't all been graded yet, but I have it on good authority that you all got A's. There's a real surprise, huh?"

We all smiled. "Thanks, Mr. Martin."

I took the opportunity to ask Mr. Martin if I could make an appointment to see him later in the day. He glanced at his schedule, and said that lunchtime would be good.

"Is this about Project Red Light?"

"No, something else."

"Okay, come to the office after fifth period."

"Thanks."

When I arrived at the office after my fifth period class, Mr. Martin was talking with one of the secretaries. When he noticed me, he stopped for a moment and said, "Benny, why don't you go into my office? I'll be right with you."

About three minutes later he came in. I was sitting in the chair in front of his desk. "Benny, come on over and sit at the table with me. I don't like being behind the desk. It's too formal. I feel like everyone's at a job interview."

I smiled as I moved over to the small conference table. "Do you have any openings?"

"Benny, you know better than that. You can have any job you want. We'll create one, if need be. No interview required."

We were both smiling when he said, "So, what's on your mind?"

I hesitated briefly. "Well, I'm not sure where to start. It's really, kind of none of my business ..." I paused, trying to find the right words.

After a few seconds Mr. Martin said, "It's okay; just tell me what it's about."

"It's about Michael."

"About Michael? I guess I didn't expect that. But that's okay, go ahead."

"Well, that Saturday when I brought the videos, we were talking a little bit ..."

"Yeah, you know that's pretty amazing in and of itself. Michael even asked me about when he'd see you again. He almost never asks things like that. Anyway, I'm sorry; I interrupted you. What were you going to say?"

"It's about his job."

"At OSC?"

"Yeah, like I said, it's not my business, but I got the sense that Michael doesn't like it there very much." I started to speed up my words. "I mean maybe it's the travel, or the number of hours, but when he talked about it, honestly, he seemed kind of sad."

"That's very nice of you, Benny, to be so concerned about Michael. And I don't think it's none of your business. Michael obviously likes you, and it sounds like you're trying to look out for him. I'd say it's okay to make that your business." He paused. "What's more, you're probably right. The last few weeks Michael hasn't been himself. And as you know, it's hard for him to explain what he's feeling. On the weekends he's like his old self. Just like when you saw him on those Saturdays, but during the week, when he has to go to his job, he barely says anything. That's not like him, at least not with me."

It was almost like Mr. Martin was saying those last few sentences to himself, like I wasn't even in the room. Then he continued. "I've been debating what to do; I've been leaning toward making a change. I think maybe this little conversation helped make up my mind for me."

He looked at me and smiled. "Thank you, Benny."

"I'm not sure I did anything."

"I'd say you did. I don't imagine it was very easy to ask to see the principal and then try to tell him to do something to help his son."

"Well, it wasn't exactly like that; it was more ..." And then I couldn't find the words.

"Whatever it was like, not everyone would have done it. So, thank you."

He stood up, and with a smile on his face, he patted me on the shoulder. As I got up, he shook my hand and we both headed toward the door to his office. He put his hand on the doorknob, but before he turned it, he looked back at me and said, "When Michael finished school, I was going to try to get him a job in a supermarket or a drug store. In fact, OSC offered to help with that. They even would have supplied a job coach. But I thought the number of times Michael would have to interact with people, even if he was just stocking shelves, would be too difficult for him. Maybe I was wrong. Maybe he's ready to do this."

I wasn't sure what to say, but I did offer something. "Michael didn't mention anything that he'd rather do. I mean, he didn't specifically say he didn't like OSC, so I didn't ask him anything else about it."

"He probably would have had a hard time explaining it to you anyway. I think your instincts are right though, Benny." He paused. "Again, thanks for telling me about this, it's been a big help." He offered his hand again, and we shook.

During the rest of the school day, I thought a lot about Michael's situation. And I figured that Mr. Martin was probably right; Michael would have some difficulty in a job where people were coming and going all the time. I was trying to think of some other job he could do in an office or someplace that wasn't quite so public.

At the end of the day I headed for the front exit of the school to catch my bus. Mr. Martin was standing outside the office saying goodbye to the students as they left.

"Bye, Mr. Martin. Have a nice vacation."

He turned as he heard my voice. "Bye, Benny. You too. Any special plans?"

"No, nothing special. How about you?"

"No. Although, I am going to take a few days away from here and just relax. Anyway, have a good one; and thanks again about Michael."

I hesitated for a moment, but then spoke up. "Can I ask you something?"

He nodded. "Sure."

"I know that Michael gets paid at OSC, but it's not much, right? ... Does that matter to him?"

"Actually, no, it doesn't matter to him. He doesn't care anything about money. How come you asked about that?"

"I was thinking after we talked earlier, what if Michael volunteered someplace?"

Mr. Martin didn't say anything for a moment, obviously mulling over what I said. "You mean like at a hospital or a nursing home?"

"Yeah, but I was actually thinking, what about the library?"

Mr. Martin looked at me and nodded his head. "The library." He paused again. "The library might really be good. I mean, he could reshelve books, and he could easily memorize where everything was supposed to go. He'd have a minimum amount of interaction until he got used to things …" He looked over at me and smiled. "He could even reorganize the video collection. What do you think?"

I smiled back at him and said, "Right."

"Benny, do you know what a 'think tank' is?"

"Sort of. Isn't that where people get together to try to solve problems?" (If you remember, we considered expanding the name of TUCK to include the initials TT for Think Tank, so actually, I had more than a passing acquaintance with the concept.)

Mr. Martin nodded his head. "Exactly. Well, I think that's where you belong. And probably right away, never mind when you get older."

I smiled again, as he continued. "I guess I know how I'll be spending one of my vacation days." He offered his hand again. "It seems like I've been shaking your hand and thanking you a lot lately. I know it embarrasses you, but I have to tell you what a special young man you are."

I got a sheepish look on my face, and just barely managed to say, "Thank you."

"Listen, you better get going or you'll miss your bus. Have a great vacation, and say 'hi' to your folks for me."

"Bye, Mr. Martin."

The Monday after February vacation, there was an intercom call during morning homeroom. Our teacher answered it, and it was quiet enough that we could hear her side of the conversation. "Yes, he's here … I'll send him right down … You're welcome. Bye."

After our teacher hung up the phone, she said, "Benny, would you please report to the main office?" There were some good-natured "oohs" and "aahs" from my classmates. (It's really hard to describe the sound that middle school students make to "razz" their classmates. It's almost as if we're granted this special addition to our voice boxes between the ages of 11–13. It disappears before puberty sets in, and then it's gone forever. The sounds we can make as middle-schoolers are found nowhere else in nature.)

I arrived at the main office, where Mr. Martin was waiting for me. "Benny, please come on in."

I went into his office and sat down as he shut the door. "I just wanted to let you know that Michael started volunteering at the library last Thursday." His voice caught as he tried to continue. Finally, he said, "What a difference. I could see it right away on Thursday and Friday morning when he was getting ready."

I smiled and was about to say something when Mr. Martin continued. "Oh, and I'm supposed to say 'Hello' to you."

I got a puzzled look on my face, and then I realized what he must be talking about. We said the name simultaneously, "Miss Frist."

I'm sure I still looked puzzled, so Mr. Martin explained.

"When I went to the library last Tuesday, I spoke with Miss Frist, told her about Michael, and asked if she would be willing to meet him, and if everything went well, to allow him to volunteer. I also said that one of the students at the school had suggested the library; and when I mentioned your name, she said, 'Oh, I know Benny'. And then she told me a story about when you were little, and something about pages missing from a book …"

"Yeah, when I was three."

"Well, I don't know if she exaggerated or not, but that story was pretty remarkable. I didn't say it to Miss Frist, but it sounded like something Michael would do." He paused. "Anyway, I just wanted you to know how well things seem to be working out. It looks like I need to shake your hand and say thank you again."

We shook and as I stood up and headed for the office door, I said, "I'm really glad for Michael. Do you think it would be okay to visit him at the library sometime? When is he there?"

"I think that would be great. It would probably have to be on a Thursday or Friday. He works until four o'clock on those days."

"Okay." I paused. "So, Michael was really all right about not getting paid?"

"I know it seems strange, but he's fine about it. He just doesn't care about things like money."

I left the office and headed for my first period class. I was smiling to myself, picturing Michael memorizing where every book and video in the library belonged. I could envision that once he got settled in and became more comfortable, someone would ask him to find the book *1001 Uses for the Right-Handed*

Palumbo Wrench. Michael would probably respond, "Aisle 10, second bookshelf on the right, third shelf from the bottom, seventh book from the left."

(The only downside to Michael's new volunteer position was that since he didn't receive any compensation, and didn't care about it, a career in politics was definitely out of the question now.)

Our first health class after February vacation was the beginning of a new unit on nutrition. As you already know, I've studied a lot about this on my own, especially about the labels listing ingredients and nutrition facts. Nevertheless, I did acquire a significant amount of new information during the unit in school. Probably the main thing I learned was that "trans fat" is the major enemy in the war against unhealthy foods. (Doesn't it seem like everything that we're trying to eliminate—like poverty, or illegal drugs, or now trans fat—involves a "war"?)

Maybe the first action in the war against trans fat should be a public service movie. Remember that film *Crouching Tiger, Hidden Dragon*, starring Chow-Yun Fat? Well, what about a documentary *Clogging Arteries, Hidden Danger*, starring **Trans Fat**?

Note to film producers: If you think this is a good idea, please feel free to go ahead with it. My only recommendation would be that it premieres in New York City. As you might know, Mayor Bloomberg has been able to get a law enacted that bans restaurants in the city from using trans fat in their food preparation. I think eliminating trans fat is probably a good idea, but I'm not sure it should be a law. There's probably enough crime in New York City without having to bust some restaurant owner for serving Twinkies.

Another thing we learned about in the unit on nutrition was cholesterol. Although at our ages it tends not to be a huge problem, we still learned the basics, so that as adults we would have the foundation we needed to make good eating choices. Did you know that cholesterol is not all bad? There's actually good cholesterol as well as bad cholesterol. When I first heard that, I couldn't help but think, "What makes cholesterol go bad?" Is it hanging around with the wrong "element", or is it just made that way?

Anyway, the unit on nutrition primarily focused on healthy eating habits. Part of this, we were told, could be achieved by reading the nutrition labels on food products and by limiting our intake of those foods that contain unhealthy ingredients. I usually did this as a regular practice anyway, especially during cross-country season. So with spring track coming up, it was very easy to get back into the routine. However, as is often the case with me (as you well know by now), I couldn't just leave it there; I had to take it one step further. So, I started to read the labels on **everything**, not just food products.

And what I discovered was that once again we've gone way overboard. In the interest of giving very explicit instructions and directions, so there should be no confusion (and I also suspect to try to avoid lawsuits), we've thrown common sense out the window. You know about my penchant for lists. Well, after visiting a number of websites that described all these silly labels, I've made up my own list of the top fifteen most ridiculous ones:

15. On an airline packet of nuts—**Instructions—open packet, eat nuts.** *Do you think there was a lady in 17b who didn't read the instructions, and put the whole foil packet in her mouth?*

14. On a frozen dinner—**Serving suggestion: defrost.** *Too bad. I think that meatloaf Popsicle might have been real tasty.*

13. On a string of Christmas lights—**For indoor or outdoor use only.** *What about underwater?*

12. On a package of bread pudding—**Product will be hot after heating.** *Yeah, but only if your oven works.*

11. On a bottle of dog shampoo—**Caution: contents should not be fed to fish.** *Why, can they become addicted?*

10. Warning on an electric router that carpenters use—**This product should not be used as a dentist drill.** *Does the character from 'Marathon Man' know that?*

9. Warning on a fireplace log—**Caution: Fire risk.** *Thank goodness! I thought I might have purchased that special kind of wood that doesn't burn.*

8. On a TV remote control—**Not dishwasher safe.** *Yeah, but if you keep it in the dishwasher at least you'll know where to find it.*

7. On a knife sharpener—**Knives are sharp.** *This one must come from the 'Caveman Dictionary', which also contains the warnings—Fire is hot, and ice is cold.*

6. On a cardboard sun shield that keeps the sun off the dashboard—**Do not drive with the sun shield in place.** *What about at night when the sun goes down?*

5. On a package of dice—**Not for human consumption.** *But wait, aren't snake eyes a delicacy in some cultures?*

4. On a steam iron—**Never iron clothes while they are being worn.** *What if you're in a hurry?*

3. On a pair of shin guards for bicyclists—**Shin pads cannot protect any part of the body they don't cover.** *What about if they're really, really good shin pads?*

2. On a package of rat poison—**Has been found to cause cancer in lab mice.** *So, this poison's pretty slow-acting, huh?*

1. On a baby stroller—**Remove toddler before folding.** *Unless you're "circus people".*

Even though the next health project wasn't due until the first week in April, I seriously considered submitting my labels list as my project. I mean, after Project Red Light, I was kind of in the teacher's good graces, but then I thought that my list probably didn't qualify as sufficiently academic. So instead, I did a comparison of diet plans.

Since we were already studying about nutrition and how to maintain a healthy diet, I figured that I'd just as soon do my project early, while the information was still fresh in my mind. There were two major conclusions that my report came to:

Number one: you can't possibly lose weight if you take in more calories than you burn off. So, if the diet plan you're looking into indicates that you can eat all you want and still lose weight, you should run, not walk, in the other direction. (Running is also better for losing weight than just walking.)

Number two: Without question, there is one diet plan that is far superior to all the others—it's whichever one you can stick to. It doesn't matter if it's low-carb, high-carb; low-fat, no-fat; just fruit and vegetables. If you can stick with it, that's the one for you.

There was one diet plan that I couldn't possibly recommend however—the Seaweed Diet. Basically you eat nothing but kelp. It keeps your cholesterol way down, but in the before and after pictures, I could have sworn I noticed gills.

At the same time that we were studying nutrition in health class, we were completing our follow-up lessons dealing with Project Red Light in advisory. For the most part we all took it seriously, although on occasion somebody would make a joke about it, or use the phrase "red light" when a teacher gave us too much homework. Interestingly though, when students did make a joke about Project Red Light, other students were the ones to put them in their place; the teachers didn't have to.

Early in March a reporter from *The Patriot Ledger* visited our school, and a few days later there was a feature article in the paper singing the praises of Project Red Light. The reporter had interviewed Mr. Martin, Dr. Foster, and then Derek, Vanessa, and me as well.

Local newspapers rarely cover middle school sports, so even though I had won all those cross-country meets, this was the first time I had my name and picture in the paper. I have to admit, although I don't like the limelight very much, it was pretty cool.

I thought the reporter did an excellent job of explaining the philosophy behind Project Red Light, and the quotes from Mr. Martin and Dr. Foster were excellent as well. But without a doubt, the last few paragraphs, which probably bordered on editorializing, really made the project come alive.

As luck would have it, the day the reporter was visiting the school, as he was leaving at the end of the day, he witnessed Project Red Light in action. And he described the situation with great enthusiasm in the article.

It seems that about ten students were waiting in line for their bus to arrive when a large eighth-grade boy came over and cut into the second spot in line. The boy who was cut in front of protested. "Hey, no cuts!"

The eighth-grader responded. "Shut up, jerk face. What are you—a seventh-grader?" Then a girl a few spots back, who evidently knew the boy who cut the line, said, "Hey, Jason (not his real name), red light."

Jason looked back at her. "What?"

"You know, red light."

Jason brushed off her comment with the wave of his hand. But then another student spoke up, "Yeah, red light." And then two or three other students joined in. Although it wasn't the middle school equivalent of the scene from *Norma Rae*, nevertheless it was pretty impressive. Jason hesitated for a moment, said, "This is stupid", but then moved to the back of the line.

The reporter indicated in the article that there was no way the scene could have been staged, although it was possible that Jason had noticed some adults in the area, including the reporter, and that may have prompted his move to the back of the line. Regardless, the reporter said he was still amazed that five or six students had spoken up for themselves. "For those of you with a short memory, middle school students and junior high students typically never do that. There's a social hierarchy in the middle level grades that doesn't permit a scene like the one I witnessed to take place. The administration and the students at O'Rourke Middle School are clearly on to something." The reporter went on to say that at least five other communities in the area were planning to adopt Project Red Light.

As you might imagine, Mom bought a whole bunch of copies of the newspaper that day. She sent the article to some of her out-of-state friends, to Grandma and Grandpa, and to the Director of Admissions at Princeton. (I'm only kidding about the last one, but I think she wanted to.)

The day after the article appeared, Mom drove me to the library. I did want to take out a book, but the main reason for the trip was to see Michael. When we entered the library, I looked around but didn't notice him right away, so we went to the circulation desk.

Although I hadn't seen her recently, I recognized Miss Frist immediately. We stood in front of the desk for a moment before she looked up and said, "May I help you?"

"Hello, Miss Frist."

"Do I know you ... is that you, Benny?"

"Yes." And then I repeated my greeting. "Hi, Miss Frist."

"You've gotten so tall ..." And then she saw Mom standing behind me. "I'm sorry. Hello, Mrs. Curtis."

"Hello."

Miss Frist turned back to me. "I'm not sure I would have recognized you, but Michael's father said you might be coming by." She paused. "And you were actually on my mind, because I saw that article in the paper yesterday about that project you did."

"Project Red Light."

"That was an excellent article, and what a great idea. See, this is terrific; I can tell everybody 'I knew you when'."

"Thanks." Mom and I both started smiling.

"I understand we also have you to thank for Michael being here. That was your idea too, wasn't it?"

"Not exactly."

"I think you're being too modest. Michael's father said that it would have never happened if you hadn't gone to see him. Michael's terrific, by the way. His memory is amazing." She started to smile. "Maybe like another certain young man I know."

Miss Frist turned to Mom again. "You should be very proud. I remember how he recited those pages when he was little, and how special and wonderful that was, and now with the project ... and Michael, well I think your son is ... I don't know ... something else entirely."

It certainly was nice of Miss Frist to say all that, but I got very embarrassed and didn't know what to say. Mom broke the brief silence. "Thank you. We are very proud; I think we'll keep him."

Miss Frist broke into a smile, and Mom said, "It was very nice to see you again."

"Nice to see the both of you as well." Miss Frist paused. "Would you like to say hello to Michael? I think he's in the reference room organizing some of the shelves. Do you want me to take you?"

I responded, "No, that's okay. I know where it is. Thank you, Miss Frist. Bye."

"Bye."

As we headed toward the reference room out of earshot of Miss Frist, Mom said, "Well, somebody certainly has a huge fan. Are you going to be able to fit your head through the door?" She glanced over at me; I think to make sure that I knew she was just teasing. "I mean, 'special and wonderful' and 'something else entirely'. Dad and I feel that way, but we're your parents; it kind of goes with the territory."

I love it when either Mom or Dad teases me like that. They can throw a whole bunch of praise my way, but because they do it with a sense of humor, I don't get as embarrassed, and it gives me a chance to tease back a little.

"I don't know, Mom. 'Special and wonderful', that would be S-A-W, and 'something else entirely', that would be S-E-E. That's saw-see—It makes me sound like dyslexic playground equipment."

Mom had trouble stifling a laugh. (Remember, it was the library.) She pulled me toward her, gave me a kiss on the top of my head, and whispered, "You **are** something else entirely."

We came upon Michael in between the reference stacks with his back toward us. In a soft voice I said, "Hi, Michael."

He turned around and got a big smile on his face. "Hi, Benny." He reached out to shake my hand. He kind of ignored Mom. It's not that he was being rude; it's just that he was focusing on me.

"How are you doing, Michael?"

Before he said anything, I noticed a change in his posture. Evidently, Michael had been given instructions on how to address patrons of the library, no matter who they were. And as you know, once Michael learned something, it stayed with him, and there was almost no chance that he would move away from the routine. So, I was treated to the standard library question—"May I help you find something?" I got the feeling that Michael even said those same words to his father when he came into the library.

"No, that's okay, Michael. I just wanted to say 'hello'."

Michael surprised me, however. He said, "I could show you where the videos are." I smiled and started to say "no", but then decided, why not?

"Okay sure, Michael. That would be great."

Michael took us to the video section. He smiled and said, "If there's anything else you need, please let me know." He started to head back to the reference room, but before he got very far he turned back and said. "Bye, Benny. Bye, Benny's Mom."

In the car on the way home, I must have had a pensive look on my face because Mom said, "A penny for your thoughts."

"I was just thinking about Michael. It was like part of the time he was reading from a script."

"It probably was a script."

"But, I think it's gonna work out for him, don't you?"

"Yes, I do. I think it's perfect for him. Most of the time he can work by himself, and yet he seems to know what to say when he has to. Plus, people going to the library will be understanding."

"I think they will too". I smiled again. "I just hope nobody asks to take out a Scooby-Doo video. Now that could be a problem."

We both laughed.

On Sunday afternoon Mrs. Witkowski came over to our house to see us. She announced that the doctors at the rehabilitation center had said that Mr. Witkowski could come home the following Friday. None of us could believe it. Dad asked, "You mean for good, or just for a visit?"

"For good." She got tears in her eyes and had a little trouble continuing. "He's still going to need therapy, but the doctors said that he's well enough that he can have it at home. And Medicare pays for everything."

Dad followed up. 'Why the change? How come they'll pay for it now?"

"Evidently, as long as there's no need for round-the-clock care, which there isn't now ... I mean Jack can get out of bed on his own and can get around with the walker. So, as long as he can take care of himself, then the cost of any therapists who treat him at home are covered by Medicare."

Mom: "He must be thrilled."

"He is." Mrs. Witkowski paused for a moment. "We won't need all of the money you loaned us now."

Mom: "You know that's not an issue. We'll figure it out once things settle down."

"We're so thankful for what you did. I really think it helped him recover more quickly."

Dad: "We're just glad he's coming home."

She sighed as she said, "Me too." Then she got a little smile on her face and continued. "I have to tell you what Jack said when they told him he was going to come home next Friday. He checked the date and saw that it was March seventeenth—St. Patrick's Day. He said he was going to become Irish for the day in honor of leaving the hospital."

We all laughed.

True to his word, when I saw Mr. Witkowski that Friday afternoon, he was dressed in a green shirt and green pants. We had made up a banner, which we hung over the door—"Welcome Home Jack O'Witkowski." And although it was a little hard to understand him, I'm pretty sure that his first words when he walked through the front door of his house were "'Tis a glorious day."

A couple of weeks later Derek, Vanessa, and I were called down to the main office toward the end of the day. When we arrived, Dr. Foster was there to greet us. He told us to follow him into Mr. Martin's office. He was grinning from ear to ear, and shaking his head back and forth. "You won't believe this."

We all looked at each other, and then I spoke up. "Believe what?"

"I'll tell you inside."

Mr. Martin was also smiling when we entered his office. He asked us to please sit down. Once we were seated, Mr. Martin said to Dr. Foster, "Go ahead, you can tell them."

Dr. Foster is usually pretty calm about things, but he was as excited as I'd ever seen him. He made eye contact with the three of us and then said, "Guess who called my office about an hour ago?"

It was obviously a rhetorical question, but I almost always feel somehow obligated to answer those. But before I got a chance, Dr. Foster blurted out, "Oprah Winfrey."

Me: "What?"

"Well, not Oprah herself, one of her staff."

Me again: "Why?"

"Project Red Light."

"Project Red Light?"

"Yes, evidently somebody sent her the article from the paper, or they monitor those kind of things, because her staff checked out our website …"

Derek: "Wow, that's really cool!"

Vanessa: "You're not kidding, right?"

"No, I'm not kidding."

Me: "So what did they want? What's going to happen?"

Dr. Foster started shaking his head again. "They're considering doing a show about it."

Vanessa: "Are you serious?"

"Yes. If you've seen some of her shows, she does them on bullying, and protecting children, stopping prejudice; things like that. So, Project Red Light would fit right in."

Derek: "This is amazing!"

"It sure is."

Mr. Martin spoke up at that point. "I know how exciting this is, but nothing's definite. So you can tell your folks and have them call me if they have any questions, but we're not making this public until we know something for sure. So, please keep it within your families for the time being. I know that's going to be hard, but please try."

Me: "When do you think we'll know something?"

"Probably in about a week."

It was a good thing it was late in the day when we found out about all this, because I don't think it would have been possible to do much schoolwork with this in the back of our minds. Well actually, it was probably more toward the front of our minds, certainly in the frontal lobe area, maybe even pressing against our foreheads. You might even say it was … Well, you get the idea.

Chapter 20

Remember that I told you how much I love anticipation—that for me, it's almost as exciting as the event itself? Well, I think that only applies to events that are definitely going to happen. Waiting for the people from Oprah's staff to call wasn't really as exciting as much as it was nerve-racking. But like most things, as each day passed, it occupied less and less time in my thoughts, although it was definitely still there.

Finally, about a week after the initial phone call from the Oprah show, Dr. Foster heard back. Derek, Vanessa, and I were called to Mr. Martin's office, where he and Dr. Foster were waiting for us.

Dr. Foster: "Hi, guys. Come on in and sit down."

He could obviously see the wide-eyed questioning look on our faces, so he got right to the subject at hand. "There's good news, and there's bad news. Well, not exactly bad news, but not what we had hoped for. I'm afraid we're not going to be on the show, at least not in person."

Vanessa: "What do you mean?"

"Well, Oprah's doing a show a week from Monday. I think that's the twenty-fourth. Anyway, she's going to have a number of different segments about schools that make a difference and community programs that work. The good news is that Project Red Light was selected, but everything will be on videotape …"

Derek interrupted. "But we'll be part of that, won't we?"

"I would assume so, but they'll decide that once they get here."

Vanessa: "They're coming here? When? Is Oprah coming too?"

"No, Oprah's not coming. She couldn't possibly go to all the places that they're doing the stories about."

Mr. Martin interjected. "But some members of her staff are coming this Friday. Again, we're not sure how this is going to work, but they faxed us some releases for your parents to sign in case the show uses any videotape that you're in."

Derek: "Do you think they will?"

Dr. Foster spoke up again. "I can't be sure, but it's hard to imagine that they wouldn't at least use your pictures on television. After all, it was your idea. Plus, they sent the releases. I doubt they would have done that if they weren't planning to use the three of you in the segment."

Derek: "Wow, this is really cool!"

Dr. Foster turned to me. "Benny, you haven't said very much."

"I guess I'm just trying to take all this in." I turned toward Derek and Vanessa. "I can't say I'm totally disappointed that we won't be on the show in person. I think I would have been way too nervous."

Vanessa: "I think you would've been fine. But you know, this is still really exciting, don't you think?"

"Yeah, it really is."

Mr. Martin got up and started to distribute the envelopes that contained the releases. "Okay, please give these to your parents, and have them sign them. If they have any questions, they can give me a call."

Even though the word about the Oprah show visit spread throughout the school and community, and there was an article in the paper, the visit was surprisingly low-key. I'm sure if Oprah herself had been there, it would have been a different story.

During the visit, Derek, Vanessa, and I were videotaped, as were Dr. Foster and Mr. Martin. I don't think you could call it being interviewed, because there wasn't anyone asking specific questions. Instead, we were asked to give a synopsis of Project Red Light and how it came about.

Oprah's staff also asked for a copy of the videotape the school had made of the evening presentation that was held for parents. Her staff indicated that the segment of the show featuring our project would consist of some of the videotape they shot that day, mixed with the videotape from the evening presentation, and it would probably last about five to eight minutes. That didn't seem like very long, considering that they had spent over three hours at the school.

Mr. Martin sent out a notice a few days before the show was scheduled to air, indicating that any students or parents who wanted to watch the Oprah show in the school's auditorium on Monday the twenty-fourth were welcome. The school was going to set up a large screen and then have the TV image projected onto it. When the big day arrived, about three hundred of us filed into the auditorium to watch Oprah. Dad even got out of work a little early so he could join us.

Oprah introduced the show by explaining that there would be five schools featured, each of which had instituted programs that made their schools and communities better places. She also indicated that one of the criteria for selecting these particular school programs was that they could be replicated elsewhere.

The first segment of the show was the longest one. But, if I'm being objective, it was probably the most impressive, because it involved finding missing children. Some students in an upstate New York high school had devised a plan to expand "Amber Alerts".

If you aren't aware, "Amber Alerts" is a voluntary partnership among law-enforcement agencies, broadcasters, and transportation agencies that activates an urgent bulletin in certain child abduction cases. When these alerts are issued, they are seen or heard on digital highway signs, TV, and radio.

The students at the school in New York created a plan to expand the notification system. Since many school districts already have automated dialing systems that can send out messages to every parent in the district on both land lines and cell phones simultaneously, these systems could be employed during an Amber Alert. In addition, the students arranged with local malls, banks, and movie theatres that have prominently displayed video screens, to include all Amber Alerts on those TV's as well.

The other three segments besides ours included a North Carolina school that had implemented a very effective anti-bullying program; an Illinois school that had started a unique program celebrating diversity; and an inner city school from Oakland, California, that instituted a program to curb gang violence.

Our segment was aired last; and while it didn't directly deal with safety issues, or even life-or-death situations, like some of the other segments, I still thought it sent a powerful message. Dr. Foster, Mr. Martin, Derek, Vanessa, and I all appeared briefly on the videotape. Oprah's voiceover introduced each of us by name, and she gave Derek, Vanessa, and me credit for coming up with the idea. Almost half of the segment focused on the evening presentation, probably because so much of that evening dealt with the potential expansion of the project. Nonetheless, I thought it was well done, and in a short eight minutes it was able to capture the whole purpose of Project Red Light.

There was a huge surprise at the very end of the show, however. Oprah announced that each of the featured schools would receive $50,000. $25,000 was a gift that each school could use as it wished; the other $25,000 was to be used to expand the program, and to provide additional information to any other schools that wanted to implement it. At the conclusion of Oprah's announcement, everyone in our school auditorium applauded and cheered.

Many of the three hundred people that were in the auditorium that day stayed for another hour after the show was over, just talking about the project and the money Oprah had pledged. Mr. Martin announced that he was going to set up an advisory committee to help decide how to allocate the $25,000 gift, and how best to expand Project Red Light. He indicated that anyone interested in serving on the committee should e-mail him. He also thanked everyone who had come, and asked Derek, Vanessa, and me to stand up and be recognized again.

It was quite an afternoon!

On the way home in the car Dad said, "Well, that was certainly exciting. You kids were terrific, and what a great thing for the school."

Mom weighed in. "It really was." She paused. "I was thinking about volunteering for the committee Mr. Martin's setting up, but with Benny so involved ... I'm not sure." She turned toward the backseat. "Benny, do you think there'll be any students on the committee?"

"I don't know. When I saw Mr. Martin after the show, he didn't talk about the committee; he was just so excited about the grant."

Dad: "Why don't you e-mail Mr. Martin, Lillian, and at least volunteer? If there's an issue, I'm sure he'll let you know."

"Yeah, you're right; that's a good idea." Mom turned back toward me. "So, how are you feeling about all this?"

"Really good. I thought the whole show was pretty interesting, and our part was well done, and then with the money ..."

Mom: "I agree. It really was quite well done. I mean the whole show, not just your segment." Mom turned back toward the front before she continued. "I'm going to give Grandma and Grandpa a call when we get home to see how they liked it."

Dad responded. "That's kind of a foregone conclusion, don't you think? I mean, their only grandchild's on national television; I'm sure they'll be very objective."

Mom gave Dad a smile and a tap on the shoulder. "Well, grandparents are allowed to be biased; and so are parents, for that matter."

"Yes, we are." With that, Dad made eye contact with me in the rearview mirror. "Benny, you know how proud we are, don't you?"

"Yeah, I do."

Dad continued. "You know, there were a lot of people from my office who were going to stay at work to watch the show, so they wouldn't miss it on the commute home."

Mom: "That's really nice."

"Oh, and in all the excitement, I almost forgot. Speaking of work, I have some news, and this involves you Benny." He made eye contact again. "We got confirmation about something today."

I leaned forward, pushing against my seat belt, so I could make out more clearly what Dad was saying.

"You've heard of MacDonald Alexander?"

Me: "The billionaire?"

"Yes. Well, he's coming to the ad agency on Thursday."

"This Thursday?"

"Right."

"This Thursday's 'Take Your Child to Work Day', isn't it? So won't I be there?"

Dad started to smile. "Yes. And you'll get a chance to meet him."

"Really?"

"I don't see why not."

Mom: "Why is MacDonald Alexander coming? It seems like he gets plenty of free publicity; why does he need an ad agency?"

"I think it has to do with that announcement he made last year. You know—when he said he was donating, what was it—two billion to charity? Well evidently, part of the donation has to do with some business venture, and that may require some advertising. But we won't get all the details until Thursday."

Mom turned back toward me. "First Oprah and now MacDonald Alexander. This is quite a week for you, Benny."

"Yeah, it really is."

After supper that night, even before I started my homework, I used the Internet to look up MacDonald Alexander. There were well over 100,000 references. I started with a capsule biography.

He was born in upstate New York in May of 1945. He graduated from Cornell and then got a law degree from Columbia. But instead of pursuing anything in the legal arena, he joined an investment firm. He rose through the ranks very quickly and could have been the youngest managing partner in the firm, but instead, he decided to go out on his own in the late 1980's. During the next ten years, his investment house didn't make many mistakes, at a time when there were many mistakes to make. A lot of investors, trying to get rich quick, started chasing the ".com companies". He didn't. By the end of the 1990's he had cracked the list of the 400 richest people in America, and last year he was ranked twelfth with an estimated net worth of **fifteen billion dollars**.

Up until last year, MacDonald Alexander had always been able to stay beneath the media's radar. However, when he announced that he was "giving away" two billion dollars, it became a huge story. Although it wasn't totally unique—Ted Turner and Warren Buffet had done something similar—it was still pretty remarkable, and got a lot of attention.

I was able to find the issues of *Newsweek* and *Time* on the Internet from the week that Mr. Alexander made his announcement. It was the cover story on both magazines.

The *Time* headline read "Alexander the Great—Conqueror of the Financial World—Giving Some of the Spoils Away."

The *Newsweek* headline read "Big Mac—Over 15 Billion Earned, and 2 Billion Donated."

I read both articles, but neither one was specific about which charities were going to be the beneficiaries of Mr. Alexander's donation. In fact, he indicated in both articles "… a large portion of the donation will involve a project that can sustain the charitable contributions for many years to come." He refused to elaborate further, saying only that when other things were in place, in about a year, there would be another major announcement.

It's usually difficult to tell from a magazine article, even one with direct quotes, what somebody is like. But in Mr. Alexander's case, I definitely got the impression that he was a "regular guy", despite his fifteen, soon to be thirteen, billion dollars.

That got me curious. If he was a regular guy, I wondered if it bothered him to be referred to as "Alexander the Great". Ever since the *Time* magazine cover story came out, the nickname had been used a lot. Despite my curiosity, I decided it probably wasn't something I could really bring up on Thursday.

Anyway, I didn't know that much about the original Alexander the Great, so I decided to Google him also. Here's what I found out:

He was born in 356 B.C., the son of Philip of Macedonia. (I was thinking that if children in modern times were identified the same way, I might be known as "Benjamin the Pretty Good", son of Joe and Lillian of Massachusetts. What do you think?) Since there were no formal schools in Macedonia, Philip decided that

Alex still needed to be educated, so he hired a tutor. Guess who the tutor turned out to be?—**Aristotle!!!**

I think there may have been another reason Philip hired Aristotle besides a commitment to Alex's education. I'm pretty sure the first year Aristotle tutored Alex was the first year Macedonia instituted the Macedonia Comprehensive Assessment System—their own version of MCAS. While passing the MCAS in Macedonia in those days was not a graduation requirement (there were no schools to graduate from), failing it had very serious consequences. Anyone who failed the MCAS could not get a permit allowing them to "pillage and plunder". (Tends to put a crimp in any conquering you're looking to do.)

There are no official transcripts still existing that can tell us how Alex fared. But I guess we can assume he passed, because his dad left him in charge of all of Macedonia just after his sixteenth birthday. A few years later, Alex conquered the whole rest of the known world. (Pillaging and plundering permits were good for up to ten years.)

While I was processing all of this information, it struck me as pretty amazing. After all, I'm only a few years younger than Alexander was when he ruled an **entire civilization**; and I'm barely in charge of my own room.

Dad and I arrived at his office at about 8:45 on Thursday morning. He reintroduced me to most of the people he worked with. Many of them commented on the Oprah show, and a few even mentioned my cross-country exploits from last fall. I couldn't help but think that Dad was sending out periodic updates on me—you know, like those Christmas newsletters that people send detailing everything the family did for the past twelve months. Only, Dad must have been sending out the "Benny Newsletter" much more frequently, certainly quarterly, if not monthly.

I knew he was proud of me. I just hoped that he wasn't boring people to death with things like, "Benny passed his Spanish mid-term", or "Benny passed his physical for spring track", or even "Benny passed a kidney stone". I mean, I can understand the Oprah thing, and even possibly the cross-country, but I thought anything else was pushing it. (I mean, I don't even think Philip of Macedonia issued regular papyrus reports on Alexander.)

Anyway, most of the morning Dad showed me the projects he was working on, and then he took me out to lunch. We got back to the office at about 1:00. Mr. Alexander wasn't scheduled to be there until 1:30, but the people in the office were already very excited in anticipation of his arrival. I'm sure they all sensed what Dad had told me—if Mr. Alexander went with their agency, it could end up being a multi-million dollar account. Plus, it wasn't every day that you met a billionaire. (You might meet some kid that had been on Oprah with his own newsletter, yeah; but a billionaire, no.)

At about 1:15 Dad's boss, Mr. Jenkins, knocked on the open door to Dad's office. "Hi, Joe. Hi, Benny. Mr. Alexander arrived a few minutes early, so he asked if he could come around to some of the offices and meet people." With that, Mr. Jenkins moved to the side, and MacDonald Alexander appeared.

I recognized him from the cover of the magazines I had read, but he wasn't as imposing a figure as I had expected. Nonetheless, he definitely had a presence about him. He walked past Mr. Jenkins with an outstretched arm toward Dad's desk. "Mack Alexander, pleased to meet you."

Dad appeared a little flustered, but he extended his hand, and managed to say, "Joe Curtis, pleased to meet you as well, Mr. Alexander."

"Please call me Mack. Actually, almost nobody does, but I really do prefer it." And he smiled.

Dad smiled back. "Okay, Mack."

Mr. Alexander turned toward me. "And this must be your son—Benny, right?" (The circulation of the "Benny Newsletter" must be more widespread than I thought.)

He headed over to me and shook my hand. If I thought Dad was flustered, I have no idea how to describe how I was feeling. I finally was able to put together a few coherent words. "Yes sir, I'm Benny. It's very nice to meet you."

He studied me for a moment. "Wondering how I knew your name, huh?"

"Well kind of, yeah."

"Warren told me—Mr. Jenkins. He also told me about you being on Oprah. That's pretty impressive. You're a few steps ahead of me. I've met her, but I've never been on her show." He hesitated and smiled. "Have you got any pull?" I just smiled back, as he continued. "I'm afraid I didn't see the show, but Warren told me about your idea. That was excellent."

"Thank you, sir."

"How old are you, twelve, thirteen?"

"I'll be twelve in a few weeks."

"There you go. Pretty impressive idea for someone your age."

"Thank you."

He turned back to Dad. "We'll see you in a few minutes, Joe."

"Thank you, Mr … uh Mack."

Mr. Alexander smiled. "Thanks for remembering." And he started to head toward the door. "Bye, Benny. Keep up the good work."

"Bye, Mr. Alexander."

Just as he exited through the door to Dad's office, he poked his head back in. "Benny?"

"Yes sir?"

"Why don't you come to the meeting with your dad? I think you'll enjoy it." There was no chance for anyone to say anything in response. He was gone.

So it ended up that there were ten people at the meeting—Mr. Alexander and two assistants, Mr. Jenkins, Dad, four other executives from the ad agency, and me. The meeting started promptly at 1:30, and Mr. Alexander spoke pretty much non-stop until 2:00. He had some handouts and some pictures in front of him, but no notes that I could see. The presentation was more extemporaneous than it was memorized, and it was flawless.

"As you know, a number of months ago I announced that I was going to donate two billion dollars to charity, but I didn't specify which organizations would be the recipients. That's because I was planning to do things a little differently. I'm using the initial two billion to create a 'structure' that will sustain the charitable donations. When all is said and done, we'll probably end up donating in the 10 billion dollar range."

Other than Mr. Alexander and his two assistants, everyone else in the room was wide-eyed with their mouths agape. He paused for a moment, taking in everyone's expression before he continued. "I know that's a staggering figure, and I know that what I'm about to say will probably strike you as even more absurd." He seemed to pause for effect. "It's—only—money." He spoke each word individually with at least two seconds between the pronunciation of each one. "How much money does any one person need?" He paused again. "I can't say I always felt that way, but I certainly do now." He took a sip of water and then continued.

"So, I'm sure you're wondering what this has to do with all of you. Okay, let's get down to it. I've been to three ad agencies in New York, one in Chicago, and now this one in Boston. The five agencies I've visited weren't chosen at random. You all have something in common." He paused again. "You have a conscience. That's very important to me ..."

"Each of the agencies has been told the same thing. You'll have about a month to create an ad campaign for the products I'm going to tell you about. And quite simply, whichever agency creates the best campaign will be rewarded with a very lucrative contract."

He expanded on those ideas for a few minutes, and then described what had been going on since he made his initial announcement about the charitable donation.

"I'm currently building ten factories around the world. There are three here in the United States, two in Asia, one in Africa, and four in Latin and South America. Each factory will manufacture children's clothing and footwear. The workers in these factories will be paid wages higher than the prevailing wages being paid to workers in those countries or geographic areas."

"The children's clothing will be sold world-wide, but at a cost to the local consumer that's just slightly above the cost to make the clothes. Our main goal is **not** to make huge profits. Primarily, we want to provide good paying jobs and offer quality children's clothing at very affordable prices."

At this point Mr. Alexander entertained some questions. In response to one, he said that yes, it was probable that the same pair of children's jeans would be priced differently in different countries and would undercut most of the more popular brands. "We'll be able to do that because, although we won't be a **non-profit** company, we will be a **low-profit** company. Any profits we do make will be donated, or will be used to fund the other significant part of this endeavor that I'm going to tell you about."

"Each factory is being built in an economically depressed area of the various countries, including the United States. Attached to each factory will be a modern-day, fully equipped health clinic, primarily to serve children. However, anyone coming to the clinic will be treated, whether they have health insurance or not. They will only be expected to pay whatever they can afford. Nobody will be turned away. We will continue to subsidize the clinics after they're up and running, even if the profits from the sales of the children's clothing line can't sustain them."

As you can imagine, the questions were non-stop after Mr. Alexander finished this last portion of the presentation. He patiently answered all of them for about forty-five minutes. Toward the very end of the meeting he made one more clarification.

"In the folders you have in front of you, the name of the clothing line is listed there—TARO. It's an acronym for the initials of my four grandchildren—Thomas, Alicia, Robert, and Olivia. And while that name obviously has a lot of sentimental importance to me, I encourage you to try to come up with something else, another name that conveys what this project is all about. Also, we don't even have a logo yet; you can work on that too. I guess you could say I'm looking for the whole package. But if you can deliver it, it will be very much worth your while. Just keep in mind that this is about children. That should be the driving force behind anything you present to me." He looked around the room briefly, and then continued. "If there are no more questions, I think everything you need is in the folders we distributed, and I will see you on …" He opened the letter binder in front of him for the first time. "Friday, May twenty-sixth."

The next day in school, Derek, Vanessa, and I held a TUCK meeting during lunchtime. I had briefly told them about Mr. Alexander when we were in homeroom, but lunchtime was the first opportunity to go into details.

Derek: "Wow, how cool is that, meeting a billionaire?"

Vanessa: "Did you say anything at the meeting?"

"No, although I got the impression that Mr. Alexander wouldn't have minded. He even made eye-contact with me a few times, as if I was one of the executives."

Vanessa: "So, when are the factories going to be finished?"

"He said in about three months. He said he'd like to have the clothing available, at least in the United States, before school starts next September."

Vanessa: "But he doesn't even have a name for the company yet?"

"Well he does. But, I think he's hoping that one of the agencies will come up with something he likes better."

Derek: "Do you think your dad's agency will get the contract?"

"No way to tell. But I do think Mr. Alexander was very comfortable with everybody there." I paused briefly. "He never said 'red light' once."

That afternoon there was a meeting for anyone interested in going out for spring track. We received parent permission cards, a schedule of the meets, and a form for our doctor to fill out if we were having a private physical. If we didn't have a physical from our own doctor, then the school physician would be there on Monday morning, and our first formal practice would be that afternoon.

Unlike cross-country, which only consists of one event, spring track has a number of running events and field events as well. However, middle school spring track doesn't have all of the events that high school track does. In middle school we don't have the javelin, the discus, the pole vault, or the two-mile.

Still, it was pretty cool that I could participate in one running event, one field event, and a relay. Since I'm better at longer distances, I decided that I'd like to try the 1500 meters (the metric mile). Without the two-mile, the 1500 meters was the longest running event we had in middle school.

Don't you think it's interesting that pretty much the rest of the world uses the metric system, but the United States doesn't? Well, actually we do, but only in **two** areas if you can believe it—**track and field** and **soda**.

I mean, we have the 100-meter dash, the 400-meter run, the 800-meter run, etc. But in all other sports we deal in yards, feet, and inches. In football for example, "first and ten" means first down and ten **yards** to go, not 2.54 meters. In baseball we sometimes say he was out by a **mile**, not 1.61 kilometers. I don't understand why we use the metric system in the sport of track and field, but no other sport.

And guess what? It's even more bizarre in liquid measurements. We purchase **quarts** of milk, **half-gallons** of ice cream, and **gallons** of gasoline. (When using this comparison, I feel obligated to inform you that gasoline is not for human consumption. It's possible that the whole "ridiculous label thing" may have made me overly cautious.) But when we buy soda, it comes in one- and two-**liter** bottles. Why? And why only in that size do we use the metric system? In the smaller sizes we have 12-**ounce** cans and 20 **ounce** bottles.

Is there any logic to this at all? And who decided it? I'll bet it's the same people who relegated Pluto to dwarf planet status. And I'll bet they're doing it just because they can. (I wonder if I still have Oliver Stone's number.)

Anyway, for my field event I thought I'd try the triple jump. I'm fairly tall for my age (I've moved up to the ninety-second percentile), so I figured that would help. Plus, the triple jump looked like a fun event.

The triple jump, for those of you who don't know, used to be called the hop-step-and-jump, and in ancient times, the hop-skip-and-jump. Legend has it that the Romans and Greeks were going to compete against each other in a precursor to the Olympic games, and the Romans wanted to add an event that would feature two hops and a jump. However, the Emperor at the time was Februus—remember him? He's the one Julius and Augustus stole the days from. Anyway, if you also remember, many Roman citizens questioned Februus' manhood—that whole bumper sticker campaign on the chariots. Well, what may have actually triggered that campaign was Februus' decision to call the new event the hop-**skip**-and-jump. The sight of Roman Centurions practicing for the upcoming games by hopping and skipping did little to enhance the reputation of the Roman army.

There's no way to confirm the authenticity of this legend, but it is a well-known fact that the genesis of most track and field events is the military, so maybe the legend is true. However, I'm not exactly sure what military maneuver involves hopping and skipping and jumping—The Battle for Peter Rabbit's Warren?

During the months leading up to spring track, I ran periodically to try to keep in shape. So, over the weekend after meeting Mr. Alexander, I ran on both Saturday and Sunday. Since Mr. Witkowski was doing so much better, he didn't dominate my thoughts while I was running as he had done for so many previous months.

Instead, I thought a lot about what Mr. Alexander had said. One idea in particular started to solidify in my head, and by the time I finished my three-mile run on Sunday, it really felt like the idea might have a lot of promise. I definitely needed to check out some things before I mentioned it to anyone else though. But if certain parts of the idea could be worked out, I wanted to let my dad know as soon as possible.

On Monday after school, I headed down to the locker room to change for our first day of track practice. To my surprise, Derek was there.

"I thought you were going out for baseball."

"Yeah, I know. I changed my mind."

"When?"

"Just today."

"Any particular reason?"

"Well, I'm okay at baseball, but I'm not sure how much I'd play. With track I know I'll get a chance to participate in every meet, and I figure in track you compete against yourself. You know, trying to improve your time. Plus, I think I'm pretty fast, and I liked the long jump when we did it in gym …"

"Hey, I think it's great, but how come you didn't say anything?"

"I just decided about ten minutes ago."

Derek and I went out to the field together to warm up. We talked about "nothing" for a few minutes, and then I told him about the idea I had come up with while I was running. Actually, I needed to ask him some questions, because he knew a lot more about some of this stuff than I did.

"So what do you think, can that work?"

"I don't see why not. That really is a pretty cool idea."

"Is there an easy way to check it out for sure?"

"Yeah, I'll get on the Internet, but I don't see a problem." He looked over at me. "You know, it's so funny that you mentioned that idea you came up with. My mom and dad took me to the doctor on Saturday for my sports physical, so Vanessa babysat for Samantha. And when we got back, they were playing with paper dolls. Vanessa had found a website that Samantha could use to design clothes for the dolls, and then she printed them out. Samantha showed them to my mom and dad. Then Vanessa said, "You did a great job of designing those outfits, Samantha. In fact, they're so good, we should show them to Mr. Alexander'."

We didn't get a chance to continue the conversation because our coach divided us up into sprinters and distance runners for our workout. While I was practicing, I continued to think about my idea and about Derek's assurance that it could work. I definitely wanted to talk to him some more about it, and probably about Vanessa's idea also, for that matter.

Chapter 21

I didn't get a chance to talk to Derek anymore that afternoon. The sprinters finished their workout ahead of the distance runners, and he was gone before I got back to the locker room. After I got home I was going to give him a call, but I decided to go on the computer instead. I wanted to see if I could find out anything more about what Derek and I had been discussing.

But since I couldn't think of any more related phrases to put into the search engine, and I figured that Derek would probably find out additional information about how feasible my idea was anyway, I decided to go in a different direction. I typed in "designing dresses".

It was probably my imagination, but my computer seemed to hesitate, almost as if it were asking me, "'designing dresses', are you sure?" As it took longer and longer, I had to fight the urge to actually speak to the computer, and tell it that I was just looking for the website that Vanessa and Samantha had visited.

I know that talking to a computer sounds odd, but in my experience a lot of people actually do talk to electronic devices. I think this is especially the case when the device isn't working as fast as they would like. For example, I've seen people who have recorded a program on TV sit down to watch it, and scream at the set when they're fast forwarding through the commercials, "Come on! Come on! What's wrong with you?" I also saw a woman on a TV reality show, who was supposedly trying to lose weight, stand in front of her microwave screaming, "Hurry up! Hurry up! Are you kidding me?"

However, I think my situation was totally different—I just didn't want the computer wondering why an eleven-year-old boy was searching out websites about "designing dresses". Doesn't that seem way more rational than the fast-forwarding and the microwave situations? Okay, maybe not. But I never did actually speak to the computer; I think that should count for something.

Anyway, regardless of what my **computer's** "feelings" might have been about the appropriateness of my search, I was very glad that Mom and Dad had always respected my privacy. I didn't want to have to explain to them what might appear to be a newfound interest in female attire.

I know the human brain is often compared to a computer. But when I watched the search engine do its thing, making all those connections, I really felt like it was replicating how **my** brain works. You know, with my ICBM, one thing connects to another, and then another, and then pretty soon I find myself in Tangent City.

That's kind of what happened in my "designing dresses" search. There were a number of sites that had those words in the title, but it was obvious that none of them was the site that Samantha and Vanessa had visited. A couple of references further down the page included the words "design**er** dresses", then "designer dresses—Paris". (Evidently, that's where the annual international fashion show is held each year.) Eventually, at the bottom of the second page was "dresses—Paris Hilton".

I didn't spend very much time at that site because I was concerned that if Mom and Dad happened to come into my room, being on **that** website would be even harder to explain away. In the brief time that I was looking at the computer screen, however, I did notice that there was a link to "exposedParisH.com". (No, it wasn't what you think.) Even though I didn't go to the linked website, there was a brief description of what was on it.

Evidently, it offers thousands of Paris Hilton's personal items for sale that were left behind in a Los Angeles public storage facility—photographs, home videos, diaries, love letters, etc. These are not being offered for sale by Paris herself, but rather by a third party who purchased the items at an auction because rental payments for the storage facility were in default. (I know we're deep into Tangent City here, but don't you think this is really too good to pass up?) Anyway, I'll just make a few quick observations and then I promise to move on.

You know that phrase—"the rich are different from you and me"? Well, I suspect that maybe that's true. Do you think the average family puts their photographs, home movies, and diaries in a public storage facility? I guess it's possible, although I would think that it's highly unlikely. But they certainly wouldn't do it—**if they owned hotels with millions of rooms in them that they could use!!!**

Also, if people did decide to put all their personal items in public storage for whatever reason, and their family is worth a "gazillion" dollars, wouldn't you think that they'd pay in advance?

I guess it's possible that this whole thing was a publicity stunt, although the fact that Paris Hilton's TV show was called *The Simple Life* was probably not an accident.

The last thing I remember thinking about before I left the website and checked my e-mail was … MacDonald Alexander and Paris Hilton … they both have a ton of money; one of them is donating billions to charity and building health clinics; and the other one is … actually, I have no idea what the other one does.

The next day in school Vanessa saw me in homeroom before Derek arrived, and she said, "I spoke to Derek last night, and he said that you were interested in the dresses that Samantha made." As she said this, she got a smile on her face and raised her eyebrows.

"Okay, okay. It was just because of the idea I had about Mr. Alexander's project. I was actually thinking about something to do with sneakers, not dresses …"

"I'm just teasing. Derek told me all about it. I think it's a really good idea." She paused. "Anyway, I did bring in some of the designs I printed out for Samantha. Do you want to see them?"

"Sure … What's the address for the website, by the way?" Her eyebrows went up again, so I tried to offer an explanation. "Oh, for Pete's sake, I'm just curious."

"Pretty touchy this morning." She was smiling again as she said this.

I smiled back. "Can I see them please? It's for my Dad's company … nothing personal."

She handed them to me, and laughed. Then she pointed to one of the printouts. "Obviously, Samantha really likes hearts. She draws them on everything. While I was babysitting, she even wrote a song called *In the Heart of My Hearts*. We typed it up on the computer." She smiled. "Every other word was 'heart'."

I started to look at the printouts. "I really don't know much about this stuff" (I didn't dare tell her about my computer searches the night before), "and no offense to Samantha, but these don't look all that great."

Vanessa continued to smile. "Well, they're actually pretty good for a six-year-old."

"I guess … so, when you said you thought Mr. Alexander should see these, you were only kidding, just trying to make Samantha feel good?"

"Yeah, kinda … about the designs anyway … but when I thought about what Mr. Alexander is trying to do, you know, help people all around the world, and I saw …" At that point Vanessa took back some of the designs and shuffled through them. "… this one." As she said that, she pointed to a dress that had red hearts around the middle of it, like a belt. "I thought about hearts everywhere, like hearts around the world. Don't you think that it would be a good slogan, even a good logo? You know, a picture of the world with hearts around it."

I didn't say anything for a moment, still studying the printout. Finally, I spoke up. "I do kind of think it's a good idea, but …"

"But what?"

"Well, I know it'll probably sound sexist, but isn't 'hearts around the world' kind of feminine? I mean, are boys gonna want to wear clothes with hearts on them?"

"I didn't really think about that … you're probably right. Anyway, it was just something that popped into my head."

I handed back the design printouts I was still holding. "Sorry …"

"It's okay. It was just an idea. I only brought these in because Derek told me about your idea about the sneakers, which—I really mean it—is excellent."

"Thanks." I paused. "You know what? I'm still going to tell my dad about the hearts idea anyway, just to see what he thinks."

"Benny, you don't really have to do that."

"Well, I'm going to show him my idea anyway, so I might as well show him yours."

"Benny, I don't think there's much of a comparison between the two of them."

"Yeah, I know … He's probably gonna like yours better."

Vanessa smiled and gave me a gentle shove.

At lunchtime we told Derek about our conversation, and I asked him if he had found out anything more about my sneaker idea.

"I did look up a few more things on the Internet. I still don't see a problem. The only thing is …"

"What?"

"We should probably talk to Mr. Witkowski."

"How come?"

'Well, I do think you'll need a special tool for part of your idea. And who knows more about tools than Mr. Witkowski?"

"Good point."

"But don't worry about it. I already e-mailed him last night. He'll probably e-mail me back later today. As soon as I hear from him, I'll let you know. Okay?"

It was really a rhetorical question, so I didn't respond. Plus, Derek appeared to be more concerned with his lunch bag. "Uh-oh."

"What's the matter?"

"My mom put in some Twinkies. She knows I love them, but with track and everything, I probably shouldn't eat them."

I tried to be supportive. "They're not as bad for you as they used to be. I mean, they still have a lot of saturated fats in them, but they took out the trans fat." I paused. "You should probably stay away from Ding Dongs though; they're worse."

Vanessa waited for just a moment, and then she added with a big smile on her face. "Yeah ... remember—You are what you eat."

Derek, not to be outdone, returned the smile and said, "Don't you have turkey for lunch today, Vanessa?"

A few days later, Derek told me that he had heard from Mr. Witkowski, and everything looked good. I decided to go next door and talk to him directly. He still showed some effects from the stroke, but he was much easier to understand, and he was getting around much better also. Mr. Witkowski assured me that my idea with the sneakers should work, but with his limited dexterity, he had to describe the process rather than show it to me. After he finished, he looked at me and smiled, and then in a halting voice said, "I think this is a better idea than that one you were on TV for."

On Thursday night right after supper, I asked Dad if I could talk to him for a minute. As usual, he said, "Sure. What's up?"

"Well, after last week when I met Mr. Alexander ..." And then I went on to describe the last few days—the idea that came to me while I was running, the conversations with Derek and Vanessa, and my visit with Mr. Witkowski. When I finished, Dad stared at me for a moment, and then said, "Some of that is very interesting, Benny." He put his index finger up to his lips and was obviously thinking about what he was going to say next. After a few moments, he made eye contact with me again and said, "I like the 'hearts around the world' idea, at least the 'around the world' part. I just wonder if 'hearts' might be too limiting in an ad campaign. I need to think about that some more."

He paused again, obviously considering something else. "You know what? I'm going to bring up the idea to our team at the agency tomorrow. We've been tossing around some things, but nothing has really gelled yet. The 'around the world' idea might have some possibilities. Let me see what happens tomorrow."

Dad got a serious look on his face, as if he were about to deliver bad news. "As far as the other idea goes, about the sneakers. I really think it has a lot of potential … But I just wonder if it's outside the realm of what Mr. Alexander is trying to do."

"I guess that's probably right." I hesitated for a moment. "Would it be okay to show the idea to Mr. Alexander and see what he thinks?"

Dad must have seen my disappointment. "I'm going to have to talk with Mr. Jenkins about all this. Let me see what he has to say." Dad gave me a half smile. Coming from most other people it would have been patronizing, but not from Dad. "Benny, it's just that when you're trying to land a contract, you have to be careful. You have to make sure you're giving the client what he's looking for. It's tricky if you throw in some add-ons that detract from the main theme of the advertising campaign. Do you understand what I'm saying?"

I nodded my head as he continued. "Mr. Jenkins really will have the final say on this. So, if he says no, you won't be too disappointed will you?"

I got a half-smile on my face. "No, I understand. I'm not even sure why this seems so important to me."

"Well, I'll tell you something. No matter what happens, I'm still amazed by the things you come up with. That goes for Derek and Vanessa too."

"Don't forget Samantha."

Dad smiled. "And Samantha too."

Dad studied me for a moment. "Benny, obviously you've always been very bright … I'm not sure we've ever really talked about … Do you have any idea how you come up with these things? I mean, some of your ideas are pretty grown-up, pretty sophisticated."

I hesitated, not knowing if I really had an answer to Dad's question, but I thought I'd give it a shot. "I guess … I get a lot of my ideas when I'm running. Running kind of clears my head, and then ideas just pop in."

Dad smiled some more. "I do remember you told us that. But I guess I mean, why do you think you're even … thinking about these things?"

I hesitated before I responded. "I don't know for sure, but maybe … it sounds kind of 'sappy', maybe because it can help people."

Dad continued to smile. "I don't think that sounds 'sappy'."

"You know, part of it is you and Mom."

"What do you mean?"

"Well, from the time I was little, I always saw things more like a grown-up than a kid …"

Dad interrupted. "That's putting it mildly."

"But you and Mom never treated anything I said like it didn't matter, like I was just a kid, and what did I know."

"Benny, don't forget, you were an only child; what did **we** know."

It was my turn to smile. "Well for whatever reason, I always knew that whatever I said and did, I don't know … that you thought it had value. I'm not sure a lot of kids get treated that way."

"That was a really terrific thing to say, Benny. Thank you."

Dad got up from his chair, came over, and gave me a hug and a kiss on the top of my head. As we separated, Dad said, "So, if any of these ideas pan out, what kind of a cut are you guys looking for?"

I smiled. "Oh … I don't know … standard. A seventy-thirty split."

"That's not standard. And who gets the seventy?"

"I figured twenty percent each for Derek, Vanessa, and me, and ten percent for Samantha."

"It sounds like when you were at the meeting with Mr. Alexander that some of his business sense may have rubbed off on you."

I put my arm around Dad's shoulder. "You know, no matter what happens, I won't forget the little people. And I'll never want them to call me boss or Mr. Curtis; I'll always want them to call me 'Benny'."

"That's good. Now go do your homework, **Benny**."

The next day when Dad got home from work, he told me about his conversation with Mr. Jenkins.

"He really liked the 'around the world' idea, and so did the people on the team who are working on the proposal. We're going to have to change some things; and we'll have to come up with some off-shoots, but I think we're definitely going to move in the direction of some sort of 'global theme'."

"What about the idea with the sneakers?"

"Mr. Jenkins liked that too, but kind of what I thought … he doesn't feel … we should devote as much time to it."

Dad studied my face for a moment. I probably looked more disappointed than I actually felt. I had kind of expected this, after our conversation yesterday, but Dad was able to make me smile with his next comment. "It's okay; I told him I'd work on it on my own, at home, if necessary."

"Really?"

"Yeah. The more I thought about it, the more I liked it, and I think Mr. Alexander's going to feel the same way. But Mr. Jenkins is still doing the right thing. If we put too much work into your idea, the main advertising proposal could suffer."

"Is there anything I can do to help?"

"Yeah, there is. I'm going to need Derek too. He understands all of this technological stuff much better than I do. And before I can translate it into a coherent advertising campaign, I need to know more about it. Can you talk to him and see if he can come over on Saturday?"

"Sure. But we have track practice in the morning. What about after that?"

"That's fine."

"Thanks for everything, Dad."

"You're welcome." He paused and smiled. "So, since I'm going to be doing a lot of work on this, are you guys willing to renegotiate that 70–30 split?"

"I'll have to talk to my people and get back to you."

Derek came over on Saturday; he, Dad and I met for about thirty minutes. Dad took some notes and asked some follow-up questions. We then went next door to see Mr. Witkowski. After another half hour with him, Dad said that he had everything he needed to get started.

For the next two weeks Dad focused on the primary ad campaign at work and the sneaker project at home. Periodically, Dad would ask me a question or show me something he was working on, but he decided to wait until the campaigns were finished before letting anyone see them in their entirety.

Then on Tuesday night a few days before the presentation was to be made to Mr. Alexander, Dad asked Mom and me to have a seat in the living room. We had just come back from my birthday dinner. (Michael Martin had been right by the way; my birthday was on a Tuesday.) Dad indicated that both ad campaigns were about 99% completed, and he wanted to give us a preview.

"You've already got your birthday presents, Benny, so this is just a bonus."

"Did working on the sneaker project give you the idea to buy me running shoes for my birthday?"

"No, it was pretty much the fifteen e-mails with the attached ads. Not to mention the subtle way you left the runner's catalogue open to the page with the picture of the shoes you wanted."

"Just trying to be helpful."

Dad had loose-leaf binders made up for us, similar to the ones he would have for Friday's presentation. At the actual presentation, in addition to the binders, however, there would be slides and DVD's projected on a large screen. But the pictures in the binders, as well as Dad's explanation, gave us a good idea of what Mr. Alexander would see on Friday.

Dad started with the children's clothing campaign. The agency was going to recommend the following:

- The newly created company would be called ATG—for "Around the Globe". (Although, as I pointed out to Dad, it could also stand for "Alexander the Great".)

- The company's logo would feature pictures of children's faces circling the globe. Although the likenesses of the children featured would be of different racial and ethnic backgrounds, pictures of Mr. Alexander's grandchildren would be scanned into the computer and serve as the models for the computer-generated images.

- Each line of children's clothing would have a different theme and a different logo. For example, one line of clothing would be called "Hearts Around the Globe" with a logo depicting hearts circling the globe; a different line would be called "Sports Around the Globe" with a logo depicting soccer balls, baseballs, and runners etc. circling the globe. Other possible lines of clothing included "Customs Around the Globe", "Flags Around the Globe", and "Peace Around the Globe", each with its own logo.

- Individual factories in the various countries could select other themes as well.

- The doctors and nurses working at the health clinics attached to the factories would be outfitted with uniforms featuring a "Health Around the Globe" logo.

Dad showed us some potential magazine and newspaper ads using the "Around the Globe" theme. He indicated that the agency had also developed some ideas for TV ads, but he hadn't brought any of those home with him. When he finished the presentation, both Mom and I applauded. And Mom spoke up first. "I really liked that, Joe; it was terrific. I love the whole global theme … and from what you've told me about Mr. Alexander, I think he's going to be very impressed."

I echoed Mom's comments. "That really was great, Dad. I think a lot of kids are going to like the sports theme. I mean, I know we haven't seen the actual clothes yet, but I think little kids especially are going to like those different logos."

"Thanks. We are really pleased with this, but you never know how a client's going to react. Anyway, thanks for your support."

Mom added, "Frankly, Joe, I don't think you have anything to worry about. And I'm not just saying that ..."

"I think Mom's right, Dad."

"Let's hope so."

Dad started to put aside the materials from the clothing campaign. And in an exaggerated formal tone, Dad said, "Okay Benjamin, let's take a look at the presentation of your idea."

For the next fifteen minutes Dad showed us what he had developed to present to Mr. Alexander on Friday about my sneaker idea. Mom and I didn't ask anywhere near the number of questions we had for the children's clothing campaign, probably because we were so much more familiar with the sneaker idea. When Dad finished he said, "So, what do you think?"

Mom: "I think it's excellent! I was worried it would be too technical, but it wasn't at all."

"How about you, Benjamin?"

I smiled. "What's with the 'Benjamin'?"

"Just trying to show the proper respect to such a creative ... individual."

"Well, Benjamin liked it a lot."

Dad smiled. "I'm really glad. I figured I was taking a little bit of a chance showing it to you on your birthday, in case you didn't like it, but ..."

"Do you think Mr. Alexander's going to like it?"

"There's no way to tell, son. But the couple of people I showed it to at the agency loved it." He paused. "And ... I've got one more birthday surprise for you."

I looked around the room. I'm not really sure why; I guess it's just a natural reaction when someone says they have a surprise for you. (I mean, our living room's not big enough to conceal a car, or even a dirt bike, so I'm not sure what I was expecting.) Anyway, if Dad noticed me looking around, he didn't let on. Instead, he just continued. "I spoke to Mr. Jenkins about you coming to the presentation on Friday."

"Really? Is it okay?"

"He said it would be fine." He paused. "The only thing is I'm a little reluctant to have you miss school."

"We don't have school on Friday."

"Why not?"

"It's Memorial Day weekend, and we didn't use up all our snow days so they gave us Friday off."

"Since when?"

"Last week."

"Where was I? Well, I guess that cinches it." He paused. "Assuming you want to come."

"Of course I do."

"The only other thing is ... I have to make sure Mr. Alexander doesn't mind. I don't think it will be a problem; after all, he invited you to the first meeting. But still, I need to ask him."

"I understand."

"Okay, let's do this. Let's plan on you coming, and for some reason if I can't get approval ahead of time, then you'll have to wait in my office until the presentation's over."

"That's okay with me, Dad."

During the next few days, I was filled with a combination of excitement, anticipation (the kind that I like), and doubt. I'm not sure why this meant so much to me. Obviously, I wanted Dad's agency to get the contract, but I also wanted Mr. Alexander to like my idea. Mom always said that since I was little, I tried to be a "people pleaser". I guess she knows what she's talking about.

The presentation was scheduled for 9:00 that Friday morning. Mr. Jenkins let everyone know that the office would be closed up immediately after Mr. Alexander left, so that everyone could get an early start for the holiday weekend. "No matter what happens, you've all done great work on this; and no decision's going to be made today anyway."

Mr. Alexander arrived at 8:30. Dad asked me to wait in his office while he went out to meet him and do a final check on the conference room set-up. About fifteen minutes later Dad came back, and Mr. Alexander was right behind him.

"Well, hello again, Benny."

I stood up. "Hello, Mr. Alexander."

"Your dad tells me you'd like to sit in on the presentation."

"Yes, sir, if that's okay."

"You weren't bored last time?"

"No, not at all! I thought it was very interesting."

"Well, I did have my eye on you, and it did look like you were pretty engaged ... either that or you're a good actor."

I smiled. "No sir, that's definitely not the case."

"Okay then, I guess we'll see you at the presentation."

"Thanks, Mr. Alexander."

"You're welcome." He started to leave Dad's office, and then he hesitated for a moment. "Oh, by the way, I watched a tape of that Oprah show. I was very impressed. Warren ... Mr. Jenkins had told me about it, but it was much more impressive when I saw it." He paused again and got a twinkle in his eye. "So, any more good ideas like the one on Oprah?"

I glanced at Dad, not sure if I should say anything, but he jumped in.

"Actually, one of the ideas we're going to present to you today came from Benny."

"Really? Well then, there should have been no question; of course he has to be there."

He came over, shook my hand, and moved toward the door. "Lookin' forward to it."

The first part of the presentation couldn't have gone more smoothly. Dad was the lead presenter, although some of the other members of the team spoke as well. The presentation was in an advanced Power Point format with accompanying DVD clips. All of the people at the meeting also received hard copies of everything they were watching. Mr. Alexander didn't ask many questions, but he did smile and nod quite frequently.

At one point, he actually raised his hand to be recognized. Dad acknowledged him by saying, "Yes Mr ... er, Mack?"

"You probably realize that if we go with the ATG idea, the media's going to figure out that it could also stand for 'Alexander the Great'?"

I looked over at Dad and saw a little concern on his face. I think Mr. Alexander saw the same thing, because he quickly added. "I mean, I don't really care, but if it comes to that, let's let them figure that out on their own, okay? We don't need to help them with it." And he gave a little laugh.

At the conclusion of the first part of the presentation, Mr. Alexander looked pensive for a moment, and then started to nod his head. "I like it. Some really good ideas there." He looked around the room, and pretended to whisper. "My assistants keep telling me I'm not supposed to say anything. But I think people deserve to get feedback, don't you?"

He continued to lean forward in his chair. "But just so I don't give you the wrong idea ... I definitely liked it ... right from the start ... very impressive. But this isn't a done deal for anyone yet. There have been two other presentations I liked too. We're going to have to take some time and sort all this out. Anyway, so far, I do like what I see." He paused. "I guess I'm getting a little ahead of myself though; you've got something else to show us, right?"

Dad spoke up. "Yes, we do. But I was wondering if you wanted to take a break."

Mr. Alexander responded. "My understanding is that Warren's giving you the rest of the day off after this. Might as well not hold you up."

That was Dad's cue to start. "Before I begin this part of the presentation, I wanted to let you know a couple of things. First of all, what I'm about to show you is somewhat outside the scope of what you asked us to prepare, although it's certainly related."

"Secondly, the original idea for this came from my son, Benny." Dad smiled at me, as everyone else in the room turned my way. "Now, I didn't tell you that to get me off the hook in case you don't like it." Everyone in the room smiled. "Whether you decide to use it or not, I think it's a great idea, and I wanted to make sure Benny got full credit for coming up with it." Everyone in the room applauded. (I'm sure I turned that color I described to you earlier—"total embarrassment red". Still nothing on that from Crayola, by the way.)

Dad looked over at Mr. Alexander. "The other reason I had to tell you that this was Benny's idea is the same reason you came to this agency—'**truth** in advertising'."

Everyone laughed, as Dad continued. "So, here's the idea we're proposing to you."

"Mack, in your initial presentation to us, you indicated that the factories you were building would manufacture footwear as well as clothing." Mr. Alexander nodded, as Dad continued. "You also indicated that the focus of this endeavor was helping children; helping them by providing quality clothing that was inexpensive; and helping them by providing access to health clinics." Dad paused for effect. "Well, Benny's come up with an idea that takes that one step further. It's not only about keeping children healthy; it's about keeping them safe as well."

Dad hesitated for a moment, obviously considering something. "Benny, I know I'm putting you on the spot a little bit here, but why don't you tell everyone how you came up with this idea before I show them the way it works?"

Everyone turned to me again. Although Dad and I hadn't specifically planned this, he had told me to be prepared to answer questions, or to speak up at the meeting if I wanted to. And even though I didn't expect it to be so soon, I wasn't that nervous. (I think the "total embarrassment red" incident a few minutes earlier actually might have settled me down.) So, before there was any chance that my nerves could come back, I just started to talk.

"After the meeting about the factories last month, I started thinking about what Mr. Alexander had said. I'm on the track team at school, and whenever I go for a run, I always do a lot of thinking. So, when I started thinking about the clothing factories, I remembered about Amber Alerts. It was one of the segments on the Oprah show. And there was an article in the paper about parents keeping track of where their teenagers were by using some sort of GPS and their cell phones. Anyway, those ideas all came together in my head, and I began to wonder why we couldn't put some sort of tracking device in kid's sneakers. Then, if they got lost or kidnapped, or something like that, the police would know where they were."

I stopped for a moment, looking for a reaction from Mr. Alexander or his assistants. They all seemed to be still processing everything I had just said, but their facial expressions seemed positive, so I started in again.

"My friend Derek knows a lot about technology, so I asked him if something like that could be done. He said that it could; in fact, at least one company had already done it." A couple of Mr. Alexander's people got a puzzled expression on their faces. I'm sure they were wondering why I thought Mr. Alexander would want to do something that was already in the works, but I quickly provided the answer.

"The problem with the sneakers that are being produced with the tracking devices is that they cost around $350 a pair. Most families couldn't possibly afford that, especially with how fast kids outgrow shoes." Most of the people in the room nodded. "Derek and I tried to think about it some more, and then … it kind of came to both of us at the same time. The only solution was to be able to take out the tracking device from the pair that the child has outgrown, and put it in a new pair." People were still nodding, which kind of spurred me on.

"Our next door neighbor is Mr. Witkowski, and he knows everything there is to know about tools." (I almost started to tell them about the bird feeders, but I pulled myself back in time. If you think I have a problem going off on tangents when I'm writing, imagine how much worse it is when I'm speaking. Anyway, I refocused and continued.) "Derek and I went to see Mr. Witkowski, and he thought of a way to do it."

I paused again to see how everyone was reacting, and then I continued. "I think my dad has some slides that will show you how it can work."

Dad stood up and was about to project the first slide, when Mr. Alexander started to speak as he turned toward me. "Young man, I don't know what else is coming, but I have to tell you, that's one heck of an idea." He turned back to Dad. "And Joe, you think this is doable?"

"I think so. I had a number of people outside the agency check it out. If you decide you want to go with this, obviously, your legal people will have to research it, but from what I understand there's no patent issues; nobody has the exclusive right to put tracking devices in shoes."

"As usual, Joe, I'm getting ahead of myself. Let's see what else you have about how this will actually work."

Dad used his laptop to project a number of slides on the screen, while he elaborated on what everyone was seeing. "Each tracking device would be embedded in one of the heels of the sneaker along a lightweight plastic track. The track, as well as the device, would be protected by the rubber heel ..."

"Each tracking device would have its own ID number that would be registered in the ATG data bank after the shoes were purchased. The ID could be registered with the local police as well. Should a child go missing, the ATG system, the local police department, and even the parents of the child, if they had their own GPS coordinating system, could pinpoint the location of the child ..."

"The key to making this affordable is to be able to transfer the device from one pair of sneakers to another. Here's how this can be done." Dad used a laser pointer to highlight the specific things he was referring to.

"This particular tool can be heated to 'melt' the material that was used to seal the plastic track and the tracking device in place. Once that is done, the tracking device would then be deactivated by entering the assigned ID for that device into a hand-held computer, and 'shutting off' the signal. The tracking device would then be inserted into a new pair of sneakers, reactivated, and then sealed again ..."

"Any attempt to remove the tracking device without deactivating it would 'red flag' that particular device in the ATG computer system and that of the local police. So that anybody who had abducted a child wouldn't be able to deactivate the device without setting off an 'alarm' ..."

"Once a child outgrows his sneakers, and his parents want to buy a new pair, and switch the tracking device, they just go to the store that sells these sneakers, and the transfer can be done in ... we estimate ... less than five minutes. At that time, the parents might be charged a small amount for the transfer, or it could be included in the price of the new sneakers. But once they buy the initial pair of shoes with the tracking device, they never have to purchase another device again; they can just have it transferred ..."

Before Dad put up the last slide he said, "Although we didn't do a full scale campaign proposal for the sneakers with the tracking devices in them, we did come up with a possible prototype." With that, he pressed a button to show the slide. It depicted a pair of children's sneakers with "sparks" on the side that changed colors. Beneath the picture of the sneakers was the word—

<u>Sparks</u>

Satellite **P**ositioning **A**ctivewear for **R**ecovering **K**ids **S**afely

As soon as Dad finished, he asked if there were any questions, and he was inundated. It was obvious that the idea had struck a chord. The discussion lasted for almost an hour. Finally, Mr. Alexander said, "Warren and Joe, this whole morning has been very impressive. As I said to you before, however, there's still a lot we have to go over and sort out, especially about the sneakers, or should I say 'Sparks'. There's cost analysis, legal issues, maybe patent issues, etc." He paused for a moment, and then said, "If we go with this, we don't want to make any mistakes."

He looked at Mr. Jenkins and then at Dad before he continued. "Let me say this much. Our plan all along has been to narrow the five agencies down to three prior to June first. I can tell you right now, you're one of the top three. Our timetable calls for us to award the contract in early July, about four or five weeks from now. We're going to probably have to stick to that. I suppose it could be sooner, but I wouldn't count on it. So around the first of July, I'll talk to you **personally**, one way or the other …"

There was some informal milling around for about fifteen minutes, and then Mr. Alexander left. Mr. Jenkins asked for everyone's attention shortly after that. "Everybody, great job! Enjoy your weekend; we'll go over all of this on Tuesday."

The next several weeks before school ended were very busy. I had MCAS tests in math and language arts, four track meets, final exams in all my major subjects, a fourth quarter health project, and discussions with my guidance counselor about next year's courses.

It probably was a good thing that I was so busy, because it didn't give me much time to dwell on what Mr. Alexander's decision might be. Of course the exception to "not dwelling" was when I was running, but only in practice, never during an actual race. Whenever I was competing in a meet, I had to focus all my attention on the race. The only exception to that occurred earlier in the school year when Mr. Witkowski had been so sick.

Speaking of running, we had a very good spring season. The track team finished 4–1. Our only loss was to a school that was comprised of grades 6–8 and that had twice as many students as we did.

Derek had a great first season on the team. He won the 100-meter dash in three of our meets, and came in second in the other two. He also finished second or third in the long jump in each meet. He told me that he really enjoyed track and was thinking about going out for cross-country next fall to build up his stamina.

I thought I had a pretty good spring season as well. I won the 1500 meters in four of the five meets we had. My only loss was by less than a second to the boy that I had beaten in our final cross-country meet in the fall. Even though I lost one race, I was undefeated in the triple jump, or the hop-step-and-jump, or the hop-skip-and-jump (take your pick). Anyway, I didn't lose that event all spring.

The highlight of the season, however, came in the second-to-last meet. It wasn't because we won, and it wasn't because I ran my fastest time, and it wasn't because Derek ran his fastest time. It was because Mr. Witkowski came, just like Vanessa had predicted he would

Our fourth quarter health/advisory project was due on the Friday before final exams. I started working on it right after Memorial Day weekend. Since I had already done one other project on dieting, and I had done a lot of my own research on nutrition, I figured I would continue in that same vein and do my project on vitamins, herbs, and supplements. It also seemed like a good idea because I thought I might come across something that would enhance my running.

Now don't misunderstand, I would never take anything like steroids, or anything even close. But I figured if there were some natural vitamin or supplement that was proven to be safe and that would increase my physical fitness, I would talk to Mom and Dad about it to see what they thought. But I would never take anything that might jeopardize my health. I guess I kind of subscribe to the idea that "your body is a temple", (although nobody would be worshipping at that particular shrine anytime soon).

As it turned out, for someone my age, the research just suggested a healthy diet and a daily multi-vitamin. As I got a little older, vitamin E looked like it might be something I should investigate further, but not for right now.

In doing research on the topic of herbs and supplements, I came across some interesting information. You already know that I believe in the Shakespearean notion of "What's in a name?". But I've gotta tell you, no matter how much it might help me, I'd have a real hard time taking any health supplement called "St. John's wort". It doesn't sound like something I think I want in my system. I checked a health website and found out that there's an alternate name for St.

John's wort. It's also known as "goat weed". (Okay, that's way better; you can pile that on my plate now.)

The website said St. John's wort is often recommended for people who have mild depression, yet the first possible side effect listed is **increased anxiety**. So … what, the malady and the cure are the same thing?

Some of the other possible side effects are dry mouth, dizziness, fatigue, gastrointestinal distress, and sexual dysfunction. Wouldn't most of those lead to more depression? My advice is to just leave St. John's wort on the shelf next to the sea grass and the kelp.

Another supplement I came across was Ginkgo Biloba. It's supposed to increase your memory, and make you more mentally alert. It would seem to me that if you can remember how to spell it and pronounce it correctly, you probably don't need it.

There were some other supplements that had names that seemed like they were the direct opposite of the two supplements I just mentioned. Who wouldn't want to take something called "Echinacea"? Doesn't that sound soothing—"Ek-i-nay-sha"? Actually, I know that Mom takes it whenever she feels a cold coming on. I discovered that there are a lot of herbs and supplements that claim to lessen the effects of a cold, like zinc. Not just because of the name, but I think I'd prefer to take Echinacea. Don't you have the feeling that if you took zinc every time you felt a cold coming on, you might set off the metal detector at the airport?

As it turned out, I got about halfway through the report on vitamins and supplements when I decided to scrap it. It wasn't really very good because I kept going off on tangents. (I know that's hard to believe, but nevertheless, true.) I looked over the guidelines for the fourth quarter projects and saw that I could do ten hours of community service instead of a report.

I was going to go to see my guidance counselor to ask if she had any ideas about where I could go to do community service. But before I had the chance, I noticed in the paper that the Massachusetts Special Olympics was going to be held at Boston University, Harvard, and M.I.T. in about a week, and they were looking for volunteers. Although I wasn't technically old enough, I thought if Mom or Dad were willing to volunteer and take me along to help out, it would qualify as community service. Mom said she would take me, and I cleared it with my health teacher.

We arrived at Harvard Stadium at eight o'clock Saturday morning and were there until six that night. Mom was assigned to be in charge of an eighteen-year-old boy named Alan who had Down's syndrome. I introduced myself to him, and we became fast friends. Alan was scheduled to compete in the 100-meter dash and the standing long jump.

As we were sitting in the stands waiting for Alan's events to be called, I happened to look a few rows down to the right and thought I recognized someone. "Mom, isn't that Mr. Martin down there?"

"Where?"

"About six or seven rows in front of us, over there."

"I think it is, and Michael too. Who's that with them?"

I tried to look more closely. "I'm not sure, but could it be Miss Frist?"

Mom was leaning forward to try to see better. "I think it is. I think you're right."

I looked over at Mom. "Should we go say 'hello'?"

"Sure. Alan, why don't you come with us? We're going to say 'hi' to some people we know. Is that okay with you?"

"Yes, I like to meet people."

We all moved toward the aisle in the bleachers and headed toward where Mr. Martin, Michael, and Miss Frist were sitting. Michael spotted us first. "Hi Benny. Hi Benny's mom."

Mr. Martin and Miss Frist turned to face us. Mr. Martin stood up and said, "Well, hello there."

There were additional greetings and introductions all around, and then a number of conversations started up. We found out that Michael was scheduled to run in the open 100-meters, just like Alan. Also, since there weren't enough volunteers, Mr. Martin and Miss Frist had offered to chaperone Michael, so some of the other special athletes could still participate.

I noticed that Michael had a notebook and was writing in it. "Michael, can I ask you what you're writing there?"

"The winners and times."

"Of each race?"

"Yeah, of the 50-meters."

That was the race that was currently being run. There had been ten heats for the boys and men, and six heats for the girls and women. And evidently, Michael had written down each heat winner's entry number, along with his or her time.

"So Michael, who has the best time?"

Michael proceeded to tell me the entry number of each winner, the winner's time, and in what place that time would put the runner. **And he never looked at his notebook once.**

"That was terrific, Michael. Thanks."

Mr. Martin looked over toward me and smiled. "So Benny, only about a week to go. Any plans for the summer?"

I told him that I always spend four or five weeks with Grandma and Grandpa each summer, from early July to early August.

"What a nice thing. Actually, now that you mention it, I think I knew that. Maybe Dr. Foster told me." He paused and smiled again. "It's been quite a year for you, hasn't it?"

"Yes, it really has."

Mom piped in. "And the excitement might not quite be over."

Mr. Martin got a puzzled look on his face, and then Mom explained about Mr. Alexander, the contract, and the sneaker idea. When Mom was finished, Miss Frist looked over at me and said, "So Benny, when do you have time to sleep?"

Alan and Michael both won their heats of the 100-meters, and received gold medals which they wore proudly around their necks. A few minutes before six o'clock we said our goodbyes and headed for the parking lot. As we were walking, Mom said, "Did you hear what Mr. Martin said about the $25,000 gift?"

"No."

"The school's going to use it to buy laptop computers."

"Oh, the ones on a cart that can be rolled into a classroom?"

"Yeah. Mr. Martin said there are 24 laptops on each cart. He thinks they can get two carts with the $25,000. Do you already have any of those at school?"

"No, just the computer labs."

"I think that's a good use of the money.'

"Yeah, I think so too."

Mom put her arm around my shoulder. "This was a nice day, wasn't it?"

"Yeah, it was."

"Why don't we stop to get something to eat on the way home? How about McDonald's?"

"Okay, but I'm only going to get a small French fry—too much trans fat."

"Actually, I read somewhere that they're not going to use trans fat in their fries anymore."

"Really?"

"Yeah, they're going to replace it with … St. John's wort."

Chapter 22

▼

"We got it." Those were Dad's first words when he came through the front door on that last Friday in June. Neither Mom nor I had any doubt what the "it" referred to, even before he started to elaborate.

"We got a call this morning that Mr. Alexander wanted to set up a video conference for two o'clock this afternoon. Since he had promised to talk personally to the people at the competing agencies, whether they were selected to get the contract or not, we weren't sure what to expect."

"When Mr. Alexander came on the screen, he said that in his experience, when you gave people either really good, or really bad news, they had trouble focusing on anything else that was said after that. But nevertheless, he decided that he was going to take the chance. And then he said, 'Warren, Joe, we've chosen your agency for the advertising contract'. I have to admit Mr. Alexander was right; the next few minutes were a blur."

Mom went over to Dad and gave him a hug and a kiss. "Congratulations, honey. I know how much this meant to you … and the agency."

"Thanks … Yeah, it is a really huge deal for us." Dad looked over toward me. "Benny, come on over here … group hug." I joined Mom and Dad, and they put their arms around me.

"Dad, that really is terrific."

"Thanks, son. So let me tell you what else. Let's sit down."

We went into the living room, and for the next fifteen minutes Dad filled us in on some of the other details. When he was almost finished, he looked over toward Mom and said, "Since I'm going to be overseeing the development of the campaign, Mr. Alexander wants to meet with me next week, right after July

Fourth. I offered to go to his office in New York. I thought we could just extend our time with your parents a couple of days when we drop off Benny."

Mom nodded. "That sounds fine; that shouldn't be a problem."

Dad looked over in my direction. "So, are you ready for this? They're going forward with the 'Sparks' idea, not as rapidly as with the clothing lines, but Mr. Alexander seems very excited about it. He said he'd tell me more next week."

I got a big smile on my face. "Really? Oh wow, that's unbelievable!"

"Well, believe it." Dad paused. "And there's more."

"What?"

"Do you remember that I mentioned to you that Mr. Jenkins had told me that if we got the contract, he was going to find some way to 'reward' everyone outside the agency who had helped out? You know, like you and Derek and Mr. Witkowski. I even think he asked me about who Vanessa and Samantha were. Anyway, he must have mentioned it to Mr. Alexander, because Mr. Alexander said that **he** would take care of that. He brought it up to me this afternoon. He said he had some ideas, and he'd talk to me about it next week as well."

Mom said, "This whole thing is absolutely incredible. Do you have any idea what he has in mind?"

"No, not exactly. But honestly, I got the sense from Mr. Alexander that Benny's idea might have been the very thing that cinched the deal. I think it fit perfectly with what this project is supposed to do … help children … keep them safe."

I think Dad could see from the expressions on our faces that we were imagining all sorts of possibilities. "Okay, you two. Let's not get too excited. We shouldn't get ahead of ourselves. Let's just see what happens."

I know Dad meant well, but it reminded me of the conversation I had had with Dr. Foster a few years back. You can't **decide** how to feel, some emotions are out of your control. It really doesn't do any good to say, "Don't get excited", or "Don't be upset", or "You shouldn't be nervous". You might as well say, "You know that 'whole law of gravity thing'?—Well, just ignore it."

So despite Dad's admonition, I couldn't help it; my head began to fill up with one incredible possibility after another. But later that summer when we found out what Mr. Alexander was actually going to do, it was even more amazing than anything I could have imagined.

We drove down to Grandma and Grandpa's on the Sunday before the Fourth of July. Dad's meeting with Mr. Alexander was scheduled for the following

Wednesday at his offices in Lower Manhattan. Dad proposed that the whole family, including Grandma and Grandpa, make a day of it in New York City.

"We can all take the train in, then grab a cab to Mr. Alexander's office ... and you can all get a chance to meet him. I'll double-check with him, but I'm sure it'll be okay. You guys can go sightseeing for a couple of hours, while Mr. Alexander and I get together? After that, I'll meet up with you at the South Street Seaport for lunch."

That Wednesday, we arrived at Mr. Alexander's office at around 9:30. We waited briefly, and then one of his assistants showed us all into a conference room that seemed about three times larger than our house. There was coffee, milk, juice, and pastries set up in one corner. The assistant told us to help ourselves. Everybody except me went over to get some coffee; I just had juice. I'm sure there was no way Mr. Alexander's staff could have possibly known about my juice preferences, but besides the omnipresent orange juice, they had grape juice. You can probably guess which one I chose. (Old habits die hard.)

Mr. Alexander came in about five minutes later. "Good morning, everyone." Dad introduced Grandma, Grandpa, and Mom to Mr. Alexander, who insisted that they call him "Mack". That seemed easy for Grandpa, but not for anyone else.

When Mr. Alexander came over to say hello to me and shake my hand, he noticed the grape juice I was drinking. "Good choice, lots of anti-oxidants." He paused and then whispered to me, "Although I often prefer to get my anti-oxidants after the grapes have fermented."

I smiled, and then he continued. "So Benny, you're welcome to stay if you'd like, but most of it's going to be legal talk." He leaned towards me and lowered his voice again. "**I** don't even like being here for that."

Although Mr. Alexander was almost whispering, Dad was close enough to have heard what was said. I looked in his direction. He shrugged his shoulders and said, "Up to you, son."

I hadn't really thought that I was going to be at the meeting anyway, and Mr. Alexander hadn't made it sound all that appealing, so I responded, "I think maybe I'll just go with my mom and my grandma and grandpa."

Mr. Alexander offered his hand. "Good choice, Benny."

We all said our goodbyes and told Dad we'd meet up with him at about 12:30 at the Seaport, after our sightseeing.

Isn't "sightseeing" an odd word? Shouldn't it really be "**site**seeing"? I mean, that's really what you're doing, looking at sites. You're not looking at looking. Isn't "sightseeing" redundant? When we dine out, we don't say, "I'm going 'taste-eating'." Or after we go to a concert, we don't say, "I had a wonderful time, 'hearing-listening'." Or on the way to the flower show, we don't say, "I can't wait to be 'smell-sniffing' the roses." (I know I've asked you this before, but do you know of anyone I can contact about my concerns?)

Anyway, after going up to Times Square, visiting the huge bookstores and music shops, and people-watching for awhile, we headed back toward the seaport area. It was a beautiful sunny day, so we waited outside the restaurant to meet Dad. He arrived about ten minutes after we did. There was an outdoor table available, and we were seated immediately. After we ordered, Dad told us all about his morning.

"Mr. Alexander wants me to get some magazine ads and a few TV spots ready as soon as possible, but just for the 'Around the Globe' clothing lines. The 'Sparks' campaign won't start right away; there's still too much to do. They're farther along than I thought, however, because Mr. Alexander's company did a lot of preliminary work even before the contract was awarded."

"Mr. Alexander said that he thought they could purchase the GPS/tracking devices in bulk for about $75 each. And with a minimum profit added to the cost of manufacturing the sneakers, they can sell them for about $99. After that, they'll cost between $15–30 depending on style and size, plus a $5 charge to transfer the tracking device."

Mom spoke up. "That's pretty inexpensive. Can they really sell them for that?"

"Evidently. He said his financial people went over the numbers and said it's doable." He paused. "Oh, and get this. Mr. Alexander is going to donate a million pairs of sneakers with the tracking devices to families that can't afford them."

Mom started to nod her head. "Boy, he's really committed to all of this, isn't he? Talk about putting your money where your mouth is."

Dad started nodding his head also. "No question." Dad paused as the waiter refilled our water glasses. "Remember I mentioned that Mr. Alexander wanted to give something to everyone who helped out? Well, I got some indication of what he's thinking about. He said he wants to use pictures of Benny, Derek, Vanessa, and Samantha on the company's letterhead. He's going to have contracts drawn up which will compensate all of them for allowing ATG to use their pictures. I'm going to e-mail him all the pertinent information, and one of his staff members will contact the families, including us, with all the details."

Mom then asked the question that we were all wondering about. "Did he give you any indication about how much the contracts are going to be worth?"

"No, but he's really not obligated to do any of this. So whatever it is, it's going to be fine."

Grandma entered the conversation. "I think it's a wonderful gesture no matter how much it is." Grandpa nodded his head in agreement.

Dad continued. "You know, he even asked me about Mr. Witkowski. He didn't remember his name, but he did remember that he lived next door to us. I told him about the stroke, and Mr. Witkowski's recovery. Anyway, he said he's going to do something for Mr. Witkowski too." Dad started to chuckle. "Although he said he didn't think ATG would include Mr. Witkowski's picture on the letterhead—'doesn't fit the demographic'."

Everyone laughed, and then Mom asked, "When are you supposed to meet with him again?"

"Well, after we talked about the clothing lines for a while, he told me he was going away for a few weeks, but wanted to get together the first Monday in August, so that's the next time we'll meet in person. He wants me to e-mail him with updates during the time he's away, however; but again, we won't meet face-to-face until August." Then Dad got a "cat that ate the canary look" on his face.

Mom saw it and asked, "What?"

"The man is full of surprises. Are you ready for this? He invited all of us to be his guests the night before our meeting ... at the Red Sox—Yankee game."

I'd been pretty quiet up until then, but I blurted out, "Are you kidding, Dad?"

"No, I'm serious."

Mom jumped in. "That Sunday, the day of the cookout?"

"Yeah, but it's not a problem. I told him all about the cookout tradition, and you know what he said? He asked me how many people were coming to the cookout. When I told him around fifteen, he said bring them all; the luxury suite at Fenway holds thirty."

Mom's mouth was wide open before she said, "You can't be serious."

"I am ... and it gets better."

I chimed in again, "What?"

"He's hiring limousines to pick everyone up at our house and drive us back and forth."

We were all stunned into silence. Finally, Mom spoke up. "Joe, I hope you at least invited him to the cookout."

"Of course I did. Actually, I invited him before I even knew about the Red Sox-Yankee game, as soon as I knew he'd be in town for our meeting on that Monday ... He's coming, by the way."

"Well, what a day that's going to be." Mom, ever the planner, took out a small notebook and started to write something down, as she continued talking, mainly to herself. "I'll have to notify everyone to see if they can go, and ..."

Dad said, "When we get back to your parents' house, I was going to e-mail everyone to ask for the information Mr. Alexander wants. Why don't you just add a note about the game?"

Grandpa spoke up at that point. "What a nice surprise! I'll bet I haven't been to Fenway in about seven or eight years." Grandpa paused. "So, does Mack root for the Yankees? He was born in New York, wasn't he?"

Dad got a smile on his face. "Sorry Marc, he's a Sox fan. He grew up right near the Massachusetts border. It looks like you and Grandma will be on your own again."

"That's okay. Victory is sweeter when you win in enemy territory."

We all chuckled.

Mom was still writing something in her little notebook when she looked up and said, "I don't think we should have hot dogs at the cookout."

Dad looked puzzled. "Why not?"

"Tough to compete with Fenway Franks."

During the first full week of my visit with Grandma and Grandpa that summer, I received a number of e-mails from Mr. Alexander, checking in to see how I was doing. He also asked for some additional information about Derek and Vanessa, including their e-mail addresses. I suspected it was related to whatever plans Mr. Alexander had to "reward" us, but it was obviously not something I could ask about.

As usual, I had a great time with Grandma and Grandpa. Although I still enjoyed just being with them at their house each day, as I had gotten older, we started going on more day trips. We visited Teddy Roosevelt's house; we went to a Native-American pow-wow; and we visited two or three of the state parks on Long Island.

As is often the case, the Yankees and Red Sox were one-two in the American League East standings, and Grandpa started needling me about how the Yankees were going to trounce the Red Sox in the upcoming game we were going to. Finally, I took the bait and we decided on a friendly wager. If the Yankees won the game, then next summer during my visit, I had to wear a Yankees hat and t-shirt every day for two weeks. If the Red Sox won, Grandpa had to wear a specially made t-shirt that said on the front, "I'm Benny's Big Papi", and on the back, "But David Ortiz Rules." (For those of you who don't know, Big Papi is

David Ortiz's nickname. He's the really popular designated hitter for the Red Sox.)

After my month-long visit with Grandma and Grandpa, we headed back up to the Boston area on the first Saturday in August, the day before the cookout and the big game. We took the ferry across Long Island Sound and arrived at our house at around two in the afternoon, just in time to watch the Saturday game between the Red Sox and Yankees.

The Red Sox had won on Friday night, but the Yankees came back to win on Saturday. That meant that Sunday night's contest was going to be the rubber game, which added even more drama to the event.

After Saturday's game was over, and Grandpa had gloated for a few minutes, Mom and Grandma went to the supermarket to pick up some last minute items for the cookout. While they were gone, Dad filled us in on some of his conversations with Mr. Alexander over the last few weeks.

"Obviously, most of our discussions were about the ad campaign. But, he also asked some things about you, Benny, and about Derek and his family, and Vanessa, and Jack Witkowski, and even you, Marc."

"Me? Why was he asking about me?"

"I don't know. Something's going on, but I don't know what … Although I'm sure it's related to what he's going to give to the people who helped out."

Grandpa said, "But I wasn't involved in any of that …"

"I don't know what to tell you. The last thing he said to me on Friday was that he'd have some surprises at the cookout."

I told Dad about the e-mails that Mr. Alexander had sent me, and Dad said, "That's probably related too; we're just going to have to wait until tomorrow to find out."

After supper we were all sitting in the living room just relaxing. The TV was on, but nobody was really watching it. Mom was reading the front section of the newspaper. When she was done with the last page, she said to me, "Benny, are you finished with the Lifestyles section?" (Which was on the coffee table in front of me)

I took a moment, and then responded nervously, "Yes … I mean no … I mean I'm not done with it, because I wasn't really reading it … anyway … uh … here." And I handed it to her.

Mom looked at me strangely and said, "What was that all about?"

I tried to cover up. "I don't know; I was just thinking of something else. Sorry."

Mom smiled. "Okay."

(Of course the real reason I got so flustered was because the Lifestyles section of the paper contains the **fashion** news. I didn't want them to think I had any interest in that subject, which as you know, I really don't. But I didn't want to open the door to possibly having to explain my Internet search of "designer dresses".)

About five minutes later, Mom half-shouted, "Oh my gosh. Look at this."

Dad was the first to respond, "What?"

Mom was pointing at the paper. "In the announcement section ... Mr. Martin and Miss Frist ... they're engaged! There's a picture of them in the paper."

My mouth opened wide, but nothing came out. Dad said, "Really?" And he got up and walked over to where Mom was sitting. I got up also, and we both looked over Mom's shoulder to see it in black and white for ourselves.

Grandma asked, "Who are they?"

Mom said, "That's Benny's principal, you remember—from the Oprah show? And he's marrying Miss Frist; she's the local librarian." Mom went on to explain about Michael and his volunteer work, and even about having seen them at the Special Olympics.

Mom held up the paper so Dad and I could read it more easily. The article read "... announce the engagement of Andrew Martin to Pollyanna Frist ... no immediate wedding plans ..."

Mom spoke up. "That's really nice. Don't you think so, Joe? I'm really happy for them."

Dad smiled. "Me too."

I asked Mom. "Do you think they were engaged when we saw them at the Special Olympics?"

"I don't know, although I didn't notice a ring. Even if they were engaged then, they might not have had a chance to talk to Michael about it. You know how difficult change is for him."

"Yeah, I know it is ... But don't you think it might not be so hard, you know, because he knows Miss Frist?"

"Probably, but it's still going to be a huge adjustment."

I glanced at the paper for another moment, and then said, "Do you think Miss Frist will change her name?"

"I don't know ... why?"

"Well ... I just noticed ... if she does, then their initials would be A.M. and P.M.—They'd kind of have the day covered, huh?"

Mom tried to give me a little push, but I scooted away. "How do you come with these things?"

Dad was shaking his head. "Never mind **how**. The real question is **why** does he come up with these things." But Dad had a big grin on his face when he said it.

The next day, everyone had arrived for the cookout by 1:00 except Mr. Alexander. He got there around 1:30, which was fine because Dad had planned to eat about an hour later, which gave us plenty of time between lunch and dinner. We were scheduled to head into Boston at about 6:30, and then to eat in the luxury suite at 7:30. The game was going to be televised nationally beginning at 8:15.

It was probably the first time in our neighborhood's history that a stretch limo was parked for any length of time on one of the streets. The limo held twelve people comfortably, and there was another one of similar size, which was scheduled to show up later on to take the rest of us into Boston. After the driver parked the limo in front of our house, Mom made sure that he joined us for something to eat.

Dad introduced Mr. Alexander to everyone he hadn't met before. He seemed to take a liking to all the new people, and they to him. It was not hard to see why he was so successful. He just had a nice way about him that was genuine and sincere.

A little after two o'clock, I noticed Mr. Alexander speaking to his driver, who then headed around to the front of the house where the limo was parked. Right after that, Mr. Alexander went over to speak to Dad, who was manning the grill. The driver returned with a briefcase and then headed back out to the front of the house. Immediately after the driver handed Mr. Alexander the briefcase, Dad asked for everyone's attention. "Mr. Alexander, or should I say Mack, would like to say a few words."

As you can imagine, all eyes were on Mr. Alexander as he started to speak. "It's very unusual in the business world, at least in my experience, to begin to forge friendships with people you've just met; partnerships, yes, but friendships, no. But with the launching of ATG, that's exactly what's happened. I've got to say that I've only been here for about an hour, and yet I feel more at home and more welcome here than at any corporate dinner or cocktail party I've ever attended, even those in my own house."

Everyone laughed.

"I don't want this to be a speech, but I did want you to know that the way all of this has come about is as improbable as anything I've ever seen … which I guess makes it even more special." He paused for a moment. "I've been extremely fortunate in my life, and I just hope that this latest venture will give back some of that good fortune to children all around the globe ..." He accentuated the last three words, smiled, and made eye contact with Derek, Vanessa, Samantha, and me before he continued. "... so they can be as healthy and safe as you are."

"But truly, none of this would be happening if most of you hadn't done some of the things that you did, particularly you four young people. So, on behalf of the children around the globe who are going to benefit from what you helped bring about, I have something for you."

With that, he opened his briefcase and distributed four oversized envelopes—one to Mom and Dad, one to Vanessa's parents, and two to Derek and Samantha's parents.

Each of the envelopes contained a similar document, which indicated that a college scholarship fund had been established in the name of each of the four of us. Each fund was in the amount of **$200,000**! The document also stipulated that any funds not expended for college would be distributed to the individual upon graduation from college, or upon reaching his or her twenty-fifth birthday.

Mr. Alexander also gave an envelope to Mr. Witkowski. It contained a cashier's check for $50,000. The intent was for Mr. Witkowski to pay back Grandpa the money that was borrowed (about $15,000), and the balance was a gift for Mr. Witkowski to use as he wished.

Finally, Mr. Alexander's driver brought two boxes into the backyard and told Grandpa they were for him. Grandpa looked puzzled, but pried at the cardboard, and was finally able to get the tape off one of the flaps. It took a few moments, but then Grandpa must have realized what was in the boxes.

It was probably only the second or third time in my life that I saw my grandpa cry. He was so choked up that he couldn't speak. Mr. Alexander walked over closer to him, and said, "Everything's there except about four or five items we're still trying to locate ... but don't worry, we will."

We found out later that when Grandpa looked into the boxes, he saw replacements of all the records, books and videos he had sold in order to set up the college fund for me.

Mr. Alexander later explained that Derek had helped him with this, but he had been sworn to secrecy. Evidently, after Dad told Mr. Alexander the story of Grandpa selling his collection, and then loaning the money to the Witkowskis, Mr. Alexander decided that just having Grandpa repaid by the Witkowskis wasn't enough. But he had no way of knowing what Grandpa's collection consisted of, until he remembered that Dad had told him that Derek had helped put the items on ebay. That's why Mr. Alexander wanted Derek's e-mail address.

Once everyone heard about Derek's involvement, we all glanced over at him. He looked a little sheepish, but he had a huge grin on his face.

Mr. Alexander explained to Grandpa that there were four more boxes containing replacements for his collection, but those would be shipped directly to his house. Mr. Alexander brought the two with him to the cookout so that Grandpa could actually see some of the items, not just hear about them.

As you can imagine, Grandpa wasn't the only one crying that afternoon. And every family who received something protested that it was way too much—that they didn't feel right accepting it.

Mr. Witkowski was probably the most outspoken, claiming that he hadn't done anything to deserve the money. Mr. Alexander responded. "Jack, I have no doubt that the idea about the transferable tracking device wouldn't have happened without your help. You deserve something for what you did. And the same goes for the rest of you." He paused and smiled. "I happen to be very rich. But Joe, do you remember what I said the first time we met? It's—only—money." He looked around at everyone before he continued. "If I hold on to all this money, it's not going to make my life any better. But, if you all accept it, it will make me **feel** better, selfish son-of-a-gun that I am. And maybe it will give your children more opportunities in life." He smiled. "Okay, try to fight me on that one."

Everybody chuckled. And then I'm not sure who started it, but everybody stood up and applauded.

Mr. Alexander said, "That was very nice. Thank you ... Now that that's over with, let's get back to the cookout." He paused and looked over at Dad. "Come to think of it, Joe, there is something you can do in return ... How about a hamburger?"

Dad laughed. "Okay, but this has got to be the most expensive hamburger in history. What, about a million bucks?"

"Joe ..."

"I know. It's—only—money."

You might expect that the interactions and conversations the rest of the afternoon were somewhat awkward. I'm not sure why, but they weren't. Maybe because Mr. Alexander's words put everyone at ease, or maybe it was the anticipation of going to the ball game that gave us a built-in topic for discussion. Whatever the reason, the next few hours were easy going and comfortable for everyone.

I hadn't had a chance to talk to Dr. Foster very much, so after I grabbed a hamburger, I went over to see him. "Did you hear about Mr. Martin and Miss Frist?"

"Yes, I did. I think it's great."

"I do too … Do you think Michael will be all right with it?"

"Yeah, I don't think that's going to be a problem." He paused. "So, this was quite a surprise."

"It's amazing, isn't it?"

"It really is." He paused again and got a smile on his face. "But you know what? It reminds me of when I found out about Mr. Martin and Miss Frist."

"How come?"

"Sometimes good things happen to good people."

I'd never ridden in a stretch limo before. I have to admit; it felt strange looking out the window, knowing people couldn't see in. It struck me that in some ways that kind of defeats the purpose. I mean, when you ride in a stretch limo, aren't you in essence saying, "Hey, look at me; I'm in a stretch limo." But if no one can see you, then what's the point. (It appears that vanity is a much bumpier road than I thought.)

We got to Fenway just before 7:30 and went through a special entrance up to luxury suite L-13. I'm not usually that superstitious, but don't you think the Red Sox would number their most prestigious suite something other than 13? What about 9, Ted Williams' number? Or 8, Yaz's number? Certainly, it should be something other than 13, at least for tonight—**We were playing the Yankees**!

I suspect that when people are seated in the luxury boxes, besides watching the game, they tend to do a lot of socializing. That wasn't the case in L-13. And even though, during the ride to Fenway, and before the game started, we talked a lot about Mr. Alexander's incredible generosity, once the first pitch was thrown, that was it. Any time a conversation began, like in-between innings, or during a pitching change, it stopped in mid-sentence as soon as the next pitch was about to be delivered. After all—**We were playing the Yankees**!

The game was a pitcher's duel until the fifth inning when the Red Sox put a four-spot on the board, and took a 4–1 lead. The Yankees tied it in the eighth and went ahead 6–4 in the top of the ninth. The Sox had their eighth, ninth, and leadoff batters due up, not necessarily the scenario Sox fans had hoped for.

The number eight batter popped out to second, and number nine struck out. Just then the hostesses in the luxury suite came around to see if anybody wanted anything else. Nobody was rude to them, but I did feel like screaming—**We're playing the Yankees**!

Our leadoff hitter drew a walk on a very close three-two pitch, and then I suspect all 34,000 fans, except for Grandma, Grandpa, and a smattering of others, started to think the exact same thing—can we possibly get to Big Papi?

It's probably true that the most die-hard fans had that idea in the back of their minds at the very start of the inning, but now it was like some telepathic thought wave that surfaced in everybody's brain.

The second man in the order was hit by a pitch (thank goodness uniforms count), and Fenway erupted. We were still losing 6–4, but Red Sox fans, more than any other sports fans, have to rely on hope, and recently that hope was—**Big Papi!**

As David Ortiz was striding to the plate, Joe Torre, the Yankee manager, went to the mound to bring in a lefty. This was a pretty unorthodox thing to do, because the Yankee closer, Mariano Rivera, who was already in the game, was arguably the best closer in baseball history.

Grandpa took this opportunity to come over and sit next to me. He smiled and said, "Just like *Casey at the Bat*." Grandpa was referring to the classic baseball poem he had read to me many times over the years.

"Big difference," I said. "**Big Papi!**"

Grandpa smiled. "I don't like to admit it, but he **is** the best clutch hitter I've ever seen, and that includes DiMaggio, Mays, Williams, even Mickey. But, how many times can you expect him to do it?"

"So you won't mind wearing the shirt then?"

"He hasn't done it yet."

"That's true … but I think he's going to."

"Are you forgetting how *Casey at the Bat* ends—There is no joy in Mudville …?"

"But that was Mudville … I think there's going to be a big blast in Bean-town."

Grandpa laughed. "I'll tell you what. If he hits a homerun, I'll buy a Big Papi shirt on the way out, and wear it for two weeks straight."

"Sounds good. Red's a good color on you Grandpa."

Everyone was on their feet as Big Papi spit into his batting gloves and rubbed his hands together. He dug in at the plate and gave an almost imperceptible nod to the pitcher, as if to say, "Okay, let's go."

I think everyone in the ballpark was expecting a lengthy at-bat. We figured the pitcher and the batter would try to get a feel for each other, try to get the smallest advantage by out-thinking the opponent in terms of what pitch to throw, or what pitch was coming. But that didn't happen.

I know the laws of physics tell us that sound waves travel much more slowly than light waves, but that didn't seem true at Fenway that night. On the first pitch, I swear I heard the crack of the bat before I had any idea where the ball was headed. And I know I wasn't the only one, because the crowd went crazy less than a nanosecond after Big Papi made contact. (The only shorter elapsed time I've ever witnessed occurs when the light turns green and the driver behind you beeps his horn.)

Somehow, in the split second that we heard that glorious sound of the bat hitting the ball, we were able to see into the future—we could see Big Papi being mobbed at home plate. And I knew in that split second that Grandpa would be making a shirt purchase on the way out. I even think Grandpa took out his wallet before the ball landed about twelve rows in back of the Red Sox bullpen.

Although I was still keyed up during the ride home in the limo, I was also pretty tired, so I slept for part of the ride. One of the dreams I had reminded me of the way I felt when I was running and all those different ideas would come into my head. I remembered most of what I had been dreaming about when I woke up; it was about lists. Specifically, about making a list of the top ten things that had happened to me this past year.

Over the next several days I started to put the list together. It was much harder to do than most of my other ones, because without question, last year had been filled with one remarkable thing after another. I probably changed the order about twenty different times. (The Red Sox win over the Yankees never finished lower than fifth, however.)

As I was developing the list, it got me thinking. You know how sometimes when something unusual happens, people say, "Wow, that was random"? Or, when they try to explain an unlikely turn of events, "Well, life is random"? In fact, Apple used that very phrase as an advertising slogan to introduce the iPod Shuffle, which **randomly** selects songs for you to listen to. So, it seems that most people believe that random means "in no particular order." And, I guess it does; but I kind of look at it a little differently.

Suppose that I asked you to list the numbers 1–5 "randomly". You might put them in this order—3,4,1,5,2, or 4,1,3,2,5, but you probably wouldn't list them—5,4,3,2,1, and certainly not—1,2,3,4,5, but why not? Actually, if numbers are generated randomly, they have just as good a chance of being in 1,2,3,4,5 order as any other, but that's not the way we look at it. 1,2,3,4,5 has meaning for us; it just doesn't appear to be random.

So, is this just a final Tangent City excursion, or is there a point to all of this? Oddly enough, there is a point. This past year when I was in the seventh grade, the things that happened to me were truly amazing. Even the bad things, like Mr. Witkowski's stroke, eventually turned out okay. So honestly, if I had to translate this past year into a sequence of numbers, even considering life's "randomness", the order would have to be 1,2,3,4,5.

And even if life isn't quite as random as we might think, there's no doubt in my mind that it's usually a lot "messier" than it was for me last year. Even so, and I know it's unrealistic to expect it, but I'm kind of hoping that next year turns out to be 6,7,8,9,10.

I'll let you know.

978-0-595-69035-0
0-595-69035-1

Printed in the United States
79434LV00004B/163-174